All the Silences

Book Three: The Hope

Geneviève Montcombroux

ISBN 9781987946161

1. World War Two
2. The Nazis in France
3. German Occupation of France
4, German Occupation of Paris
5. Women during Occupation
6. Resistance
7. Women in the Résistance

Cover by: Stunningbookcovers.com

Published by Whippoorwill Solitude Publishing
solitudepublishing@gmail.com

Dedicated to all those who rose up to fight against Nazi oppression so that I and others could live in a free world.

To the memory of Rose Ernstberger who, in Germany, and I in France as children suffered hunger, cold and fear during WWII.

To my late English teacher Germaine Bodénan

Acknowledgments

My grateful thanks to June for her enthusiasm, to Tanis for her enduring support and friendship, and to my Gilmore knitting club fans.
And last but not least, to my husband Michael, who relentlessly encouraged me to write this series when I was plagued by doubts.

All the Silences

Book Three
The Hope

Notes

All the historical facts are meticulously researched and include fragments of diaries and other original documents. A more comprehensive author's notes can be found at the end of this volume. The language used corresponds to the era. So do the behaviors. Most situations and incidents are based on true stories, although the characters are fictional.

This book is not a romance, nor is it about the exploits of some fictional heroine and hero during WWII in France although some of the characters will see action. Mostly, it is about what life was like for the everyday people, particularly women, what they did because they wanted to do something to get rid of the occupying Germans, and how they were drawn into actions they had never planned on doing and never thought they were capable of.

In this book, Paris is liberated. The women, who had struggled to feed their families, while helping the Résistance as much as they could, are still desperate to find food as famine looms on the horizon. As events come to their paroxysms they have to cope with losses and betrayals.

Recap of Book Two

Julie's official assignment to reunite lost children with their parents has ended but leading downed airmen to the safety of the free zone along with vulnerable children continues fraught with danger.

While Julie is meeting her friend Rébecca, SS-Obersturmbannführer Meinhard appears. Julie is forced to introduce her friend. Meinhard is intrigued by Rébecca's mathematical skills and says they should be put to use helping the Nazi ideals. He tells Julie about a planned Gestapo raid on the printshop. In return for the favor she has to have dinner with him. Julie gets word to Yolande to warn her parents about the raid. The dinner date ends with Meinhard raping Julie.

General von Trennen learns about the assault and promises to report it to Meinhard's superiors. Pursued by the Gestapo, Sylvain has a narrow escape, only to be later arrested after meeting Julie. She is taken to the Avenue Foch Gestapo to identify him. Sylvain's fellow resistance fighter, who was arrested with him, sacrifices himself to spare Sylvain who, being high in the Résistance hierarchy, knows much vital information. He is released but has to disappear. Philippe drives him to the demarcation line. The Gestapo come back for Julie but she slips out of their grasp and travels to Montauloup, along with François and the younger children.

Julie discovers she is pregnant, but by whom—Sylvain or Meinhard? At the end of the summer, Julie and François are eager to return to Paris. An incident at the demarcation line is a reminder that tomorrow may never come and it's important to seize the moment.

Rodolphe, wearing a Waffen-SS uniform, abducts his daughter Lyse-May. General von Trennen helps to locate the child. Julie and Bérangère with Captain Langen's help bring Lyse-May back home.

Julie makes an unsuccessful attempt to rescue Rébecca from the Pithiviers detention camp. Yet, due to Julie's intervention, Rébecca's life is spared. She is sent to Germany to work on a top-secret weapon project.

Pearl Harbor brings the Americans into the war.

Julie goes to the remote village of Le Monastier to have her baby, a boy. She works for the local Résistance and has a narrow call. Back in Paris, Rébecca resurfaces, having escaped from Germany. She takes refuge in the Ritz Hotel. With the help of her Luftwaffe boss, Yolande organizes Rebecca's travel to the free zone.

Meinhard catches up with Julie, now in Paris. Bernard's réseau is in danger from a traitor in their midst. For safety, Julie moves with her children to a new address. Meanwhile, the net is closing in on the traitor. Discovered, he is taken care of by the Résistance.

Meinhard orders Julie to meet him. To avoid him she has again to go into hiding.

Characters of importance late August 1942:

Gontrand & Bérangère de Montregard, patriarchs of the family. They live in the family's ancestral mansion named Le Manoir, but now in the west wing.

First son, Philippe (collaborateur) m. to Madeleine = Mireille 22, Pierrette 20, François 18

Second son, Bernard m. to Marie-Ange = Paul 12, Micheline10

Third son, Rodolphe = Lyse-May 5

Fourth son, Sylvain m. to Julie = Claire 3 (deceased)

Arnaud, Gontrand's brother, pétainist, m. to Huguette, supports de Gaulle = Mathieu (deceased), Jean-Jacques, live in Montauloup family country home, in the Auvergne.

Camille, Bérangère's sister, m. to police captain Hilaire Malleville = Christophe, live in Pontcharra, near Grenoble in the Alps

Lorraine, Gontrand's sister, m. to Jean-Luc Bourgmestre = son Hughes 17, daughter Yolande 29, print shop owners.

Brigitte, close friend to the de Montregards, m. to Hubert Marchand = Damien 9, Estelle 7, Sylvestre 4, Christiane 2

Charmaine, close friend to the de Montregards, m. to Alexandre Lebeau = Marianne 14, Baptiste 12, photographic studio owners

Maude Pleynet, Bérangère's best friend.

Jacques Werner, commandant of the Paris gendarmerie, Gontrand's friend.

Léonie Bodénan, Julie's close friend.

Xavier Despins, escapee became friend of the family

Madame Durand, Julie's concierge.

General Reynard von Trennen, Aide-de-camp Captain Gerhardt Langen, + orderly Günter Klein, reside at the requisitioned Manoir; driver Karl Froeder + groom in apartment above garage

Kurt Meinhard, Julie's hated suitor

Ernst Lhose, Yolande Bourgmestre's boss at the Ritz Hotel

Baron Dieter von Hauffen, Mireille's lover

Rose Sauter, son Helmut 18, German refugees, new names: Rose and Daniel Sauterel, friends of the de Montregards.

Armand, SOE agent, becomes head of Bernard's réseau

Pedro, Elissa Poveda, Spanish refugees in Montauloup

René, résistant in Le Monastier
Denis, mayor and résistant in Le Monastier
Marguerite, in Le Monastier
Dédé Dumonteil, m. to Gertrude = Francine, Lucette, and son Robert 17, farmers in the Auvergne.
Joseph Lavergne, mayor in Le Falgoux
Marcel & Louise Boyer, résistants in Le Monastier
Toine, Hortense and Serge, farmers, résistants
Claude Auzello, m. to Blanche, Director of the Ritz Hotel
Monsieur Biquette of Fromageries Biquette (cheese business), passeur across the demarcation line.
Popaul, leader of Résistance group and café owner, Chez Popaul.
Dr. Bignon, physician to the Résistance groups
Dr. Katzenberg, German surgeon-major
Madame LePlouhëc, general manager at the Majestic Hotel

Chapter One

Paris, End of August 1942

With a cigarette butt dangling from his lip for effect, Bernard glanced up at the derelict façade of the apartment building in the Passage du S. He pulled his béret a little more over his ear and hitched his baggy pants with his elbows. His blue workman's jacket hid his athletic frame.

He pushed the entrance door open. A foul smell assailed his nostrils. The walls oozed damp and mildew. He climbed the stairs two at a time to the fourth floor and knocked on door 42.

"Uncle Berna—"

"Shush! Only Olive."

Pierrette pulled a face. "Sorry, Olive. How did you find me?"

"I have my ways."

"So much for me hiding in this commie neighborhood."

Bernard took in the large room with a cot at the back, a sink and a hot plate on the side. "It isn't even sanitary."

"Well, the Germans won't be poking their noses around here."

"The Gestapo are less fussy."

Pierrette pulled a rickety chair toward her uncle and took one for herself. "Please sit down. I like your outfit."

"It suits the district. Now, I want to know how you came to throw a grenade."

"You heard! Fine. Foufard chickened out. I knew he was a coward the moment I saw him, but because he's a male, he was entrusted with our one and only grenade. You men should listen to women more often."

"I've nothing to do with that outfit, but point taken. Now, back to you."

Pierrette sighed. "The idiot had already pulled the pin out. What was I to do? Let him be blown up and everybody else in the vicinity? I grabbed his hand and slipped mine around the grenade. I ran to the canal and threw it in. The explosion was something! But it only killed a few fish."

"You're absolutely crazy grabbing a live grenade from someone's hand."

"There was no choice."

"A botched job that operation was. Now you're on the run. What about the others?"

She grimaced. "The four men who had entered the guard post were caught."

"Why on earth did you join up with Yves Lamont's bandits? Are you becoming communist?"

"No, but François said he needed a couple more bodies."

Bernard took off his béret and raked his hair. "I'll have to lengthen your brother's ears. You are not to involve Hughes and Daniel. They're too young."

"They didn't ask my permission. There are boys younger than seventeen in with Yves."

"It's wrong! That's how cells get busted by the Gestapo. Immature idiots who think that killing a German or two is going to make a difference to the outcome of the war."

Pierrette exhaled a deep sigh. "Someone was indiscreet and suddenly all the youths knew about the operation. I think Foufard is responsible. He's so immature for a twenty-year-old."

"Who's speaking!"

"I'm nineteen."

"Only for another month. Tell me from the beginning."

"The guard post has only one sentry at night. I lured him out and Yves knocked him unconscious. The others rushed in to grab the guns and ammo in the post. The grenade was only to be used if the other guards woke up and we needed a distraction to get away. But because of Foufard, it didn't go according to plan."

"You were seen, and who else?"

"I had my bicycle. But, yes, a soldier with a spotlight saw me as plain as daylight and they pursued me. I lost them through the Buttes Chaumont woods. My bicycle is hidden in a bush against the rocks by the lake."

"You can't stay here."

"It's safe. There's no policing in this district, except at the train station. The rest of us got away."

"Foufard?"

"I didn't see him."

Bernard shook his head. "On my way, I saw a couple of Gestapo Citroëns circulating in the streets."

"I'll hole up here. I have enough food."

"What about Xavier?"

"He wasn't involved. He brought me supplies. Since he works for the Société Nationale des Chemins de Fer, he isn't being bothered when he walks by the station. I'll be all right, mon oncle."

"I'll find you a safe house. For the moment, stay put until you get a message."

Pierrette spontaneously hugged her uncle. "I think that's was what is called baptism by fire. I'll know better next time."

Lips pinched into a repressed smile, he tugged her braid and left. A worried frown didn't leave his forehead.

A few days later, François, wearing his scout shorts and sporting close-cropped hair, whistled outside the apartment building in rue du Passage du S. He wheeled two bicycles. A curtain briefly lifted and dropped on the fourth floor. Minutes later, Pierrette bounded into the street, her braids flying around her face.

"Do I look suitably young and innocent?" she asked her brother.

"You sure don't look like a grownup lady."

"Good."

They mounted and pedaled toward the Manoir. They arrived in time for lunch. Bernard chuckled and teased her. Pierrette, saucily, put out her tongue at him.

Jacques Werner burst out laughing. "Well, you two are a sight for sore eyes. I'm glad you made it safely."

A beaming Madeleine stood up and hurried to put plates in front of her two children.

Those around the table turned and looked at one another. When no explanation was forthcoming, everyone concentrated on their plates on which mashed turnips was the main ingredient.

Jacques leaned back in his chair. "As I was saying, the Paris police are letting a unit of the SOL operate in Paris."

"What's the SOL?"

"Service d'Ordre Légionnaire. A bunch of Vichy's paramilitary organization. I never thought I'd see that in my lifetime. All because of Bousquet and his ambitions." At the inquiring looks, he added, "Secretary General to the police."

While Jacques kept on ranting, Brigitte pulled Charmaine aside. "Are you still getting threats from your neighbors?"

"It's calmed down a bit. Gus put out a few threats of his own. I wish Alexandre would agree to go to the unoccupied zone. Bernard said he could even get us to England and my husband could forge papers there just as easily as here."

"Some men put their duty before their family."

"That's for sure. I'm worried for Marianne. She's just fourteen and she's far too pretty for comfort."

Brigitte chuckled. "Usually, it's the dad that worries about his daughter growing up into a young woman."

"Fortunately, she doesn't try to look grown up. She must realize she's safer looking like a young girl. Baptiste is very protective of her. He goes with her everywhere."

Brigitte shook her head. "Not even twelve and already a man."

"Like your Damien. Only nine and acting like the man of the house."

"That's what that war does to our children. It robs them of their childhood."

"It isn't our war, though."

"Yes, it is. To me, the German Occupation is the same as the war when we were bombed and fleeing south."

Painful memories cast a gloom over the two friends.

Brigitte broke the silence. "I suppose the Allies are fighting, so it's our war too. Do you have stockings on? Your legs look fabulous."

Charmaine laughed. "No stockings. I won't accept anything from Wolfang. I shared his gifts of stockings between my neighbors. He got the message and no longer brings anything. Alexandre painted my legs, and I got those superb antique shoes from maman-Bérangère's attic, also painted to look fashionable."

"That's what comes from being married to an artist!"

"I can borrow his paint and do yours, if you like."

"We'll do that. I wish Julie would come back. I miss her."

"Me too."

Gontrand's entrance with the rest of the family interrupted their tête-à-tête in the sitting room.

Bérangère's voice rose. "In church this morning our curé read the pastoral letter from Monseigneur Saliège publicly denouncing the treatment of Jews by Pétain."

"Not him! Not Marshal Pétain!" Gontrand bellowed. "The French State! Those useless ministers in the government."

"Isn't Monseigneur Saliège the archbishop of Toulouse?" Lorraine asked.

"He is."

"How come you know about his letter if he is in zone nono?" François asked.

"If you went to church on Sundays, you'd hear about it and a lot more."

"No need to go to church, grand-maman," Pierrette said. "We hear that Cardinal Gerlier is protecting hundreds of Jewish children."

A sudden silence followed her words.

"And how do you know that?" Gontrand's tone was almost belligerent. "Through some of your unsavory friends, *hein*?"

Jacques and Bernard lifted their heads from their private conversation.

"It's a matter of opinion, grand-papa."

It was time to defuse the mounting tension. Jean-Luc got to his feet and motioned to his wife to follow suit. "Thank you everyone. It's been another beautiful Sunday, but we've got to get back and prepare for tomorrow's printing."

Hughes lifted his eyes from his book. "Do I have to go, too, papa?"

Lorraine gave a wave. "Be home before dark."

Gontrand's sister hugged him and joined her husband outside.

Madeleine burped Félicité "How's the garden, belle-maman?"

"I planted all the space with potatoes."

Gontrand grumbled. "You dug up all my rose bushes that I planted and nursed for years."

"Sorry, dear, but we can't eat roses. Lyse-May is growing lettuce and radishes in boxes. She also sowed a seed of chrysanthemum in each one. You'll have some flowers later."

Just hearing the name of his granddaughter was enough to calm Gontrand.

Jacques turned to Bérangère. "Are you handing over your brass?"

"Absolutely not! Why should I give the Fritz brass so they can make weapons to kill our Allies?"

Jacques loved to see his friend's wife riled up. "Officially, people must take their brass items to the town hall and other municipal buildings and it goes to Vichy to hel..."

"Wrong! It goes to those hoodlums so they can offer it to their German buddies. Not my brass or any of my friends' brass."

"Those hoodlums, as you call the thugs of the criminal underworld, have turned themselves into the richest, most respectable citizens." He waited for a reaction.

His audience remained speechless.

Jacques Werner sighed. "All show, of course. They have become the prime suppliers of goods to the Germans. They have buying offices everywhere in the city. They get what they, and their masters, want. Because, make no mistake, they think they are getting the best of the bargain, but in the end those Boches get what they want and are magnanimous enough to let the gangsters get a small share. They go into houses under the guise of a legal search and just help themselves. Stealing, extortion, racketeering, you name it, all means are good to achieve their end."

Charmaine spoke in a quiet voice. "What about the French police?"

"Powerless. The brigands are protected. Each one carries a card that says German police."

"And no doubt their first victims are the wealthy Jews who are still here," Alexandre said.

Bérangère squared her shoulders. "If they come here, I'll bash them on the head with my brass candlesticks."

Chuckles greeted her words. The children ran into the house. It was the signal for everyone to go home.

Bernard sidled up to Pierrette. "Foufard got away..."

She gave him a questioning look.

"He took his own life."

Pain etched her features. She had no words.

Chapter Two

Le Monastier

Julie had barely put her bags down when the door opened behind her. All smiles, René greeted her.

"How was Le Puy-en-Velay?"

She laughed and turned to Marguerite, who held a squirming Claudine. "Here, ma chérie, I'm back." Her adopted daughter came into her arms with squeals of delight. "Bonjour, Marguerite. Ah! Monsieur René Lafleur, I didn't hear you." She bent and kissed sleeping Mathieu's head.

They chuckled.

René adopted a contrite look. "Nice to have you back. Did you have a good trip?"

"Actually, yes, the contacts are all in order. Security is being taken more seriously and is being tightened. The cells are now observing the rule that each member knows only two other members."

René scratched his head. "It can work in the city, but here everybody knows everybody else."

"It also has its advantages," Marguerite said. "Our rural cells are a lot more difficult to infiltrate."

Denis had quietly let himself in. "Right. I'd say impossible."

Julie shook her head at the mayor. "I'd say nearly impossible. You could have a member enticed by reward from the Vichy police and who becomes a traitor."

"Alas, you're right. It could happen."

"To change the subject, I saw a radio detection van in the streets of Le Puy."

Denis' eyes widened. "But those are Germans! This is the free zone."

Marguerite rummaged in the box of newspapers. "Here, it says in La Gerbe that the government, meaning Vichy, has allowed German technicians into the non-occupied zone to fight the terrorists."

Julie shrugged. "What they call terrorists are the résistants that are blowing up things in the occupied zone. Nothing like that here."

"No, but there are radios sending messages to London. They got wise to it," René said.

"Of course. I wasn't thinking."

Denis leaned over and gave her a hug. "You think just fine. You've done a fabulous job helping with the organization of our réseau."

"I recognize that tone of voice. You have an assignment for me?"

Marguerite picked up a sleepy Claudine. "I'll put her back to bed. Mathieu hasn't woken up."

"Merci."

After Marguerite left the sitting room, René poured boiling water in the coffee pot. "Ersatz, I'm afraid. The real coffee reserves are exhausted. I don't know what Vichy thought when they ordered us to mix one third coffee and the rest chicory or barley. It wasn't going to last long enough. Bunch of idiots!"

"You were saying you had an assignment for me."

"Forgive me, yes." René paused a few seconds. "We have a barge full of weapons and explosives. They're needed in the north."

Julie frowned. "So, someone can blow up more installations and trains?"

"I've no say in what they decide. In fact, nothing either, to do with our escape line. I was asked because the suppliers need someone who can speak German and distract the guard at the Écluse Chassenard. The barge must reach the réseau in Briare. Chassenard is the best lock, as it has only two guards."

"And I am the one who speaks German. My geography isn't too accurate. Where exactly is Chassenard?"

"Right on the demarcation line. The canal latéral de la Loire joins up with the Loire River farther downstream."

"What do I have to do exactly?"

"You'll be a government supervisor. Yes, we have a set of

official papers for you. The barge will arrive at the lock at dusk."

"I suppose I have to seduce the guard on duty."

They burst out laughing.

"Darling Fox, you have a real sense of humor," Denis said. "Seriously, you'll hand him all the transit papers. We think they're well done and in German."

Excitement coursed through Julie's veins. She tiptoed into the nursery and dropped a tender kiss on Claudine's and Mathieu's foreheads. She contemplated him for a moment. Remorse flooded her. She hadn't bonded with him, not like she had with Claudine, her adopted daughter. Not like she had with her own angel, Claire. She loved him because she loved all children.

Her heart pulsed with anxiety. What if she were caught and couldn't come back to them? Her fingers lightly stroked the silky hair on their heads before joining Marguerite.

Two days later, Julie met her contact, who turned out to be a nervous young man named Théophile. She took an instant dislike to him. Nonetheless, she greeted him warmly. "*Salut,* Théo."

"And you're supposed to be a Vichy official?"

Her dislike deepened when Théophile didn't have the courtesy to return her greeting. "And what do you suppose a female Vichy official should look like?"

"Sorry."

Just a curt apology for his stupid question didn't bolster Julie's confidence. "Where are we going now?"

"The barge's waiting for us."

He led the way down the towpath to a moored barge loaded with coal. She presumed the real cargo was buried under underneath the coal. Luckily the local inhabitants weren't hanging around to help themselves to a little of the black gold. The boatman stood next to another man whom she assumed must be Moustique, an ironical name for the large-shouldered résistant.

"Welcome to my péniche. It's also my home. I'm known as Marinier. Let's move."

Obviously a false name.

Théo unfastened the ropes from a bollard and jumped aboard. He joined Moustique aft to puff on a cigarette.

Marinier watched the two men and addressed Julie. "Let me tell you how it goes. You will be with me, about half-way on the port side, while I hand the papers to the guard, after which, I'll go back to the cabin. That's where the guard on duty will walk up to check and stamp our transit papers. The other guard is being kept busy in the lock house." He winked at her. "After he checks the papers, he walks upstream to close the lock gates behind us, then goes to the front to open the downstream sluice gate It's a slow process, but as the péniche gets lower, he goes back to the guard house. Your job is to flirt with the guard so he doesn't look at the papers too closely."

"What are the two men's roles?"

"They're supposed to be my workers. Never dealt with them before. They're responsible for the explosives and arms hidden under the coal."

"Do you do this often?"

"First time with a cargo of explosives."

"What do you normally carry?"

"Food and other essential items not available in the occupied zone."

"Black market stuff?"

He shrugged. "Whatever. It's good money. Alright, we're approaching the lock."

Julie watched Théo take a few steps forward. He stopped half way to light a cigarette, then sat on the edge of the cargo hold. Marinier maneuvered the vessel into the precise middle of the canal and entered the lock. He cut the engine, and the laden barge drifted between the narrow walls, the deck level with the towpath. A guard emerged from the door of the lock keeper's house, hastily buttoning his uniform jacket.

"*Guten Abend*, Herr Marinier. And you have a lovely lady with you today," he said in German.

"*Ah, bonsoir.*" Marinier handed over the sheaf of official papers. "Madame Latour is the Supply Ministry supervisor." He returned to the cabin.

The guard looked puzzled. He tilted his head and shook it.

Julie smiled at him. He didn't understand French. "*Guten Abend, Herr Wachemanne. Ich bin der Aufseher.*"

"*Sehr schön. Sie sprechen sehr gut Deutsch.*"

After she told him she was the supervisor, the beaming guard delighted in telling her how he missed being home with his fiancée, while flipping through the transit papers. Julie empathized, giving him words of comfort. Théo strode up to them.

"What's going on? She's betraying us!"

Alarmed, Julie turned toward him just as he pulled a pistol from under his jacket and fired at the guard, who collapsed.

"No!" Horrified, Julie watched the scene unfold as if in slow motion.

Marinier rushed to Théo.

"You fool! Stupid idiot!" He snatched the pistol from the young man.

Moustique ran to tackle Théo. The second guard came out. Without giving thought, Julie dove into the canal, between the barge and the wall. The last thing she saw was a grenade in Théo's hand. The guard fired his submachine gun. Spurred on by her survival instinct. Julie swam deeper below the barge, swimming upstream with all her might. Her lungs about to burst, she was suddenly projected forward. She hit the hull of the barge. Another explosion threw her against the wall of the lock. She gripped strands of moss growing on the wall and kicked herself free of the careening barge, confined in the narrow space, before it crushed her against the stone wall. Another explosion created a violent upsurge of water. Powerless, Julie concentrated on holding her breath. As the water fell back, she threw herself forward with renewed energy. She cleared the lock.

Only one thing occupied her brain, to get out alive. For her, swimming had been only a holiday pastime in the days before the war. She wasn't an adept swimmer, but she refused to die. She refused to give up even as she swallowed another mouthful of the grimy water.

Julie lifted her head just enough to breathe and again swam underwater against the slight current. On her next breath, she risked a look backward. Fire and explosions rocked the lock. Suddenly, the current became stronger. In a flash, she understood what had happened. She kicked with the strength of desperation without moving as much as an inch. The explosions had blown the downstream gate open and the water rushed down the six-meter gradient. It had transformed the canal into rapids.

Julie's legs began to cramp. Her arms were numb. But she remembered passing a wooded area on the way down. She strove harder. By now she was sure people had been attracted by the explosion and flames. The last thing she wanted was to be spotted. The evening was fast darkening. In the gloom, perhaps no one would see a head bobbing in the water. Trees bordered the canal on the opposite side to the towpath. She grabbed a low branch and forced herself to breathe evenly.

She had escaped. She was alive.

But she was unsure whether she was far enough away from the scene of devastation. The woods she had seen appeared to be a long way off. Her stomach heaved, and she brought up the water she had swallowed. She wasn't going to take chances. Despite the cold that now invaded her tired limbs, she kicked herself off again. The current ceased to pull her backward. It was now a gentle, buoyant flow. She kept her head out of the water and switched to an easy breaststroke, which made no splashing noise. Her eyes became accustomed to the increasing darkness. The mass of the forest rose to her right. The towpath was on her left, to be avoided at all costs. That's where the Germans and the Vichy police would search first if they suspected someone had escaped the explosion. She must now be in the free zone. She hauled herself out of the water and stumbled into the trees. Somewhere, either in the water or on the barge, she had lost her shoes. She couldn't remember when or how.

When she was away from the canal, she leaned against a tree and looked around. To her dismay, it wasn't a forest, just a small clump of trees. She could make out a field beyond. The clouds parted to flood the earth with the light of the full moon.

Her legs refused to hold her up. She swayed. To prevent herself from falling, she circled the tree with her arms. A field. There'll be a farm. She pushed her dripping hair out of her face and took a long breath. Her dress clung to her body. She pulled it down as best as she could. The day being warm, she hadn't worn a sweater. She wished she had one now as she shivered uncontrollably. Adrenaline still flowing in her veins, she set off toward the row of trees bordering the field. In the silvery light of the moon, she could see some way into the distance. No farm in sight.

Just as she thought she couldn't take another step, her sore, bare feet grazed flagstones. In front of her stood a small stone building surrounded by shrubs. She closed her eyes and opened them again. It was real. It was a hut. She made out a door and reached for it, hoping it wasn't locked. It wasn't. She stumbled inside the pitch-dark shelter. An immense sense of relief overcame her.

She took two cautious steps forward, one hand on the wall, the other feeling in around in the dark. A bench of sort barred her way. She continued and found it wasn't a bench but a low platform covered with sweet-smelling hay. Then the wall again, two more steps and she was at the door. She pushed it closed and went back to the platform. She dropped onto the hay. An intense fatigue hit her body now raked by a violent trembling. What had she learnt about survival in the girl guides? Her thoughts melted away from her brain. Instinctively, she dragged as much of the hay as she could over herself, until she fell into the abyss of sleep.

In her cocoon of hay, Julie opened her eyes. Shivers made her teeth chatter. The previous night's ordeal smacked her awake with a wave of fear. It was still pitch dark in the hut, but she had to get out. She stood up and made her way to the door. Cautiously, she lifted the latch and peeked outside. A rosy dawn streaked with turquoise was tearing at the night. A robin sang in a nearby tree. She listened to the sounds of nature. There were no human sounds. She risked venturing outside and took stock of her surroundings. The ground was wet. It probably had rained during the night. Against the stone hut, raspberry canes still had some dried fruit on them. A handful later, an intense thirst spurred her on, toward the babbling of a brook. Its clear water promised relief. Although exposed, she dropped on all fours, her face just above the rippling current, and drunk avidly. Then she washed her face and her hands. The sun burst out over the tree tops. A residual heat rose from the earth with the rich scent of decaying plants.

She pivoted, carefully looking about in all directions, and there to her left stood the dark forest she had been hoping to find. Her damp clothes began to dry. Trees and low bushes separated two fields. In their meager shelter, she started off on shaky legs toward the forest. It would be easier on her bare feet to walk on the tilled earth of the field, but there, she would be too exposed. Protruding roots dug into the soles of her feet. She gritted her teeth. The forest would hide her until she could think of what to do next.

At that moment, nothing counted except walking toward the welcoming trees.

Finally, the soft carpet of pine needles soothed her feet. She looked at her watch and laughed. To her amazement, it still worked. The leather strap had shrunk against her wrist. For once it stayed put on her slimmed down wrist. She rewound the watch and held it to her ear. Its faint ticking reassured her. She didn't know why, in her dire situation, the fact her wristwatch still worked was such a huge relief.

Dense evergreens slowed her progress until she burst into a clearing where a clump of oak trees surrounded a pond. Frogs bounded into the water as she approached. The damp moss oozed water between her toes. By now her clothes were dry, as was her hair. She made an attempt to finger comb it before braiding it.

On one side, an animal path led through the thick forest of mixed evergreens and deciduous trees. She remembered the airman Kevin who had taken refuge at her cousin's cabin in the Froidmont forest. He had lived many days in the woods. But it had been summer and wild berries and other edible plants had been plentiful. He had collected mushrooms and watercress. He also had boots and clothes, and a Swiss Army knife. She searched the ground before venturing down the track. A low bush scratched her leg, and she squealed with delight. The bush was a bramble patch laden with ripe fruit. She ate, careful not to spill juice onto her already stained dress. Ahead, the ground rose slightly, and she arrived at another clearing, this one crossed by a stream. She could see the bottom strewn with gravel. Fish swam leisurely, now and then gobbling an unlucky fly. It didn't appear to be deep. Her now dry dress hitched up, she waded into the stream. The glacial water up to her knees cut her breath. The light current eddied around her legs. She reached the opposite bank. There she found watercress, gooseberries and chanterelle mushrooms. Though, at that moment, she didn't dare eat them raw.

It was a lovely place to camp, if only she had some equipment. She explored her surroundings and found a narrow path. Was it an animal trail or one made by humans? Her eyes darting from side to side, she followed the track. Farther on, the trees thinned out. She didn't know where she was. Was she really in the free zone or still in the occupied one? She had swum upstream in the canal, therefore toward the free zone, but she didn't know how far or in which direction she had walked in the night. Still, she hoped she had put enough distance between the scene of the incident and herself. Beyond the edge of the wood, lay a field of potatoes awaiting harvest and beyond still, farm buildings. A glance at her watch told her it was noon. If she put the sun behind her, she'd be facing north, as she had learnt in the girl guides. At noon, in the fall the shadows are short as the sun is still high in the sky. Undeterred, she watched the compressed shadow her body projected, and hoped the theory was right. The path pointed due north.

Julie crouched to observe the activity at the farm. She saw a flock of sheep on the far side of the potato field. Exhaustion and hunger threatened to overcome her. She sat against an oak tree. Maybe she could eat raw mushrooms. She took a bite of the yellow chanterelle. It tasted sweet. She ate three of them and dozed off before she had the strength to eat another one.

A wet tongue and a warm body jolted her back to reality. She stifled a scream. Beside her sat a black and brown dog, tail wagging as fast as it could go. Tears streaming down her face, Julie laughed and cuddled the dog. After a few minutes, the dog bounded away, and she withdrew hastily into the thicker shelter of the forest, back to the stream in the clearing. Dusk was already darkening the forest. After eating more gooseberries and a few blackberries from a straggly bush, she crawled under the low-hanging branches of a pine tree. There on the soft needles, she had enough room to stretch out. The thick branches provided a warm cover, at least warmer than in the open.

Well, Julie, you're in a pickle! You can't stay here long. Tomorrow, you'll have to find out what that farm is like. Friends or foes. Where are you exactly? In the zone nono, you could get away but in the other? Does anybody know I escaped? If the guards are dead, no one will know... but it's dreadful to think they're dead. What about Marinier and Moustique, did they survive the explosions, the fire..? There's a haystack toward the sheep pasture. It would be warmer to spend the night there... A fitful sleep put an end to her rambling thoughts.

Curled up and shivering, Julie stifled her cry as her brain identified the wet tongue on her face. "You came back and found me. Good dog."

A few minutes later, her canine companion bounded away. She dragged herself from her improvised shelter. The cold of the dissipating night fell on her shoulders. With much effort, she began to run on the spot, her arms flailing the air to restore circulation and create a semblance of warmth. After collecting chanterelles and blackberries, along with a handful of watercress, she pretended she was eating breakfast at Maxim's.

A quick wash in the frigid water made her skin tingle. Julie finger-combed her hair and braided it in the hope she didn't look like a scarecrow. Once more, she followed the animal path to the edge of the wood. Before she reached the field, she stopped in alarm. What looked like a basket lay on the ground, in the middle of the path. Holding her breath, all senses on alert, she strained her ears. The only noises she heard were the chirping of birds and the scurry of small animals, as the sun made an appearance in the cloudless sky. She released her breath and took one careful and silent step and listened again. A subtle fragrance reached her nostrils. Not the dampness of soil that rose as the dew began to evaporate. Not the pines awaking from the night to release their pervading essence. What assailed her nostrils was the mouth-watering aroma of freshly baked bread.

Julie's eyes scoured the woods and the field as she advanced with cautious steps. The farm lay quiet. Off in the distance a sheep's bell tinkled. She lowered herself to the ground and crawled toward the basket. It rested on top of a blanket. A flow of gratitude for the farmer washed over her. She had been discovered, and this offering was a friendly gesture. She pulled the bounty toward her and retreated into the thicker shelter of the trees. Why did the farmer leave the food and the blanket without calling to her? This was obviously an act of kindness, a token of peace. Her mind functioning now in high gear, she envisaged multiple scenarios, none of them realistic.

Back at her camp, she wrapped herself in the blanket and lifted the cover of the basket. It wasn't a cloth as she expected, but a well-worn woolen sweater. She promptly pulled it on and attacked the slices of bread and butter underneath. A small jar contained what she thought was milk. The taste was strange, but it did feel like milk. She saved two slices of bread and half the jar of the unknown liquid.

Moments later, sated and exhilarated, she tried to decide why the farmer, probably the farmer's wife, had brought the food and blanket but didn't make herself known. In the end, she concluded it wasn't safe to be seen at the farmhouse. Maybe she was on the occupied side of the demarcation line. Maybe the farmer's wife was friendly, but her husband was not. Maybe she had walked in a circle and was close to the lock. Whatever it was, she knew that sooner or later she would have to make herself known and hopefully be directed toward Le Monastier again. Though it seemed to be a long way off. Throughout the day, she collected mushrooms and berries and filled the basket. As the sun began setting, she carried the basket to the end of the path and put it down where she had found it. Back at her camp, she looked forward to a comfortable night and hope for the morrow.

The friendly dog again came to wake her in the morning. She folded the blanket and carried it with her. At the end of the path, the basket was already there. Along with food, there was a note in the basket. *Come to the farm at nightfall.* She retreated to her camp by the stream. While she ate, she decided she had to trust her anonymous benefactor. And if it was to turn her in to the police, so be it. She couldn't hide in the forest forever. Images of Claire, her angel in heaven, floated in her mind's eye, merging with those of Claudine and Mathieu, both safe and well-loved by her friends. What would her beloved Sylvain do in her place? She shrugged, a man would start walking south through the forest, then go to a farm and ask for work, until he found his way to a Résistance group. Women didn't go to an unknown farm and ask for work.

Night fell. Julie could barely see the path in front of her. She stopped before emerging from the wood. She surveyed the fields and the farm beyond. No light shone from the buildings, and there was no discernable movement anywhere. She took a deep breath and set off along the margin of the potato field toward her fate.

Chapter Three

Paris, Tuesday, September 15, 1942

More bombing in the suburbs last night, and some again this morning· We have to accept now that our Allies will inflict much destruction on our cities in the guise of destroying factories, railroads and whatever they think will make them win the war· What are the pundits thinking when they know that bombs also fall on houses and kill people who want nothing else but to be left in peace? They think that people are expandable and a small price to pay compared to the cost of the total war· Human lives don't count for much in a war· Soldiers don't count for much either in the political aspect of the war· The excuse is that they have to do their duty· What duty? The duty to kill and die?

And the attacks against the Germans continue to increase· I want to respect everybody's opinions, but I don't like what the communists are doing· Why don't they save their people to act at the right time, when the British and the Americans are about to land?

Food· Food· That's all we hear everywhere on the streets· A family's rations are barely enough to feed one person, but it has to be shared among two or three· I'm so worried about the younger children· Their growth is delayed· Lyse-May's milk ration as a J1 is no more than a cup· I registered her as a six-year-old to put her in the J1 category so she'd have the larger milk ration· How can a child grow strong bones on so little? Not to mention there's never enough milk to serve everyone at the crèmerie· The child is so skinny· She doesn't complain, but I see her scrunch her face when hunger twists her insides· I ought to convince Gontrand to let her go to school· Damien said they get a vitamin biscuit· There are canteens in the elementary schools, but Micheline reported that some days there's no food, just pieces of dry bread. She said moldy, but I can't believe they'd give children moldy bread. My husband maintains she gets more at home. I've seen him slip her some of his own food. When I confronted him, he needs food too, he said he only needs energy for one leg.

Since the rafle du Vel d'Hiv, women are outraged at what happened. It's a general topic in the queues when we can stop talking about the best recipes on how to cook without ingredients. I guess that horrific events like those are awakening the population's conscience. About time, too. Gontrand still venerates his Marshal Pétain but is a little less vocal about respecting his wishes or laws, or collaboration.

In the queue I delight in telling the women over and over that earlier in the summer four résistants, in Belgium, dressed up like Germans, went to burn all the papers of the census of the Jews. That will save a few lives, at least for a while.

I wish Julie could come back. I love her like a daughter. I'm so sorry Agnès decided to make her own life the way she wanted. I wasn't going to interfere but her father can't accept she has different ideas, didn't want to go to university and didn't want to get married. I don't think living in common with a black man is necessarily the sign of a débauchée but that's how he sees our daughter.

I wonder where I failed in raising my children. If it wasn't for Bernard and Sylvain, I'd be thoroughly depressed. Where are they now? Bernard is playing such a dangerous game in the Résistance. He won't admit he's in it. I suppose it's for security reasons. My heart still grieves for my Florent. His life was so full of promises.

I wonder how difficult it is to get an Ausweis. I would like to go and see my sister in Pontcharra. I could take Lyse-May. The mountain air would be good for her and they have better food in the zone nono.

Pierrette is late again. It's curfew time. She'll give us a heart attack one of these days.

The door being closed quietly brought Bérangère to her feet. She saw Pierrette step into the kitchen as if she had conjured her.

Gontrand put the newspaper down. "And where have you been that you missed the curfew? *Hein?*"

"Sorry, grand-papa, I couldn't avoid it. There was another raid on Jews today."

Bérangère sighed. "And what did you do?"

"Nothing. I was in rue du Puits de l'Hermite when I heard crying behind some garbage cans. It was a little boy. He said his parents had to go on the bus with his big sisters, but they forgot him. He knew he had to hide, but he was hungry so he came out to look for food and couldn't find any. It was already almost curfew, so I was going to bring him here."

"Why didn't you?" Gontrand said.

"Because when we walked past the mosque, a man was looking in the street and asked why the boy was crying. I said he was an orphan. Well, he isn't yet, but we've never seen any of the Jews that were taken by the police come back home. The man looked at the boy's yellow star on his chest and bent down to talk to the boy."

"By which time it was curfew," Bérangère said.

Pierrette nodded. "The man said *mektoub*. I think it means something written in the sky because he looked up at the sky. He said he was an Iman. Then he said the mosque would take care of the child."

"But the boy's a Jew," Gontrand said. "And an Iman is a Muslim."

Bérangère pointed her pen at him. "He is a compassionate human being. And so must be all the people who go to the mosque."

"I'll be darned what we see these days!"

"I should be registering for university tomorrow, but the program has been changed to kowtow to the master race."

Bérangère frowned. "What do you mean, the program has been changed?"

"Political Science courses have to reflect the new ideology. The Vichy one, that is, but it's no different from the Nazi beliefs."

Dismayed, Bérangère said. "Mon Dieu! They're indoctrinating children now."

Pierrette kissed her grandparents goodnight and ran upstairs to her attic bedroom.

Chapter Four

Julie took another deep, calming breath and glanced around. She heard rather than saw the farmhouse door being opened. The friendly dog ran up to her. It struck her that the dog never barked. Then she was at the door.

An unseen hand pulled her into a warm room. “Come in.”

“Merci.”

The door shut behind her. The light came on. Julie stood in front of a wiry man, his face weather-beaten. Streaks of silver ran through his short hair. The woman who had pulled Julie inside dropped her hand.

“My poor dear, what an ordeal for you.” The woman’s tone was warm and kind.

“I’m so grateful to you...”

The creak of a door sent a shiver of fear into Julie.

“It’s our son.”

A young man entered accompanied by the black and brown dog. He dropped the armful of logs he was carrying. He added one to the stove, then shrugged off his coat and threw his béret on a chair. The dog sat obediently at his hand signal.

“Nothing to report. Bonsoir, madame.”

Julie swayed on her feet.

The farmer’s wife pulled out a chair from the table. “There, sit. You’re at the Beugney farm. I’m Hortense. Pip, here, our Beauceron, found you and decided you were a friend.”

The two men sat at the table while Hortense fetched a steaming soupière from the stove.

“Antoine,” she nodded toward her husband, “we call him Toine, has arranged the room in the attic. I dry herbs and apples up there. Now, help yourself to soup. There’s plenty. You must be starving. You can stay here until all the hoo-hah is over.”

Julie held her spoon mid-way to her mouth. "You mean the accident at the lock?"

Toine nodded.

"Serge, cut another piece of bread for madame," Hortense said. "Eat plenty, I have some hidden reserves."

"I suppose you need to know that we are in the occupied zone," Toine said. His deep bass voice reverberated against the stone walls.

Serge raised a hand. "But you're safe."

Julie wiped her mouth. "Thank you! I have no words to express my gratitude to you."

Hortense shrugged. "No need to. We do only what's right."

Now relaxed, Julie smiled at her hosts. "I'm known as Anna. I was on the barge. It's a miracle I escaped." A deep sigh rose from her chest. Her throat constricted.

Serge reached out and put his callous hand over hers. "I'll tell you our end of the explosion. I was with some friends a little way downstream when we heard a shot, then machinegun fire and almost right away an explosion, like maybe a grenade. We knew something had gone very wrong."

"So, you were the recipients of the weapons."

"Yes. I'm relieved that you're one of us, and not just some girlfriend Marinier took along."

"How can you be sure I'm one of you?"

Toine laughed. Serge smiled. Hortense rolled her eyes.

Serge laughed. "The way you said you're known as Anna. Only someone with a fake identity would say it like that."

Hortense took the empty soup plates away and put a dish of baked apples on the table. She served the crisp, hot dessert into small bowls and passed them around.

Julie took a deep breath. "You're right. I was asked to go along to distract the guard. It was the first time the cargo would be weapons and explosives." She tilted her head and stared at the wall. "There were two men besides Marinier."

Serge raked his hair. "Marinier didn't make it. One man, we assume it's Moustique, got away. We didn't know about a second man."

"Théo. I disliked him on sight. Forgive me, but that's what I felt when I met him. He panicked while I was flirting with the guard, who wasn't looking at the papers while he stamped them. Théo shot the guard. The last I saw he had a grenade in his hand, the other guard came out and fired his submachine gun, but by then, I was already jumping overboard. It all happened at once, in a split second."

"Less time than to tell about it." Hortense smiled.

"*Dieu*, you jumped in the canal between the barge and the wall?" Toine's eyes widened.

"I had no choice. Somehow, I didn't think. I acted. It was hard, but when I thought I was far enough. I got out and walked along the fields. It was night and I just about bumped into a stone hut."

"Ah! the *gariotte*," Hortense said. "A shelter for the shepherds. Not used anymore."

A chuckle from Serge drew attention to him. "The door hinges are well-oiled, the latch very smooth and the hay is kept fresh."

Hortense looked surprised. "You didn't tell me."

"Maman, we can't tell you everything. It's safer not to know the details." He turned to Julie. "Then you made your way here."

"Not exactly. I didn't know where I was, but I'd seen the forest from the barge and aimed toward it. I'd be able to hide there. I couldn't see any farm."

"The Beugney forest is pretty big, but it is bordered by fields, so you'd end up at a farm sooner or later. I'm glad you found the way to us," Hortense said. "I'll get you some clothes and shoes." She raised her head toward her son. "How long before it is safe to move Anna?"

Inwardly, Julie smiled. That's how she and her group talked when they had an airman or someone fleeing. They were packages and, like packages, they were moved from one safe house to another.

"Right now, the Germans are combing the area around the lock because there was a report by a local that a man was seen swimming away."

"If that was Moustique, he probably swam upstream like I did. The guard hadn't already closed the gate."

Toine chuckled. "He was distracted by a beautiful woman."

Hortense playfully slapped his hand.

"We were expecting Moustique. He was to help us, teach us about the weapons. He was from England. From what you say, he logically swam all the way back into the zone nono."

"If Marinier didn't make it, what about Théo, the other man?"

"If he had a grenade in his hand, as you said, he must be pulverized."

The women pinched their lips, then sighed.

"What about the guards?"

"They were taken by ambulance, most likely to Digoin. The gendarmes are also searching, slowly, very slowly. The Germans' tracker dogs didn't find any trail."

"Not even mine?"

Toine shook his head. "We had a light rain in the night. Sometimes the *bon Dieu* is on our side."

"Yes, sometimes God is good. For the time being, you're safe here," Hortense said. "Come with me, I'll get you clothes and shoes and show you your bed."

"I smell of stagnant water," Julie said.

They burst out laughing. "No worse than the sheep after the rain."

"If it makes you feel better, I can put some hot water in a crock and pour it all over you in the laundry tub. Your dress is ruined anyway. It'll wash off some of the smell."

At Julie's nod, Hortense drew the hot water from the tank on the side of the woodstove.

After a restful night, Julie rejoined her hosts, who had just come in for breakfast. "Oh, you did chores and didn't wake me up to help."

"You needed to recover, Anna. The Chleus will probably stop by again today. They have extended their search area," Serge said.

After a hearty breakfast of bread, butter from ewe's milk and a slice of cold mutton, Julie helped Hortense hang the laundry. The men went to begin digging the potatoes.

"Our neighbors usually come and help with the potatoes but since the Fritz are nosing around, everyone is staying close to home."

Julie didn't reply immediately for at that moment the sound of a car arriving broke the morning peace. "Gasoline, not gazogène. That'll be the Fritz," Julie said.

The two women continued hanging the sheets on the line. A gendarme came up to them, followed by a German soldier.

"Bonjour, mesdames. I won't take time away from your chores. Did you see a strange man around here?" the gendarme asked.

"No. It's just me and my daughter," Hortense replied.

"Where's your husband?"

"My husband and son are in the potato field."

"That's fine," the gendarme said. He started to move away. The soldier tapped him on the arm.

"*Niemand*?" the soldier asked.

"*Nein*," replied the gendarme. "Au revoir, mesdames."

Nobody. The Fritz was satisfied with the answer. Julie's heartbeat returned to normal.

"Don't worry, they won't come back. In another day or so, we'll have you on your way."

***

The taciturn young man led his mule cart to the door of Le Monastier's post office. Julie jumped down and thanked him. For the first time since Solignac, he smiled at her before turning back. Julie had already been seen. Thérèse Lafleur ran out of the building and engulfed her in a hug. Running steps behind them brought Denis, who enveloped both in his brawny arms. Now half a dozen persons surrounded Julie. René pushed his way through them to hug Julie, who was a little surprised at the reception.

"*Bon Dieu de Bon Dieu*, you're alive!" René said.

Tears flowed freely. "Oh, God the good Lord!" Someone intoned.

Puzzled, Julie noticed the unrestrained tears on her friends' faces. "Thank you."

"How did you survive? They said everyone had been killed in the explosion."

They dragged her to the café. Coffee and a couple of forbidden croissants were put in front of her. "Someone went to fetch Marguerite."

Julie was in the middle of recounting her ordeal when Marguerite with Julie's children arrived. More hugs and, with Claudine and Mathieu on her lap, she finished her tale.

"But they were still looking for a man when I left."

"Moustique's safe," Denis. "Everything is quiet now. The Fritz are busy repairing the lock. The Chassenard mayor persuaded them that it was arms for the garrison in Digoin and that the barge master had dropped his cigarette in the hold, hence the explosion."

"And they believed him?"

Joseph shrugged. "They have no reason not to. The résistants in the area have not been attacking their troops."

"That's lucky."

"There's a saying that you catch more flies with honey..."

General hilarity prevailed until finally Julie and Marguerite were able to go home.

"How long are you going to stay?" Marguerite asked.

"A few days at least. If René and Denis don't need me, I think I'd like to go back to Paris."

"You're safer here."

"But there's a lot of work to be done in Paris. Maybe it's selfish, but I want to take my children with me. I miss them so much. It's been arranged for me to have a new address in Paris. In a new place, I can live a normal life."

Marguerite laughed. "You'll soon be drawn into helping a group or two. Didn't you do that already?"

"Yes, I know. But at least I know I can bring my children to you if the need arises. What was Denis complaining that the Service d'Ordre Légionnaire has become as bad as the SS?"

"True, but there are no one from that phony force supposed to keep order here in Le Monastier."

"That's why I'd prefer to go to Paris. If I, or one of us, was caught, they'd soon fall on the village. Being local, I think Denis or René have ways I don't."

"True. Although everyone in the village holds the same beliefs, you never know what one person can succumb to. When exactly do you intend leaving?"

"When it can be arranged with Dédé."

"Ah, yes. Your friend with a pass."

Julie smiled. "He does business for the Fritz at the same time as he does for us."

"This war makes us all do things we never thought of doing before." Marguerite shook her head. "Some know how to do it, though."

Claudine threw her arms around Julie's neck, who kissed her sweet face and made her laugh.

Chapter Five

Dédé surveyed the paraphernalia in the middle of the sitting room.

"If you don't mind, I'd like to hide something below the baby's mattress, in the carriage."

Julie knew that Dédé would be transporting some legal matter and some not so legal, starting with herself and her children. She didn't think the Auweis she'd been provided would stand scrutiny, but these days, one had to have blind faith.

"Where are we crossing the line?"

He scratched his head. "I could cross at a busy post late in the day when the Fritz are getting tired and want to be finished as fast as possible in order to get to their supper, or I could try a track in the forest but it can get very bumpy. I'd risk it on my own, but with the babies, if I get a puncture or breakdown, it wouldn't be very good."

"Are you thinking of the Givry Forest with Michel Curie's help?"

"I did a couple of runs with him."

"Then let me pack an emergency backpack, just in case I had to go through on foot with my children."

"Go ahead. I'll load all this."

Denis and René came in to give a hand. Marguerite dressed the children in warm outfits. It came time to leave.

"Return any time you need to," René said.

Marguerite hugged her. "It's your second home."

Sadness accompanied Julie who watched in the side mirror until her friends disappeared from view. October had arrived with its shorter days. Leaves floated gracefully to the ground. It wasn't cold yet. They met up with Michel in uniform with the police wagon.

"I'll lead the way. We shouldn't have any problem. You'll get to Givry in the occupied zone in no time. There's been no rain. It's all dry."

In Givry, Dédé drove to a small hotel. "I'm known here. No need for identity cards."

Next evening, Dédé pulled into the Manoir's courtyard in the dark. Once more, they had succeeded in making a clandestine crossing of the demarcation line.

***

Lyse-May was ecstatic at Claudine's return and embraced Mathieu joyfully. The rest of the family was no less happy about meeting Julie and her children. No word was mentioned about Mathieu's appearance or age.

Bérangère brought attention to herself when she announced her intention of going to Pontcharra to visit her sister.

"Surely, you can get me an Ausweis, Bernard."

He looked dubious.

"I can make you a perfect one," Alexandre said. "But recently, the Frisés have been modifying them almost daily. There's no guarantee that a border guard wouldn't spot a fake."

Bernard raised an eyebrow. "Why do you want to go to Pontcharra now that winter is coming? Not a good time to travel."

"We can't even write like we used to. In Camille's last letter, she said she had no reply to her previous two letters and wondered if something had happened to us. I never received the letters. The post office is either negligent or the censors destroy them. It happened to my friends too."

"I'll see what I can do."

"I'm taking Lyse-May."

Bernard nodded. "Of course."

To Lyse-May's regret, her mama Julie had to leave in the afternoon to go to her new apartment. As tears pooled in his little niece's eyes, Bernard picked her up.

"Let's go and help mama Julie settle in."

That and the promise to go on a train soon dried her tears.

I was dark by the time Dédé pulled up in front of Number 38 rue de la Lancette. The two men quickly installed the child's bed and an antique crib from the Manoir's attic.

"It's all basic furniture, but I'll ask mother for some more for you."

Julie laughed and punched him on the shoulder. "It'll do just fine." Her helpers left. She made the beds and sat watching her babies play on the floor. *What a pity we can't go to the apartment rue Victor-Hugo. It's more spacious and Madame Durand had offered to look after the little ones. But it wouldn't be safe. Meinhard knows that the concierge doesn't have grandchildren in Paris. Tomorrow, we'll explore the area.*

A knock interrupted her train of thought. She opened the door to a middle-aged woman with hair pinned into a tight bun.

"Are you the new concierge?"

"Uh... er... no. A friend who lives nearby told me this was vacant. Do you know the landlord?"

The woman gave a forced laugh. "Long gone... he's Jewish, you know."

"That doesn't bother me. Do we deposit the rent somewhere?"

"No, the Fritz let you deposit the money, but the landlord wouldn't be able to take it out. He needs food like everybody..." Hand over her mouth, she stopped aghast.

"Let me guess. He's in hiding and you're helping."

"You're not going to denounce us, are you? Because we'd get friends to teach you a lesson. A permanent lesson."

Julie smiled. "I'll help too. Tell me how."

The woman exhaled a long sigh. "Me and my big mouth. Do you want the concierge's job? You get a stipend for keeping the place clean and taking care of the twelve tenants. You collect the rent and hide it."

"That'll suit me just fine."

The woman hesitated. "I'll take you to him and his wife. They live in the attic. The front is full of furniture. The back is where the living quarters are. You can't tell from the door unless you know."

"What about footprints in the dust?"

"Lydia, that Joachim's wife, thought of it. We turned the space in front of the old furniture into a playroom. The other tenants' children come to play and my daughter Colette takes care of them."

"How many tenants know about the hiding place?"

"Only the two who have young children. I told everybody that the rent had to be deposited in the mailbox, but some don't. They take advantage."

Julie nodded. "Then I'll call myself the concierge and see to it."

"I'm Germaine."

"I'm Josiane. Claudine is eighteen months. Mathieu is six months. We'd gone to the country and just came back."

Germaine frowned and tilted her head. Julie stretched her lips in a tight smile. "Claudine's adopted."

Relief spread on Germaine's features. She patted her chignon back in place. "Husband?"

"He was caught in a raid. Sent to Germany, I suppose."

"It happens a lot. Is he..?"

"No, he isn't a Jew."

"Then he has a chance, right?"

The lies flowed easily. By now Julie was adept at embroidering the truth. "I hope so. What about you?"

"My youngest daughter and her four-year-old daughter, that's Colette and Viviane, came to live with us when her building got unstable after the bombing. Her husband was killed in '40. My oldest daughter, she's twenty-two, and my son, he's seventeen, were already living with us. We're crowded in the two bedrooms. I was planning to settle Colette in the loge."

"I'm sorry. Do you want me to try to find something else?"

Germaine sighed deeply. "Are you going to get a job?"

Julie nodded. "I'll be looking, yes."

Germaine hesitated. "If you're going to have a job, Colette could look after your children. She could move in?"

Julie smiled. "That would be perfect. She can have the second bedroom with Viviane."

"She's... she's a bit shy. She's been really... disturbed, like shocked at her work. She's just going to turn twenty. She can't go out to work, yet. The fear, you know."

"I understand. The only problem is I don't have much money right now, not till I find work."

"Oh, that's alright. She has her widow's pension. Not much really, but she can buy food. I'm glad we can help each other. I'll go and fetch her."

While Germaine went upstairs, Julie gave a snack to Claudine and a last bottle of diluted milk to Mathieu. She readied them for the night. Germaine came back with Colette and her daughter.

"I'll let you two get acquainted." Germaine left.

"Nice to meet you, Colette. And this is Viviane?" She

crouched by the four-year-old who was sucking her thumb.

"You're taking me?" Colette reddened.

"If you would like to care for my children while I look for work. I'll give you my ration cards. You can do the shopping..."

Colette burst into tears. "I... I don't go out."

"Sorry, you don't have to do the shopping." A silence stretched. "What happened?"

Colette cried louder. Viviane rushed to her mother and sobbed.

"Dry your tears, Colette. I think I can guess."

The startled woman looked up. "You..."

"Yes, me too."

The two women fell into each other's arms. When the tears dried, they re-arranged the meager furniture. Colette went up to fetch her belongings, and her brother brought Viviane's cot down.

Julie made an ersatz which claimed to have one grain of real coffee in it. "Where are the best places to buy food?"

"Mom says that if you go at the end of the street where there's a dead-end alley, La Brèche, you'll find a woman at Number Five. She's a bit expensive, but she has products."

"Black market stuff?"

"Yes, but without it, we'd starve."

"We would. I know. I have enough money for a few things. Now about the children, Claudine is toilet trained during the day."

"We'll manage. We go up to the playroom every day, except Sundays. Mom told you about the playroom. The older children join us on Thursdays as they don't have school."

"Very good. Does the elevator function?"

"It does. Mom and I bring supplies to madame Lydia. She's very nice."

They chatted a while longer and went to bed, happy with the new arrangement.

***

On Joachim's advice, Julie wrote the name of the last tenant she collected rent from on a sheet of paper and put it in the money box, which she inserted into a cleverly hidden crevice in the cellar wall. Her search for a job had been unfruitful, but she had no doubt that she'd be contacted sometime soon. With the Allied bombings intensifying, the Gavroche escape line must be busy. Early in the morning, she dressed warmly to go and take her place in the queue at the bakery. October was pleasantly warm, but standing without moving soon chilled a body.

"Colette, I'm going."

The young woman winked. "I hope you get a lot."

At the bakery, Julie obtained two bâtards. Three would have been better, but the kindly baker's wife couldn't fulfill all the tickets.

"And it's only eight o'clock, ma'am. My Aldo worked all night. I don't know what we're going to do if the Chleus keep on stealing the flour."

"We'll all do our best."

"You're new here."

Julie had tried to watch how she spoke in order to fit into the district. She gave a sad smile. "I came to share an apartment with a friend. It's cheaper. We have children. Three between us."

"Ah, oui, *p'tite madame*. Life's difficult with children." While talking, she served the next customer. "That's it. No more."

A discouraged grunt answered the storekeeper. Julie didn't mind being called little lady, but it also means she didn't quite look like the people in the quartier. She went out under the envious stares of the women who were too late. They dispersed to try to find bread somewhere else. The queue at the grocer's was shorter, and Julie wondered whether it meant there would be nothing left by the time her turn came.

The women and an old man were holding an animated conversation. "It's a shame our police helping the Huns like that. What does it matter if people are *Youpins* or not, people are people."

"The Fritz lie, you know. They say they're sending the Jews to work in the east, but little children can't work. It's monstrous taking the children."

"Vichy is supposed to do the administration. How come they're letting the children go?"

"They're no better than the *Doryphores*."

Julie bent her head to hide her smile. Doryphores, after the Colorado beetle, was only one of the derogatory names people called the occupiers.

"Were you in the rue de Bucci last May?"

"You bet I was! It's us women who have to demonstrate against the damn Boches!"

"Who killed the policemen?"

"Nobody knows."

Julie nodded imperceptibly. Of course, nobody knows, nobody will denounce a camarade.

"Quite a few of us were arrested."

"The men in the government are all traitors sold out to the Boche!"

"They should remember that when women get angry, they're the ones who bring about revolution, like in 1789. It's us women who marched clamoring for bread."

"We've got to throw the Boches out!"

"We thought Marshal Pétain was going to get the armistice army and push the Chleus back to where they came from."

"What d'you think an eighty-four-year-old was going to do?"

"Have a siesta before the parade."

More raucous laughter erupted. "Eighty-six now, you know. Probably quite senile."

"It's depressing."

"When are the Americans coming?"

"They were late into the last war, an' they'll come late again in this one," the old man said.

"But they're already fighting alongside the Anglais. That's what I heard, camarade. They're coming to land here."

"In the meantime, the meat ration is so small you can wrap it in a Métro ticket."

The quip sparked some guffaws in the line. "Make sure it doesn't fall through the punch hole."

Julie joined in the laughter. She left the store with five potatoes and two rutabagas in her filet. It wasn't a meat day, and she already had the milk ration for the babies and Viviane. On her way back to the rue de la Lancette, she almost bumped into a well-dressed businessman.

"*Pardon, monsieur*." She bit her lip to contain her laughter.

On the pretext of steadying her, Bernard apologized for being in her way, and added for her ears alone, "Four this afternoon at Café de la Paix."

Energy flowed in her veins. Bernard had work for her! Back in her new home, Colette helped her dress smartly for her rendezvous.

"Let me do your hair."

Julie dutifully sat while her friend expertly styled her long brown hair. Satisfied she looked her best, Julie took the Métro in the direction of the Opéra.

***

Madame Durand held her breath and tried to squash the panic in her chest. The tall, and admittedly handsome, SS officer climbed out of the gleaming red car she knew only too well. She squeezed her eyes shut. If she didn't move, maybe the man will think she wasn't there. But Madame Durand forgot the door of the loge wasn't locked.

Meinhard knocked twice. As there was no response, he opened the door.

"You need not hide from me. Go and tell Madame de Montregard that I wish to speak to her."

Madame Durand remained stock still for a moment, not understanding why he was so polite when the last time he came he went straight to the second floor. "I'm sorry, monsieur. Madame de Montregard is away."

"Where? When?"

"She's gone to the country. She didn't confide in me."

"Where is she?"

"In the country, monsieur. I can show you the empty apartment, but you can't requisition it because she'll be coming back."

His anger was mounting. "Did she have children with her?"

"Of course. That's why she went to the country. For their health."

He looked at the concierge as if she spoke from another planet and took a threatening step in her direction. "Two children?"

"Oui, monsieur."

"Her children?" He seized her arm.

Madame Durand didn't like being manhandled. "How would I know? It's her job with the Red Cross."

"Two babies?"

"Two children, oui, monsieur."

"Where is the child she adopted?"

"I presume with her, monsieur."

He shook her. "And the baby?"

Although her heart beat too fast, the concierge lost her fear.

"What baby?"

"She had a baby. Where is he?"

"The Red Cross and the *Soeurs de la Piété* are doing all they can to get orphans adopted."

He gritted his teeth and pushed her arm away with enough force to make her stumble. He turned on his heel and strode out. The door slammed, making the glass rattle.

Meinhard got into his car and peeled away from the curb. Madame Durand wasted no time to walk as fast as she could to the bakery to have a message sent to the Manoir.

The Obersturmbannführer burst into the Gestapo office, pushing aside the adjutant.

"Sturmbannführer Kiefer, I need to find Madame Julie de Montregard."

"Address?"

"She is not there."

Kiefer sighed. "Address?"

"Number 198 rue Victor-Hugo. Now get on it."

"With due respect, Herr Obersturmbannführer, I have to know what the person looks like and why should my men be taken from their duties to look for your woman."

Anger coloring his tone, Meinhard spat out, "She is my wife-to-be."

Kiefer toyed with his pencil. "Is she French?"

Meinhard looked hard at the official sitting nonchalantly at his desk. "Only for the moment." He knew that marriage with an inferior race wouldn't be allowed, even if the Alpine race was second only to the Aryan race.

"But she is not your wife, Obersturmbannführer Meinhard."

Meinhard reddened.

"SS men, officers especially, must marry good German stock and provide children for our Führer."

The man was getting on Meinhard's nerves, but he needed his services. "I gave her a beautiful Aryan baby."

"That's interesting." Kiefer enjoyed making a superior officer squirm, particularly Obersturmbannführer Meinhard, universally disliked. "I'll see what I can do for you. Do you have a photograph?"

After a long moment, a furious Meinhard pulled out his wallet and extracted a photograph. "It was taken eight years ago, but she hasn't changed. Just more beautiful."

Kiefer curled his upper lip in a mocking smile as he took the photograph. He contemplated the lake at the foot of the mountains and the couple in profile looking into each other's eyes in the sunset. "Very well."

Meinhard made a gesture to retrieve the photograph.

Kiefer shook his head. "My men need it. I will return it to you after we make copies."

"Send it to me. I won't be back for a while. I'll be in Berlin."

Kiefer watched him go and threw the photograph onto his desk. "As if I was going to spend my time searching for the man's kept woman."

Kiefer's adjutant had come in. "Did you call me, Herr Sturmbannführer?"

"No, Schmidt, I did not. But since you are eager to work, would you like to find a missing woman?"

"If it helps you, yes."

"Good, find the woman in the photograph. Slowly. There is no hurry. And only when you are not on duty. I believe you can get a copy or two made at the photographic studio on boulevard Saint-Germain. It is highly recommended by some of our own people."

Adjutant Schmidt saluted and left. When he arrived at the studio, Charmaine was alone behind the counter.

"*Bonjour, madame. Est-ce que c'est possible de faire une copie de la photographie?*"

She put on her commercial smile, so used was she to foreign customers mangling the French. "Oui, monsieur. It is possible to copy the photograph. It will be ready tomorrow, Saturday."

"Do not rush. Monday will be good enough."

"We are closed on Mondays." She smiled. The young man was so gauche, it was amusing.

"Perfect. Tuesday then."

She wrote up the order. He handed her the photograph.

Charmaine looked at it and froze.

"Beautiful photograph, do you not think?"

She stilled her erratic heartbeat. "Most beautiful. Do not worry. I'll take good care of it." She forced herself to wait a few more minutes, just in case Mr. Schmidt came back, before rushing to the studio room where Alexandre retouched and colored photographs.

"Oh, chérie! What makes you so agitated?"

"This." She put the photograph down on his drafting table.

"Julie?"

"With that Meinhard fellow."

"What is it doing in the hands of a SS man? I saw him come in."

"I didn't ask. Could he or his boss be looking for Julie?"

Alexandre drew his hand across his face. "When is he coming back for the copy?"

"Tuesday. He said there was no hurry."

"That gives me plenty of time to do a little arranging."

"How?"

He caught her by the waist. "Trade secret, but I'll tell you. I'll make a negative, alter it suitably and print two copies."

Charmaine heaved a sigh and let herself drop on the only chair. "She's in danger."

"I think so too. If your Mr. Schmidt needs a photograph, he may not have seen her in person before."

"He wouldn't need a copy if he had."

"How can we warn her?"

The door chime tinkled. "Sunday at the Manoir. We'll see her or Bernard. I'll go and serve the customer."

***

A few hardy patrons sat on the terrace of the café. Inside, Julie saw Bernard at a table beyond the fluted columns. The gold decor and elaborate ceiling impressed her, but the men in gray-green uniforms sprawled on the velvet chairs promptly brought her back to grim reality. In his impeccable dark gray business suit, Bernard stood up and held a chair for her.

"I ordered wine and a dessert for us. No tickets needed."

"Thanks." She threw covert glances around the long room. "Isn't this a bit dangerous for me? Meinhard could come to a place like this," she whispered.

Bernard shuffled the brochures in front of him. "He's in Berlin playing politics."

Relief flooded over her. "I trust you. What's next?"

In an assumed voice. "As for your country house, could I recommend a chalet in the Alps?"

"Let me think."

The waiter approached and deposited a Fontainebleau au chocolat with a dash of crème Chantilly in front of her. He then served Bernard, while the sommelier opened a Saint-Émilion rosé. Bernard nodded his approval of the wine. The sommelier filled their glasses.

Julie made short shrift of the delicate Fontainebleau. "You were saying?"

Bernard made a show of opening some real estate brochures and handing her one. "There are many possibilities."

"Where would my knowledge of German be most useful?" She whispered while turning a page.

Their heads bent over photographs, he murmured, "Intelligence work where you can hear the Fritz's planning?"

"That would suit me fine," she said, her voice normal. Several Kriegsmarine officers had taken the next table.

"You said you didn't like Brittany."

"That's right. I'd never go there.

He threw his arms in the air as if he was weary of a difficult client. "What about this other one?" He pushed a brochure toward her, his voice low, "Supervisor of chambermaids at the Majestic." Then in a normal voice, "Take it home and peruse it at leisure."

"Well, thank you. You were most helpful. I'll make up my mind soon."

Julie carefully wedged the brochure, no doubt containing her instructions, into her purse and left. As she waited for the Métro, she wondered whether they really needed to go through such elaborate charades in order to meet. Would those Kriegsmarine officers have been interested in hearing that she was offered a job at the Hôtel Majestic? They probably didn't care about what the Militärbefehlshaber was doing at the Majestic. For a brief period, they were enjoying the good life in Paris.

Back home, she examined her instructions. Since her nemesis was in Germany, Julie decided it was safe to go to the Manoir for Sunday lunch and take Colette with her.

"Colette, I'd like to introduce you to the de Montregard family. You need to know just in case something happened to me."

"Oh, no! Don't let anything happen to you."

"My job could become dangerous. It's a fact. It's the reality under this Occupation."

"I really prefer to stay here. I can't go out."

Julie patted her friend on the shoulder. "I understand your fears. We'll get a vélo-taxi. Anyway, with the children, travel on the Métro gets too complicated."

"Are you sure?"

"You'll be safe with me, and my family will be welcoming. Trust me."

"I wish I had your courage."

"It'll come. I'll go and get a vélo-taxi."

***

Paris, Sunday, November 1, 1942

When I heard that the employees at the Grands Magasins like the Printemps and the Galeries Lafayette had asked the bosses of the department stores to lower their wages rather than dismiss them, I just about fainted. Employees are always asking for a raise, not a decrease in pay. These are the times we're living. Everything is upside down.

Pierrette said even the police are changing. She was caught with rather compromising documents and was let go.

I'm happy that Julie is back, but I worry that it is too much risk for her. And those raids against the Jewish population continue. What can we do to stop them? When our pro-Nazi government in Vichy made wearing of the yellow star compulsory, non-Jewish youths everywhere stuck yellow stars on their chests. A brave gesture that sent them to prison, but I admire their defiance.

Society is breaking down. People trade, sell, hide money, steal too, so they can buy on the black market. But will it stop when the war is over?

Gontrand is reading the paper. We don't want to read that garbage from Vichy but that's where there are announcements of food arrivals. It also states the rations for the month. Why do they bother? Rations just get smaller with every passing month. What is not right are the children in the poorer districts who have no shoes and can't go to school. They need their education to get a better life. They'll get sick going about barefoot in the cold. Not right!

Marie is raising a couple of rabbits in hiding. Lyse-May was in a state when she learned rabbits were to be eaten.

But I hear the door

Julie introduced Colette to her in-laws. They embraced the young woman. The chaos that usually came with the children astounded her. She stepped back against the wall on seeing the hugging and kissing of the women friends. Julie included her but Colette's strength was waning. Pierrette saw her withdrawal and came to take her arm.

"Come with me. It's too noisy here. I'm Pierrette. I'm twenty and I study political science. What about you?"

"I'm Colette Lemoine. I'll be twenty next month." She reddened. "I don't go to college."

"But you have a lovely daughter. See how she plays well with the little ones?"

Amazed, Colette watched how the children accepted Viviane as if she had always been part of the family. "Thank you. You're all very nice."

"And you're a bit overwhelmed. You'll get used to us."

After lunch, the adults stayed in the kitchen while some children played in the sitting room, the older ones having rushed upstairs to the playroom in the attic.

Colette tugged Pierrette's sleeve. "Do they have someone hidden in the attic?"

Taken aback, Pierrette had to think fast. "No, that's where my brother and I have a bedroom. And another couple of bedrooms for when our cousins stay with us. We made a playroom because there's not much room downstairs for the tribe."

"But the house looks enormous."

"Didn't Julie tell you? The Manoir has been requisitioned by a Wehrmacht general and his staff. So, we prefer to live in what used to be the servants' quarters. Come and see the attic. Why did you ask if we had someone hidden there?"

Colette bent her head, her lips pinched.

Pierrette smiled. "Attics are good places. I'm glad you have an attic to hide someone. And if you need help sometime, let me know. I have contacts."

Eyes wide and mouth open, Colette stared at her new friend.

After a moment of seeing Pierrette's smile, she passed her hands over her face. "You won't tell?"

"Of course not. Here, this is my room."

With the children playing elsewhere, calm returned to the kitchen.

"Surely, Bernard, there's a way to get an Auweis. Should I go to the Kommandantur and apply? Going to see my sister that I haven't seen in two years is a good enough reason. And I can bring back provisions."

"Here is your Ausweis, mother. And no, you better not bring provisions. They'd get confiscated at the line."

Surprise followed by happiness played on Bérangère's face. "You, rascal. You let me gnaw at my fingers all that time."

"I wasn't going to say anything until I was successful."

"It has Lyse-May on it."

"You said you were taking her. And the stamp is genuine."

François snickered. "Who stole it?"

"Arsène Lupin," Bernard replied in a deadpan voice.

No one had heard Lyse-May come in. "Who's Arsène Lupin?"

"A very famous thief in a book," Gontrand said.

"Can I read the book?"

Her question drew a few chuckles.

"Later, if I can get it," Julie said. "So, you'll be going on a long train ride with your mémée?"

Serious, Lyse-May said, "I am. I have to take care of mémée."

Brigitte carried Christiane and Julie carried Claudine to the spare room for a nap. The two little girls fell asleep hugging each other.

"What is it like in the south?"

"Quiet."

"Are you going to tell us about your epic adventure?"

Julie laughed. News had a way of traveling fast. Charmaine poked her head into the room.

"Come and tell us."

"I don't know whether everybody needs to know."

"Don't worry, Marie-Ange doesn't come anymore. Bernard and the children are quite happy."

"I might tell you the story, but I'll abridge it for the company. Some young ears could misinterpret."

They knew she meant Lyse-May always popping up where she wasn't expected. "Right, tell us here."

The three friends sat close together on one of the beds and Julie recounted the part on the barge and the explosion. "But to the rest of the family, I'll only say I was on a boat that sank."

Charmaine shook her head. "You're incredible."

"She's got nine lives," Brigitte said.

"She'll need an extra one. A SS man came to the shop to get a copy made of a photograph with Julie in it."

They looked at each other in alarm. Julie recovered first. "I know Meinhard is looking for me but his minions have never needed a photo, or so I think. Don't worry more than necessary."

"Anyway, no one should recognize you. Alexandre has done a little surgery on your face."

With a laugh, they went back to the kitchen where Julie gave an amended version of her survival in the forest.

Chapter Six

Shortly after noon, there was a knock on the door of the house rue de la Lancette. A man in the Printemps department store livery handed a heavy box to Julie and went back for a second one. She let it drop in the middle of the floor. Intrigued, Colette knelt down while Julie untied the string and unwrapped the brown paper. They weren't surprised that it had been used once before.

Colette carefully lifted a sheet of blank dressmaking pattern paper. "Look at these dresses!"

"From grands couturiers, no less. Let's see. This one by Madeleine de Rauch."

"And this one by Jacques Fath."

"I thought they had all closed down."

Julie sat on her heels. "Most of them are thriving, providing high fashions to the Fritz for their wives and girlfriends."

"But you're going to wear these, right?"

"Of course, my duties require me to dress in the epitome of fashion." She fingered the envelope she picked up from the second box. Her instructions. "I better put that in my purse. It's to give to my boss." She was lying, but Colette need not know the nature of her job.

"It must be your references."

"That's correct."

Colette shook her head. "The Majestic Hotel is full of Germans."

"Alas. But patience, they won't be there forever."

"Is it true that the Americans and the English are going to come and fight them?"

"I believe they will. You must believe it too."

Colette pouted. "I wish I could help."

"You are."

"I mean doing something real..." An incredulous look came over Colette's face. "You mean..." Then it dawned on her. "You are helping the comrades resist."

"Not so loud. Walls have ears."

"Sorry, I should know." She pulled the smaller box toward her. "There's enough makeup in here to last a lifetime."

They laughed. Colette unwrapped two tiny hats from the box. "You're going to look beautiful in these."

"I have to report at five o'clock."

"Then let me do your hair and makeup. I like doing hair for my mom and my sister."

An hour later, Julie looked as if she had stepped out of Le Petit Écho de la Mode, or *Marie-Claire*, two prized fashion magazines.

Colette grimaced. "The Fritz are going to look at you."

"It's part of the job, and I can look right back at them."

Colette full of admiration watched Julie stride toward the Métro station.

***

A fiacre waited in the courtyard of the Manoir. Gontrand leaned against the doorway of the west wing, chewing on the stem of his empty pipe, while Ernest and Marie helped Bérangère and Lyse-May settle in the carriage. As soon as they were away, Pierrette rushed out carrying her backpack. Her braids flew sideways as she turned to wave goodbye to her grandfather. He shook his head.

"Ernest, I wish I knew why a proper young lady goes round with boots and socks and little girl's braids. Where's she going with her backpack?"

"She didn't tell me, monsieur Gontrand. Our youths are very busy these days."

"You mean they still tear up posters?"

"Possibly."

"Don't tell me they're blowing up things and getting the Chleus riled up."

"Possibly. I must go and turn the soil over for next spring planting."

Gontrand groaned. When his long time helper, never servant, didn't want to answer questions, nothing could make him. "And I better go and tutor that groom how to take care of the general's horse. Such a lummox."

***

At the Gare de Lyon, Bernard discreetly watched his mother and his niece show their tickets and proceed to their platform. Worry creased his forehead. He hadn't told her that a man would be following her, all the way to Pontcharra where his cousin Christophe would then take charge. Hopefully she wouldn't notice. If she did, perhaps she'd have the presence of mind to ignore him. Bernard had rehearsed with the English airman the potential situations that could arise. He made another round of the concourse and spotted Pierrette. She had connected with the family she was to take to a safe house. He feared for her. At the start of the Occupation, adolescents like her, her brother and their cousins had made a choice and brazenly pursued their goal.

Bernard watched a moment longer as she shepherded three children, all under ten years of age, and a young man also carrying a backpack. *He'll never pass for the father. He's too young.* Bernard wished he could go with them and help, but he couldn't take the slightest risk to endanger the réseau and all the résistants that depended on his leadership. At the gate to her platform, Pierrette charmed the German soldier and the ticket controller. A rush of pride came over Bernard. His niece could hold her own, despite being so young.

Shoulders slumped, head inclined as if looking ahead at the ground in front, but with eyes covertly scanning the concourse, Bernard exited the station. He maintained that typical posture of Frenchmen burdened by the Occupation and shambled along Quai de la Rapée toward the Austerlitz bridge. He hadn't gone far before he sensed he was being watched. His responsibilities weighed on him. If he really had a tail, he had to shake it off without alerting suspicion. He turned into rue Traversière, entered an apartment building, crossed the lobby under the severe gaze of the concierge. Would she denounce him if the Gestapo came to ask? She didn't call out to him. He trusted that meant she'd not say a word if his pursuer turned up. He continued across the courtyard to another apartment building and came out into boulevard Diderot. He ran across to avoid a German car and dove into the nearest apartment building, hoping the door wasn't locked.

Relieved it was open, he found his way to the courtyard.

"You looking for somethin'?" Leaning against the wall, a man in a worn coat smoked a foul-smelling cigarette.

Bernard's training kicked in. He turned slowly. "The way out."

"Same way you came in."

"I'd rather not." He took a half-empty packet of Gauloises from his pocket.

The man's eyes shone briefly. "There's a corridor."

Bernard handed him one cigarette. A crooked smile lightened the man's surly air.

"One more?"

"Show me."

"Com'n."

Mindful of his instinct to be cautious, Bernard followed the man through a door and down a less than well-kept hallway. They turned two corners. The man opened a door and pressed the timer switch. A dim bulb flicked on.

"There's the corridor. Comes out on rue Audubon."

Bernard shook five cigarettes into the man's hand and stepped into the smelly corridor. He hurried to get to the end before the timer cut off the electricity. He reached the door just as darkness invaded the corridor. The well-oiled hinges opened silently, bringing a smile to his lips. Whichever side of the law the users of the door may be didn't matter. He'd remember the place.

***

Madame LePlouhëc's eyes took in every detail of Julie's outfit. "Perfect. You have a flair for clothes. Follow me. I'll show you the layout of the hotel. We have four hundred rooms. Except for a few suites, they are all offices for the Militärbefehlshaber. Let's start with Carl-Heinrich Stülpnagel's floor. You'll spend quite a bit of time here. He has a suite on the floor above, but he also has a suite at the Hôtel Raphaël, just next door and another one somewhere. Last May we had to host a social occasion when no less than Reinhard Heydrich introduced the new chief of police and of the SS, Carl Oberg. They're intent in exterminating all the Parisian Jews. I'm glad that Heydrich man went back to wherever he came from. He looked like a vampire."

Julie chuckled. "Nice description."

"Not that Carl Oberg looks any better. Ugly Nazis, all of them.

Now we come to the Grand Hall where conferences are held."

At a glance, Julie took in the potted palms, the intricate woodwork and the rich Persian rugs. Officers from the three branches of the German military were holding a heated discussion at a nearby table. A Luftwaffe officer stood up.

"Madame LePlouhëc, I am sorry, we are having a private meeting."

"Of course, Herr von Schäfer. I'm showing the ropes to our new supervisor, Madame Josiane Lesbois."

He turned to Julie. "Enchanté, madame."

Julie extended her hand, and he duly bent his head to kiss it.

"Please to meet you, Herr von Schäfer."

His eyes shone with appreciation. "The pleasure is all mine."

The two women withdrew to Madame LePlouhëc's office. "You'll soon learn that those gentlemen are in a constant battle with the Gestapo. That's what they were on about."

"The little that caught my ears sounded like a familiar refrain."

"That general at your in-laws? It's true. The military cannot stand the SS. It has got worse since Herr Joseph Göbbels established his propaganda HQ here. Anyway, the MBF has eleven hundred employees here. You'll only deal with the top brass, like Oberleutnant von Schäfer."

"Do I go around making sure the staff is serving properly?"

"Right. Several of our staff know to watch for your hand signals."

"I see. My cousin works at the Ritz. She explained about hand and head signals. One finger for food, two fingers for drink, patting the hair for an emergency. Do you do the same here?"

A smile lightened the Madame LePlouhëc's severe expression. "Yes. Just remember never to let on that you understand German, even if you hear something extremely outrageous."

"You needn't worry."

"I won't. I've already heard that you always keep your cool. Now I'll show you your own room. When a meeting goes on late in the evening, you'll have to stay the night. Bring some clothes. There're already some dresses in the wardrobe. If they fit, keep them. At the Majestic we collect intelligence. You write it on this onionskin paper, roll it up and slip it under the ink well on my desk."

Julie started. "Write it in clear?"

"Yes. It then gets coded and sent on."

A dubious look drew lines on Julie's face. "That won't do. What if someone forces his way into your office while I'm writing?"

"You eat it."

They laughed. "And I'll be arrested on the spot. I've carried messages that sounded perfectly innocent except to the recipient."

Her boss sighed. "The Militärbefehlshaber personnel are very respectful."

"Don't count on Oberg's staff to be as polite. He's SS, and they are a law unto themselves."

"You're right. Coding takes time. What do you propose?"

"If a message is to go to the south to be passed onto London, I'll write a letter to uncle George. If it's urgent and concerns Paris, I'll write about food."

"Such as requesting a factory to be bombed would be something like lots of potatoes wanted there?"

"Simple, isn't it?"

"Absolutely!" Madame LePlouhëc unlocked a cabinet and handed Julie a gift box. "You'll need this."

Julie opened the box. "A compact? A compact from Cartier? They don't deal in makeup."

"But they make gold boxes. Makeup in the possession of a beautiful woman isn't suspicious should you be arrested."

Talking about being arrested had become as casual as talking about a Sunday walk. It was a reality of life underground. Julie turned the delicately decorated gold box in her hand, opened it and laughed. "Clever. It's a camera. How does it work? Oh, I see. The lens is hidden in that intricate rose garland."

"It's a lovely design from our American friends. It may not be a true Cartier. They may have just borrowed the name. There's an important meeting tonight, but you won't need it."

At the appointed hour, Julie entered the meeting room. Oberleutnant von Schäfer greeted her in German. She looked at him as if he had gone mad.

"Sorry?"

"*Sprichen Sie kein Deutsch?*" he asked.

"I'm sorry, Herr Schäfer, I'm only here to make sure you're

comfortable and that the staff serve your food in the appropriate manner. I won't interrupt."

He continued in German. "You didn't answer my question."

"Is there something wrong, Herr Schäfer?" Her heart beat faster as fear began to creep down her back.

He smiled and switched to French. "I was just thinking that an educated woman would speak German."

She returned his smile. "I learned English with a view of working in a hotel. I was going to learn other languages, but I got married."

"Ah, voilà! And your husband?"

"A casualty of the war, Herr Schäfer."

"I am sorry to hear that. I shall let you get on with your work."

With a theatrical smile on her ruby red lips, she inquired about the welfare of each officer, noting which of them didn't speak French, and conferred with the head waiter before rejoining Madame LePlouhëc. She told her about the Oberleutnant asking whether she spoke German, before returning to the conference room.

The meeting broke up well after midnight. Julie couldn't wait to write down the stupendous information she had learnt. Madame LePlouhëc had fallen asleep on a chaise longue. Julie sharpened a pencil. Dear Uncle George. The friends who are staying with us want to go on holiday in the south before winter. They are already gathering a few things for an extended stay. The demarcation line is no problem for them. Prepare to welcome them. Your faithful niece, followed by an illegible signature.

Madame LePlouhëc woke up and came to read over Julie's shoulder. "Mon Dieu! Are the Germans really going to invade the free zone?"

"You got the meaning right away."

"One has to be in the right frame of mind to understand the hidden words. But is it true?"

"That's what I heard, loud and clear. They call it Unternehmen Anton. They discussed how to proceed without annoying Marshal Pétain. The Luftwaffe is in a sulk at being left out. Not allowed to bomb anyone. There was no mention of a date."

"I'll send the message."

"What about curfew?"

"The kitchen superintendent has a pass to go to the Halles and buy food for the hotel. He'll be going in a couple of hours."

"That's the other nightlife in Paris."

Madame LePlouhëc snorted and went to wake up the superintendent.

***

In Lyon, Bérangère took Lyse-May to the café de la Gare to have an early dinner while they waited for the Grenoble train.

"Y'a pas de Fritz, ici," Lyse-May said.

"Of course not, there are no Fritz here, we are in the non-occupied zone."

"Zone nono. Can I have more bread?"

Bérangère didn't reply and mechanically pushed her own slice of bread onto her granddaughter's plate. Her attention, and everyone else's, was attracted by two youths, wearing a uniform dark jacket over khaki shirts, who entered with a swagger. They strode straight toward a man in work clothes at the bar. A hush fell over the patrons. When the boys were at arms' length, the worker pivoted, seized the bar stool and threw it at them. Without wasting a second, he vaulted over the nearest table and in a couple of strides reached the door a patron held opened for him. The two youths picked themselves up and ran after the fleeing man. At the now closed door, the man thrust out his foot. The two stumbled and landed flat on their faces. Guffaws broke out.

Mouth open, Lyse-May stared at the door being closed behind the two boys.

"Eat your bread. Don't speak," Bérangère said.

Dutifully, Lyse-May complied, until they took their seat in the train for Grenoble.

"What were they doing, the people at the bar?"

"The boys in uniform help the German police."

"But you said, there're no Germans here."

The child's logic always astounded her grandmother. "It is very complicated. The German police in Paris give orders to the Vichy police and some young people go to a school... oh, *ma chérie*, it's too complicated. I can't explain. You'll ask tonton Hilaire to explain."

"He's the commissaire de police."

"That's right. He'll know."

The woman sitting opposite Bérangère laughed. "Ah, children! Always so curious. Look at the mountains, poppet. You don't have mountains in Paris. See how big they are."

Lyse-May knelt on the seat and pressed her face against the window to see better. A moment later a man looked into their compartment and took one of the free seats. Bérangère tensed. She had seen the man on the platform in Paris, then in the train. He had remained in the corridor opposite her compartment door. His appearance had something foreign about it. His long angular face didn't fit the French types. The thought that he may be a downed English airman germinated in her mind.

It dawned on her that his presence was no accident. He was following her to Pontcharra, probably to meet her nephew. According to her sister, Christophe was busy with a youth group. Now, she guessed what the youth group was about, helping airmen escape. No doubt Bernard was behind it. She promised herself to give him a talking to. He could have told her.

***

Pontcharra, Tuesday, November 3, 1942

My diary is safe at home under the marble top of the mantlepiece. But there are so many things I want to note before I forget them that I'll use this sheet of paper. I can always tuck it in the diary when I get back home.

What a change being in the non-occupied zone! It's a rest for the eyes not to see German soldiers on every street corner. But I'm surprised at seeing a few uniforms of that new Vichy creation, the Service d'Ordre Légionnaire. They have a school to indoctrinate children like those two in Lyon.

I think the sudards, that's how we in the north call the people in the zone nono, are talking much too loud. Maybe it's just my suspicious mind, but it can't be safe to express opinions against the Fritz as some do. When I mentioned it to Hilaire, he just shrugged. Then I told him about the youth incident in Lyon, he said the police follow orders from the government, and Marshal Pétain is the government. As for the SOL, he shrugged again in that typical Gallic way. "Idiotic fascist youths. Their stay in the Chantiers de Jeunesse didn't do them any good. When they came out they went straight back to praising the National Revolution and joined the SOL·" I don't like it· My sister says Hilaire follows the edict from the Vichy government conscientiously, yet burnt the directive to send twenty-five Jews to a holding camp·

There's a lot of complacency in the zone nono· Camille said that the brainchild of Vichy to encourage young men to volunteer for the Relève isn't working· Whoever thought that young people would sign up to go to work in Germany, even if it meant that a few prisoners could be returned to their families? Now the rumor is that they will make it compulsory· Mon Dieu, what sin did we commit that so much grief falls on France?

On the other hand, my nephew is so totally opposed to Vichy that he antagonizes his father at every turn· His mother and he hold quiet conversations· They both must be involved in the Résistance· I didn't know there would be a Résistance movement here in the free south, but come to think of it, it makes sense· They want the Germans out so that France can be whole again· How long will it take? We need help from the Americans and the English· I have to chuckle a bit· When anyone talks about the English, Jeanne d'Arc is no longer mentioned· Not unless they are Pétain supporters, in which case the English are still the enemy that burned our national heroine at the stake·

Christophe has taken Lyse-May to climb a "little" mountain· She already looks healthier·

I ought to go and help make dinner·

Chapter Seven

Paris,

Julie opened the door to a frazzled Brigitte and swiftly dragged her inside.

Brigitte pulled herself together. "I'm sorry to barge on you so early in the morning. I was followed."

With Mathieu in her arms, Colette told Viviane to help Claudine to the kitchen.

Alarmed, Julie strove to keep impassive. "Take a deep breath. Ten o'clock isn't too early. What happened?"

Brigitte handed her a cloth bag with knitting needles sticking out of the top. "I met Rose as agreed at the Marché aux Puces. There're some urgent documents in the pattern book. It has to be given to Léonie as fast as possible."

"Where did you notice you had a tail?"

"Rue Victor Hugo."

"But Léonie is at the Manoir cleaning the general's office in the morning."

"Not today. She's expecting the documents."

"I see." Julie chewed her lip. "Do you know if your tail followed you right up here?"

"I pedaled fast. I lost him in the Parc the Bercy, by the canal."

"You mean he was on a bicycle too?"

"Yes."

"Strange. I can't imagine a Gestapo on a bicycle."

A forced chuckle later, Brigitte said, "Don't tell me he was after a woman. Before I got to Léonie's, I saw a man sitting on a bicycle by the curb. Nothing special, right? The fact it's a little too cool to just idle in the street didn't grab my attention until he started behind me. Of course, I passed Number 198, and kept on a little faster. He was still behind. That's not just a man hoping to entice a woman. With those plans and documents from the Hôtel

Crillon in my bag, I wasn't going to take any chances."

"Ah, the Crillon! That's where the offices of the army headquarters are located. That's hot stuff to deliver to Léonie."

"It's obviously for the general."

Julie chuckled. "Ah, yes. I'm seeing a pattern, don't you?"

"So she can give it to the general and he can send it, let's say, abroad?"

"Cunning. What pretext does Rose have to go to the Crillon? She is not supposed to carry dangerous stuff, or anything at all. If arrested, she'd soon be identified as a German refugee, an enemy of the Reich."

"She sells her beautiful hand-knitted, or machine-knitted, I'm not sure which, sweaters to the officers and staff."

"I wonder who arranged that."

"Anyway, since I was seen in rue Victor-Hugo, I can't go back and I don't know who can go except you."

"Fine. I'll go. I don't start work till later."

Julie tied her Hermès head scarf over her hair, put on her split skirt, a coat and left while Colette and Brigitte chatted. She approached her apartment from the Place de l'Étoile, bicycling without hurry to make sure she didn't miss any out-of-place car or cyclist.

A last glance, and Julie hurriedly opened the coach gate and wheeled her bicycle into the courtyard. Still cautious, she entered by the back of the lobby. Empty. Madame Durand mustn't be back from shopping. The queues were getting even longer of late. She climbed the backstairs two at a time.

"Julie?"

"That's still my name. Brigitte was followed, but she evaded her tail."

"Merde, it's getting tighter and tighter."

"We have to be extra vigilant. Did you notice anything out of the ordinary in the street?"

"Not really. A man on a bicycle comes often and waits a couple of doors down. I saw him chat up the girls from the Foyer de Jeunes Filles."

"If he's trying to interest a girl from the Young Ladies Home, that might explain why he followed Brigitte. Unless, of course, he's waiting for me on orders from Meinhard."

"He isn't there every day. He's not here today."

"Must have been if he followed Brigitte. Maybe he won't recognize me anyway. Alexandre had the incredible chance to alter a photo of me, which is presumably used by Meinhard's goons to find me."

Léonie pursed her lips. "Don't trust those SS bastards. I'll go now. You follow in ten minutes."

Except for light bicycle traffic, rue Victor-Hugo was quiet. Julie dropped down to avenue Dufrenoy. None of the cyclists behaved in what she'd call a suspicious manner. At the Champs-Élysées, she was obliged to stop for the daily parade. A quick glance behind reassured her she had no reason to be concerned. Yet, she began to have the odd sensation of being followed. Close by, a man with a bored look, leaned on his bicycle. A young man, eager to show off, tried to keep his balance on his stationary two wheels. Around her, unsmiling women, with bulging paniers, grumbled at being held up by the marching troops. Bérets on men's head, woolen scarves wrapped around women's heads to keep out the chill and threadbare coats were the norm. She chastised herself for being paranoid and made it to her apartment on the rue de la Lancette.

Schmidt, the bored man with a béret pulled down over a woolen scarf, came alongside the curb and watched the woman enter the modest building. He'd been lucky to arrive just as she exited Number 198 rue Victor-Hugo, though he wasn't convinced she was the woman in the photograph, even though she had come out from the address he'd been given. Ready to return to his surveillance duty, he caught another glimpse of her just as she swung back the shutters of the ground floor apartment. No matter that she wasn't the right woman, he'd give the address to the Sturmbannführer, and call off his dreary surveillance task. Herr Kiefer could tell his Obersturmbannführer that there was nobody matching the photo. Schmidt would tactfully omit to mention the first woman whom he'd lost track of, like a rank amateur, in a park. Anyway, she hadn't come out of the building. He only thought she was behaving suspiciously. But then, dozens of people could be said to behave suspiciously. It didn't matter as neither women matched the photograph.

He blew warm breath on his hands and returned to his office.

"So, Schmidt, you followed that woman to... what is the name of the street?"

"Rue Lancette."

"And you think she lives there?"

"Why else would she open the shutters if it was not her residence?"

"Never mind, Schmidt. I shall give the address to Meinhard. And if it is not the woman, it will gain us some peace before we are ordered to search for her again."

"Herr Kiefer, could I look at the photograph again?" He raised his hand. "No, no, the original, not the copy."

"I sent it back to the Obersturmbannführer's office. He has phoned every day from Berlin! Why?"

Schmidt raised a shoulder. "The copy is slightly fuzzy, but never mind. It really isn't the same woman."

***

Docteur Bignon comforted Colette's father. "The cold brings on the pain. Take an aspirin. I can't get any medicine to kill the pain." He paused for a second. There was so little his friend could steal from the German requisitioned Lariboisière hospital. The résistants were taking more and more risks, which often resulted in injuries. He had to share his meagre resources to the best of his ability. "Now, believe me, monsieur Raynal, you'd feel better by taking a walk every day. Do you have a flannel?"

"Oui, I can help wrap it around him," Madame Raynal said.

She accompanied the doctor to the landing just as screams came from the concierge's loge. Madame Raynal recoiled and inhaled sharply. "Colette!"

As she made a move to run downstairs, Dr. Bignon grabbed her arm and held her back. "Don't," he whispered. With his chin, he indicated the two Feldgendarmes in the vestibule and a woman in a German nurse's uniform coming out with baby Mathieu in her arms. The guards preceded her and held the outside door open. A tall SS officer followed them.

A screaming Colette ran after them but was brutally thrown backward by the officer.

As soon as the door closed, Dr. Bignon ran down the steps. "Did they abduct the baby?"

Through her tears, Colette replied, "That German said it was his son."

Without waiting for more explanation, Dr. Bignon opened the door and saw the SS Opel pulling away from the curb. The two guards overtook on motorcycles. Dr. Bignon climbed into his Delahaye, glanced at his gas gauge and, cautiously keeping a discreet distance behind, set off after the car. After traversing half of Paris, he saw the motorcade turn into the rue Boissière. Since it was one of the shortest streets in Paris, Dr. Bignon continued along avenue Kléber, turned around the median and slowed to a stop opposite rue Boissière. He saw the motorcyclists ride away, but not the SS car.

From his vantage point, Dr. Bignon could see the Opel parked, almost blocking the street, in front of what he thought was a hôtel partculier. He decided to come back later and talk to the concierge of the luxury apartment building opposite.

He returned to rue de la Lancette.

"Now, Colette, take a deep breath and start from the beginning, slowly."

Her mother handed her a glass of water and pulled her hair away from her face. Viviane had stopped crying and was mothering Claudine.

"The officer said Mathieu was his son, and he was taking him. I said it was Madame de Montregard's son, adopted as she told me to say. Then I said you can't take him, and he pushed me away. The nurse took the baby. I was screaming." She sobbed. "What will Julie do?" Colette wrung her hands and sobbed louder. "I made a mistake, I said Madame de Montregard instead of Madame Lesbois."

Dr. Bignon flinched when he heard the name de Montregard. He straightened. "I saw where they went. You stay here. We're going to get the baby back." He left and returned to where he could observe what was happening in the rue Boissière. To his intense relief, the Opel was no longer in sight. He pulled up in front of the luxury apartment building and went to knock on the concierge's door.

***

Eyes red and swollen, Colette righted her posture after the doctor left. "Maman, I have to find Julie and tell her." She grabbed a head scarf and tied it around her hair.

"I can go. You don't have to go out."

"Maman, Julie needs to know as soon as possible. I must tell her. It's my fault I couldn't prevent him from taking Mathieu."

"It's not your fault..."

But Colette was already out of the door, leaving her mother astonished. She wrestled her bicycle out of the shed. The tires didn't need pumping, they had been filled with kapok since there were no repair kits for the tubes. She prayed she'd remember where the avenue Kléber was. It was one of those avenues leading up to the Arc de Triomphe. Colette found it and the hotel, but she knew the staff entered at the rear. Undeterred, she passed the hotel, turned in rue des Portugais, turned again on rue La Pérouse and there, beyond the bunker, was the staff entrance. She dropped her bicycle at the curb and ran... straight into the arms of a concierge.

"I need... it's urgent, really urgent. I must speak to Jul... Madame Josianne. Josianne Lesbois." Her breath came in short, sharp burst.

The concierge helped her into a small room and sat her down. "Don't move." He came back moments later with Madame LePlouhëc. Still out of breath, Colette managed to tell the staff manager her name and the reason for her disheveled appearance. Madame LePlouhëc wasted no time in taking Colette to her office.

Soon after, Julie came in. "You called for me?" She blanched on seeing Colette. "What? What's happened?"

"That SS man." Colette told what had happened at the rue de la Lancette apartment.

A rush of pain stabbed through Julie's heart. Her baby, her little Mathieu. The possessiveness of love rose in her chest. The mother and child bond finally grew and submerged her. No one on earth was going to harm him. Cold fury washed over her.

"I'm going to see Meinhard, right now. Excuse-me, Madame LePlouhëc—"

"Wait!" Her boss took her by the shoulders. "First, you get beautifully dressed, beautifully made up and your hair done, and I'll call a fiacre. You can't go confronting the vermin without all the aces in your hand."

Colette stood up. "I'll help do your makeup and your hair."

They adjourned to Julie's private room. It didn't take long, with the help of her friend, for Julie to assume the look of a poised aristocrat. Madame LePlouhëc nodded her approval and announced that the fiacre was waiting.

***

It was a short ride from the Majestic to Number Eleven rue des Saussaies. Julie's anger roiled up, threatening at any minute to spill over. She nimbly jumped from the fiacre and strode up to the entrance. The two sentries moved to bar her way. Unable to contain her white fury, she brushed them aside with an imperious gesture. An Unteroffizier stepped out of the guardroom.

Julie shot him an unsmiling glance. "Herr Meinhard... *Bitte*."

Unfazed, and slightly amused, as if he'd been expecting her, he bowed. "*Kommen Sie mit mir*."

He led her to the elevator. On the fourth floor, the grille was not even fully opened before Julie stormed out, her heels beating a tattoo on the oak parquet. The Unteroffizier had just enough time to knock before Julie threw the door open. It slammed back against the wall. Kurt Meinhard raised his head from the thick file he was reading.

"Julie, *liebling*." He directed a frown and abrupt gesture of the chin to the junior officer.

The Unteroffizier withrew, the smirk hastily erased from his face.

Julie turned on Meinhard. "What got into you that you abducted my child?" The anger in her voice was palpable.

"I removed my son from unsanitary conditions."

A rush of hate threatened to submerge her. "Mathieu is not your son."

"Seven months old, blond and blue-eyed, he is my son. Our son, *liebling*."

"No, he is not! He is nine months old. An orphan from the bombing on Boulogne-Billancourt." The lie came spontaneously. She watched the slight wavering in Meinhard's eyes. "You don't know the babies I adopted after you killed my own daughter. Babies your people made orphans."

The Obersturmbannführer tensed. "You did not adopt him. That blond and blue-eyed baby is my son. Our son." He accentuated the last two words.

"No, he is not!" Her rage sent sparks flying. "Where is he?"

He leaned back in his chair. "He is safe. That Lancette street is not a fit place to bring up my son. And you will give up that address too. It is not proper for my wife-to-be to live in a slum."

"You're delusional. I won't ever be your wife and the baby is adopted."

Meinhard jumped to his feet. "If he is not my son, then he will be raised by a good Aryan Nazi family."

He towered over her.

"Over my dead body!" The fleeting thought she'd have to pay dearly for that remark didn't stop her defiant attitude.

"That would not work."

Stupid SS man didn't understand the imagery. "Mathieu only knows me as his mother. He must be very distraught. Take me to him."

"In a few days, I have to go back to Berlin. Come with me."

"Fine. I'll take my children with me."

He took a step toward the window and glanced outside. "No, I will introduce you to many influential people. You cannot have children with you."

The quick thought that maybe he had been trying to repair his image after being sent to the Eastern front crossed her mind. That had been his punishment for raping not just any woman but a de Montregard. She was convinced General von Trennen had emphasized the aristocratic status of the name de Montregard. "My children will come with me. End of discussion."

The ghost of a smile floated on his lips. "My son is well taken care of by his German nanny and is learning German."

"You, pig! Despicable pig! I demand to know where the baby is." Her voice rose with an imperious tone.

His eyes shone with excitement. "This does not concern you. Not until you admit he is mine."

Before she could check herself, Julie landed a resounding slap across his cheek. Time froze for a fraction second. No French person, not even a woman, would strike a German officer and expect to get away with it. She expected death. But Meinhard laughed out loud. His adjutant cracked the door open.

"I do love your spirit." He glowered at his aide, who wasted no time in retreating. "You are coming with me to Berlin. You will be a sensation. I need you."

It was unbelievable that she had committed a major offence by striking him and he dismissed it as if nothing had happened. Triumph began to surge within her. She was right, he had need to restore himself in the eyes of his superiors. He needed her. That admission was the strongest weapon she had. She still did not understand his obsession with her, but she'd play it until she could retrieve Mathieu from his clutches, even if she had to suffer his assaults. "I think you're right. I'll go with you. I'll go home and plan my wardrobe now."

"I'll drive you."

"No thanks. It's just around the corner, and my neighbors don't need to see you."

"Women happen to like me."

Dieu, he's even more arrogant than I thought. "Women are jealous. Do you want them to throw acid at me?"

"That would be a real pity. I love how beautiful you are. But, as you wish, walk by yourself."

Julie hurried out, head held high with a disdainful air about her, Meinhard following two steps behind. Office doors closed softly as they passed. Clerks, with armful of files, averted their eyes. The sentries came to attention. Meinhard watched her retreating back for a few seconds before re-entering the hushed building.

Julie's heartbeat slowed. She assumed she'd be followed and went straight to the rue Victor-Hugo. Madame Durand rushed out in an agitated state.

"Madame Julie! Madame Julie! Monsieur Bernard came to fetch Madame Bodénan and said you're to go to the Manoir if you come here."

"Thank you. Did you see anything wrong around here in the last little while?"

The concierge wiped a tear with her apron. "I didn't see that Nazi. I heard that he... he took your baby. The only thing I noticed was a man sitting on a bicycle for hours, watching the young ladies from the Home down the street. A pervert, I thought."

"He must have been one of Meinhard minions."

"He looked like an ordinary person."

"That's what a good detective looks like."

"But the baby isn't his, the Nazi's?"

"No. My husband was hiding in Paris at the time."

Madame Durand smiled, apparently relieved. "You need to disappear again?"

"Indeed. I don't know where, though."

"These are the keys to my sister's apartment, Number Eight in Passage Lepic, third floor."

Uncharacteristically, Julie patted the concierge's shoulder. "Thank you. I'm grateful. Tell no one. I'm going up to pack a suitcase ready for a trip." If she'd been followed, it would look as she was doing what Meinhard had ordered.

As she stepped onto the sidewalk with her suitcase, an empty vélo-taxi cruised by. She signaled. Once on her way, she kept a close watch on the street and used her Cartier compact as a rearview mirror. She didn't detect any tail.

***

In the late afternoon, Dr. Bignon cut the engine in front of Number Twelve rue Boissière, and, with his black bag in his hand, knocked on the concierge's glass door. The woman lifted the curtain before answering.

"*Bonjour, madame.* I've been called to examine a sick baby."

"Oh? No sick baby here."

"Would that be across the road? I'm not sure now what number I was given."

The concierge frowned. "Well, let the brat die. That'll be one less Boche to worry about."

"Ah! You did see a car, and a baby taken in... would that be the Hôtel particulier across the road?"

"I'm not telling. Germans in the big house."

"What if I told you a good French baby had been abducted and taken to the big house, or perhaps one of the other apartment buildings?"

"Why the Fridolins do that?"

"Let's say the mother refused to go out with a German."

She frowned. "What d'you mean?"

"That a Fritz is taking revenge."

"*Mon Dieu! Mon bon Dieu! Jésus, Sainte-Marie! Joseph!* What will they do next?"

Dr. Bignon waited for the litany of saints' names to fall from the woman's mouth. When she paused for breath, he said, "Nothing good, madame, nothing good."

"The big car stopped across the street. You can't see much with all the greenery in the garden. They expelled the owners, you know."

"I'm not surprised."

"They were Jewish, you know. But they caused no trouble. It's not right all the same. Are you going to get the baby back?"

"I'll come back tomorrow with a few friends... When it's dark."

"I see."

"Don't tell anyone. Are there other Chleus in the house?"

"Two of them. They leave in the morning and come back very late, like at twenty-three hours, even midnight."

"So, tomorrow evening you could tell me if they're still out?"

"I'll leave the front door unlocked if you need a place to hide."

Jubilant, he kept his professional tone. "You're very good, madame. Can I do anything for you?"

The concierge sighed. "What can you do for my headaches?"

"I'll take your blood pressure first."

He finished examining the concierge and gave her a small vial of pills. "Only half a pill when the aspirin has not worked. That's all I have. Make it last till the war is over."

"Do you think it will end soon? The Fritz will go home?"

"Not for a while, but our Allies are making progress."

Back in his car, he sacrificed a page of his precious prescription pad to write a brief message.

***

At the Manoir, Julie could barely contain herself. Gontrand didn't know what to do and ranted about Bérangère and Lyse-May's absence. He urged Julie to wait until Pierrette came back. It was late when Julie's niece made an appearance.

"We know where Mathieu is." She put her hand out to check Julie, who had sprung from her chair. "Bernard has alerted some of our members. We're meeting at the Cave at eight o'clock tonight. You and I will walk there."

Julie gave a nervous laugh. "The sixteenth arrondissement has been requisitioned by the Boches, but it's chock-full of résistants' hideouts."

"Hiding in plain sight has a lot to say for itself."

"Let's go."

Bernard introduced Dr. Bignon to Julie, Xavier, Pierrette, François, Léonie and a handful of men Julie had never seen before.

"I called this meeting because Oberstumbannführer Meinhard has abducted Julie's baby, Mathieu."

A collective gasp went up from the crowded room.

"It's my fault." Julie couldn't repress a strangled sob. "Brigitte had been followed while delivering some urgent documents. She succeeded in losing her tail and came to me. I delivered the package. Although I made sure I wasn't followed, I must have missed something. Meinhard would never have found me, us, otherwise. I made a mistake." With an angry gesture, she wiped her eyes.

Pierrette stopped her aunt. "It's not your fault. Either the man on the bicycle was a French snitch, in which case we'll find him, or he was a well-disguised Gestapo goon."

Bernard thanked his niece with a nod. "Thanks to Dr. Bignon, and incredible luck, we know where Meinhard has hidden Mathieu. We're here to plan the best way to extract the child from the house without attracting unwanted attention and in a manner that will give us ample time to secure a hiding place for him."

Léonie handed around cups of ersatz coffee and sat down. Cigarette smoke drifted up to the ceiling while various scenarios were being bandied about.

Dr. Bignon cleared his throat. "First, I have a safe place for Mathieu and, I'd like to suggest, for young Colette and the other children. My mother lives alone in La Celle-Saint-Cloud in a villa shrouded by trees and shrubs."

"Maybe that's too close to Paris," François said.

"It's too far out for the German brass to reside, and there are no industries to interest them. My sister used to spend time there with her two young children and a newborn until the German invasion. She fled to stay with family in the south. The arrival of a young woman and children wouldn't surprise the few neighbors who might become aware of the new arrivals. Besides, we pretty much keep close together in that neighborhood."

"Thank you," Julie said. "What does your mother think about having strangers in her home?"

He smiled. "She'll be delighted. I've already arranged with a market gardener friend from Suresnes who leaves the Halles at closing time in the morning to take Colette and the children to my mother tomorrow."

"Thank you, doctor," Bernard said. "Now to get Mathieu out, I called on our members who have experience in, let's say, kidnapping."

"Ah, Pink Rabbit's concierge!"

Guffaws greeted Pierrette's exclamation. Even between dedicated résistants, only code names were used, even by family members who knew it was Yolande.

Dr. Bignon continued. "The good concierge told me there was no one else in the house, except for two German tenants. We know a German nurse is caring for Mathieu."

One of the specialists raised his hand. "How about one of us will knock on the nurse's door? When she opens, we gag her, bundle her up and drop her in the Catacombes with all the bones and skulls for company."

Dr. Bignon repressed a smile. "A bit brutal, but not a bad idea. Maybe we could refine it."

"She'd die of fright or get free and wander through the Catacombes wailing," Léonie said. "She'd be heard and rescued. Retaliation would be grievous."

Xavier contained his laughter. "The Lioness's right."

Dr. Bignon chased the smoke from his face. "I can go in and say that Obersturmbannführer has asked me to examine the baby. I'll prepare a cloth with chloroform. Once she opens the nursery door, the men can jump in and hold her while I apply the anesthetic. It's pretty quick, but I'll have a syringe ready just in case. It will make her sleep twelve hours and she'll wake up very sick for another four hours at least before she'd be strong enough to raise the alarm."

François coughed and stubbed out the cigarette he'd tried smoking. "We could leave several empty bottles of calvados around and pour some on her to make believe she had a hangover."

Applause greeted his suggestion.

Dr. Bignon approved. "That'd work, especially if we pour some into her mouth. The swallowing reflex will send it into her stomach."

"And when she pukes, it'll be very realistic," Léonie said.

Bernard stood up. "Sounds good. We'll rehearse it and time the action."

The four specialists and Dr. Bignon took their positions by the door. Julie stood behind them. Léonie volunteered to act as the nurse. Xavier, Pierrette and François flattened themselves against the wall, watches at the ready.

"One moment." Pierrette spotted a leather bag on a far shelf. She brought it down and put it on a chair before returning to her place. "That's the baby."

'Nurse' Lιonie attempted to fight off her attackers, as the squad presumed the nurse would. When it was down to five minutes, Bernard shook his head and declared, "It's taking too long. The nurse has enough time to get a good look at Dr. Bignon."

"That's because the doctor is doing everything. We're only holding the patient," one rιsistant said. "Ace and Bobard can hold the woman. Jambon can apply the chloroform cloth. Then I make her drink with a bulb. Fox and Doc can grab the baby and get out. We'll turn the lights off on the way out."

A chuckle greeted his last words. The revised plan was rehearsed and adopted. The other members would hide in the lobby of the helpful concierge and act as distraction should the two Fritz come home unexpectedly.

Xavier waved his hand. "The getaway has to be quick. By the time Fox gets into the car carrying the baby and Doc runs around the front to the driver seat, you've lost precious minutes."

A murmur of appreciation greeted his comments.

Bernard nodded. "I was thinking that too. What do you propose?"

"I sit in the driver's seat. Colombine in the back will take the baby from Fox while Doc climbs in the front passenger seat."

"Excellent. Let's do it."

Her fists against her cheeks, Julie asked, "You mean I can't go?"

Bernard placed his arm around her shoulders. "Not unless you want to stay with Madame Bignon for the rest of the war."

Julie bent her head. "No. I have work to do. Madame Durand has offered me her sister's apartment in the Passage Lepic. I'll move there."

A flash of interest lit Bernard's eyes when she mentioned Passage Lepic located in the heart of Montmartre. "But you can't go and visit the children."

"I guessed as much. But without me, they'll remain safe."

The meeting broke up. Julie returned to rue Victor-Hugo accompanied by her brother-in-law.

"I'll get someone to move your things to Passage Lepic. When you're there, make contact with Popaul at the café-tabac hotel. Order a Cinzano and ask him if he has an olive to go with it."

"Oh, clever. But I don't usually drink apıritifs."

"Sip it slowly. It's ersatz anyway." He waited until she entered the west wing and turned back, hurrying to get home before the curfew.

***

Paris, Sunday, November 8, 1942

Although it's good to be back, I couldn't help having a shock when we re-entered the occupied zone· I had brought a bag of walnuts· I couldn't leave Grenoble without some of the town's specialty· At the line it was the French douanier who wanted to confiscate the walnuts· Lyse-May clutched the bag, which was almost too big for her to hold, and told him, "You take the walnuts then you take me with them·" Fear was turning my insides to liquid· When the border guard reached for the bag, my fearless granddaughter pushed herself into the back of the bench· "It's not yours· You can't take it·" The other passengers murmured louder· The douanier, aware of the hostile stares, turned and left·

What is that wailing? Oh! Something happened···

At the news that Mathieu was safe, and hidden away, Brigitte and Charmaine let out shrieks of joy. They hugged Léonie and Julie.

Bérangère entered the room. "Young ladies, what's all this noise? It's hardly becoming."

They sobered up. "Léonie was just telling us that she's secured a wagonload of turnips," Charmaine said. Her usual calm composure dampened the excitement.

"I doubt turnips would cause so much hilarity if that were true."

"Sorry maman-Bérangère. We were really just being silly."

"Ah, oui. We do need to be silly and laugh sometimes to survive the grimness of the times. On another topic, I was coming to thank you Charmaine and you Brigitte for having come every day to cook and keep company for my husband while I was away."

Brigitte smiled. "Maman-Bérangère, you took care of us when we were little. We couldn't do any less while you had a holiday. How was it?"

***

Yolande had hoped to get away and join the family at the Manoir. Luck wasn't with her. She was summoned to Oberleutnant Lohse's suite. Before she could knock, Ernst's adjutant opened the door, bowed and took his leave. Ernst, hair wet from his shower, sat bare-chested on the edge of the bed.

"You asked for me, Ernst?"

"I did, chérie. I have to travel down to your beautiful Provence."

Yolande frowned. "You mean in the free zone?"

"Alas, free no longer will it be in a short while. I see by the expression on your pretty face that you do not understand. The British and Americans and probably some French, like your Général de Gaulle, have moved to capture North Africa."

Although it took only a fraction second for Yolande to grasp what was happening, she wanted a detailed explanation from Ernst. "Are they landing in Algeria?"

"As we speak, yes."

"Then they'll land in Provence?" She had to hide the joy that sprung in her heart.

"They will try. That is why we have to go and prevent them. We have troops at the ready. I do not know the role of the Luftwaffe. We are not supposed to bomb or fight the French in the free zone, but I am to leave with my unit tonight. Come close."

This was capital information she must pass on. She had grown genuinely fond of Ernst. "I'll miss you. You'll come back here when it's over?"

"I hope so." He pulled her onto his lap.

She wasn't sure it was love that united them or gratitude on her part for the number of times he quietly helped her smuggle Jewish children, or a whole family away from danger. He was well-aware of what the Auzellos, Frank and she were doing. Yet he never said a word. He'd even make sure to let her know when the Abwehr and other German spies met. Some of the intelligence thus gathered had been helpful.

Chapter Eight

Clad in a worn dress, Julie entered the Café Popaul and took note of the mix of German soldiers and low-ranking officers. A couple of waiters circulated. One of them approached Julie's table and gave it a perfunctory wipe. "What will it be for you, mademoiselle?"

"Un Cinzano."

The waiter brought her a glass of a reddish drink. She took a sip while he waited.

"Today is a no-alcohol day."

"That's fine with me." Was it a code? Bernard hadn't told her anything else. Would Popaul come to find out who this new customer was?

Some ten minutes later, the garçon returned. "Are you waiting for someone, mademoiselle?"

"Oui. Popaul."

The garçon went away again. Another five minutes passed before a tall man with a comfortable waistline ambled over to her table. He inclined his head.

"Mademoiselle wishes for something?"

"Do you have an olive?"

He gave her a warm smile. "I can always use someone. Your name is?"

"Fox. Mademoiselle Fox. Sometimes, I'm in need of extra work."

"Then you come here."

Julie thanked him and left, followed by the appreciative stares of some of the soldiers. Her mind reviewed the café-tabac layout. The recess on the far right probably had a piano and the door to the outdoor W.C. She'd also seen the end of a billiard table. A doorway with a bead curtain opened opposite the main entrance. The whole place was clean and welcoming with its marble-top tables and upholstered chairs belonging to another era.

***

Tuesday, November 10, 1942

"Is it Sunday?" Asked Sylvestre. He had just turned four.

With all the maturity of her fourteen years, Marianne knelt next to the little boy. "It is Tuesday. We decided to come to the Manoir and celebrate like it's Sunday because the French and the Allies have landed in North Africa."

"Where's that?"

"I'll show you on the map." She hoisted him onto a chair and placed a finger on the map. "We're here."

"It's a long way. Will they come to see us?"

Lyse-May climbed on the chair next to him. "Nope, they're going to fight the Huns and get them out."

"I fight too." Sylvestre jumped off the chair and flew to the sitting room in his imagined airplane.

"I wish mama Julie could come," Lyse-May said.

"She's working, poppet."

Lyse-May sighed. "I know."

***

Julie slipped into Madame LePlouhëc's office. "I've just heard they are crossing the line tomorrow at dawn."

"Go and deliver the message verbally. It's essential that the Résistance does not interact with the German army, unless the latter start shooting at people. Stress that the Résistance doesn't have enough weapons, and it'd be foolish to try to fight." She shook her head. "We knew all along they were going to invade the south. Now they'll stay there and we're losing the safety the zone nono afforded us."

"For an excuse, I'll take a basket of food to my contact."

Julie checked herself in the mirror and walked to the kitchens. Chef Raoul smiled at her.

"I need a basket of food for an old man."

"Coming right up, madame. Do you need to include papers in the basket?"

"Not today."

"Then, that's easy."

While he talked, he filled the basket and covered it with a cloth. She thanked him and left by the kitchen door. An officer with the dreaded lightning bolts on his collar pushed hmself off the wall. Julie recognized him. He had been in the meeting she had just listened to. She smiled and started walking. He fell into step next to her.

"May I accompany you on your errand?" His French was poor. "*Z'il fous plaît.*"

"Er... I'm flattered, but you don't want to walk all the way to my friend's place."

He put his cap on. "I do, to be *vith* you."

"It's a long way."

"I like *valking*. *Vat* is in your basket?"

"Leftover food."

He lifted the cloth. "Why would anybody want to eat leftovers?"

"My elderly friend gets very tired queueing up and he doesn't have much money." Inwardly, she was relieved that this time there were no documents in the basket.

He persisted. "What about the ration cards?

"Even with a ration card, there's hardly any food in the stores."

"The French could have avoided all that. You started the war."

He was a confrontational man. She had to watch her words. "No, I did not. If it had been left to me, there would have been no war."

"So, you agree with our Führer's ideology?"

Julie compressed her lips. Here it comes. "I have read *Mein Kampf*."

He inclined his head toward her. "That is unusual for a maid."

She wasn't going to react on his put down. "Not at all. French women read a lot of serious books. Since your lot was coming, I thought I ought to read it."

He laughed. "Your lot, you mean us Germans?"

She nodded.

"I'll tell you the truth. I didn't read the book, although we have to carry it with us at all times. I know it. I heard enough in the Hitlerjugend and in the army. Of course, I thoroughly support our Führer."

"Truth is, I started reading, but it's too hard for me."

He laughed again. "Are you a communist?"

"Never! But here we are. Thank you for your company."

"I'll wait for you."

She hoped he wasn't going to ask to go in and meet her friend. "As you wish."

She entered the modest apartment building. The elderly male concierge came and greeted her, appearing not to notice the SS officer on the sidewalk. They stepped into the loge.

"*Ah, mon enfant. Des bonnes choses à manger*."

'My child' and 'Good things to eat,' was her code. If it was safe to speak she had to reply, 'We mustn't leave anything go to waste.' In a low voice, she imparted the message. "I must get back to work, now."

"Be careful."

"I have an escort."

"I saw that."

"I couldn't refuse."

In a normal voice, he said, "Thank you for the food."

***

Wednesday, November 11, 1942

The sirens wailed in the early morning. Gontrand and Bérangère looked at each other. Bérangère frowned. "Surely the Americans aren't bombing us on Armistice Day?"

"The Americans have no respect. They don't understand why that day is important to the French people."

"We'd better go down to the shelter. Lyse-May, come, sweetheart."

"I'm making up a story."

"You can do it later."

"There's no need to go to the basement."

The mutinous expression on Lyse-May's face made Bérangère laugh. "Fine. I'm going."

"If we wait long enough, it'll sound the all-clear," Gontrand said.

"We are not waiting!"

Bérangère strode to the backstairs. General von Trennen, his aide-de-camp and adjutant arrived at the top of the basement steps at the same time. They exchanged greetings. They were barely halfway down when running steps made Gontrand smile. His granddaughter hurried after them, followed by Marie and Ernest.

"General, do you have any idea why there's an alert?" Gontrand asked.

"None at all, except that since dawn today the troops are marching into the free zone to occupy it, and the Italians have invaded Corsica and extended their occupation of the Alps."

Bérangère held her head in her hands. "*Mon Dieu!*"

"Do not worry, madame. It is not war, just a precaution. Hitler even wrote to Marshal Pétain to tell him it was necessary to protect France from the American enemy."

"*Pfft!..*" Gontrand's disgusted exclamation brought a smile to Reynard's tired features.

"Can I go down the corridor? It's all dark. Can I have a lamp?"

They all turned toward Lyse-May. "What corridor?"

She pointed. "Down there."

The adults stood and followed her. Captain Langen produced a flashlight. Where there used to be a solid wall of limestone, there now was an opening large enough to let a person through.

"Stay back while I inspect it," Captain Langen said. "Just in case."

"It leads into an ancient underground quarry," Gontrand said. "And there's another passage to another quarry. It goes a long way under Paris. I bet François made the opening. When we were boys, we traveled all the way to Pigalle."

Reynard shook his head. "Amazing how Paris is built on top of those old quarries."

"They used the limestones to construct Paris' fine buildings."

"Even more amazing."

"So, I can go now?"

Gerhardt rejoined the others. "It is in a very good state, and dry."

"I want to go."

Gontrand patted his granddaughter's head. "Sorry, *mon trésor*, it may look like fun but it is very dangerous. You wouldn't know where to go. You'd get lost, my little treasure. There are many paths and some are very low or drop into another lower quarry and you could break your neck. You're not allowed to go, especially by yourself."

A disappointed pout was the child's response.

"And don't think you'll escape and explore when I take a nap. I'm going to lock the basement door from now on."

The muffled all-clear sounded from above and everyone went back upstairs.

"What does the radio say?"

"That Marshal Pétain made a formal protest and accepted the new status. His ministers tried to make him leave to go to Algiers, but he refused."

Bérangère grimaced. "So he can continue to play at being the head of state and send Jews to an unknown fate."

Lyse-May skipped around the table singing on top of her lungs.

"*Chut*! Silence! Listen."

When the broadcast was over, Gontrand leaned on his elbows. "That's it. Nothing left. Not even a semblance of France."

"They haven't got into Toulon. There's a stand-off. Do you think the fleet will pound them off and they'll withdraw?" Bérangère asked.

"The politicians are busy talking. The Germans want the fleet. It's still powerful despite the losses in Mers-el-Kébir in '40. Vichy wants to keep it, in accordance with the Armistice Convention. This is a disaster. Vichy will give in. So will the admirals. There are too many of them. Vichy is the Society for the Protection of Admirals."

Bérangère laughed. "Society for the Protection of Animals, that's a good one."

"They're so Pétainists, they're totally useless."

"We'll soon make a Gaulliste out of you."

Bérangère's quip didn't amuse her husband. In a dark mood, he went out.

Lyse-May stood, fists on her hips. "Pépère didn't take me."

"He needs to walk and grumble on his own for a while. You'll go later. In the meantime, you can help me prepare lunch."

***

Montauloup

From the top of the ridge on Puy Chavaroche, with binoculars pressed against his eyes, Pedro watched the tanks roll into Le Falgoux. "Why the blazes do they come here to such a small village of no military value?"

Marcel and Dédé spread out a map. "They must be lost," said Dédé.

Chuckles greeted his words.

Marcel shielded his eyes. “Just a moment. They’re stopping. Is that our mayor talking to the lead tank commander?”

“That’s Joseph. all right,” Pedro said. “I hope he gives them the proper directions.”

Marcel guffawed. “Send them to the Pas Peyrolles. It’s snowed in. The tanks wouldn’t get through. They’d somersault down the mountain. That would be the end of a few doryphores.”

“Seriously, I hope he gives them the quickest way out. You don’t want an accident to bring more of them. They’re not interested in Le Falgoux. They want Toulon and the fleet,” Pedro said.

Dédé sighed. “Why isn’t the fleet sailing to Algiers?”

Pedro shrugged. “Politics, my friend, politics.”

“Now they’ll install garrisons everywhere.”

Marcel’s grimace of distaste was reflected on his friends’ faces.

“They won’t make it to Teulon today or tomorrow,” said Pedro. “The mountain roads are treacherous this time of year with all the hairpin bends icing up. I reckon they’ll have to camp three nights before they reach Aurillac, and that is if we don’t have snow before that.”

“Then they’ll set up house there.” Marcel’s joke drew smiles.

“No more coming. Time to go home,” Dédé said.

Chapter Nine

Julie hid her worry. "François, are you sure you know where we're going?"

"We've been walking down here one hour already," Pierrette said.

François shone his flashlight on the limestone wall. "See the mark?"

"It says troc."

"Because we are under the Trocadéro. Another twenty minutes and we'll be at the Manoir. We're more or less following a Métro line."

They climbed a flight of steps. Another step up and François announced they were in the Manoir's basement.

"We can't just irrupt in the middle of the family and give them a fright," Julie said.

Pierrette assumed a theatrical air. "Not to worry, we'll walk in casually from the backstairs."

François pointed ahead of them to a narrow staircase. "There's the door."

At the top of the stairs, he turned the doorknob. The door didn't budge. He tried again. Pierrette tried. Julie tried.

"*Mince, alors!* It's locked."

"Drat! Now we'll have to scream until someone comes," Pierrette said.

Julie burst out laughing.

"What is so funny, tante Julie?"

Julie's hilarity calmed down. "We walked half-way under Paris so that I could join the family for Sunday lunch only to find the door locked."

François shrugged. "I did my best."

"Alright on the count of three we call out. One, two, three!"

Their united voices resonated in the vast basement. Nothing

happened. They tried again. A light knock on the door raised their hopes.

"Are you the ghosts?"

"Lyse-May!" Pierrette shouted. "Lyse-May, sweetie, can you open the door?"

"Pépère took the key."

"Please, sweetie, can you go and ask him to open the door? Your mama Julie is here."

"Mama Julie?"

"Yes, chérie, I have come to see you. But we're locked in the basement."

They heard the girl's running steps and waited.

"Pépère, mama Julie is locked in the basement. You've got to open the door."

"Ah! A good try, darling! Go and play now."

"But it's true! Cousin Pierrette and cousin François are in there too."

"Nice story. Go and write it on your slate."

"I tell you it's true! It's true." She stamped her foot.

Charmaine and Brigitte looked at each other and ran out of the kitchen. At the locked door, they called out, "Julie? Pierrette? François?"

"Yes, we're in here," Julie replied.

"Hang on, we'll find a key."

They hadn't heard Lyse-May. "I know! I can see it. Pépère put it high on the wall."

Minutes later, the door was open and the three women embraced each other and hugged François and Pierrette. Overjoyed, Lyse-May clung to Julie, who carried her on her hip into the kitchen.

They had to relate how they had traveled underground. Jacques listened intently. Later, he took François aside. "Can you draw a map?"

"I can try. I'd have to do it as I go. My flashlight battery won't last more than the return trip, though."

"I'll get batteries for you. Are you planning to take your aunt back the same way?"

François shook his head. "I'd like to. She shouldn't be seen around here. But it takes one and a half hours."

"Tell you what. I'll come back here with a police car and I'll take her home."

"She lives on Passage Lepic."

Jacques squeezed François' shoulder. "I know." He gave a low laugh. "A police car doesn't draw any attention in that district."

"I know other ways through the Catacombes."

Jacques ruffled the eighteen-year-old's hair. "So, that's what you've been doing instead of going to school?"

"No, sir, I'm registered at the Sorbonne."

"Why aren't you attending classes?"

"I did... I take turn going to class and exchanging notes with my friends from the lycée Janson de Sailly who... who have ideas."

"You'll have to share them with me. Whatever you do, don't join the communist Bataillons de Jeunesse. It's not the right way to resist at this time."

"I understand."

"We'll talk again."

***

Sunday, November 22, 1942

Everybody has left now, and the west wing is so quiet. What a surprise to see Julie arrive by those secret passages. If it hadn't been for my granddaughter's acute hearing, they would still be down in the basement. We're not locking the door again. Lyse-May solemnly promised her mama Julie not to go down to the basement by herself. I know she'll keep her word.

What a tempestuous day it's been. We ranted and raved against the Boches invading the free zone, which is no longer free, and that weakling Pétain who gave them permission. Permission indeed! My husband still tries to defend his Pétain, though not quite as vigorously as before. No, he was rather subdued in his words. He's making a distinction between the hero of Verdun and the government in Vichy. Fortunately we had plenty to talk about, what with the victory of the Allies at El Alamein.

Brigitte and I were lucky at the grocer's. He had secured some topinambour, which he called Jerusalem artichokes, and some squash. We couldn't find a recipe in the cookbook and decided to slice the topinambour bulbs. They were white inside. The slices, cut very thin and fried in the little bit of oil we had saved from yesterday, were delicious. Maybe because Brigitte drowned them in garlic and onions from the garden patch.

I had promised my good friend Bernadette Ducharme to find her a length of cloth for a coat. She has taken to sewing. My two girls and I went to the Marché aux Puces. Charmaine is always looking for either a dress or material to go out singing with that SS officer of hers. I suppose she has to look her best in front of his guests. Anyway, our man, I won't go into what he's doing, stealing is stealing even if it's from the Fritz. And we're just as guilty buying from him. So, our man showed us a new fabric. He called it rayon. It's made from wood fibers. He told us it's an invention of a Frenchman for the collaboration.

We almost turned our backs on it, but there's precious little else to buy. Sometimes, we have to put our principles in our pocket. I bought a length for Bernadette and Brigitte bought a couple of meters for herself. I noticed she's overly fond of Captain Langen. He's so attentive, I can't blame her, but I see trouble for the future. The moment our man cut the rayon, I knew it was going to be difficult to sew. It frayed badly along the cut. But it's lovely looking, a little like silk.

I must go and see what my husband's grumbling about.

***

"Fox, would you like a holiday in the Auvergne?"

Julie artistically laid out the appetizers on her tray. "I'd love to. Popaul, but I have a job at the hotel."

"I'm sure we could arrange something. We could let your boss have one of the wheels of cheese we're expecting."

"Did you see the direction finding van this afternoon?"

"Of course! A couple of our German gentlemen went out and told the goons they were making a mistake."

"You were lucky, but you have to move that transmitter."

Popaul scratched his head. "The gentlemen that frequent my establishment have rooms in the hotel to entertain their ladies, which contravene their army rules and regulations. They won't let anything happen to me, in order to keep up the good time they're enjoying."

"They're not high up enough in the hierarchy to have any influence. It's pure luck the sergeant was able to talk the technicians out of probing further. I wonder what lie he gave."

He scratched his head. "True, high-ranking officers go to the chic cafés. On the other hand, the Gestapo never come around here. Aw, alright, I'll let the Auvergne know we're changing transmission time."

"You should change it every day and keep it short. Their direction finder only works on fixed and lengthy emissions."

"Where did you learn that?"

A dreamy look came over her face. "Let's just say from a London agent."

"Ah, the SOE! Why can't we communicate directly with London?"

"Their trained agents have specific codes. If you could communicate with London, so could the Fritz posing as French Résistance."

"Point taken. So, about that holiday?"

She gave a wink. "I'll get your cheese. I'm sure Olive has a few things, too."

Julie was right, there was a lot more to do. The Résistance was intensifying their actions, as were the Gestapo.

***

Harassed, Madame LePlouhëc thanked the SS officer and closed the door behind him. She turned to the head waiter. "Tell the staff that spilling soup on officers' laps is not resisting. That sort of retaliation because they invaded the zone nono is childish. There're better ways to resist."

"Sorry, ma'am. Please tell us a better way. Some of my waiters are looking to do something."

Madame LePlouhëc smiled. "Good. We'll have a meeting in my office at the end of your shift."

After he left, Madame LePlouhëc turned to Julie. "What do you think?"

"If they're accidently spilling soup, they're ready for more precise action."

"We're only collecting intelligence here, not blowing up things!" She tugged on, and repositioned, the hairpins that threatened to fall out of her immaculate chignon. "And now I have a couple of unwanted guests I can't even disguise as waiters or janitors since they don't speak a single word of French."

"That's why I'm taking a holiday in the south."

"You're taking them off my hands?" Madame LePlouhëc tilted her head. "Now that the Fritz are everywhere, what about the line?"

"It's still in force, but there are ways through it."

"What do I say to your admirers when you don't turn up for work?"

With a chuckle, Julie moved to the door. "I'll leave that to your imagination." She left via the cellars of the Majestic and the Hôtel Raphaël next door, and emerged in the street opposite the Métro Kléber. All senses on high alert, she scanned the avenue. Not that her nemesis would be hanging out in front of the hotel, but she left nothing to chance.

When she arrived at the Cave, only Bernard was present. "Anybody else coming?"

"Later. Ace will bring the two Americans we're supposed to take to the next safe house. Jambon thinks they are not genuine. Our agent from Creil expressed the same doubts."

"Enemy agents trying to infiltrate our réseau?"

"They were passed on by a cell in Beauvais to Creil and directly to the Majestic."

"I know." She chuckled. "Seriously, this is a breach of procedure. Why did the Creil agent come to the Majestic? It sounds fishy, but I didn't tell Madame LePlouhëc. She was a bit frazzled today. Why the hotel? It isn't on the circuit."

Bernard nodded. "Precisely. Xavier will bring them in. After they arrive, we'll let you interview them."

She didn't have long to wait. Xavier entered with two tall men, with their light brown hair cropped short, American style.

"Tell the men we're making dinner. Keep them amused," Xavier said.

Julie swallowed hard. A familiar gut feeling of danger roiled through her. In the hope that Xavier and the others hadn't been talking freely, believing the airmen didn't understand French, she immediately changed her planned interview tactics. In laborious English, she greeted the men. The feeling they understood French perfectly gnawed at her.

"Thank you, ma'am. We're so glad to find someone who speaks English."

"I don't speak very good."

They beamed at her. “But you do.”

Her eyes darted from one to the other noticing the quality of the suits they were wearing. After more than three years of rationing, no one in the réseau possessed anything but worn out clothes scavenged from the bottoms of various wardrobes. Rarely did a suit fit the usually tall flyers, especially the Americans. “How did you come to Paris?”

“We met many of your people. They were very nice taking us to safety.”

Contrived American accents crossed her mind. “That is good. Where you are going now?”

“We don’t know. We’re trusting you.”

She played coy. “I’ve never met Americans before. Where do you live in America?”

“In Seattle.”

“Is that by the sea?”

The speaker gave a condescending laugh. “It is, *mademoiselle*.”

She laughed. “Hey, you speak French!”

He laughed with her. “That’s the only word I know.”

“What do you do in Seattle? Americans play a lot of sports. Is it true?”

“Yes, yes. We do. We play football.”

Julie racked her brain for the name of a team to no avail. She took the interested air of a student. “Who’s your favorite football team?”

There was the barest hesitation. “*The Seattle Mariners*.”

It didn’t sound right. She didn’t know why. It was just one of those unexplained feelings. “So, you were bombing the *doryphores*?”

The second man burst out laughing, then became serious. “Who?”

There, she got them! Their accents were like none that she knew. They were Germans. The nickname offended some and amused others. Americans arriving in France wouldn’t have a clue about it. They understood French perfectly well or they wouldn’t have reacted to the word doryphores. “I meant the Germans.”

“Yes, we bombed them.”

She smiled prettily. “What sort of plane do you fly?”

Both of them appeared taken aback by her question. The

shorter of the two replied after a brief pause. "We fly a Hawk."

"And drop bombs on the Germans, that's really good." Yes, really good. The Hawk was a fighter plane. She'd learnt that at the Manoir the previous Sunday. Damien, Paul and Baptiste were passionate about planes and could draw silhouettes of all of them. The young boys had been so happy to find a listener that Julie indulged them until they'd exhausted their knowledge and went out to play. "I wonder if dinner is ready. I'll go and see."

In the other room, she made a negative sign. Xavier drew his hand across his throat. Julie nodded and picked up the soup tureen. Bernard followed with Xavier. The latter excused himself. "I'll go and get the man who knows the way."

Julie continued a meaningless conversation while they ate, pretending to translate for Bernard from time to time, even though he was fluent in English, but it kept up the charade. Not long afterward, Xavier came back with Aristotle. A man who fitted the stereotypical image of the Frenchman with a béret on his head and a cigarette dangling from the corner of his mouth.

"Ari, here, will take you to the safe house."

Julie translated. The three men left. Julie dropped her head in her hands. Without a flicker of remorse, she had just sent two men to their deaths. Her humanity was slipping, and it frightened her.

In silence, Bernard washed and put away the dishes.

Eyes unseeing, Julie leaned against the wall. She brusquely straightened. "He said *Seattle Mariners*. It's wrong, I'm sure it's wrong, but it's just an impression. I don't know much about sports teams. But what clinched it was the Hawk."

"Isn't the Hawk a fighter plane?"

She nodded. "I asked what plane they flew to drop bombs. They didn't expect a technical type question. I had fresh knowledge thanks to my nephews, your Paul included. They meant the Goshawk. No pilot would mix up the name of the plane he flew."

Bernard gave a shake of the head. "We should pay more attention to children. You did well with your schoolgirl English."

"I wasn't going to let them recognize my American accent when I speak English. I couldn't place their accent and they were too well dressed."

"That was my feeling too, and why our people got suspicious

in Creil. Far too well dressed." Bernard threw up his hands, then dropped them. Life and death had to take their course. "We'll bicycle back to the less-desirable quartiers where we live."

"I came by Métro."

"There's a spare bicycle hidden in the other cellar. We're going to Armand's."

"Armand?" Her surprise made Bernard laugh.

"My second-in-command. He's the one who's arranging the cheese delivery. He'll explain."

The blue paint on the bicycle lamp lens gave so little light it didn't make a dent on the blackout darkness. They puffed hard to the top of rue de l'Abreuvoir, tied the bicycles to the street lamp and climbed the three flights of stairs. Bernard rapped his code on the door panel and a second later the door opened.

Bernard pulled a pouch from his coat pocket and handed it to his lieutenant. "That should cover expenses till Christmas." He put his gloves back on and took his leave.

A shiver shook Julie. She took her gloves off and opened her coat but kept it on. The chill in the room was the same as in her apartment. "It's going to be another cold winter."

A chair seemed to invite her to sit. She leaned against the kitchen table. Armand sat across from her. He took both her hands in his and brought them to his lips.

She shuddered. "What do you feel when you have to kill a man?"

He raised his eyes toward an unknown horizon. "In the army, before sending us to the front, we're trained not to think. We're told the enemy opposite you intends to harm you, your family, your neighbors, your friends. Get angry and prevent him from violating your country. Kill him and go on to the next, and the next... I, in my army unit, had no time to think." He took a breath. "Now we're facing a different war. It's more personal, but the same enemy. I have time to think, to think about the silent soldiers of the shadows, their lives, our goal. Sometimes, I have to make a terrible choice, and I make it even when his eyes are pleading for mercy."

Armand fell silent. Julie contemplated their joined hands, the tremor in his. She thought of Charlot, and the tragedy in the sewer. The silence continued for a time.

"What if I made a mistake? What if these men were genuine? What if my ear isn't sufficiently attuned to different American accents? What if they weren't interested in sports? Airmen have the habit of giving a name to their plane. What if Hawk was just a nickname?"

Armand opened his mouth but had not time to speak. He rushed to the door just as hurried footsteps pounded on the stairs followed by the staccato code on the apartment door. Armand opened the door and a young woman collapsed in his arms. He kicked the door shut. "Pierrette! Pursued?" He was already heading, with her and motioning to Julie, toward the bedroom to the emergency exit.

"No."

He relaxed and with Julie's help sat Pierrette in the only armchair. Julie brought her niece a glass of water. Her face red with exhaustion and hair matted with sweat, she took several gulps of water.

"Arrests at the safe houses in Beauvais, Breuil-le-Vert and Creil. Liancourt is still safe, but they evacuated their guests. I bicycled to Aulnay-sous-Bois to warn them. They're warning Wémars and St-Witz." She blew out a long breath and drank more water.

Armand stared at Julie. She hugged herself. "Those spies must have been able to pass a message to the Fritz in Beauvais. It's crawling with Luftwaffe and Feldgendarmes because of the airport."

"I'll give orders that no matter how long an escapee has to wait, he must never be let outside. I'm going to see someone."

Pierrette stood up. "I'm recovered. I'll go there on my way home and pass the order to him."

Julie and Armand watched her retrieve her bicycle and disappear down the street

"I didn't know she worked for you."

Armand laid his arm on her shoulders. "You have a dangerous enough job. You need not know where everybody is. And talking about dangerous, let's sit and talk about cheese. How about a cup of ersatz? I have some saccharine to sweeten it."

She nodded. The bitter taste didn't matter so much. The black liquid was warm. He poured two cups.

"Do you know what a fourme de Cantal is?"

"A very large wheel of smelly cheese from the Auvergne."

An amused smile floated on Armand's lips. "Quite right, to be more precise, a fourme is a tall cylindrical cheese weighing thirty-five kilos. Can you lift that weight?"

"You're joking?"

"Are any of your nephews or nieces about that weight?"

She thought for a moment. "I guess Marianne is fourteen. I guess she'd be about thirty-five kilos. Yes, I can pick her up and twirl her around. Not far and not for long, though."

"You'll be fine handling the cheese, even if you had to do it by yourself. But don't worry, you'll have help. You're going to Le Falgoux and you'll stay at the Boyers' farm. Pedro has secured a good landing field."

"Let me guess. We'll unload some nice TNT, which will get hidden inside the cheese that I'll bring back to Paris."

"By train. But don't worry, we have the necessary papers. All genuine."

"Live dangerously is the norm of the day. Can't Dédé get the cheese and me to Paris?"

"Only as far as the station in Aurillac. Dédé has other work to do. He's ingratiating himself into the new garrison supply departments in the region."

"So he can pass people and goods under their noses. But it's viewed as collaboration."

Armand casually drummed his fingers on the table. "He's also the head of a Résistance cell."

"I know. He lives a double life."

He shrugged. "Don't we all?"

"Will we ever live normally again?"

Eagerness colored his voice. "That's why we're here, to help throw the invaders out."

Julie smiled. "Count on me! Is there more than the cheese?"

He sighed. "The invasion of the south has disrupted our escape routes and safe houses. You'll be followed by an English fellow. We'll see if we can establish more connections."

Two yawns later, and having memorized her instructions, Julie stood up to go.

"I'll see you home. Leave the bicycle here, I'll take you on my crossbar. That'll look less suspicious."

Less suspicious was a sort of mantra. It was a common sight to see a lover carrying his girl on the crossbar. They mounted the bicycle, Julie perched on the crossbar cocooned in his arms. They then free-wheeled down Montmartre's narrow and tortuous streets as far as the Passage Lepic.

Chapter Ten

Paris, Monday, November 29, 1942

My poor husband's going to have an embolism or an infarction the way he's raging about the Vichy government· Even Lyse-May got scared and ran to her room· I called her for lunch and she said, "No thank you· I'm not hungry·" Gontrand has lost faith in his Maréchal Pétain since the French fleet scuttled itself in Toulon two days ago· Why are those admirals so stubbornly stupid? The Fritz invaded the south on November 11 in defiance of the Armistice Convention· There was ample time for the fleet to get away and join our allies· Not to mention Mers-el-Kébir when another doddery admiral refused to join the English who had no choice but to fire on the ships· Does that admiral sleep at night knowing he caused the death of some two thousand sailors? I think what has really hurt Gontrand is the fact that Pétain himself gave the order to surrender the fleet to the Germans· I admire the commanders who defied the order and successfully destroyed over hundred ships· But what a waste!

And now the Italians are in Grenoble· I wonder how Hilaire is going to react· Of course, being the commissaire de police his allegiance is to Vichy, but to the Italians? No· He is strongly patriotic· He won't put up with them on French soil·

Will all this ever end?

***

With two hours to spare in Clermont-Ferrand, Julie went to the Café Restaurant de la Gare. There she found more Germans, loudly enjoying the food, than there were French. The plat du jour was cabbage soup, but not for the Fritz. Their fare comprised of sausages atop a mound of mashed potatoes. She watched her charge nod to the waiter. Moments later he was served his soup. Julie closed her eyes, gritted her teeth and willed him to look at her. He didn't and continued to eat, tilting the soup plate with his left hand while scooping up the soup away from him, English style.

Fear crept in when her eyes caught sight of two civilians sitting at a table against the back wall. Seemingly focusing on the bottles in the bar, she observed them out of the corner of her eye. They were methodically scrutinizing each civilian customer, herself included. No doubt, Gestapo. She lowered her gaze to her soup. The airman still ate unawares. In a swift movement, the Gestapo agents were on their feet and grabbed the airman under the armpits. The soup plate flew to the floor, the chair tipped, the table tottered. They dragged him outside. Julie kept her head down, her hand mechanically bringing the spoon to her mouth.

A waiter cleaned up the mess. The waiter who'd served Julie came to her table with a basket of bread. "He was with you?"

"Er... non."

"They'll come back for you. You came from the occupied zone."

She flinched. "Is it so obvious?"

"When you came in, you paid no attention to the soldiers. You're used to them. The locals wince, hesitate and some go back out. Take a train anywhere, but don't wait for them to come back."

She picked up her purse. The waiter waved her on. "Never mind. just go."

"*Merci!*" In calculated haste, Julie left the restaurant by the kitchen door and wasted no time in putting distance between herself, the café and the station. She turned a corner and another and arrived at a park and children's playground. An empty bench was just what she needed. Her mind replayed the events that had just taken place. She was thankful for the waiter's comments and decided to find a bus to the nearest small town and maybe take a micheline to Aurillac. There she'd be in familiar territory, though Pedro didn't expect her so early. She shivered from the cold and from her narrow escape.

A young woman pushing a baby carriage and holding a toddler by the hand came and sat beside Julie. The toddler went to play in the sandbox. The woman picked up the baby. A pang of regret hit Julie. She could be hiding with her children, away from the heartache of being powerless at seeing a man arrested. What would happen to him? He would be beaten up and tortured until he revealed the names and location of his helpers, then sent to a prisoner of war camp. That was the information that circulated throughout the networks.

A scream from the toddler jolted both women. Entangled in his long woolen scarf, the more he thrashed, the more the scarf tightened around his throat. His faced turned purple. Julie jumped up, ran to the child and freed him.

The mother had put the baby down to help her toddler. "Merci, madame."

The women sat again, each holding a child. The little boy's messy gloved hand touched Julie's face. He laughed while he tried to put the scarf over her head. Julie chuckled.

A Citroën traction-avant cruised down the street. Julie bent her head to the delight of the toddler. The mother's eyes followed the black car.

"Michou, don't mess up madame's hair."

"Actually, I'm enjoying the play," Julie said. A quick glance to see that the car had gone, and she breathed freely again. "Is there a coach going to Aurillac?"

"You're from the north?"

"Am I so obvious?"

"The way you speak. No there isn't. And with them here, I don't know if we can travel."

"We can still travel, it's just more difficult." She sighed. "And my suitcase is in the station baggage room. I left it to go and have lunch. Someone was arrested. I don't feel like going back."

"You think you'd be arrested too?"

Julie smiled. "You recognized I came from the occupied zone right away. I mean from the north, since we're all occupied now. I have the right traveling papers, but I'm just scared."

The young woman's face showed concern. "Do you want me to go with you? If we see the Boches, we'll keep walking."

"You'd do that for me?"

"You saved my Michou's from choking by being quick on your feet."

Julie didn't think the toddler's life was in peril, but she didn't voice that opinion. The area around the station was calm. In the station, Julie retrieved her case and would have liked to change her ticket for Toulouse to Le Puy, but didn't dare. Outside, the young mother was in conversation with a rugged looking man next to a horse-drawn carriage. She signaled to Julie.

"Jean, here, will take you to Pérignat. You can catch the micheline there."

Relieved, Julie kissed the woman and Michou. Jean had already taken her case and helped her up onto the foot-plate and into the carriage.

***

Snowflakes fluttered about her face like butterflies. Outside Le Falgoux station, Julie glanced down at her low-heeled pumps and went back inside. She sat on a bench and retrieve her mountain boots from her suitcase. Case in hand, she set off toward the mayor's house. The brilliance of the snow rent the darkness of the night.

"Julie?"

"In person."

Jeannine Lavergne grabbed Julie's suitcase and slammed the door shut behind the traveler. "What happened? You weren't expected for a few days."

Julie's shoulders drooped. "I didn't go to Toulouse as planned."

The scraping of boots outside the door signaled Joseph's arrival. "My councilors were all in favor... Fox!"

"Can you put me up for the night? I'll go to the Boyer Farm tomorrow."

Jeannine busied herself making dinner.

"You need not ask. What happened?"

"The English airman got spotted and arrested in Clermont-Ferrand simply because he hadn't been taught the French way to eat soup." She sighed and shook her head. "We ought to pass on a recommendation to our safe houses to make sure the escapees know a few basics, like how to eat, and how to hold a cigarette."

"Like this?" Joseph looked at the cigarette in his hand held between his thumb, index and middle finger, then took a puff, letting the smoke curl upward in lazy spirals. "All the helpers are volunteers risking their lives every day. They do their best feeding and clothing the men. You're right, though, we'll circulate a message about those two small but important French habits."

Jeannine put the soup on the table along with a round country loaf. "When we heard the Chleus were coming, I bought all the flour I could find, so eat your fill."

A dog barking, clanging and scraping noises heralded Gabriel's arrival. A gust of cold air preceded him into the kitchen. A large Pyrénée dog shook snow off his back before flopping down in front of the woodstove. The twelve-year-old hooked his cap and coat onto the doorknob. "Hey, madame Julie! Did you see the Boches tanks? They went down Main Street."

"We have them in Paris, too."

The boy's questions were cut short by his mother ordering him to eat.

***

At the Boyer's farm, Julie heartily threw herself into the work. The apple rings that Louise had dried in the fall had to be layered in wooden containers to keep them over winter and spring. There was also the special work that involved hollowing out four of six matured fourmes stored in the buron, a one-room stone shelter in the far field. The snow wasn't yet deep and the sheep, herded by two Beaucerons under the watchful eye of the shepherd, were still going out to the pasture by the farm.

The evening before the drop was due, Joseph came to the farm with Gabriel, who tried to monopolize Julie to talk about Paris.

His father frowned. "Gabriel! If you want to be a résistant you have to learn to obey, and that means not speaking until you're required to do so."

"*Oui, papa.*"

Joseph turned his attention back to the adults. "We have a problem. We have good reasons to suspect there's a traitor and the drop tomorrow is in danger."

"Who?" Marcel asked.

Louise jabbed her finger in the air. "Lulu! I never liked that small man. He's got something shifty about him. But that's just a woman's intuition."

Julie scrunched her mouth to hold back her smile. The men wanted more concrete evidence than a woman's feelings.

Joseph passed his fingers through his hair. "Well, Louise, you may be right. He's been helpful, but a couple of our men wonder how can his mother go around wearing new, quality clothes." He looked at Julie. "We know he supports his widowed mother, but he doesn't have a job. He goes to Aurillac too frequently. Since the Boches have arrived, there's been two raids in Le Falgoux. Why would they come from Aurillac to our sleepy town unless they knew they'd find something?"

Louise sighed. "Right. How did they know there was a Jewish family living with the Pestouris'?"

Joseph shook his head. "And yesterday morning, Jaroux was arrested, and they found the mimeograph machine in his basement."

"No!" Julie and Louise exclaimed at the same time.

"What are you planning?" Julie asked.

Joseph scratched his head. "I hope it'll work. Pedro suggested changing the drop location. Instead of your field, Marcel, we gave London the coordinates for Font de Lemars. They agreed and the drop will be advanced by one hour. We'll tell the men at the last minute about the change."

"The Font is quite a steep plateau. A bit narrow, too." Marcel said.

"There's enough room on the north-east side and it's flat there. Since it's high up, we'll be down and away before the Germans realize they've been had and try to climb up."

Marcel nodded. "And get lost on the forested slopes."

"Right. Pedro has two trusted men who will hide and follow Lulu. We'll go as planned toward your field. Pedro suspects Lulu will drop behind because he won't want to be caught with us."

"What if he goes with you?" Julie asked.

"Then we'll have to keep a close eye on him," Joseph replied.

Marcel lit a cigarette. "Now that the Fritz are in the region, we need to be more careful."

***

Despite having to perform farm chores, the day passed at a slow pace. Darkness fell. All eyes were on the sky. Finally, the moon rose, throwing long shadows over the snow. The group arrived from Le Falgoux. The Boyers and Julie joined them as they walked through the woods toward the designated field.

Louise discreetly brought her lips to Julie's ears. "That's Lulu, over there."

"He seems to be vomiting in the bushes."

Louise went over to him. "You don't feel too good, Lulu?"

"Sorry, no. I'm really sick."

"Go home, then." Louise hastened back to the others.

Julie slipped behind a tree. Pedro came behind her.

Lulu glanced behind him, straightened and ran toward the farm and the road. He hadn't gone far before two men jumped him. Pedro pulled Julie away.

"Joseph has now told our people. We'll climb up a goat track up to the Font."

They hurried on in silence. Julie didn't want to ask what would happen to Lulu. A traitor wasn't allowed to live. She concentrated on following Pedro till they connected with the rest of the group.

While they waited, Pedro murmured, "Julie, do you want news from Montauloup?"

"Of course."

"Arnaud is finally seeing the light. He no longer claims that Pétain is playing a double game fooling the Boche. Huguette and my wife Elisa are busy with charities."

"You mean hiding people?"

He made a throaty sound. "There's lots of room at the old château. Little Reine is an adorable five-year-old. Elissa wants to adopt her. But Jean-Jacques... I wish I could slap some sense into him. Joining the Service d'Ordre Légionnaire is the same as joining the Gestapo."

"What does the SOL do?"

"It's a Vichy paramilitary force. We'll talk later. Midnight. It's time to get ready."

From a distance, the growing drone of an approaching plane could be heard. The men dispersed to their posts to form a triangle with their flashlights directed toward the sky. The lens of the flat box was surrounded by a tin cylinder which concentrated the light to a single point. Pedro handled the miner's lamp to blink out the agreed signal. The Lysander flew low, banked and came back to land on the bumpy field. Julie had to marvel how the plane was able to land in such a short distance.

Two men exited the Lysander. Julie's heart beat at triple speed.

"Sylvain," she murmured. Their eyes connected for a brief second. She made to rush to him, but the two agents were whisked away. She clamped her jaw. That was life in the Résistance, so close yet so far. A package landed at her feet. "Move it!" She sprung to action. Within five minutes, the plane was taking off and a dozen heavily laden men made haste along the mule track. Although stumbling more than once, Julie kept up the pace. As they approached the valley, they ran across the flat ground, crossed the stream and headed up the mountain pasture to the buron, where Julie and the men deposited their burdens under Joseph's and Pedro's directions.

The men dispersed into the forest bordering the pasture. Back at the farm, Joseph secured the radio set onto Gabriel's pulka.

"I'll take it home, papa."

"It's heavy. Are you sure you can ski with it?"

"I'm used to pulling much heavier loads."

"All right, go now and keep to the back roads."

Gabriel shrugged. "Of course!"

Pedro came in. "I've put the ammunition under the straw in the sheepfold."

"There it is!" Marcel extracted a bottle of Beaune Les Marconets from the back of the pantry. Louise set five glasses on the table.

The moon waned as night began to shake off the darkness, but they had to wait until the end of the curfew. They were savoring the fruity red wine and talking about the success of the operation when the dogs jumped up.

"Shush!" Pedro ordered.

The Beaucerons whined softly. The unmistakable sound of a car engine laboring on the tortuous track leading to the farm. A gas-powered vehicle, not a gazogene.

Without a word, the men grabbed their coats and were out the back door in a flash.

Julie listened intently. "Two cars." She seized the wine bottle and topped up all the glasses. Fortunately, she hadn't begun to drink hers after they had clinked. Meanwhile, Louise had passed the dry mop over the floor where boots had left melted snow. Julie lowered the wick in the lamp. The less light, the better. Moments later, with beads of anxious perspiration trickling down their necks and backs, the two women stood by the table. The cars screeched to a halt in the yard. The Beaucerons barked in unison. Julie lifted a corner of the blackout curtain and distinguished three men striding toward the house. A loud knock.

Julie held one Beauceron. Louise held the other while she opened the door. Two soldiers, rifles pointed at the dogs, hesitated on the doorstep.

"Couchez!" Louise ordered the dogs. They dropped to the floor, noses between their paws. The soldiers entered the kitchen. At that moment another soldier dragged in a bloodied boy. Side by side, the two women stepped back against the table. Though they recognized Gabriel, they didn't move. They shuddered, the concern on their faces genuine. Without any ripples, Julie's hand found Louise's and squeezed it for reassurance. The soldiers saw the glasses .

"*Wo sind die anderen?*" One of the soldiers said.

Julie guessed they didn't speak French. "*Hier sind nur wir.*"

"Where are the others?" He repeated.

She didn't think wise to say there was nobody else again. He was low ranking. Maybe a corporal. "I don't know what you mean, *Herr Offizier.*"

"Your son was carrying a forbidden radio. The plane landed here."

"No, Herr Offizier. We heard the plane, but it didn't land here. May we clean up the boy?"

He narrowed his eyes. "The boy won't talk."

"Please let me ask him."

His face twisted in disgust. He nodded.

Now she prayed that they didn't understand French. In a quick low voice, she said to Gabriel, "You were coming to work on the farm and found the suitcase on the roadside. Repeat that to me."

With effort, Gabriel obeyed. Julie translated and added the boy didn't understand why he was beaten up. The soldiers holding Gabriel threw him forward. Louise caught him and sat him down. The soldiers saw the glasses.

"*Was ist das? Wo sind die anderen?*"

"That's for you, messieurs. We saw you arrive and prepared the wine for you."

"*Fünf?*"

"*Ja*, the four of you and madame Boyer." She pointed to her rather flat belly. "No wine for me. I'm pregnant."

The men grabbed the glasses and downed the wine in one gulp. "Search the house," the corporal said.

One soldier remained with the women. Louise washed Gabriel's face. It was no more than a bloody nose and a bruise on his cheek. The three soldiers stomped to the parlor and upstairs, opening wardrobes' and cabinet' doors. The soldier guarding the women and Gabriel smiled at the boy.

"*Fous troufer radio?*"

Julie saw Gabriel pull his eyebrows together. He was assimilating the bad French, *vous trouver radio*. On tenterhooks she waited, ready to intervene.

"Yeah! Me, find radio on road."

Relief flooded Julie. By speaking with single words like the soldier, the smart boy boosted the Fritz's confidence. It was going to be all right.

"You see plane?"

"Non, me hear plane."

"Curfew. You out?"

"Me, work farm. Start early."

That was the extent of the soldier's French. He looked at Julie. "*Wo ist dein Mann?*"

"You mean my uncle. He's tending the sheep in the sheepfold." She turned her head toward Louise. "He asked where is your husband, I said my uncle's in the sheepfold."

Louise nodded.

The other three soldiers came back to the kitchen. They pointed at the empty wine bottle. The meaning was obvious. Louise raised a finger meaning wait here and stepped into the cold pantry. She emerged seconds later with a bottle of Beaune Les Marconets, which was reserved for special occasions.

Julie took the bottle from her. "Here, Herr Offiziers, enjoy this good French wine."

"*Danke*!"

A line of pink spread across the sky. Dawn took its time to chase the night away. The women didn't move until the sound of the cars faded away down the mountain. A worried looked on his face, Marcel rushed in.

Louise raised her hand. "Calm down. Everything is alright."

"I aged twenty years waiting in the barn. What happened? I was ready to come and surrender, but I didn't hear any shots or screams. What happened to Gabriel?"

The boy lowered his head. "I'm sorry. I was going home as planned when I heard the cars coming round the hairpin bend. I threw myself into the ditch, but too late. They saw me. I didn't talk, so they slapped me."

Julie pursed her lips. "Actually, their French is more than limited."

"They came here and looked around. Fortunately, Julie can speak their language. It costs us a bottle of your best wine."

Marcel exhaled a big breath. "They could have had the whole cellar as long as you're safe. But they got the radio."

Both women raised their hands at the same time. Julie shook her head. "I know Pedro had the crystals, so it's useless without them. We have to rejoice that the agents got away safely, and the men got the cargo away. We're lucky it was Wehrmacht guards, not the SS."

"My skis and the pulka are still on the road," Gabriel said.

"We'll get them on our way to church in the morning. I want to find out about the others."

"What about my father?"

"He and Pedro were watching from the woods. He'll be relieved you're staying here."

In church. Julie was only vaguely aware of the mass, kneeling and standing automatically. A man's life was ended because greed drove him to betray his compatriots. Even when it was clear that he was a Gestapo informer, no one in the village had come forward to stop him, to make him see the error of his ways. Julie was oblivious of the end of the sermon. Louise nudged her to get to her feet. Julie's somber thoughts returned. Did the villagers share the responsibility of Lulu's death? Her mind drifted to the SOE agents who had disembarked from the Lysander. The look exchanged between her and Sylvain, was it a message of love or an adieu? Was he safe?

The service over, people gathered in small groups on the square to exchange the latest gossip. The Boyers went for news. Huguette and Elissa, holding Reine's hand, joined Julie standing alone to one side of the steps. Soon, Pedro joined them. His smile told the women all they wanted to know. Julie pulled him apart. "Why didn't you let me talk to Sylvain?"

"You know the answer. Anyway, there was no time."

She sighed. "Yes. What happened to..?" The words died on her lips.

"They took him to Aurillac. Keep this place clean."

"How much do you think he revealed?"

"We won't know for some time. We agreed to disband and lie low for two weeks while we monitor developments."

"If any. I always wanted to ask you something. How did you come to speak such good French, almost like a native?"

A dreamy look came over his face. "I was a teacher of languages, French and English, in Madrid... I see Dédé at the end of the street. Are you ready?"

"My suitcase is at Joseph's."

***

No incident marred the journey to Clermont-Ferrand. The specially constructed four-wheeled hand cart contained the six tightly packed fourmes, which, together with the cart, were loaded onto the train without a problem. To make sure no one would want to examine the cheeses too closely, Marcel had made sure his three goats slept in the buron for the last month so the crust of the fourmes would absorb the odor of goat. Julie was glad the porter was amused when people gave him plenty of room. The baggage car attendant was less amused, but he grabbed the rope handle and maneuvered the cart inside. As Julie gave a generous tip to her porter, she saw the attendant wrap a waxed sheet over the fourmes.

In Paris, a dour porter took charge of her cart and directed a few insults at those passengers who weren't moving out of his way fast enough. Julie handed over her papers at the control and removed the wax cloth from the fourmes.

With a terse, "Put it back on!" from the guards, she was let through. A glance at her watch dismayed her. She hadn't enough time to get the cheeses to the Majestic before curfew, nor had she been told of a plan. Undaunted, she improvised.

"Monsieur, I'll give you a good tip if you pull the cart to the Hôtel du Lion."

"They won't let you in."

"I'm sure Gustave will let me."

The porter scratched his head, then wiped his mouth. "Where are you going tomorrow?"

"I have to deliver the cheese to the Hôtel Majestic."

"Maybe I can help."

"You're on. Let's go see Gustave."

The hôtelier's warm welcome heartened her. She watched the two men drag the laden cart through the lobby and the kitchens to the courtyard.

"It's all arranged, madame," Gustave said. "Tomorrow at eight o'clock, we'll take the cheese to the Majestic."

"Mind the anti-tank defenses on avenue Kléber."

"Don't you worry, ma'am," the porter said. "We'll go to the back, rue la Pérouse."

"Big blockhaus there."

"*Bah*, that's not a problem, we'll go around it," Gustave said.

"Thanks. I'll get there before you."

***

The Hôtel du Lion was far from being a luxury establishment and was closed at night until Gustave or his wife opened the doors in the morning. Julie slipped out as soon as the curfew ended. She squeezed into a Métro car, already packed with workers but, thankfully, no Germans. She listened to the low grumbles that emanated from the disgruntled workers, a change from the early days of the Occupation. Tonight, on the return trip, the workers would be silent and morose as there'd be not only Fritz, but their collaborating hangers-on.

At the Majestic, Julie eyed the bath in her room. An immense fatigue descended on her. An hour later, refreshed and ready to take on the rest of the Boches, she strode into Madame LePlouhëc's office.

"Gustave is coming with a friend, I believe, at about eight o'clock with the cheese."

"Can you trust them? That's a dangerous cargo."

Somewhat fatalist, Julie shrugged. "I didn't think I could drag the wagon through Paris on my own. Gustave offered his help. I was already having help from a grumpy porter. They appear to know each other. I didn't question."

"But how safe is your Gustave? Here we only deal with intelligence gathering and transmission."

"That's why I wondered why you had ordered those cheeses."

Madame LePlouhëc stifled a yawn behind her hand. "Some brass made a request for Cantal cheese. He was told it'd take a little while and, well, we couldn't miss the opportunity when we had a duly signed and stamped safe-conduct pass for cheese from the Auvergne."

Julie burst out laughing. When she recovered, she wiped her tears. "I needed that good laugh."

"About Gustave?"

"I left enough money for them both. I came to know Gustave serendipitously. Olive cleared him for various tasks." She smiled. "Tasks that need a bit of brawn."

Madame LePlouëc laughed. "Let's go downstairs and watch them arrive."

The resourceful men arrived pulling the cheese cart behind two bicycles. It was a sight to see. The men and Julie manhandled the fourmes into the elevator and down into the food cellar. Gustave and his friend refused the tip Madame LePlouhëc offered but didn't refuse the meal she put in front of them.

"The two edible fourmes are standing alone to the right of the cheese larder. I noticed the cellars seemed to go down a long way," Julie said.

"They're vast. I haven't explored them. Now, when will your people come and take the explosives away?"

"They'll let you know when. I'm not on the planning committee."

Madame LePlouhëc re-arranged the papers on her desk. "There's a meeting tonight. Are you up to it?" Julie nodded. Madame LePlouhëc continued. "Those Americans airmen got away?"

Julie sighed. "They got a long way away, where they will no longer harm anyone."

"You mean..." Stunned, Madame LePlouhëc dropped on the nearest chair.

Julie straightened. "We lost some good people because of them."

"Damned war! Damn Nazis!"

Julie went to get ready for the evening.

Chapter Eleven

Maude groused as Brigitte opened the door to her. "I shouldn't be coming to your apartment like this, but there's no other way!"

Alarmed. Brigitte pulled up a chair for Auntie Maude, as she was affectionately known, and served a cup of the ersatz she had made. "What's up?"

"The newspaper kiosk was raided. Nothing found, but the blasted Gestapo closed it. If it re-opens, we can't use it as a letter box. It'll be watched."

The children had gathered around Maude. "Sorry, my sweeties, nothing to eat today. I was in Paris for a few days. Next time I come from Meudon, I'll bring you something."

"Damien, Estelle, it's time to leave for school."

"Do we have to? It's cold in class."

"My darlings, it's cold here too. It's December. It'll soon be spring. Go, now. You'll get a meal at the canteen."

"*Pouah!*" Estelle's exclamation left no doubt about what she thought of the canteen food.

"It's never very good, maman," Damien said.

"I know, but it's something."

With an outpouring of sighs and dragging of feet, they edged to the door. Maude took a handful of coins from her pocket. "There's enough to buy you a piece of bread pudding from the baker, but hurry before he sells it all."

Seconds later, they were running down the stairs.

"That must have been your Métro fare."

Maude shrugged. "I'll walk. No big deal. Can the kids get ahead of the queue to buy the bread pudding? Women can get pretty iffy when they've been queueing for a long time."

"We all know one another. I've never used my priority card to get served first and they know it. So occasionally, if Damien or

Estelle go in for that heavy, indigestible stuff that passes for pudding, the women let them through."

"What do you think the baker puts in it?"

"It's supposed to be unsold bread, as if that existed! He makes it by thoroughly scraping the blades and sides of his mixer. He adds a little flour and a lot of water."

"The flour is disgusting. It's got sawdust in it."

Brigitte had to laugh at Maude's expression. "You didn't come here to talk about flour, did you?"

"No. You have to pass on the message that Yolande is being watched."

"I thought our Pink Rabbit was quite safe at the Ritz."

"Nobody is safe anywhere, chérie. Nobody. She needs to be warned and security put in place."

"You're going back to Meudon?"

"I have messages to send."

A noisy dispute between Sylvestre and Christiane put an end to the friends' conversation. Brigitte dressed the children as warmly as she could. At four years old, Sylvestre insisted on walking everywhere, but two-year-old Christiane had to sit in the pushchair, despite her protests. They set off as a brisk pace for the Manoir.

On arrival, Lyse-May took over and Brigitte sat with Bérangère for a few minutes.

"Maman-Bérangère, may I borrow your bicycle?"

"Of course. You look worried. Anything I should know?"

Brigitte twisted her lips. "You're not supposed to know."

"Which makes me feel like a useless relic."

Brigitte laughed. "It's for your safety."

"Tell my son that I've survived a war on the front lines, caring for poor souls who had been hit in the trenches, and I've survived raising five boys to manhood. That alone qualifies me to know what my family is up to."

"The Gestapo is watching Yolande. I've got to go and warn her. She shouldn't go home tonight."

"Tell her to come here."

With the customary kiss, Brigitte left. She pedaled in haste to the Ritz entrance on rue Cambon. One of the concierges rushed up to her.

"Ma'am, you cannot..."

"An urgent message for Mademoiselle Bourgmestre. Let me in and take care of my bicycle." The German sheltering in his sentry box glanced at her and kept on smoking his forbidden cigarette. Brigitte pushed the bicycle into the mystified concierge's hands and ran up the three steps into the hotel. A clerk, carrying a sheaf of papers, nearly collided with her.

"Mademoiselle Bourgmestre's office, please."

He looked at her curiously. "I'm going there, follow me."

At the door, he knocked. A young maid opened. "I'll get mademoiselle Yolande."

Brigitte didn't wait to be invited, she went in and sat on a chair. Still puzzled, the clerk waited by the desk. Brigitte decided he was born with that owlish expression. Shortly afterwards, Yolande came in. She promptly dealt with the clerk before acknowledging Brigitte's presence.

"What's up?"

"You've got a target on your back. The Gestapo have been watching you. What made them suspicious?"

Yolande's hands flew to her face, and she collapsed on her office chair. "The line is over-crowded. The invasion of the south has created a bottleneck. I took a woman and two children to my place. Then two men."

"Your concierge?"

"Likely."

"You can't go home. Maude has contacted Olive, I think."

"Can you let Julie know?"

Brigitte nodded. "But what will you do in the meantime? Is Ernst back?"

Yolande smiled. "Reichmarschall Göring needs him to maintain order in the hotel."

"Then tell him you need a safe place. I'm off to see Julie."

Yolande composed herself and went to see Frank Meier.

"Mademoiselle."

"I'm burnt."

Impassible, Frank took the wine glass he was polishing and hung it among the champagne flutes. Yolande debated whether to find Blanche or go to Ernst. Her dilemma was solved when Blanche sidled up to her and led her to the office. "What?"

"Gestapo on my trail."

"*Merde!* What did the Obertleutnant say?"

"Nothing yet. I was on my way."

"Good, then leave by the front door. The Gestapo must be watching rue Cambon."

This worried Yolande. Brigitte had come by the staff entrance. Hopefully, she looked like she might be applying for a job or hoping for a handout. Yolande used her passkey to let herself into Ernst's suite, after sending a message with a maid.

He came promptly. "Where will you be going, *chérie*?"

"I'll go to my grandparents and see what we can do."

"*Vacherie de* Gestapo! Is that how you say bloody Gestapo?"

Yolande smiled. "It is. You're acquiring a wide vocabulary."

"But I don't want you to go. You must stop smuggling Jewish people, even little children. It's too dangerous."

"If the situation were reversed, wouldn't you do what I'm doing?"

He pulled her into his arms. "Yes, I would. But in order to continue that work, I would have to take a rest. So, it is time for you to suspend your work."

Yolande knew the Gestapo watched the officers' mistresses but didn't think they'd be interested in her. Unlike others who took their paramours to the opera and to restaurants, Ernst never did. She also would have refused. Their relationship was one of casual convenience based on similar ideas and friendship. She thought about his happiness when he shared the news of his niece's birth.

"I'll go home to pack a bag of essential things and I'll go straight to the Manoir."

Ernst looked at his watch. "I must go back to the meeting." He kissed her. "Promise to keep safe."

"I promise."

In the street, Yolande tried to apply the advice Julie had given her to detect a tail. She realized how woefully inadequate she was compared to her friend. Tense and worried, she opened the door to her building and stiffened at the crunch of steps next to her.

"Julie!"

"Get in."

They both hurried inside and up the stairs.

"I didn't see anybody following me."

"There wasn't. I froze watching your street. I'm sorry you have to disappear, but that's inevitable in the life we lead."

"I thought I was safe at the Ritz."

"Mistake. We aren't safe anywhere. Especially that you took people to your apartment instead of the safe house."

Yolande punched the air. "Damned concierge! I'm sure she must have squealed."

"She forgot the lesson she was taught. Trash like her don't learn. We'll have to do something about her. I'll take your bag with a change of clothes. I'll go first. If the street is still clear, I'll stop to tie my shoelaces. If I keep walking go to your hiding place. We'll change the procedure."

The coast was clear, and they both arrived at the Manoir to Lyse-May's exuberant welcome, seconded by Sylvestre and Christiane.

"Silence!" Gontrand yelled.

"*Chut*, children! We're listening to the radio," Bérangère said. "Come sit at the table for lunch."

Yolande pulled bread and potatoes from her bag. "There's also a camembert. You have it, since I'm going away for a while."

"I didn't think you were coming here just to say hello."

While Bérangère dealt with the children, Julie signaled to Yolande to step aside. "You'll go to the Gare d'Austerlitz at twenty-two hundred hours. A young man will hand you a bouquet with instructions in the middle of the flowers."

"Where am I going?"

"Your final destination is Le Monastier. A lovely place with even more lovely people."

Despondent, Yolande helped clear the children's dishes and partook of the meager lunch with her uncle, aunt and Julie. Charmaine and Brigitte arrived soon afterwards.

Charmaine handed papers to Yolande. "Here is your new identity card and Ausweis."

They laughed at the stupefied look on her face.

"That was fast!"

"Alexandre has photos of all of us and sets of identities. It takes minutes to put them together," Charmaine said. "He did that just in case we need them in a hurry, like today."

"I'll follow you when you go to the station," Julie said.

Pierrette entered the kitchen. "No, you're not! You're going back to your home through the quarries. I'm the watch for Yolande. Those are the latest orders."

A silence fell. Julie sighed, hugged everyone and headed toward the cellar. Lyse-May caught up with her.

"You can't go, mama Julie."

"I have to, chérie. But I'll come back through the secret passage. You'll be a good girl, right?"

"I will, and after the Christmas holidays, Mémée said I could go to school."

"Are you excited?"

"I don't know. Pépère says I don't need to go."

"You'll have fun, I'm sure. 'Bye for now."

***

On her return to the Majestic, Julie called in at the office.

Madame LePlouhëc was in a happy mood. "Here, have a piece of Cantal and a freshly baked bun."

Julie chuckled. "I have the feeling I know this cheese. What make you so lighthearted?"

"The fourmes are gone, only the cheese is left."

Julie understood that the special cargo had been collected. "Anything happening that needs my presence late tonight?"

"Nothing scheduled. They've got their way with Vichy and are busy talking about Christmas. A new law will be passed in the new year to send young men and women to Germany as forced labor."

Julie paled. "They can't do that! Sorry, of course they can and will. There are not enough volunteers, so now they'll raid houses in search of young people."

The two women ate in silence.

"Are you working at Popaul's tonight?" Madame LePlouhëc asked. "Tell him I don't want any more cheese. My hair turned gray out of fear that some brass would want to ship one of the fourmes home."

With a laugh, Julie set off for Café Popaul. Notepad in hand, she lingered around the German soldiers. Along with the orders for beer, wine and food, in her own coded notes, she recorded snippets of conversations which indicated a low morale among the troops. She didn't bat an eyelid when Pierrette and Xavier nonchalantly took a table as far as they could from the soldiers, like most French customers did.

Without haste and after transmitting the Fritz's orders to the bar and the kitchen, she stopped by her niece's table.

"Yolande's been caught at the station," Pierrette whispered.

Only a trembling in her hand betrayed Julie's emotion. "I'll bring it right over." A minute head movement and Popaul followed her to the kitchen. "Two ersatz," she said.

Bertrande glanced at her husband's serious face and took the ersatz to the young couple herself.

"Tell me," Popaul said.

"Yolande has been caught."

"Alone?"

She nodded and saw the relief on his face. The young man with the bouquet was one of his men. They didn't normally work across the cells. Each had their specialty and they made sure to keep separate, but sometimes it was unavoidable.

"Go now and make arrangements. I have men if we need to mount an operation to intercept a prison van."

Julie went back to the room, smiled at the soldiers, swatted away an errant hand and stopped at Xavier and Pierrette's table. "Anything else I can provide?"

Xavier nuzzled Pierrette's neck while she whispered, "Lunch at the Manoir tomorrow."

In a louder than necessary voice, Julie said, "Believe me, this is the nicest ersatz in the whole of Paris."

Xavier stood and pretended to pull Pierrette along. The soldiers made crude comments in German. She didn't need to know the language to understand. She blushed.

As Julie hung up her apron, she whispered to Popaul, "I'm going to the Manoir tomorrow morning."

"Fine, I'll move the wine rack at ten o'clock."

In the morning, Julie met François in Popaul's cellar.

With an impish smile, François said, "I thought I'd show you the way, tante Julie."

She punched his shoulder. Gone were the days when she could ruffle her nephew's hair. He was too tall now. "You made some pretty good blazes and I've followed them."

"I know, but I like this way of traveling, hidden from sight. Everybody has heard that the youths eighteen and over will be conscripted for labor in Germany. I'm not going."

"I hope not."

They negotiated the drops and a narrow tunnel, finally emerging in the Manoir's cellar.

The mood was somber and no one talked until the children had been fed and sent to the playroom under Madeleine's supervision, with help from Marianne.

When the dishes had been cleared, the discussion resumed.

"We know for sure Yolande's been taken to avenue Foch," Bernard said.

"We can only attempt an intercept when she's transferred to one of the prisons," Jacques said.

Sitting close together, Jean-Luc and Lorraine held hands.

"How long do the Gestapo keep their prisoners at avenue Foch?" asked Alexandre.

"It depends on the type of information they trying to get. Sometimes a few days in solitary. When they start beating them up, they send them to Fresnes to be brought back next morning," Jacques said. "What are you frowning about, Julie?"

"The longer she stays in their clutches, the more she'll be beaten."

Lorraine let out a sharp gasp.

Bernard leaned toward Julie. "I hear your mind working."

"I'm prepared to go and see Oberleutnant Lohse and ask him if he can pull some strings."

"Why would he bother?" Gontrand's voice rose with an accent of defeat.

A glance around the table told Julie that some of the family agreed with the question. She squared her shoulders. No one needed to know about their special relationship. "Obertleutnant Lohse is Yolande's boss. He really appreciates her skills at avoiding scandals at the hotel. He must have connections, even with the SS."

Charmaine nodded. "He frequently comes to the musical evenings where Wolfang and I perform. I have seen them talk and surmised they were friends."

Jacques snorted. "A Luftwaffe officer and a SS officer?"

"Stranger things happen," Bérangère said.

"That settles it. I'll go and see him first thing in the morning."

"Just so you know," Brigitte said. "I met Madame Durand and

she told me Meinhard has come to see if you were back from the country."

"Has he gone to rue de la Lancette too?" Julie asked.

"He has," Jacques said. "One of my patrol calls in regularly to talk to Colette's mother. She and her husband have moved into the loge. From time to time a man comes, a different man each time, and asks for Madame de Montregard. When told there's no one by that name, he apologizes and says he must have the wrong address."

"And that doesn't fill me with confidence about your job at the Majestic. Avenue Kléber's too close to your apartment in the rue Victor-Hugo, which he probably also keeps under watch."

Julie stood up. "I don't go to my apartment. And at the Majestic, I take care never to start or leave at the same time. Sometimes, I leave through the Raphaël Hotel and not always use the same Métro station. I must go now."

"Me too," Pierrette said.

It was the signal for everyone to leave except for the Bourgmestres.

Bernard elbowed Julie. "What would you think about working for Popaul full time?"

"You know yourself that we gather useful information at the Majestic, sensitive information. The MBF hates, absolutely hates the Gestapo."

He sighed. "All the same, be careful."

***

Elegant in her best Jeanne Lanvin dress and coat, Julie opened the blackout curtain. "Oh, no, it's snowing!" She glanced down at her high-heeled shoes. "I need a fiacre." But she knew there would be no fiacre in the Pigalle quartier at ten in the morning. Determined to carry out her mission, she descended the stairs slowly and racked her brain for a solution. Moussou, the boy from the ground floor apartment, sauntered into the lobby. There was no concierge in the building.

"Moussou, ten francs for you if you go and get me a fiacre."

He looked her up and down. "I can only buy one egg on the black market with ten francs."

"You get me the fiacre and I'll give you twenty."

His eyes lit up. "Deal, ma'am. Ten now."

She put a ten francs bill in his hand and hoped he'd be reliable.

Glad she had put on the pair of silk stockings she reserved for the most important conference at the Majestic, Julie walked on the spot to keep warm. He was taking a long time. She wondered if he'd decided to go and buy his egg first.

The door burst open. All smiles, Moussou gave a wave of his hand. "It's right outside."

Julie glanced at the car and jumped up. The driver was coming toward her.

"This rascal said you were urgently needed at the Majestic."

"Dr. Bignon!"

Julie gave Moussou the promised tip and climbed into the car.

"Actually, I'm going to the Ritz today."

"That's perfect."

"How did he find you?"

"On Mondays, I help at a dispensaire in the Batignolles quartier. He knows. Are you going to the Ritz about Pink Rabbit?"

"Oui."

"Then I'll wait for you at a little distance. I guess we're going to the grand entrance."

"I'd think so, and if all goes well, I might get a ride home."

"If I see you walk and I'll come to the rescue." He paused. "You're not asking."

"I dare not."

"You're putting your mission ahead of your feelings. Both Claudine and Mathieu are thriving. My mother dotes on them, and Colette is very competent. She has a photo of you and tells the children, maman will come soon."

Tears threatened to undo her carefully applied makeup. "Thank you."

Dr. Bignon pulled up in place Vendôme. The sentries looked on. A concierge rushed to open her door.

Once inside, she thanked him and, shoulders pulled back, approached the desk. "Oberleutnant Lohse, s'il vous plaît."

A blasé clerk dialed the internal telephone. Moments later, he summoned a bellboy.

"Take madame to Oberleutnant Lohse's office."

She wondered why the clerk hadn't asked her name, perhaps it was because they were used to seeing French women cavorting with German officers? She reddened at the thought.

The bellboy ushered her into the office, which was empty. A Louis XVI style chair in front of the desk was inviting. She sat down. Shortly afterwards, Oberleutnant Lohse, a displeased expression on his face, came in.

"*Ich war in einem Treffen. Was wollen Sie?*"

"I'm sorry to interrupt your meeting, Herr Lohse. What I want is to inform you of a grave matter."

He narrowed his eyes in scrutiny of his visitor. He appeared surprised to hear her speak his language so fluently. "And you are..?"

Julie had thought carefully about which identity she'd use. "Julie de Montregard." She saw him flinch.

"A relative of Mademoiselle Bourgmestre, I believe."

"Right. I've come because Yolande has been arrested by the Gestapo."

He blanched and lowered himself into his chair. "She was going on holiday. I told her I did not want her to have anything to do with saboteurs."

"No, Herr Lohse, not sabotage. She was helping people get to safety."

"Yes, I know, smuggling little Jewish children." His tone softened. "Why is she so stubborn?"

Julie caught the change in his voice. "You'd be the same if we had invaded your country and wanted to kill Prussians just because they were Prussians."

He gave a short burst of laughing at her logic but quickly become severe again. "Tell me what happened."

"Her concierge denounced her to the Gestapo. They waited for her and caught her. She is at avenue Foch."

A murderous expression marred his handsome features. "That concierge! What do you think I can do?"

"You appeared to be a good friend of SS-Hauptsturmführer Ziegler."

"I love music. He plays better than Elly Ney or Emil von Sauer, and Madame Lebeau has the voice of an angel."

"Will you talk to him?" She sensed she had the advantage and feigned candor. "He's connected with the Gestapo, like all SS men."

He smiled with indulgence. "It doesn't exactly work like that. But I'll go and see him, and I'll get Yol... Mademoiselle Bourgmestre out of their clutches... if I can."

"Thank you, Herr Lohse." She stood up. He hurried to open the door for her.

"I'll find my way out and let you return to your meeting."

On her way out, Julie met Blanche Auzello.

"What did he say?" Blanche asked.

So much for discretion. But then she did come in through the front door. No matter what, in the Ritz Hotel, news travels at the speed of light. "He's seeing a SS friend and I imagine will apply the right pressure to get Yolande released."

Relieved, Blanche gave Julie her professional smile, as she would to any client.

***

Ernst Lohse commandeered a car to take him to Hôtel du Louvre, where he sought out SS-Hauptsturmführer Ziegler.

"Bonjour, Ziegler."

"Ah, Lohse."

"Shall we take a walk in the Jardin des Tuileries?"

"If you wish." Wolfang nodded and shrugged into his greatcoat. It didn't take long for them to reach the Jardin.

"I'll come straight to the point. I am very annoyed that your Gestapo took my girl from the Ritz."

"Damn, I'm so sorry, Lohse. And it is not my Gestapo. Your friend must have been involved in something they didn't like."

"Not at all. She is just a maid. Besides, The Ritz is neutral. It is Swiss, did you not know? And all the staff have been screened and vetted."

A look of disgust came over Wolfang's features. "Gestapo! I really have nothing to do with that bunch. I only deal with workers for the Reich."

"You must know someone. After all, you are all Schutzstaffel."

"I am not that high ranking."

"I know you do not care for women, but I do."

Wolfang sighed. "I know, you know. I will try to see Joseph."

"Joseph?"

"Sturbannführer Kieffer. He heads the Sicherheistdienst."

"Thank you."

They parted and Wolfang Ziegler went back to his hotel. He dreaded meeting his old friend and railed against the Gestapo. Like everybody else, he had to make an appointment and the earliest was the following Wednesday, two o'clock in the afternoon.

On the day and right on time, he arrived in a bundle of nerves, at the avenue Foch. To his surprise, he was shown in right away.

"So, Ziegler, are you trying to enroll me for one of your soirées?"

"Your talent would enhance any concert. You were a top bassoon player."

Josef Kieffer pinched his mouth. "Those were the days. We had good fun. It is all behind us now. So, what brought you here?"

"A friend of mine has been arrested and I find it very annoying."

"Who?"

"Mademoiselle Yolande Bourgmestre. I believe she was brought to this building."

"A woman? The name does not ring a bell. Do you really have a woman… friend?"

Wolfang smiled to hide his fear. "I do."

"I thought maybe that gorgeous singer… Well, well, well, I will have seen everything." Kieffer rubbed his hand over his chin. "I shall see what I can do. Is she a terrorist?"

"Absolutely not. She works at the Ritz and as we all know, it is neutral territory."

"Indeed!" He picked up the phone and gave rapid orders. "Do you have your car here?"

Wolfang nodded.

"Have some coffee while we wait. It's freshly made." He picked up the silver coffee pot and poured the fragrant brew. Wolfang took a cup and helped himself to sugar.

They talked about the old days and shared a few laughs until the phone rang. Kieffer picked up.

"You can go downstairs now. She will be brought up to the door. And by the way, I will be at the New Year musical evening, but to listen only. I no longer play."

Wolfang made haste going downstairs, trying to ignore screams that the stone walls couldn't contain.

He reached the door at the same time as two guards holding Yolande. They pushed her into his arms. He supported her and hurried outside. His Duesenberg had been brought to the front door.

"Where do you want to go to, Mademoiselle?"

She made an effort to speak clearly through her chattering teeth. "To my uncle, rue Chantemesse."

"*Ja*, I know Monsieur de Montregard."

With a stammer and stutter, she managed to speak. "Of course, you played at the general's receptions a few times... Thank you for getting me out."

Yolande directed him to the courtyard. He insisted in helping her into the house. Bérangère's eyes widened at the sight. Her nursing training kicked in. Without a word, she pulled up a chair and had her niece sit. She wrapped her woolen shawl over the young woman's shoulders. Yolande's trembling prevented her from speaking. While Bérangère prepared a warm drink and some food for Yolande, Wolfang stood awkwardly to one side not knowing what to do as he took in the sight of Yolande's torn dress, her swollen face and limp hair. Only then he realized she had no shoes. He paled and heaved. Lyse-May, who'd been watching the scene, came up to Wolfang.

"I liked it when you played the piano. I can play too. Do you want to come and listen? The general isn't home."

Stunned and still ill at ease, he followed the child to the music room. She lifted the lid of the grand piano and sat on the stool, while he gratefully sank into an armchair.

"I'll play Bach Prélude in C."

When she finished, he had recovered his composure. He appeared surprised. "You played very well with a lot of feeling. It is a difficult piece for little hands."

Lyse-May beamed at him. "I like it a lot."

He stood up and came to the piano. "Rock your right hand from side to side a little more, like this." He bent next to her and demonstrated, giving her an impromptu lesson.

Ten minutes later, Wolfang, fortified by the music, thanked Lyse-May. They went back to the kitchen. Wrapped in a warm robe, her face washed and her damp hair held back with a clip, Yolande was drinking soup from a bowl.

"I must go now. Bonsoir, mesdames."

"Merci, monsieur l'officier," Bérangère said.

On his way out he saluted Gontrand who was coming in, stupefaction painted over his face. Rather than phone Lohse, he drove to the Ritz to deliver the message in person.

It didn't take long before Charmaine and Brigitte burst into the kitchen, followed by Bernard and Julie, rubbing her backside. "Someone stole the saddle from Bertrande's bicycle. So Popaul made one out of wood. It looks good, but, oh my!..."

Stunned, Bérangère stood up, her arms hanging by her sides. "How did you hear the news so fast?"

No one replied, as at that moment François and his sister arrived. Pierrette carried a basket whose aroma made everyone look up. "You're guessing right. It's a roasted chicken."

Gontrand frowned. "And how did you procure a roasted chicken?"

Titters were heard in the background.

"You don't really want to know, grand-papa."

His thunderous voice resonated in the kitchen. "Speak up!"

Her tone flippant, one shoulder moving slowly up, she said. "It just flew into my basket."

Gontrand's cane hit the back of a chair. "Take it back! You're not to steal! It's a sin!"

The laugh that erupted from Bérangère's throat stopped her husband in mid speech. "A sin! You can't label an action a sin, because you never go to church and don't even know what the word sin means. Anyway, we're at war and there's no such a thing as sin, except on the enemy's side."

With a calculated nonchalance, Pierrette leaned both hands on the back of a chair. "It's simple. I occasionally work at a collabo restaurant. When the Fritz pinched my bottom, I told them I was going to punish them by taking the bird. They laughed, and I walked away with the chicken. But, enough about me. How is Yolande?"

Everyone's attention turned to Bérangère. "She's better..."

Yolande entered the kitchen on Julie's arm. "I am, thank you."

Lorraine bounded off her chair and wrapped her arms around her daughter. Bérangère ordered everyone to sit and eat before allowing Yolande to relate her ordeal.

"They grabbed me when I was coming out of the Métro on my way to the train station. They were hiding in a couple of apartment buildings opposite. A car was waiting. They took everything from me and threw me in a cell." She shuddered. "It was so cold and dark. A dungeon, I guess. Nobody came. Nobody brought me anything to drink or eat. Then on Monday, I think, I don't know what day or time it was because they had taken my watch. They interrogated me for hours, through the night too. They slapped me. Someone from the cell across mine said they start with slaps and if you don't talk, it gets worse. I kept saying I didn't know anything. The same happened again, yesterday, Tuesday." She paused to catch her breath. "The hardest part was having to listen to the muffled screams, the cries from nearby cells... The smell was awful. I understood then that they were not so much wanting information about résistants but about which officers were anti-Nazis, those visiting and living at the hotel. Today, I couldn't hold myself up. I was so thirsty I couldn't speak. My tongue stuck to the roof of my mouth." She paused in the general silence. "Then they dragged me out and Herr Ziegler drove me here."

She stopped talking. The silence lengthened. François brought out his violin and played. Afterwards, words of love and sympathy dominated the conversations.

***

At the end of the week, Yolande went back to work. She had barely hung her coat when a maid brought her a message to go straight to Oberleutnant Lohse's suite.

"I believe I owe you my freedom, Ernst. Thank you."

"I was only a link in the chain. How do you feel?" His eyes examined her from head to toe.

"I'm feeling much better."

"*Chérie*, you must stop helping the Résistance."

"I was only helping little children. The orphanages are full to overflowing."

He sighed. "Children should not be pawns of war. They ought to be kept safe."

"You're not angry with me, then?"

He pulled her into his arms. "I cannot stay angry at you for more than two minutes. When are you smuggling little children to Switzerland again?"

She laughed. "When the need arises."

He directed a small smile at her. "Does it not all the time?"

"Alas! How did you manage to convince the Gestapo to release me?"

He waved away her question. "Simply a friend of a friend doing me a favor."

"Why did you intervene for me?"
"Because I am Luftwaffe, not SS."
There was no more talk after that.

***

After giving instructions to the staff for the following day's party, Yolande hastened to the kitchens with the intention of begging a plate of food from the chef before going home. She didn't have to. Ernst stepped in front of her and showed her the basket in his hand.

"My chauffeur is waiting outside."

She recognized the basket and smiled. "That's nice of you."

Head held high, although anxious, Yolande went to push open the outside door of her building. It was locked. Anger surged while she inserted her key in the lock. Her belongings had been returned to the Ritz, and she'd had to sign a receipt. "What's all this about, locking the—"

She stopped in surprise at the sight of the middle-aged woman coming out of the concierge's loge. Uneasy, the woman stood on the spot looking at the Luftwaffe officer standing beside Yolande.

Yolande recovered first. "Who are you?"

"Lucienne Cabestaès. The new concierge." She glanced at Ernst and back to Yolande. "You must be Yolande Bourgmestre. I didn't expect you, not with company."

"This is Herr Lohse, my boss."

"*Enchanté, madame.*"

"*Bien le bonjour, monsieur.*"

Ernst extracted a *Bourdin* from the basket and handed it to the concierge. The aroma of cooked apple and pastry escaped from its foil wrapping. "We are celebrating the safe return of Mademoiselle Bourgmestre. Please share in the happiness."

Bemused, Lucienne took the delicacy from him. "Merci, monsieur."

***

The brouhaha of children's squeals, the scraping of boots and the laughter of adults preceded the entrance of the family into the kitchen.

"Where's Lyse-May?" Brigitte asked.

Bérangère shrugged. "Sitting by the cellar door."

Amused but worried, Brigitte went to the cellar door and sat on her heels at the level of the little girl. "What are you doing, poppet?"

"I'm waiting for mama Julie. She comes through the secret passage."

"You know she can't come every Sunday. Sometimes she has to work."

"I know, but she's coming today."

The mutinous look on Lyse-May's face didn't prevent Brigitte from continuing her probing. "How do you know?"

Lyse-May tapped her chest. "I know it in here. See, it's my heart and it knows."

Any comment Brigitte wanted to make evaporated when Lyse-May jumped back from the door. It opened slowly and noiselessly. Lyse-May flung herself into Julie's arms.

Flabbergasted, Brigitte got to her feet. "Happy to see you. The bond between the two of you is out of this world."

"It's one of those mysteries of love. Here, take this bag of food courtesy of the Majestic."

Pierrette appeared, framed in the doorway. "If you ladies would move out of the way, we could come in."

The fact she laughed and François pushed her into her aunts lightened the mood.

As the adolescents entered the kitchen, Bernard frowned, anger tangible in his voice. "Where were you last night?"

A silence fell. Spoons in the air, Bérangère and Charmaine stopped stirring and mixing food.

François reddened and looked sheepish. Defiant, Pierrette straightened her shoulders. "We helped Yves Lamont. He was short of manpower."

"What did I tell you about working for a communist cell? Do I have to hammer it into your thick heads again? The Bataillons de Jeunesse are reckless communists. They get caught every time. Killing a German or two creates no more damage to the enemy than a mosquito bite and puts other lives needlessly at risk, not to mention our entire réseau. As from this minute you are no longer working for me."

François cleared his throat. "Sorry, uncle, but we aren't doing anything in Gavroche."

Jacques didn't normally interfere with the family. His severe tone made the youths sit up. "*Petits imbéciles!* I thought you'd grown up. But no, once more you're disobeying. How do you think we're going to help the Americans and the English win the war if you are not disciplined enough to take orders? Yes, the Francs Tireurs Partisans are organizing like an army, nothing too wrong about that, but you, you two, cannot endanger the réseau and your family by hobnobbing with the FTP. They are being caught like flies all the time. It's a miracle you weren't arrested last night."

Subdued, Pierrette said, "We were only on watch duty and we escaped into the Catacombes."

"One day, you'll get lost in that labyrinth." Bernard was still angry. "And you Daniel?"

"Although, I wanted to go, I have to protect my mother. I stayed home. She didn't come today because Madame Ducharme has a *guest*."

"Sensible young man."

"Hughes?"

Jean-Luc chortled. "I caught him when he tried to sneak out. We had a talk."

Embarrassed, Hughes kept his head down.

Jacques stood to let the women feed the children. "François, Pierrette, I'll arrest you myself and let you rot in one of my cells for months if you pull another stunt like that. And as for the réseau doing nothing, young idiots, you better learn again a few things I thought you knew. Hiding and leading escapees, or people in need, is of vital importance. Just as it is to gather and pass on intelligence. That's why we don't go around shooting people and sabotaging things which draw a lot of attention."

A silence ensued while his words were absorbed by the company. Gontrand looked on bewildered. "Is that what's going on under my roof?"

"Yes, father."

"You could have told me."

"As long as you believed in Marshal Pétain, there was no point in telling you."

"But he's playing a double game..." His words trailed away without conviction.

Bernard blew out a breath. "Father, you're an intelligent man. You listen to the BBC Les Français parlent aux Français broadcast, don't tell me you still believe that idiocy about Pétain."

"Well, don't involve your mother in your shenanigans."

A general laugh punctuated his words. The attention veered away from the adolescents and Bernard signaled to François to follow him. In the sitting room, François took his violin from a high shelf and tried to open it while shielding it from his uncle's view.

"You can't hide whatever you've got in there, François." He stepped closer and reached for a handful of papers. "Hum, that is... an organizational chart of the FTP. The Gestapo would so much love to have these. And they would torture you until you told them everything and then, throw your broken body in the Seine."

"Sorry, uncle. I promise I won't do it again. Here's another microfilm from von Trennen."

Anger surged in Bernard's voice. "You dared take your violin out of the Manoir after you had the microfilm? Are you crazy?" He shook his head. "Sorry, François. I thought I could trust you, but I can't anymore. As I said earlier, you will no longer have any role in our organization. That microfilm falling into the hands of the Gestapo would spell death for many good people, including our German friends in the Manoir, who are taking huge risks to pass on that intelligence. Yes, I said friends, and they are since they are anti-Nazi and used their resources to save Lyse-May. Don't you ever forget that. But for the time being, you go and attend your university classes. There'll be no assignment for you."

Head low, François murmured, "Herr Fashingbauer often has messages for me to hand to Reynard."

"The orchestra conductor is still teaching you?"

He lifted his head. "Yes. He and Reynard don't want to be seen together other than for official business."

"So, you see now the repercussions that your recklessness could have caused, had you been caught?"

"Oui, parrain."

Bernard hugged his godson. "Let's go and eat."

"I'll tell Yves I have reasons not to go along with him. There are other students at Janson de Sailly who have formed a cell, but not like Yves. They're not communists."

"But you are not joining them either."

"I'll keep my word. I promise."

Chapter Twelve

Bernard stood up. "It'll be dark soon. We should go home."

"I'm going back through the quarries, but my flashlight's pretty dim. It might give out before I get to Popaul's cellar."

Bérangère handed Julie a couple of replacement batteries. "Ernest managed to get his hands on a small supply."

"While Julie is warm and sheltered on her underground road, we freeze our behinds in the slush," Brigitte said.

Her complaint earned her a round of good-natured teasing.

Bernard tapped her on the shoulder. "I'll help you with the children."

Yolande readied herself to leave. "Well, I braved the weather and bicycled." She went to retrieve her bicycle from the rack and set off. Back on the street, she splashed her way to rue Laugier and was relieved to find the door unlocked. As she struggled with her bicycle, Lucienne rushed to help her.

"Merci, Madame Cabestaès. I'm glad to see you're the new concierge. What happened to the old harpy?"

Lucienne cracked a smile. "Black market. She was caught... by the French police."

"Indeed!" Yolande wondered whether Jacques Werner had anything to do with it. The coincidence seemed rather obvious. "I'm not unduly sorry. She wasn't very nice. Downright obnoxious, in fact."

"Unpatriotic citizens get their just desserts."

Yolande tilted her head and looked at the concierge. "You knew about her?"

"You have a lot of friends, Mademoiselle Bourgmestre. You were arrested."

Yolande laughed. "Word travels fast."

"In some circles it does."

"Do I assume that the same friends told you there was a loge available?"

"They did. But they didn't say a Fritz would also come. That's why I wasn't so welcoming when you got back."

"That man saved my life. He might visit from time to time. Sometimes with children. No, not his. Just children who need a safe place. And I have other friends too."

"Anything to help. But what if he comes when you have other visitors?"

"If it happens, they'd disappear via the servants' stairs."

"They can come here. The loge has a trapdoor to the cellar."

Yolande nodded. Many buildings' cellars were connected. Not everyone was aware that beneath the streets and courtyards of Paris existed an unsuspected life. "Sometimes I bring leftover food from the hotel. We can share."

"That's most generous of you. I only have my widow's pension from the First War. I lost my job when the Fritz took over the management of the factory and purged the staff."

"You'll be fine here."

***

"Gontrand, get your best suit on right now. We're going to the reception, whether you like it or not."

"I don't want to rub shoulders with the Hun. Tell your ambassador that he can stick his invitation..." The glare from his wife ended his tirade.

"General von Trennen kindly offered to take us in his car. He isn't any happier than you, but no one in their right mind would refuse an invitation from Otto Abetz. And Charmaine will be singing."

Gontrand limped to the bedroom muttering the loudest grumbles he could produce.

Bérangère followed. "Would you prefer to heed the words of that worthless minister? I mean Laval? Did you hear what he said? *The German victory will prevent our civilization from sinking into communism. An American victory would see the triumph of Jews and communism.*"

"Enough, woman!"

The reception was getting under way when Julie arrived. Ever vigilant, she scanned the foyer before handing her coat to the attendant. She stood on the threshold of the spacious reception room and took a step forward just as a whirlwind of a woman seized her and drew her back into the foyer.

"Charmaine!"

"Meinhard's here. Get back home." While speaking, Charmaine signaled to the attendant who didn't appear to care which coat, she was handing out. At the same time, Charmaine helped Julie wrap her shawl about her head, then pushed her through the door.

Julie squeezed her friend's hand. "Go back in. I'll be alright."

She flew down the carpeted stairs as fast as her heels permitted. A fiacre arrived. As soon as the passengers got down, Julie climbed in.

Charmaine watched through a side window and sighed with relief when the fiacre departed. She hurried to join Wolfang.

Always polite, Bérangère complimented a German Countess von something or other on her elegant Maggy Rouff dress. On being introduced, Bérangère hadn't grasped the name of the aristocratic woman but was disinclined to ask her to repeat. Instead, she went to take her seat in the adjoining room where the concert was being held. On her way, she was stopped by a tall SS officer.

"Madame de Montregard." He gave a stiff bow.

Heart beating fast, Bérangère didn't offer her hand. "Monsieur."

"Allow me to introduce myself. Obersturmbannführer Meinhard at your service, madame. You may know me as Kurt, as I am well acquainted with your daughter-in-law, Julie."

Anger roiled up inside Bérangère. Her high-society-lady mask slipped. She pinched her lip and bit hard enough to draw blood so that she wouldn't utter the words that crowded her throat. Her lack of response didn't appear to deter Meinhard.

"Julie and I have been close since our youthful days. I am distressed that she has not been home for some time. You may know where she is?"

With supreme effort, Bérangère mollified the acid tone of her voice. "She's a married woman and doesn't report her whereabouts to me. She may have gone to the country. This dreadful war has disrupted normal life. Now, if you will excuse me, I wish to listen to the music."

Since he didn't move, she stepped around him and, with all the regal bearing she could muster, swept into the next room. She spotted Gontrand sitting next to General von Trennen. A chair was free next to her husband. Rigid and still seething, she sat down. Reynard leaned forward and looked at her. He raised his eyebrows and followed the tilt of her chin at Meinhard walking down the aisle scrutinizing the rows of people. He took a chair in the front row.

Under Wolfang's pianist fingers, the music cut short the hum of voices. It seemed as though the room's collective breath was held when Charmaine began to sing.

Once the performance was over, Otto Abetz beamed his satisfaction with the success of his party. The Tout-Paris and the cream of the German military elite mingled again. More than ready to leave, Charmaine headed toward the exit, threading her way through the well-wishers complimenting her on her performance. Close to the door, she came face to face with Meinhard.

"Madame Lebeau."

"Monsieur."

"Let us not waste time in civilities. Where is Julie?"

A shudder of terror ran down Charmaine's spine, but her face showed an utter surprise. "I don't know."

He came close and towered over her. "Yes, you do. You are close friends. Where is she?"

Soft, well-mannered Charmaine had a natural theatrical talent. Her haughtiness hid her inner turmoil. "I can only repeat what I just said. I do not know."

Her eyes flitted over the room in search of Wolfang. She saw him looking in her direction.

Obviously not pleased with her reply. Meinhard grabbed her arm and pushed her back against the door jamb. He spoke through gritted teeth. "I asked you a civil question. Where is Julie?"

Before she could make a reply, a voice came from behind the belligerent Meinhard.

"Is this gentleman bothering you, Madame Lebeau?" General von Trennen edged closer. "Ah, Meinhard, I do think you are hurting Madame Lebeau's arm. That is hardly becoming of an officer in polite society."

Meinhard ground his teeth, but released his hold on Charmaine. "I was asking the lady a polite question."

"It appears that Madame Lebeau does not know the answer."

"I have not finished talking. You may return to your business, von Trennen."

The general gave a flicker of a smile. "My business has already led me to a cargo train of gold bars. Does that interest you? Besides, may I remind you that it is General von Trennen to you?"

His face twisted in fury, Meinhard swung round and strode away.

In a minute, the de Montregards, Wolfang and Captain Langen surrounded Charmaine and Reynard.

Charmaine rubbed her arm. "Thank you for your intervention."

Reynard smiled. "I am afraid I had to pull rank on him. As a Generalfeldmarschall, I still carry a little clout."

Full of assumed innocence, Charmaine addressed Reynard. "Would that be a gold clout?"

At Reynard's chuckle, Wolfang offered his arm to his musical partner and led her out.

***

Paris, Sunday, December 20, 1942

What a do it was last night at the ambassador's reception. That dastardly Meinhard still looking for Julie. I'd have thought that those SS, (aren't they all Gestapo?) could find people at the drop of a hat. But just as well their organization isn't as good as they are reputed to be, otherwise we'd all be in their prisons. Reynard made that SS man really furious. If I understand the play on words, it looks like the general was able to blackmail Meinhard. More than once when we play music together, he's let out that the Wehrmacht, and with it the Abwehr, thoroughly detest the SS. He also hinted that the Nazis in Berlin were working to get rid of the Abwehr. Why on earth did God allow National Socialism to grow as it has? We hear that there are labor camps that are not exactly what they seem. We don't know because nobody who's been sent there ever comes back.

It can't continue like this. We have to queue for hours for a loaf of bread. Children are going hungry, they don't grow properly. In the meantime, the Boches are getting fat, eating sumptuous meals. That's what my dear Charmaine reports every time Wolfang takes her out. She tells me she only eats the main course and refuses desserts. Her sensitivity prevents her from eating her fill. She's as proud as we are and doesn't accept gifts from him. Just, she said, the occasional cans of food for the children.

I fear for the future. The Chleus are closing French factories, those that were allowed to keep running, so that they can ship the workers to Germany. Jacques mentioned a census for workers. True, some of them are unemployed men, but mostly they don't want to work for the Fritz. He said Vichy will pass a law to institute a compulsory labor service.

It's the wholesale destruction of the fabric of our country. The Americans and the British can't come soon enough.

Time to stop my ramblings, I hear the outside door.

Julie and Brigitte cornered Charmaine before she had time to take her boots off.

"Tell us! What happened? After you literally threw me out to save me from harm," Julie said.

Charmaine recounted the previous evening.

"The damned man was supposed to be in Berlin."

"I'm glad I saw him arrive long before the majority of the guests."

"So, you think General von Trennen was blackmailing that despicable man because he's got something on him?" Brigitte asked.

"Possibly. He hinted something about a train load of gold bars."

The three friends shrugged. It didn't mean anything to them. Disaster had been averted and that was the main thing.

"Anyway, thank you for saving me. What shall we do for the réveillon de Noël?"

Madeleine joined them. "Félicité wants to put a gift under the Christmas tree for every child. You won't disappoint her, will you?"

"Of course she can." Bérangère came and sat with the friends. "At two years old, she understands the concept of giving, but please, Madeleine, keep the gifts simple."

"We will, belle-maman."

Giggles greeted François' entrance. His gym shorts still fitted his lanky frame. No one dared ask him who cut his hair. It was short on the sides, but unequal, and brushed back on top.

"You look so much younger than your eighteen years. I thought you wanted to look like a man," Brigitte said.

"If I look very young, I won't be taken for a worker and be seized."

"Shorts in December? Did you see how much snow there is outside? It wouldn't fool anybody for very long. You'd best stay off the streets. There're bound to be raids to snatch young people who forget to register in the census." Jacques snorted. "Attend classes as usual and hurry home. But you're on holiday right now. So, stay home."

"What about my violin lessons?"

"Send a message to Mr. Fashingbauer. He'll understand."

"Reynard will keep giving you lessons," Julie said.

Bernard winked at his nephew. No one except Julie saw it. François went to change.

***

Christmas Eve and the snow continued to fall. Everyone made an effort to attend. Captain Langen borrowed the general's Mercedes and collected Brigitte and her children. Bérangère and Gontrand swallowed their pride and accepted the basket of food Reynard brought. In keeping with the custom they had established two years previously, they gathered in the ballroom and when the children had found gifts under the Christmas tree, everyone sang carols with Bérangère at the piano and Reynard on the violin.

***

New Year's Eve started ominously with bombing raids on the industrial suburbs. Defiant Parisians queued earlier than usual in the hope they'd get a little extra to celebrate the New Year. They were more interested about the prospect of beans being handed out under the counter than worried about yet another attack on some factory working for the Germans.

At the Manoir, everyone gathered again, including Yolande. From time to time, a sad smile flitted across Julie's lips.

"Are you thinking about your little Claudine and Mathieu?" Reynard asked.

"I do when I see Félicité and Christiane. Claudine is about the same age. As for Mathieu, I'm missing out on so much of his growth. I miss holding him."

"I could drive you to their hiding place."

A flash of hope lit Julie's eyes, only to be extinguished by reason. "I don't know where they are and as long as I don't know and don't go to see them, they are safe."

"You are very brave. Your sacrifices will pay off."

"Is Hitler really losing the war?"

"It is too early to tell. Is Jacques grumbling about the new laws?"

Jacques overheard the question. "Yes, I am! It isn't official yet, but Vichy has taken measures to paralyze the gendarmerie. Bunch of fascists!"

Bérangère lifted an eyebrow. "The police were all for supporting the new order at the beginning."

"So were thousands of other people, and if we all had quit who'd have ensured order in the city?"

"The Boches," Gontrand said.

Pierrette stretched her lips in a mock smile. "We'd all be dead if they had."

Reynard coughed into his fist.

"You're not like them. It doesn't apply to you," Bérangère said.

"Thank you for your expression of confidence."

Jacques wasn't done. "I'll remind you that I, and a few other gendarmes, were opposed. Now lots of them are outraged, especially with that travail obligatoire law they will impose to recruit young people to go to work in Germany."

As midnight approached, everyone stood with a glass of wine. The children who hadn't yet fallen asleep struggled to keep their eyes open.

"Let's make a wish that the coming year brings us closer to the liberation of our country," Bernard said.

The clock hands came together on the numeral twelve and cheers erupted, including from the general and his staff.

Chapter Thirteen

Sparkling snow added a festive air to the drab streets. But everything changed the moment the alert sounded and the surly growl of bombers, each eager to drop its payload on the industrial north and western suburbs of Paris, shattered the peaceful day.

The inhabitants of the quartier des Invalides rejoiced when a company of German soldiers was attacked and left sixteen dead on the third of January, the day of Sainte-Geneviève, the patron saint of Paris.

The school holidays were over and Lyse-May, holding her ardoise, strode confidently along next to Gontrand. He had grudgingly agreed to let her go to the local parish school. He had cleaned her slate carefully and found a new piece of chalk for the holder. The school gates closed at nine o'clock and Gontrand from outside the yard continued to stare at the door that had swallowed his granddaughter. With a sigh, he trudged back home in the deep snow.

"Stop moving the cold air about," Bérangère said. "It's only half past ten."

"I think I should go and wait for her. There is so much snow I had to carry her part of the way, because her legs are too short."

Bérangère laughed. "The snow isn't that bad. It only takes ten minutes to walk to the school. Do you want to freeze until noon?"

Gontrand didn't have to reply. The outside door banged open. Moments later a distraught Lyse-May burst into the kitchen, without coat or boots.

Her grandfather jumped and picked her up. "What the devil happened?"

"Where are your boots and coat, chérie? You walked from the school in your slippers?"

Cocooned in her grandfather's arms, her feet vigorously

rubbed dry by her grandmother, Lyse-May allowed herself a tear.

She showed her slate with a crack in the middle. "The Mademoiselle threw my ardoise at my head."

Rage made Gontrand grind his teeth. "What?" he managed to say.

"It was arithmetic. She said the numbers and we had to write the answer. I did right away. The other students were writing for a long time. Then she took our ardoises. Then she took mine and threw it at me. But I have the right answer. I know it. So, I left because it's broken now."

"I'm going to go and have a word with that woman. You're not going back!"

Bérangère raised her hand in peace. "After the noon recess, I will take Lyse-May and talk to the teacher. Lyse-May probably didn't know the instructions on how to present her work."

That afternoon, Bérangère's interview with the institutrice did not go well.

A frazzled Mademoiselle tried to push Bérangère out. "Lyse-May is smart but inspectors are coming this afternoon, with a German one too. I don't have time."

"Throwing a slate at the head of a six-year-old child is not acceptable, Mademoiselle. I'll leave you now, but I'll be back tomorrow."

Mademoiselle sat Lyse-May at the front of the class. Two inspectors from the Ministry of National education came in, accompanied by a German inspector in civilian clothes. The visitors sat at the back of the class.

Mademoiselle asked Lyse-May to recite the alphabet, then to name the river flowing through Paris. Her clear answers pleased the teacher.

"And now who can tell me who governs France?" There was silence. "Lyse-May?"

"The Boches."

A horror-stricken teacher looked at her, dumbfounded. She quickly recovered. "Wrong! Wrong! You must have heard that from your parents. They are wrong. You come to school to learn what is right. The correct answer is Marshal Pétain. Marshal Pétain, our savior. Repeat Marshal Pétain saved us."

Lyse-May stood up. "Pétain is a senile old goat. School is bad. I'm going home."

She stood up and walked toward the door.

Horrified, Mademoiselle started behind her. "Come back here and apologize."

She tried to grab the little girl. Lyse-May slipped from under the teacher's hand and ran along the aisle to the back of the class, past the three astonished inspectors, Mademoiselle in hot pursuit. Lyse-May reached the door and slammed it shut behind her. She snatched her coat from the rack and thrust her boots under her arm. The principal came out of her office just in time to see Lyse-May reach the outside door and run straight into her grandfather's arms. Gontrand meant to give the institutrice a piece of his mind, but decided it was more important to take his granddaughter home. He carried her and ignored the principal's shouts behind him.

In the kitchen, her hands warming on a drinking bowl of hot water with half a teaspoon of sugar in it, Lyse-May had to explain her behavior. Bérangère tried to be conciliatory, while Gontrand remained belligerent.

"That's that. She isn't going to any school."

"The public school would be different."

"That Vichy nest of infamy?"

Bérangère was getting impatient. "They still learn good things."

"I thought you read those darned Vichy newspapers. Don't they tell you anything about collaboration, and all that Service du Travail Obligatoire? Compulsory work, indeed!"

"I capitulate." Bérangère hid a smile at seeing how much her husband had changed.

***

The snow finally was beginning to melt to a messy slush. Brigitte carefully folded the documents and inserted them into the inner pocket of the battered baby bag. She wrapped Sylvestre's scarf around his face, leaving only his eyes visible. He was running a fever and was lethargic. Downstairs, she sat him in the pushchair and lifted the footrest for Christiane to sit on. She tucked a blanket around them both. She'd have preferred to leave her sick little boy home, but Amélie wasn't there to babysit. The bookstore on rue Victor Hugo wasn't too far. She didn't intend to be long.

Sylvestre fell asleep. She stopped to lower the backrest to make him more comfortable. Full of concern, Christiane snuggled next to her brother and put an arm around him. “I keep him warm.” Brigitte sighed in relief, adjusted the blanket and pushed harder.

Someone ran past her. “Don’t go there!”

Shocked, she came to an abrupt stop. Black cars, tires squealing, converged on the street just meters ahead of her. She was about to turn round and go back, but too late. A man in a black coat stepped in front of her.

“*Halt!*” he shouted.

Her heart gripped with terror, she took the decision to bluff her way and took a few steps, looking like the frightened young mother she really was.

“*Halt!* I said.”

“*Bonjour, monsieur.* I’m going to church. Saint-Honoré d’Eylau, at the end of the street.”

Christiane lifted her head and smiled.

The man bent his head to look at the child. “You go somewhere else. Street closed.”

Brigitte gracefully bowed her head. “Merci, monsieur.” She turned the pushchair round and feigning nonchalance, strolled back the way she’d come. Her heart beat erratically, and she desperately clenched her belly muscles so she wouldn’t wet herself. As she passed Julie’s apartment building, she saw Madame Durand peeking through the half-open door.

“Madame Brigitte. Come in quickly. This doesn’t look good.”

Brigitte entered and ran to the bathroom. Sickness came over her and she fetched up her meager breakfast.

“Pardon me, madame. Being caught in the raid made me sick with fright.”

“I see that. And Sylvestre is sick too. Sit down, I’ll make you both a tisane.” She cut a sprig of a green herb from her pot on the windowsill and rubbed it in her hands. “Did you see what was happening? I won’t ask you what you were doing out there.”

An amused grin on her lips, Brigitte said, “I was going to Saint-Honoré d’Eylau church to find out whether I could enroll Damien in catechism. I saw the Gestapo at the bookstore.”

“Going to church, *hé?* That’s a good one. The bookstore probably has newssheets for the Résistance. I saw monsieur Bernard going there.”

“Oh, no, not Bernard!”

"Some time ago, before you walked by. I thought maybe you were to meet."

Brigitte went to the window but couldn't see much.

"Here, drink this tisane. It's made with hyssop. I'll give some to Sylvestre."

The beverage was mildly aromatic, tasting somewhere between aniseed and licorice. Sylvestre drank avidly. Christiane wanted some too. Brigitte returned to the window. "Here's Bernard, now!"

At that instant, the wail of sirens rent the stillness of the wintry day.

"I'll get him."

With surprising agility, Madame Durand bounded to the outside door. "Psst! Monsieur Bernard!"

He ran the last few meters and stumbled into the foyer. At the same instant, a traction-avant followed by another sped down the street.

"Not for me, thanks to the alert." Bernard's voice conveyed his relief.

"Are we going to the cellar?" Brigitte asked.

"It must be the Americans. They bomb during the day and the RAF at night. It sounds like the north-west suburbs are getting a pasting. "We're alright."

"What about the bookstore?" Brigitte asked.

"It's finished."

Madame Durand, who was holding her chin in her cupped hand, let it drop to the table. "You can leave your messages here."

Bernard shook his head. "We know you have already helped a lot, but the Gestapo keep a close eye on this building. I don't want you to take more risks."

"It's only one man that comes and asks if Madame de Montregard is home. Then he goes away for a couple of weeks."

Brigitte cuddled Sylvestre who'd just got off the pushchair. "It doesn't look like the whole Gestapo is after Julie, more like Meinhard alone paying a private detective."

"You may be right. No need to take unnecessary risks, though. We'll only leave messages here in an emergency."

"Always leave them in the box on the wall. That's where the postman leaves the mail if I'm not in the loge."

Finally, the all-clear sounded. Bernard escorted Brigitte home. "I wonder if the bookstore has been denounced."

"It's so pro-Vichy and collaboration up front, how would anyone suspect the owners of being a letterbox?"

"We've got to tighten security and find out whether there's a mole in the réseau."

***

"Are you coming with me?" François asked his sister.

"The law for the Service du Travail Obligatoire includes women, and for the moment, I'll just be careful and stay at the Manoir. In case you haven't noticed, the police avoid the sixteenth arrondissement. They don't want to clash with the upper echelon of society."

"That's what Jacques said. But when the SS take over with their own goons, all that'll change."

"Even the despicable SS show a smidgen of respect for the upper strata of society."

"Only if they're pro-Nazi, and there're plenty around here who are." François rubbed his forehead. "Women might be a little safer than men as they can claim essential service exemptions, motherhood and all that. But I no longer look like a boy. I don't want to hide here. I'd go crazy. I'm going to make my way to Montauloup."

"A dangerous journey, especially now that the south is no longer the free zone."

"We send downed airmen there all the time. I'll be alright. I'll follow our own Gavroche line."

Pierrette clasped her hands in prayer. "Promise you'll curb that impulsive nature of yours."

"Very well. I'm doing much better. Bernard pulled my ears a few times."

They burst out laughing and hugged each other.

"Service du Travail Obligatoire. It's abbreviated as STO," Pierrette said. "We printed a new version of it in the next newssheet: Don't be *SOT*, get away."

François laughed. "That's rich! Don't be stupid, get away. Who came up with that?"

"Actually, Hughes and Daniel did. They also said they are not going to wait their eighteenth birthday to get away."

"There's plenty of room in Montauloup and no Boche. It's too far for them."

***

Thursday, February 4, 1943

Those Boches! We heard they razed a whole district in Marseille, and now hundreds of people have no home. They said it hid terrorists. Now, I'll give that to the French police who were, of course, required to help blow up the district nicknamed Le Panier, but went to warn its inhabitants, mostly Jews, beforehand. Those who didn't manage to leave in time were deported. Poor people! They thought they'd be safe, and safe it was when it was still the free zone. If I believe the rumors, twenty thousand other people were ordered to leave their homes while the despicable Boches carried out their destruction. But when they came back, they found their homes ransacked. The Résistance's ranks swelled up with angry young Marseillais. So, where are all those rebellious youths going to go and hide?

Since the weather is so mild, my husband took Lyse-May to the Bois de Boulogne. Earlier, she climbed up to the attic and found some books. Unfortunately, all the books suitable for her age have been given to the grandchildren. She is too old for the baby books, but I don't think she can make sense of Madame Bovary. The old copy of Le petit chose is not relevant. Bullying in school isn't relevant unless she understands that the bullying concept can also apply to a teacher. And Hector Malo's Sans famille has already made her cry.

What are those Boches going to do next? What are they doing here that the electricity keeps going off?

I never saw Jacques so furious. Vichy now has its own little Nazi army: La Milice. The French police and gendarmerie have been stripped of their powers. Jacques and some of his men are seething at having to obey those upstarts in the milice.

More attacks against the Fritz. We now avoid being on the same sidewalk as them.

Gontrand and Lyse-May are back. I better go and see if those turnips are cooked.

***

Jacques made a triumphant entry. "Did you hear the news? Of course, you must have."

Even the children paused a moment from eating.

Gontrand slapped his old friend on the shoulder. "I never thought we'd ever see a German army surrender."

"That's because Hitler thought he was invincible. Napoleon was defeated at the gates of Moscow and the Boches are defeated in front of Stalingrad. The Russian winter kills all who dare invade," Pierrette said.

"Léonie, what does the general say?"

"That it was inevitable. We all knew when Hitler attacked the Soviet Union in June '41 that he had lost the war."

Bernard sighed. "But it isn't yet over."

"I heard that they're having a bad time in front of Kursk. Morale is low among the Wehrmacht troops," Julie said.

"That didn't mean you could bicycle all the way here!" Bernard was not pleased with her.

"I wore Charmaine's coat and a blond wig."

General laughter greeted her words.

"I haven't seen François for a long while," Madeleine said.

Julie and Pierrette looked at Bernard. His body language expressed his unwillingness to answer. Julie grimaced in his direction.

"You know that all young men are being recruited for the STO?"

"I heard that. But it's a good thing, isn't it? Philippe says so."

Julie took a deep breath. "You don't really want your son to go to Germany, do you?"

"No, he could work here when he finishes university."

"But that's the point. All the young men and women are being sent to work in Germany. We don't know of anybody who went to Germany and has come back."

Madeleine looked horrified. "You mean they don't come back?"

To make Madeleine understand, Julie stretched the truth, though in all honesty travail obligatoire was really forced labor, 'compulsory' was too mild. "It's forced labor. The young people are being pulled out of the jobs they already have here, or from their studies. The workers who volunteered haven't come back home. They can't. They live in camps and are not allowed out."

"Philippe said it is their duty to go." Madeleine looked perturbed. "But that's not right. Is it?"

Jacques cleared his throat. "The workers can only send a postcard home once a month. It's always the same picture, and the same printed words. Only the signature is genuine. A couple of upset women from the twelfth arrondissement went to their commissariat de police with the postcards and asked the gendarmes to get their sons back home. They suspected that their sons were being held prisoner. But there's nothing we can do."

"Then, François mustn't go."

"Don't worry, maman. He's in hiding."

The conversation shifted to Yolande, who raised her voice. "It's no joke, father. I know your contribution to the Résistance is invaluable, printing all those documents, but we heard that the Gestapo is closing in on the printshop."

"True, Monsieur Bourgmestre," Léonie said.

Lorraine put a hand to her mouth. "We have so much material in the basement."

Bernard held a hand. "We'll help you take it out. We'll be there tomorrow."

With these words, everybody dressed to go home.

Yolande accompanied her parents. "It's my day off tomorrow. I'll stay with you tonight and get a head start in the morning."

"I'll help," Hughes said.

"You are going to school, young man," his mother said. "And it's bedtime."

Hughes groaned. Night brought sleep to the household.

The squeals of tires and car doors slamming shattered the silence of the night. Hughes jumped out of bed and looked into the hallway.

"Upstairs. Go, run, hide!" Yolande pushed him out onto the landing, locking the door behind him, and hurried to wake up her father and mother.

Barefoot and in pajamas, Hughes ran up the stairs as the same time as the clatter of booted feet resonated downstairs. A door opened on the landing above.

The neighbor motioned him in and closed the door noiselessly. He flicked on a lighter on and put a finger to his lips. Heart beating fast, Hughes followed him to the kitchen at the back of the apartment. The neighbor lit a candle and whispered, "I'm a light sleeper and I'm often awake at four in the morning. When I heard car engines, I knew what was going to happen to the printshop. I was hoping your parents were behind you."

Hughes let a tear drop. "Merci, monsieur Pascal. My sister stayed the night to help us move out. I don't think they had time to get away."

"Don't lose hope."

"I know what the Gestapo do. Yolande was arrested. She told us. Someone was able to get her out."

"Maybe that person can do it again."

"I hope so."

They fell silent as banging continued. Hughes ventured to the window and lifted a corner of the blackout curtain just enough to peer outside. The light of dawn emerged from the darkness. Pascal blew out the candle and joined Hughes at the window. In the street below, Gestapo men were carrying boxes and bundles out of the printshop. Two trucks drove off. Finally, the men were manhandling Jean-Luc, Loraine and Yolande handcuffed into the back of a van.

Hughes bent his head and cried openly.

After a while, Pascal put his arm around his shoulders. "I'll give you my son's clothes. He's gone to England two years ago. They'll be a bit too big but better than bicycling in your pajamas to go to your uncle's."

"Thank you. I'll bring them back later." Hughes dressed over his pajamas and tightened the pants' belt beyond the last hole. The jacket and coat floated around his skinny frame. He put on three pairs of socks so the shoes would stay on his feet. Pascal went down first. Piles of broken furniture and machinery lay everywhere. The shattered door hung askew. He took Hughes's bicycle out of the shed and brought it through the lobby to the front door. Still shaking, the concierge came out of her loge.

"I'll hold it. They're all gone. *Si c'est pas malheureux!*"

Pascal let his head waggle in disgust. "Indeed, it's a crying shame. Poor lad."

The hugs Hughes received from the concierge and Pascal threatened his composure. Hughes climbed on the bicycle and pedaled off as fast as he could, avoiding the main streets. He finally arrived in the Manoir's courtyard.

His white face and tear tracks were sufficient explanation for Bérangère. She opened her arms.

"They took my parents and my sister."

Fresh tears wet his cheeks. After a moment, Bérangère made him sit in front of the stove. She added a little of the coal that Dédé had smuggled in. Lyse-May pulled a chair next to her cousin. Her scrawny arms encircled his neck. An aroma of chocolate attracted Gontrand into the kitchen.

"What smells so good?"

Bérangère looked at him pointedly. "A Fritz gave Lyse-May a whole bar of chocolate. I'm melting half of it to make cocoa."

At that moment, Gontrand caught sight of his nephew and sat next to him. Although he wanted to ask, he didn't. He took Hughes' hand in his and remained quiet. More and more nowadays, silence was his refuge when events overwhelmed him.

"The Gestapo got my parents and my sister."

The cocoa ready, Bérangère put two bowls onto the table and a slice of bread. "Drink and eat, Hughes. Lyse-May, make sure your cousin does. I've to go out for a while."

Stricken, Gontrand didn't acknowledge her. Although the weather remained mild, Bérangère wrapped her head in a woolen scarf. She pondered who could best pass the message to Bernard. She bemoaned that her son didn't want to give her a way to contact him directly. Since Julie's safety was at risk every time she went out, Bérangère opted to go to Brigitte's and hoped she was back from shopping.

"Maman-Bérangère! Come in. I'm sorry there's no elevator in this building."

"I'm not that old and decrepit that I can't walk up a flight of stairs." She picked up Christiane. "Both of them have the sniffles?"

"Alas, between the lack of heat and the lack of meat, they seem to have a permanent cold."

"Do you have enough lentils and beans to make a good meal?"

"Yes, but they don't like lentils, and beans give them colic."

"I'll give you a cooking lesson, but I came here with bad news that needs to be relayed to Bernard. The printshop was raided. Jean-Luc, Lorraine and Yolande were taken by the Gestapo."

"No!" Brigitte's hands flew to her face. Tears welled up. A worried, Sylvestre clambered onto her knee.

"We have to be strong."

Brigitte rubbed her face. "I must go and pass on the message."

"I'll stay with the children." Bérangère didn't let on that she was worried Brigitte could be caught and the children could be left with the neighbor. Although she was proud of her family's actions, she lived in constant fear for their safety.

With precise gestures, Brigitte wound a scarf around her head and donned her threadbare coat. She held her children tight and kissed them, in the desperate knowledge she might not come back to them.

It was noon when Brigitte, cheeks flushed from exertion, let herself into the apartment to a sight that warmed her heart. Her children were eating with gusto under Bérangère's supervision.

Bérangère looked up. "How did it go?"

"A message left at two places, then across Paris to Popaul's in case Julie doesn't get word at the hotel. There may be an informant in the réseau. Since we added several safe houses, things haven't run smoothly. Could you go to visit your friend Bernadette and tell her to move her guest right away?"

"I'll go now. By the way, both Sylvestre and Christiane are enjoying lentils. I cooked a pot when the electricity came back on."

"How?"

"I mashed the lentils lightly. Then I used one potato and a big onion to make a sauce, et voilà. Come this evening. I'm sure we'll gather at home to talk about the situation."

Bérangère hurried down just in time to see a man trying to break the padlock on the chain that secured her bicycle to the street lamppost. "My man, would you like the key?" Her haughty tone of voice startled the thief. He jumped so high, he dropped the tool he was using and fled as fast as his legs could carry him. Bérangère kicked the tool into the gutter.

She arrived at her friend's hôtel particulier to find the household in an uproar.

A disheveled Bernadette was trying to comfort her upset tenants. "Bérangère, we've had the most dreadful time. Those uncouth men from the Gestapo insisted in checking every room. We are alright now. Ladies and gentlemen, please return to your suites. Rose will cook a special supper to help us recover." She took her friend's arm and marched with her into the kitchen. "I look a fright. Give me a minute to tidy up."

Rose pulled out a chair for Bérangère. "It was scary. Pierrette had come, just half an hour before the Gestapo, to take our guest somewhere else. She said it wasn't safe. How lucky we were."

Composed and re-coiffed, Bernadette made a dignified entrance. "I ought to tell you that Rose saved our lives. She put on a perfect French accent and told those frightful Gestapo in broken German that we were a home for old and sick people. The Gestapo men have no manners. Despite being told there was nobody else, they still wanted to check the rooms. They ordered my tenants into the salon. Rose told us to cough and sneeze. I joined in. What a comedy! But it worked. When Rose told that horrid Gestapo fellow that half of us had tuberculosis, they couldn't leave fast enough."

"Everyday something happens to scare us. Fear is becoming a constant part of our lives."

"I heard one of them say their tip off was wrong. Do you think someone denounced us?"

"Alas, I suspect that might be so. There's someone who knows about what we're doing." Then Bérangère told her friend and Rose about the printshop.

Chapter Fourteen

At the end of the afternoon, the family gathered in silence around the table. Tension rose. Bernard still hadn't arrived.

"Does anyone know if Julie can come?"

A negative shake of head was the reply. Brigitte and Pierrette looked at each other. Someone had to break the silence.

Pierrette cleared her throat. "Since—"

Footsteps sounded on the backstairs. All heads turned toward the kitchen door. Bernard and Julie came in. They hugged Hughes before taking their places.

"Is Jacques coming?" asked Bernard.

"He'll be here after six," Pierrette replied.

The patter of little feet distracted the assembly. Marianne scooped up Christiane. "Come on sweetie, Lyse-May will tell us a story."

Bernard gave a deep sigh. "Julie and I had a talk while we were walking through the quarries. We've had two of our couriers arrested in the last twenty-four hours. Three safe houses have been raided. And now Madame Ducharme has had a visit from the Gestapo. Fortunately, Pierrette had the presence of mind to run there and spirit the airman away just in time. Where did you take him?"

"To the closest apartment... Julie's. Madame Durand gave me a key. He's settled, with orders not to open the curtains. Madame Durand will take care of him."

"Unfortunately, two of our escapees were caught in the safe house they were at."

Charmaine raised an eyebrow. "A traitor in our midst?"

"I'm thinking more like someone talked to a friend in all confidence but the friend saw it as a profit making opportunity. We had to scramble for safe houses and perhaps didn't have time to make a thorough enough security check."

"But the printshop has nothing to do with the escape line."

Bernard scratched his head. "If they arrested someone in possession of a newssheet from the Bourgmestre Printshop, plus having already ransacked the printshop once, is enough motive for them."

"Could it be related to Meinhard?" Looks of incredulity were directed to Julie. "What if he's hitting at the family to force me to come out of hiding?"

"We can't exclude that possibility," Brigitte said.

Julie bit her lip. "In which case, Alexandre is at risk."

"Surely, they wouldn't try to raid the studio and arrest us, when Charmaine is close to a SS officer?"

Jacques entered at that moment. "Don't you believe it. They would and they will. Time to lie low, Alexandre."

"But there is so much need for identity cards, ration cards and so many other papers we have to have simply to exist."

"I know." Jacques sighed and shook his head. "You all need to curtail the activities for at least some of the time. The news, now. The Bourgmestres were not taken to rue des Saussaies nor avenue Foch. They were driven directly to the Drancy camp."

There was some relief knowing that they wouldn't be beaten and tortured.

With sadness in her voice, Julie said, "Unfortunately, it means they will be deported to a forced labor camp."

"Can they escape from Drancy?" Bérangère asked.

Bernard tugged his ear nervously and grimaced. "Nobody's succeeded so far."

"Jacques," Xavier called. "Is it possible to know when and who is put on the trains going east?"

"Theoretically, the gendarmerie administers the camp under the command of Obersturmführer Röthke. In reality, they do what they are told. I'll make some inquiries among the staff. It's not my jurisdiction, as Drancy is outside the city limits, but I could talk to someone. Why?"

"Because if I were to know which train, I could organize to have the bars on the window of the cattle car loosened. When the train gets to the Lérouville gradient, near Bar-le-Duc, it slows down considerably. The train engineer sounds the whistle. People could jump."

"Providing they know the bars are loose," Pierrette said.

Jacques tilted his head toward her. "Right. I think that information could be passed on if I can make contact."

"The end car would be ideal," Xavier said.

"When my friend Rébeca was interned, I took her a parcel of clothes. Maybe I could do the same at Drancy. There's always a guard willing to be bribed."

Pierrette's hands fluttered. "Auntie, I'll do that. It's too dangerous for you."

"I want to go too," Hughes said.

An animated discussion followed and it was agreed that Pierrette would be the one to take a parcel to the camp. After Hughes said his parents and Yolande had been in their night clothes, the parcel would contain a sweater, a couple of dresses, a shirt, a pair of pants, socks and walking shoes for each of them.

Gontrand broke his silence. "You know there are rebus puzzles in the newspapers. My sister is an ace with them."

"What do you have in mind?" Bérangère asked.

"If you painted or embroidered a window with bars on the left side of the shirt pocket and a bird on the right side, Lorraine would solve it right away."

A round of applause marked Gontrand's words.

Alexandre was already designing the picture. "We can pass a whole message that way."

"All activities are to cease until we figure out if there's a leak in the rıseau."

Pierrette waved both hands in the air in an animated gesture. "There's so much to do to keep our guests moving to safety. At least now that the demarcation line has been suppressed, it's one less obstacle. I can't stop."

"It isn't any easier since the Fritz are everywhere now. And they are getting jumpier and jumpier by the day. Remember that a dead body is no use to the Résistance. You'll do like the rest of us. Lie low for a while."

Pierrette bent her head. Sighs were heard. It was time to go home.

***

Hughes, Daniel and Marianne stood clutching one another in front of the Lycée Buffon. Behind them, Damien, Paul and Baptiste imitated their older cousins, as did hundreds of other students. The young people kept a haunting silence to honor the five fifteen-year-old students who, two days earlier, had been executed by firing squad at the Balard rifle range for being résistants. Still silent, they turned to go home, just as police vans arrived. The students continued walking home without another look at the gendarmes who watched, arms folded on their chests.

At the Manoir, Pierrette dropped into a chair, one boot in her hand. "*Dieu*, you gave us a fright! I was coming after you."

"We're safe. The flics didn't bother any of us," Hughes said.

Bérangère boiled a kettle and put drinking bowls onto the table. She added a spoonful of the apple jam she and Marie had made with apples and beetroot in lieu of sugar. It made a pleasant warm drink.

***

Paris, Tuesday, April 6, 1943

What's wrong with the American bombers? They bombed the Renault auto factory on Sunday, and more bombs fell on the surrounding buildings than on the factory. So many people killed! The radio reported almost six hundred dead and thousands of wounded. How does that advance the war? Do they gain much by putting the factory out of action for a month or two? The damage to Renault will be repaired and production resumed. Then it will start all over again and more people will be killed. Tongues were wagging in the queue this morning, but although everyone deplored the casualties, the women and a couple of men were all for pounding the Fritz out of existence. I didn't like to tell them that all the casualties were French.

And there's no limit to what those Boches will do. We heard that a train was derailed by the Résistance in the north at Ascq. The first thing the Chleus did was to shoot all the station employees. Then they went into the town and rounded up all the men and killed them. Of course Pétain goes to salute the victims of an allied bombing, but not a word about the massacre at Ascq. What am I expecting? Of course he'll ignore the excesses of the Germans. He sold his soul to the devil himself when he shook Hitler's hand in Montoire three years ago.

The bread ration has been reduced yet again. We are dangerously close to a starvation diet. My grandchildren are underweight. The soup kitchen lines are getting longer. There are many workers' wives who don't have the resources to buy on the black market. At first, I was against it. Now, whether it's morally wrong or not, I buy whenever I can. It's a question of survival, no luxuries, just the basic food. The only income we have comes from Les vêtements d'enfants Robi. They still buy my designs and give me finishing work I can do at home. It makes me angry because those beautiful children's garments are going to Germany or to the collaborators' children. Madeleine came the other day with Félicité beautifully attired in one of my designs. I don't begrudge her that fact. I only wish my son would see the light, like his father did, and leave all that collaboration business alone.

Still no news from my niece and her parents. Pierrette doesn't know whether the parcels she takes get to them. The gendarme she talks to appears sympathetic, but who knows. At least the weather is mild.

***

"Madame Gonthier, to my office, please," Madame Le Plouhëc said.

With a last glance at the lounge, Julie joined her supervisor in her office. "Not about Cantal cheese again, I hope."

"Ah, non! Not this time. We're done with that. There's a new guest of the MBF, a civilian, and since we're not open to tourists, I'm curious to know who he is and what he transported in a big heavy case."

"A guest? Not an employee?"

"He was assigned a suite."

"Interesting. So you want me to go and interview him?"

"How about checking that the maids have done their job?"

"As in snooping?"

Madame LePlouhëc waved her arms. "Do whatever you need to do. You're as cunning as your namesake, Fox."

With a chuckle, Julie made her way to the reception desk to find out where the new arrival was lodged. In the elevator, she displayed the blank expression of someone who didn't understand the language. It was hard to repress her satisfaction when an officer mentioned the terrible losses in Tunisia and how the troops were happy to be made prisoner. Even more so when he was reprimanded by another officer for undermining morale by relaying negative news.

At her floor, she observed the hallway while pretending to check the dust on a gilt and bronze half-round table. She knocked on the door of the suite. There was no response. She let herself in with her passkey. The object of her boss' curiosity sat on a table under a cloth. Without wasting time to determine what it was, she brought her compact-camera out of her reticule, threw aside the cloth and photographed the unusual machine.

The rattle of a key in the door startled her. She took three steps backward and powdered her cheeks.

"What are you doing here?"

Julie turned slowly. The man's French was correct, but he had an accent. Not a German accent, more of an eastern European, Hungarian perhaps or Czechoslovakian or even Polish.

"I'm sorry to disturb you, sir. I'm the manager and was checking that the staff had prepared your suite in the proper fashion."

"What's in your hand?"

She put on a contrite air. "A powder compact. I took a minute to repair my makeup." She took the puff and shook a small cloud of scented powder.

He grimaced and coughed. "I see. Put it away."

Julie complied. "I'm supposed to be always perfectly dressed with impeccable makeup."

The man chuckled. "Don't worry, you look ravishing."

Now, adopting a coy air, she smiled and said, "I better get on with my job."

A shrewd look came over his face. "You were interested in this machine?"

Total innocence painted on her face, she said, "What? The typewriter?"

"Yes."

"I'm sorry. I shouldn't be so curious. I wanted to know the brand. I could do with a typewriter to type all sorts of propaganda."

He laughed. "I think you're a spy."

"No, not me." She looked at her finger nails. "I have no abilities to be a spy."

"You do, but you slipped up. You left the cover off."

Julie made a show of biting her upper lip. Her mind worked at double speed for a solution to extricate herself out of the situation. "Forgive me. It has the shape of a typewriter, and I was toying with the idea of stealing it."

He laughed even louder. She was beginning to be reassured that he took her banter to be just fun. Her prospects were getting better by the minute.

"Go ahead, steal it."

"Of course not. I don't want to end up in a Gestapo cell. Besides, it isn't a typewriter as I know typewriters. So, I'm not interested."

"You're right. It isn't a typewriter. It's a coding machine."

A shiver of fear went down her back. He had just revealed what should obviously be kept secret and now, she was part of the secret. "I know nothing about code." She had to divert his attention. "You speak good French, but what is your accent?"

"You're a smart spy, madame. I'm from Poland."

"Surely, you don't work for the Germans?"

He made no reply but went to the desk in the room and withdrew a thick folder. He gave it to her. "That's the manual, all the diagrams for the machine and the code system. Take it now and bring it back before midnight."

Would he ask her to sleep with him as repayment? "Really? You know I'll send a copy to the British."

"I know the English have a machine to decode the Enigma machine the Germans use. This one is the latest amended version of the Enigma. That's what the machine is called. They don't know anything about this one. My French partner is out of commission with the Occupation and my English partner had to go back to England and our in-between contacts have broken up. It's up to you now."

Dumbfounded for a moment, she cleared her throat. "Thank you... I think. But why trust me?"

He smiled. "You were taking photographs with a sophisticated camera, therefore you work for the Résistance. Before midnight, alright?"

She was amazed. In seconds he had identified the camera and herself. She definitely wasn't cut out to be a spy on a grand scale. "I'll be back before then."

Without bothering to maintain her poise, she snatched up the folder and rushed to Madame LePlouhëc's office. "Top secret. We must photograph all the pages and get the manual back to him before midnight."

Stunned, her boss' jaw dropped. "How did you...?"

"Caught in the act. He's a Pole and I have a hunch he has no love for the Germans."

While they talked, Madame LePlouhëc extracted a micro-photographic camera and a stand. She locked the door, while Julie told her about her encounter with the Polish man.

"I also have photographs of the machine on my compact."

"Go and see chef Raoul and give him the compact and tell him twenty-three hours and have him send a tray for us."

Julie delivered the compact. She picked up a tray of food herself. Madame LePlouhëc had already photographed several pages. Between the two of them, the work went faster. At ten to midnight, Julie carried the manual on the food tray with a white cloth over it and a carafe of coffee on the side.

"There you are, sir, your order." She placed it on the desk.

"Thank you."

About to leave, she turned to him. "Why did you do that?"

"For the same reasons you did."

She nodded. Their eyes held. He smiled. "Keep safe."

"And you too."

Julie went back to Madame LePlouhëc's office.

"Good?"

"All good."

"I thought maybe you would have had to sleep with him."

Julie laughed. "I believe he was more concerned about the manual getting to England than having a fling with me."

Madame LePlouhëc raised an eyebrow. "We now have to get that microfilm to Switzerland. I'll have to find an excuse for your absence while you travel. I asked Raoul to send a message to my chief. He'll come in the morning with suitable papers. Thank goodness we don't need an Ausweis for the line."

A wave of excitement passed through Julie. She quelled it. In the morning she and Madame LePlouhëc concealed the microfilm container in Julie's hair and then styled it with rolls around her head. To go with her Nina Ricci dress, she wore an elaborate hat secured with hatpins through the rolls to reinforce the safety of the microfilm.

At the rapping of a coded signal, Madame LePlouhëc hurried to open the door. Julie's eyes grew wide as Armand stepped in. Their gazes locked for a brief instant. An awareness passed between them.

"Your new name, Marjolaine de Beauharnais."

Julie chortled. "Why not Joséphine? I'd be Napoleon III's wife."

They joined in the laughter.

"Seriously, if asked, you're a baroness. You have a château in the Auvergne and a manor in Geneva. You'll go to Hôtel de Genève and meet your contact at the café Remor at eleven-thirty."

"Password?"

"Sit at the same table as the person who is reading *Les fables de Lafontaine*, and say, 'do you like all those fables?' The person should reply, '*I like Le corbeau et le renard*' best."

"The Raven and the Fox!" She laughed. "I'll try to keep a straight face."

"And you'll be traveling with your children."

Julie straightened on her chair.

"Sorry, not your own children. These two are protégés of Mr. Bernard-Émanuel Lefschetz. He has a network of volunteers for children whose parents have been deported or are in danger, not all of them Jewish. I'm getting a fiacre and you'll detour via rue d'Artois to collect the two children. There's a bit of police activity around there, but you should be fine."

Madame LePlouhëc opened the door to a knock. A bellboy announced the fiacre was waiting.

"Tell the cabman we're on our way."

Julie frowned. "Something else?"

Half a smile stretched over Armand's lips. "If a couple of men appeared to be following you, just ignore them. They're only following to make sure they get on the right train and to the Restaurant de la Gare in Lyon. They'll be taken care of there. Let's go."

In the elevator, Armand whispered to Julie. "We have an envoy from London to help unify the different Résistance movements so they work together. We'll win this war." He gave a hug to Julie. "Good luck."

In rue d'Artois, the fiacre had to stop behind a police van.

"Sorry, ma'am, I can't go right up to number Twenty-Two."

"Don't worry, I'll walk. It's only a short way down."

With the cabman's help, Julie stepped onto the sidewalk. As she approached her destination past a manor's garden, she witnessed an argument between a policeman and the concierge of an apartment building just beyond Number Twenty-Two. She was trying to prevent him from taking a toddler from her arms.

Julie accelerated her steps. "What's going on?" Her imperious tone made the policeman turn toward her.

Without wasting a breath, the concierge raised her voice in anger. "He wants to take this two-year-old and send him to a labor camp. I tell you, it's outrageous!"

Julie straightened even more. "Monsieur, you do not send babies to labor camps. Leave that child here. Have you no moral conscience?"

"I'm only doing my duty. So mind your own business."

"This is precisely my business." Julie took a quick decision. "I'm with the Red Cross and I forbid you to take that child away."

He looked her up and down. "Everybody's with the Red Cross these days."

Julie already had her hand in her purse reaching for the secret pocket. She brandished her Red Cross identification card. The policeman scrutinized it, squared his shoulders and gave her the card back.

"Madame de Montregard, I have orders."

The concierge had followed the exchange with shrewd eyes. "Monsieur l'agent, come and have a cup of my very special ersatz."

The policeman hesitated, glanced down the street where other gendarmes were herding people into vans, and stepped into the lobby. Swift as lightning, the concierge handed the silent toddler to Julie who was already holding out her arms. She pivoted on her heels cooing to the child and went to the address where she was supposed to collect the two children.

The worried cabman had been watching and rushed up to open the door for her. "I'll wait here, ma'am. That's a brave thing you just did."

"Thank you. We won't be long now."

In the foyer of the building, Julie saw an elderly concierge trembling in the loge doorway.

"Third floor. The elevator doesn't work because of the electricity cuts. I saw you argue with the police."

"Well, madame, some of them need a boot up the cul."

She sighed. "The little Jewish boy is Samuel."

Julie wondered how many other people had watched the scene. At least none of the other gendarmes, and their Nazi supervisors, appeared to have seen her. She climbed the stairs as fast as she could with the child resting on her shoulder, still silent but with eyes open wide in terror. The door opened before she knocked.

"You made it! We watched from the window. What happened?"

"I will have three children instead of two now." Julie then laughed. "Forgive me, my nerves are about to break."

Two girls dressed to the nines came and stood behind the woman.

Julie took a deep breath. "A fiacre is waiting to take us to the station. Do you happen to have clothes to fit a toddler? I'll call him Gilles."

"Yes, we get many children through here and the wardrobe is well-furnished. I'll get him something and a bag for spares."

Julie turned to the girls. "Francine?"

The oldest smiled. "That's me. I'm ten. My sister Annie is eight."

"Very well. Now you have a brother who is two."

"And his name is Gilles," Annie said.

Moments later, the girls bounded downstairs ahead of Julie, who carried Gilles clutching a stuffed bear and looking contented in his sailor suit. The cabman helped them into the fiacre and set off toward the Gare de Lyon.

Although there was no longer a demarcation line, Germans still exercised some control in the trains. When a jolt shook everyone, and the train ground to a halt, Julie was sure the Fritz would board the train. She hoped they'd be Wehrmacht. A man sitting by the window looked out.

"It appears there's damage on the line. Hmm... must be sabotage. Uh-Oh! The Boches are getting onto the train." He sat back and like the other passengers assumed an air of indifference.

The first-class compartment door opened and a SS soldier stood framed in the entrance. His eyes slowly examined the six occupants.

"*Papieren!*"

Julie sensed he was in a bad mood, he hadn't said please. A shiver of fear ran down her spine. She didn't move. Gilles was fast asleep on her lap, but her purse was on the lower luggage rack. No one moved.

"*Papieren!*" He repeated.

"He wants our papers," Julie said. "Francine, chérie, get my bag, will you?"

The young girl obeyed. Without haste, the other passengers brought out their identity cards. Julie pulled their three cards. The SS soldier briefly looked at them.

"*Was ist mit dem Kind?*"

"*Kinder brauchen keine Karte.*"

He tossed the cards back at her and strode out leaving the door open. The man sitting nearest pulled the sliding door shut. Francine picked up the cards. Julie's fear evaporated.

"What did you tell him?" a woman asked.

"He wanted the identity card for the baby and I told him babies don't need cards."

"It didn't seem to make him happy," a man said. "Good job you could tell him in his own language. It helps, but I refused to learn it."

Finally, the train was on its way again. By late afternoon, they arrived in Lyon. Julie went to the Restaurant de la Gare with her charges and asked for a table at the back against the wall. The garçon nodded. He moved an empty table and invited her and the girls to sit. He came back with a highchair for Gilles. The toddler was reluctant to leave Julie's arms, but when the garçon came back with plates of food and a glass of milk, Gilles made no fuss at being seated in the highchair. He was surprisingly adept at eating, with only occasional help. The girls' hungry eyes looked at Julie. She nodded for them to go ahead and eat.

The garçon bent toward Julie. "Real meat sausage in the potato purée. Don't tell. It's from their supplies." His chin made a brief movement toward a group of Wehrmacht soldiers.

"Thank you, monsieur."

He went away and she noticed the slight hesitation of two men entering the restaurant. They must be the ones supposed to follow her. The garçon also noticed. He took them by the arm and led them to two different tables near the bar. He spoke to each of them in the ear while making a show of cleaning the table. Julie relaxed. The little game went unnoticed by the other patrons. She concluded the garçon was the résistant and his sharp eyes had detected the foreigners he was supposed to take care of. She shuddered. She wasn't a foreigner, but he had identified her, unless he'd been warned to watch out for her as well.

Night had fallen when the train neared the Swiss border and stopped in Annemasse, now occupied by the Italians. The border guard wasn't interested in her passport and, after a couple of *bellissima* to Julie and the girls, pointed the way to the transborder train.

In Geneva, Julie and the children left the train. The Swiss custom officer demanded her passport.

It crossed Julie's mind that he looked familiar. "I'd give it to you, but I'd have to awaken my baby. You don't want me to do that."

"He screams," Francine said.

The child's self-assurance made the guard raise his eyebrows. He looked again at Julie as if he recognized her. He shook his head. "Your name?"

"Marjolaine de Beauharnais."

He stroked his chin. "You remind me of someone. Let me see. Josiane? Ah, yes, she had children too."

After a silent prayer, Julie adopted a conciliatory air. "I have a large family."

Fists on hips, he shook his head. "You have a nerve like I've never seen!" He then motioned them to go. "And don't come back!"

An anxious woman was waiting outside the station. She promptly ushered the girls into a car, while Julie sat in the front seat, holding Gilles.

The woman drove away. "My name is Marthe. Is the boy your son?"

"No, he isn't. The Boches are about to make him an orphan. I had no choice but to bring him. I can't adopt another child."

Francine leaned over the backrest. "Madame de Beauharnais fought with a nasty policeman and took Gilles away from him. Now he's our brother."

"I was only expecting two girls. I have to make arrangements."

Annie shouted. "He's staying with me."

Marthe chuckled. "I only meant I have to get another bed and some boy things. He's adorable."

"Annie and I can sleep in the same bed. You give him my bed," Francine said.

"You're very sweet girls. Everything will be alright."

Gladness filled Julie. The girls had played with and taken care of Gilles during the whole journey. The little family would be alright. Once the children were settled, Marthe's husband Timothé called a taxi for Julie.

At the Hôtel de Genève, Julie carefully removed the hatpins securing her hat. With a great deal more patience than she'd normally have, she undid her hair and extracted the microfilm. She inserted it into her purse's secret pocket and put the purse under her pillow.

Next morning, she had no trouble finding Café Remor and entered at eleven-thirty. A young man leaning against the backrest of his chair was reading *Les fables de Lafontaine*. He looked like a student. By force of habit, Julie scanned the room and approached the reader.

"Do you mind if I sit here?"

"Not at all." He return to his book.

"Do you like all those fables?"

He smiled. "I like *Le corbeau et le renard* best."

"You're right. It's the best."

Julie made to go. The young man held her arm. 'Enjoy some coffee. It is safe here."

A waiter placed a cup of coffee in front of her. "In Paris, we don't hang around. It's too dangerous."

"Enjoy the tranquility of Switzerland for a while longer. We'll go for a walk by the lake and you can give me your... advice."

Julie gave half a chuckle and savored the coffee, real coffee for once.

Chapter Fifteen

Jacques arrived at the meeting in the Cave. "Fancy digs you've got here."

"Perfect, with three exits through two cellars and an ancient quarry," Bernard said.

The core nucleus of the Gavroche réseau was assembled. All eyes turned to the new arrival. A hand offered a pack of cigarette. He took one, lit it and pulled on it with relish.

"Xavier, explain the train system."

"I obtained a transfer to the Gare de Bobigny. The first train to leave from that station will depart Sunday, April twenty-fifth."

"That's Easter!" Pierrette said.

"It is. Up to now the trains left from the Bourget station, but it's been bombed repeatedly. The trains usually have twenty cars, though sometimes as many as twenty-five. A SS officer and twenty personnel will arrive from Berlin the day before to escort and supervise the train."

Jacques nodded. "I learned that the German bureau of Jewish affairs makes up the list of Jews to be put on the train. Some political prisoners also end up on it, especially if there are more than twenty cars. The orders are that the prisoners are not to be searched and can take luggage with them."

Léonie raised a hand. "That's new. How come?"

Armand, who had sat in the shadow, leaned forward. "The camp is getting a new commandant later on this year, a certain Alois Brunner. He sent orders ahead of his arrival that the departures had to look like the people were going on holiday with family and luggage."

"How will we know that the Bourgmestres will be on that train?" Julie asked.

Bernard signaled to Pierrette to speak.

"In the messages we sent with the clothes and food parcels, we told my aunt and uncle and, of course Yolande, to exchange places with three Jewish persons assigned to the last car. The bribe being clothes. We sent a lot in the hope that the people staying in the camp will live a while longer."

"How do we know that they received the parcels?" Léonie asked.

"The gendarme I have successfully bribed confirmed they got them all."

"Even though it became difficult when the SS took over the security inside the camp and the French gendarmes were relegated to the outside, but Pierrette is very persuasive," Jacques said.

"With your help, too. Nothing like a gendarme talking to another gendarme to make life easier for me."

"The day before departure, we have to check all the cars to make sure they are in order," Xavier said. "I've heard that on some trains the SS were putting barbed wire over the window. Although Pierrette has already included two small wire cutters in one of the parcels, a friend and I will hide an additional two in the edge of the window. We tried it on a car and, unless you know it's there, it's not visible. Also, the engineer will sound the whistle when the train begins to slow down at the foot of the hill."

Julie chased smoke from her face. "Where is the Boche escort?"

"We, at the SNCF, are given the order to assemble the train. We have to put the right engine and the cars together at Bobigny, the designated station. The SS ride in three cars, front, middle and rear. And before you say it won't work, the escort car will be the penultimate one."

Julie looked sceptical. "Won't they order you to change it to the very end?"

"When they discover the extra car, I'll kindly explain that it's impossible without dismantling the train which would take two days because the station is not equipped with sidings for a train that long."

Julie nodded. "They'll be eager to get back home and once the cars are locked, they won't give it another thought."

Bernard turned to Dr. Bignon. "What's the plan?"

"Jumping through a small window from a moving train could well result in injuries. I shall position myself at the bottom of the Lérouville hill where the first person will jump. Our kidnapping squad will be spaced along the track up to the top."

The participants chuckled at the mention of the kidnapping squad. Ace, Bobard, Jambon and Ari waved their hands.

Pierrette fanned smoke from in front of her. "Does everyone realize that this place Lérouville is in the restricted zone of the Lorraine department?"

A silence fell. "Yes, I know," Bernard replied.

"How do we get there?" Julie asked.

"By train to Saint-Dizier where we connect with a local cell. They have contacts all the way to the Reich border, which is at Novéant since they annexed the Lorraine region. That's where the French *cheminots* are replaced by the Germans train personnel. The Saint-Dizier people will have a doctor's car and two farm trucks with suitable passes. Several men will ensure our security. We only need to let them know the day and time."

"It doesn't look like Pierrette and I will be called upon to help," Julie said.

"No. This time, we can't have too many people who don't belong to the region hanging out there," Bernard said. "The escapees are going straight to Montauloup. We have identities ready for them."

Dr. Bignon cleared his throat. "Actually, Olive, I wouldn't mind having a couple of nurses who can keep their cool. Despite the parcels we sent, our friends may have suffered from the unhygienic camp conditions."

Bernard smiled. "It looks like I'm overruled."

"Could we revise the part after the Bourgmestres are on the ground?" Armand asked.

"What's on your mind?"

"We have a safe house in Saint-Dizier. Rather than bring everyone back to Paris, I suggest that we leave the Bourgmestres there with Julie and Pierrette, who will then escort them from the town."

Bernard stroked his chin. "That's a very good idea." He turned to Julie. "You know the way. You'll be in charge."

More details were sketched out with the help of a Michelin large scale map. There was a whistle of admiration at the detail it provided.

"Julie just happened to meet a member of the Michelin family while in Clermont-Ferrand. They have a few hidden treasures," Bernard said.

***

Saturday, April 24, 1943

What awful news we heard! The Jewish population in Warsaw had been confined to an area of the city, a ghetto where conditions were simply appalling. Last year the SS deported two-hundred and fifty thousand people from the ghetto. A few days ago, the brave people revolted and fought the Germans. How courageous of them! The BBC called it an uprising. I don't see the difference. In the end, the Germans are massacring everyone. They are setting fire to all the houses. I can't begin to understand what's driving the Nazis.

Tomorrow's Easter, but only Madeleine and Brigitte will come for lunch. I haven't heard from Charmaine, but I'm sure they'll come. So where is the rest of the family? Something's afoot.

It's time for me to rehearse the last movement of part two of the Messiah with Reynard. I wonder why he chose the Hallelujah to play, surely not to celebrate the German's victories. He said the Reich is on its knees. It may be a little too early to celebrate the end of the war. But there's reason to hope. Without hope, we'd all die.

***

Dr. Bignon, holding his black bag and flanked by his two elegantly dressed nurses, was met at the end of the Saint-Dizier platform by a chauffeur with white gloves and cap. The man bowed to him and led them through the controls without stopping. The German controllers stood to attention. The chauffeur showed the way to a gleaming Packard 180. Julie, one of the nurses, wasn't surprised that they were passed through as special persons. Embracing diverse personas at short notice had become a way of life for her. She itched to see how the men in their SNCF workers clothes and carrying tools were faring at the controls, but she didn't dare turn to look.

In a low voice, the chauffeur said, "I'm the chauffeur for the Kommandant in Bar-le-Duc, but we'll avoid the town."

The Packard was the first to arrive at the selected clearing in the Sussonval forest. They didn't have long to wait before the farm trucks, laden with sacs of grain, barrels and some crates of early vegetables, drew up alongside. The men emerged and rapidly took up their assigned positions.

The whistle of the approaching train startled a flock of magpies. Julie's heart beat faster. She could hear the train but not see it.

Inside the railroad car, Jean-Luc swiftly wrenched the bars off the window. As it had been ordered, much to his chagrin, he was to be the first to jump. The train slowed and a second whistle was heard. With Yolande securing his foothold, Jean-Luc hauled himself up to the window, straddled it and threw himself out.

He hit the ground and rolled the way he had seen paratroopers do and flattened himself onto the clinker of the roadbed. In the distance he saw a person jump out of the train. He turned over and rolled down into the ditch. A hand grabbed his arm, and he was pulled into the cover of the trees.

"Bon Dieu, it's good to see you!" Bernard embraced his uncle.

Dr. Bignon glanced at him. "All in one piece?"

"I think I am."

Soon, Armand and Jambon burst into the clearing, holding a man by the arms, soon joined by Ace and Bobard unceremoniously pushing a second man in front of them

"What's the meaning of this?" Bernard's voice shook with anger.

At that moment, Xavier and Ari arrived, half carrying Yolande. She didn't waste time on niceties. "Those men pushed me and mother out of the way to get out. Because of them, maman couldn't jump."

Jean-Luc bounded forward. His hands seized the nearest man by the throat. Bernard put a gentle hand on his shoulder.

"Not here. Let's find out who they are first."

The man held by Armand spoke up. "This man escaped prison but was caught again and put on the train. I'm Alouette. I work with Colonel Rol."

Bernard turned to Pierrette. "Question him."

Julie finished helping Dr. Bignon care for Yolande's cuts and bruises. She joined the group.

"Charlot?"

"Fox! I never thought we'd meet again."

"Your unlucky day. You prevented my aunt from jumping off the train and now she's on her way to one of those awful camps we have heard about."

Bernard crossed his arms over his chest. "He's yours, Fox."

They moved aside.

"I also work with Colonel Rol," the other man said.

Pierrette planted herself in front of him. "You just heard that. You don't even know who he is."

"I do, more than you."

"So you know Tanguy?"

"Of course. We work together."

"Liar. It's Colonel Rol Tanguy." Pierrette turned to Armand and slid a hand across her throat. Ace and Bobard twisted the man's arms behind him. He whimpered. Armand grabbed him by the back of the neck and the three of them marched him into the woods.

A muffled shot was heard.

The chauffeur came up to the group. "Time to go."

Jean-Luc was sitting on the ground, his head in his hands, shoulders heaving. Bernard and Armand lifted him and pushed him into the Packard. Bernard indicated the car to Yolande.

"No. I'm going back to Paris with you!" Yolande said.

There wasn't enough time to argue. Pierrette led her cousin to one of the farm trucks.

"Julie, take Charlot with you," Bernard ordered. He reached in his pocket and handed her an envelope.

Her ears still resonating with the sound of the shot, Julie sat on the front seat and the two men in the back, ready to duck down. Her mind whirled trying to make sense of one more death.

Charlot put his hand on her shoulder. "There are hundred and hundred thousand people, most of them Jews, being killed by the Nazis. The death of that fink will save many lives."

Julie shuddered. "I know. It's just hard to accept, that's all. I think you men see it as par for the course. Women give life. We protect life."

The chauffeur interrupted. "Messieurs, get down out of sight."

The car once more passed the Saint-Dizier control with guards standing to attention. Soon after, they arrived at the safe house.

Chapter Sixteen

After changing trains where the railroad was damaged, and dodging bombing, Julie led Jean-Luc and Charlot through back streets to avoid controls as she feared Charlot's papers wouldn't stand close scrutiny. They arrived tired and weary in Moulins.

"There must be a disreputable hotel nearby," Julie said.

Jean-Luc stopped a moment to catch a raspy breath. "Why disreputable?"

"Because the Germans avoid them." She glanced at her companions' clothes. "And we won't stand out in such a place. Now, tomorrow morning we'll go to the distribution center and I hope Monsieur Biquette still delivers cheese there despite the invasion of the south zone."

On a quiet back street, Julie saw the sign for a Pension de famille dangling on its chain above a door. Memories of being welcomed in similar bed and breakfasts houses gave her hope. "Wait here, I'll inquire." Minutes later, she signaled to Jean-Luc and Charlot to join her.

Their host, Madame Huss, busied herself in the kitchen. "It's no trouble. I had made a lot of preserves from the garden last summer. My husband and my sons took off for the hills when the Boches invaded us in the free zone. We believed we'd be safe here when we evacuated from Alsace. I found the sign in the attic and thought I could make a little money. My husband's job didn't pay much." She stopped talking to put bowls of thick soup in front of her guests. "After the Huns came last November, we hid bags of flour. Many people used to come across the line begging for food. Now that the Boches are here, we'll all be hungry. Hopefully, the Americans will come before we run out of food. Here, have some of my sourdough bread. I make it myself because the bakery can't supply everyone, even with ration tickets. The Huns take everything."

"You're very kind, Madame Huss. I have a little money to pay for our meals and rooms."

"Well, that is nice. Merci."

In the morning, Julie, in a freshly ironed dress, walked to the distribution center. She composed herself to appear carefree as she didn't know how long she'd have to walk around. As far as the réseau knew, Monsieur Biquette still came on Monday mornings and helped lead *guests* to safety. She met some German soldiers who greeted her and she politely returned the greetings. No need to draw attention to herself by being ungracious. She spotted Monsieur Biquette's truck in the street. At her wave, he stopped and she climbed into the passenger seat.

"Welcome! I haven't seen you in years, but I'd recognize you anywhere, madame Julie."

"I never forgot you."

He drove to the control in front of the distribution center and was waved through. Once his delivery was completed and he climbed back into the cab, Julie said, "I have my uncle and a friend at Madame Huss'. We need to go to Le Falgoux. Could you take us as far as Saint-Pourcin?"

"You even remember where my farm is."

She chuckled. "You maybe not aware that I recommended a number of the people you helped one way or another. Yes, turn right here."

"Wonderful of you. I've been so happy sneaking people from under the noses of the Boches. You'll stay at the farm tonight. Ah, here is the Pension."

"I won't be long."

"Here, take this block of cheese for the lady."

The journey to the farm near Saint-Pourcin took no time, thanks to the jovial Monsieur Biquette and a surprisingly witty Charlot.

In the morning, Monsieur Biquette called Julie to the goat stable. "The best way to get to Le Falgoux is by bicycle. Can monsieur Jean-Luc bicycle? He isn't in a very good shape. That stay in the Boche camp didn't do him any good."

"He's also suffering because his wife remained on the train." She briefly recounted the events that brought them to Moulins. "Charlot has tried to make amends by helping and supporting Jean-

Luc, but it must be hard to be with him knowing he pushed Lorraine out of the way."

Monsieur Biquette scratched his head. "There's a big garrison in Clermont-Ferrand. I know a collabo who's going there. I could ask him, but he wants to be paid."

"He's done it before?"

"He's an opportunist. And as long as money is offered, he does whatever is required."

"Not my favorite type of person, but we have no choice. I can give him three thousand francs. That's all I have. Would that be enough for three people?"

"I'll offer him one thousand and we'll haggle up to two. You need to keep some money."

Monsieur Biquette departed on his bicycle. Julie relayed the information to Jean-Luc and Charlot.

Not long afterward, a Peugeot 402 pulled into the farm yard. Julie paid half the money demanded. The trip to Le Falgoux passed in silence. Julie noticed how adept their driver was at taking deserted side roads. When they were within sight of the village, the driver stopped. Although the evening was darkening, he said he didn't want to be seen in the village. Julie paid him the balance minus one hundred francs. "We have to walk to the house now." The driver looked at her. Charlot had lost much weight while in detention. However, the good meals and rest over the last few days had built up his strength. He stood tall and straight by Julie. The driver pocketed the money and left.

"We're not far from Joseph's place." Julie reached into her travel bag and pulled out a loaf of bread and slices of cheese. "Courtesy of Madame Biquette. Have a bite to get strong, Jean-Luc."

They munched on the food, stretched their legs and set off on the last part of their journey.

***

Joseph and his guests were sitting at the table waiting for Pedro. A knock on the door announced his arrival with François.

"Aunt Julie!"

"I'm glad to see you, François. You look good."

"Uncle Jean-Luc. I heard." He threw a malevolent look toward Charlot.

Jean-Luc gathered his nephew in his arms. "Take it easy, son. It was a most unfortunate happening. I should have made sure Lorraine got out first. We did as we were instructed, only obeyed orders. As for Charlot, he hurts as much as I do. He will be a great asset to your maquis."

François clenched his jaw. "You're not coming with us, uncle?"

"I'm not that strong right now. I'll go and see my brother-in-law at Montauloup. I'm going to set up a printing business. It's badly needed." He hugged his nephew. "We're at war, François. The better we work together, the sooner peace will come."

François bent his head and nodded. Julie watched the men leave. Joseph came back in with an oilcloth bag in his hand.

"You may as well take this putty to Paris. I'm sure you can use it there."

"Don't you need it here?"

He laughed. "We have a good supply and more on the way. Dédé should be here any minute. He's only going as far as Clermont-Ferrand on this trip. I have a bicycle to spare. Do you want it?"

"With all the destruction to the railroad, I'd be happy to have an alternative means of transport."

They laughed. Just then Dédé pulled into the yard.

***

At dawn, the train arrived in Melun. The travelers learned there would be another delay while the tracks were being repaired. After two days in the train and being shunted onto other lines, Julie decided she'd be better off bicycling to Paris. She retrieved the bicycle from the baggage car and calculated she could cover the sixty kilometers to Paris in a day. She was not the only bicycle on the road. At Ivry-sur-Seine, just before entering Paris, she stopped to tidy her appearance before rejoining the flow of cyclists. She noticed that the majority were leaving the main road for a secondary road to the east. Instinctively, she followed. Street after street as if in a maze, the group entered the Vincennes forest. Julie almost laughed aloud. This was the way to avoid the checkpoints at the gates of Paris. She followed the footpaths through the Bois de Vincennes and came out onto rue de Picpus. Tired and suffering from cramps, she reached boulevard Dumesnil. From there, it was but a little way to Passage Lepic.

In the morning, she went to see Popaul.

"Anna! We missed you. There's a message for you to go and meet Armand. He's home till ten every day until you get there."

"How's it been around here?"

"Rather quiet. Do you think the Fritz are getting ready to pull out?"

"That'd be too good. It's the quiet before the storm. Alright, I'll go now."

With the oilcloth bag securely tied inside her pannier, she pedaled toward rue de l'Abreuvoir.

"I'm relieved to see you," Armand said.

"It went well. There are no reports of safe houses being raided and no one arrested in our network." She handed him the bag. "Some candy to liven things up."

Armand burst out laughing. "Thanks, but it's very quiet here too and I don't like it."

"The suburbs have been hit again. I saw bomb sites still smoking on my way into Paris."

Armand sighed. "The bombers fly high to avoid the flak and we had strong winds. Most of the bombs fell on habitations. If only the factories would let us sabotage inside them, we could create huge damage without loss of life."

"The Germans are their only customers. If the production is stopped by a bomb, it's not their fault but sabotage, they'd be suspected and the management would get arrested and deported."

"Maybe. Maybe not. The Peugeot factory has let us do a couple of strategic sabotages."

Julie inclined her head. "Bravo!"

"Are you going to the Majestic? We've heard about some new construction in the Nord, or Pas de Calais, department at a place called Moyecques."

"I have to change into my finery. I don't bicycle to the hotel."

They shared a laugh and she went home.

At the Majestic, Madame LePlouhëc with an uncharacteristic show of exuberance, hugged Julie and kissed her. "I'm so glad you're back. The brass is after me to rehire you."

"Oh, was I fired?"

"I had to explain your absence. These gentlemen didn't get good service after your departure. I made sure everything went wrong when they had important meetings, and they've had a few sometimes lasting into the night. Give a show of authority with the staff. They're expecting it. I'm sure they'll enjoy the theatrics. They've put on some good performances. Only the Fritz didn't know it was all for show."

Amused, Julie directed her steps to the main meeting room. She heard the shouts before she reached the door. "*Geh zum Teufel!*" If they want to send someone to the devil, the scene must be good inside.

She threw the door open. "What's the problem here?" Her voice dominated the tumult.

The immediate silence was broken by the two maids bursting into tears. All faked, Julie realized, as she saw them quickly stick their fingers into the slices of lemon and wipe them across their eyes. The waiter dropped his tray. There was a collective groan from the various officers at the table. Hiding her enjoyment, Julie gave a few harsh orders and dismissed the staff.

"Messieurs, I apologize for the disruption caused by the staff."

Oberleutnant Schäfer stood up and bowed to her. "We are very pleased that you have come back to take charge of the staff. They are useless when you are not here."

"I'll do my best, of course, Herr Schäfer."

"Those scatterbrain maids dropped those documents and mixed them all up. It would greatly help if you would put them back in order." He walked with Julie to a sideboard. "The pages are numbered with a number and a letter."

"I will do that for you right away. Can I get the sommelier to replace your drinks?"

"Yes, please, do," a SS officer called out.

Julie hurried out. Madame LePlouhëc was hovering nearby. "It was a grand spectacle!"

"Just run of the mill. Now, get a couple of maids who haven't been involved in the disaster to clean up. I'm getting them drinks, strong drinks, then I'll return to put their most secret documents in order."

Her boss whistled and rushed to her task, while Julie called the head sommelier. She then returned to the meeting room, not believing her luck to be entrusted with the top secret papers. Of course, they didn't know she could read German. She didn't flinch when the SS officer kept asking others like Oberleutnant Schäfer if she was safe.

The maids cleaned up the mess. The head sommelier himself and two waiters brought in bottles and glasses.

"Thank you, I will serve the drinks myself."

They withdrew, trying to hide a wry smile. By the time Julie had finished classifying the documents, she had an earful of Hochdruckpumpe and additional push for the shell traveling at 1500 meters per second and a whole lot of technical information she couldn't remember. She guessed that was a new project they called Tausendfüssier. Julie at the same time kept an eye on the glasses and refilled them as soon as they were empty, wondering what a millipede had to do with a war machine. Some participants excused themselves for short moments.

By the time the meeting finished, Julie had concluded that the Boches were developing a new weapon, which was in its trial stage in Germany, and were planning to construct it in the north of France. What she had gleaned, while carefully smoothing out the secret documents, pointed to a super weapon for the destruction of London.

Later, in Madame LePlouhëc's office, she wrote all she could remember in her tiniest script and tucked it under the inkwell.

***

On her way out of the hotel, Chef Raoul intercepted her and handed her a cloth bag.

"For me?"

"You have to celebrate thirteen escaped résistants."

"Merci!" She could smell the appetizing aroma of saucisson and ripe Camembert as well as the heavenly scent of still warm bread. After a careful look outside, she turned left to go to the Manoir. Paul, Micheline and Lyse-May needed the extra food.

In the courtyard she bumped into Reynard, who had just come back from riding.

He raised an eyebrow. "Lovely smell of freshly baked bread."

"A surprise gift from my favorite chef at the Majestic. He wants me to celebrate thirteen escaped résistants." Her tongue-in-cheek response made him smile.

"Fourteen."

"What?"

"Not thirteen, fourteen who escaped from the Abwehr headquarters."

Julie stared at him, mouth agape, for a few seconds. "You arranged it!"

"Me? Non. I was riding in the Bois de Boulogne."

Julie burst out laughing. "You're worse than we are. Do you want to share the saucisson?"

"Non merci. You probably intended it for the children."

He bowed and walked into the house under Julie's amazed eyes.

Chapter Seventeen

At La Combe-aux-Loups, eager young maquisards awaited the signal. In single file, they came down the mountain, and weapons at the ready, took up positions overlooking the road. Pedro watched François and shook his head. The captain came up to him.

"That young guy won't do. Send him across the road to the ruins of the old mountain refuge. You can see all the way down the slope from there. Have him raise the red flag when the Boches appear at the bottom of the hill. He must stay there until the shooting is over. Forbid him to shoot unless he is attacked."

Pedro observed François holding his great-uncle's hunting carbine. Although he had followed orders and participated in the camp life, François didn't fill him with the confidence needed in an armed operation. The post of lookout would boost the boy's self-assurance even though it was totally unnecessary since the engine noise of the German truck they were ambushing would be heard long before it appeared at the foot of the hill.

With his semi-automatic slung over his shoulder, Pedro led François across to the ruin, and installed him so he would be hidden from view and protected against stray bullets.

"Let's hope there is only one ammunition truck. If there are two, or if there is an escort, we'll have to abort the operation. You understand?"

François smiled. "I do."

Only one truck came in sight. François signaled, then watched through a hole in the dilapidated wall. Fired upon, the Germans returned fire. François saw a German soldier bound over the ditch and take shelter in the trees on his side. The man kept climbing toward François. In that split second when the brain gives a cruel choice, either him or me, instinct prevails. François fired.

Below him, the combat was over. The maquisards began to

unload the truck. Hands trembling, François brought another bullet into the chamber and started toward the prone soldier who was moaning.

I didn't kill him, was François' first thought. The young soldier straightened himself. He had no firearm.

François froze. "Wilhelm!"

"François?"

"You're bleeding. I'm supposed to kill you. We don't take prisoners."

"Do, François. I'm happy to die."

"Merde!" François shook out the length of rope he was to use to carry his share of weapons and promptly applied a tourniquet to Wilhelm's thigh.

"I am deserting. I never wanted to be a soldier. I can't shoot at people."

At that moment the captain arrived. François stood to attention.

"Wilhelm is my friend from before the war. I wounded him. I don't want him killed."

"You know the rules."

"Wilhelm is deserting. He's true to his word. He won't give us trouble. You can trust him."

The military man's voice boomed. "Get down there and help carry the ammunitions."

François held Wilhelm's hand for a second. Blinded by tears, he made his way down the brush-covered slope to the truck.

Later, a shot rang out.

Somber and silent, he performed his duties. At camp, when everyone was in a jubilant mood, he gathered his meagre belongings, and came face to face with Pedro. "I'm leaving. I'm sorry to disappoint you. I'm not cut out for this life. I know about keeping the secrecy."

Pedro put his hand on the adolescent's shoulder. "Go back to the Boyer's farm."

Night was approaching. François pushed on. In his mind, he still could see the bodies on the road.

Wilhelm.

He greeted his teeth. Is it really worth it? What will the maquisards do with the guns? Kill more human beings. That was what they call my baptism by fire, and I failed. Now, I know why uncle Bernard was a medic. And the SS will retaliate on the nearest village by killing people.

François gagged but swallowed back the bile. Darkness had enveloped the mountains by the time he reached the farm yard. A Beauceron bounded to him. He dropped to his knee and hugged the dog to hide his tears.

***

Wearing a jaunty scarf over her blond wig, and with dark glasses, Julie left her building and climbed on her bicycle. She soon noticed Bernard riding some distance behind her. They arrived at the Manoir in good time and parked their bicycles in the courtyard. Julie carried two bags into the kitchen. She handed them to Bérangère. "Courtesy of the Majestic."

The younger children mauled Julie with their kisses until Lyse-May told them to go and play, provoking a great deal of hilarity. It died when François entered the kitchen.

Bernard frowned. "When did you get back to Paris?"

"Yesterday."

Julie's jaw dropped. "What about the maquis?"

François bent his head and took a deep breath. "I decided to come back to resume classes at the Sorbonne."

"It's summer. Classes are over," said Brigitte.

"I'm preparing for October."

The conversation ceased as it was time to feed the children. Bernard faced François.

"What happened?"

"I decided I want to study medicine and become a doctor."

"I'm glad to hear that. Now what really happened?"

François drew a long breath. "I couldn't kill. When I saw the maquisards kill the Germans, I understood why you chose to be a medic."

Bernard hugged his godson. "So now you won't be going to help your friend Yves, right?"

François nodded.

"I'll ask Dr. Bignon to take you on as an assistant. He has too much work on his hands. You'll learn that the work involves extracting bullets from flesh and setting broken bones in the backrooms of cafés and in cellars. Still want to do it?"

"I do." He straightened.

Bérangère ordered everyone to sit down. "Charmaine, did you call on Marie-Ange to bring the children?"

"I did, maman-Bérangère. Once more, she was in a bad mood and just about threw me out."

At that moment, the door opened. Paul and Micheline, flushed and panting from exertion, came in. "We bicycled," Paul said.

"Does your mother know?" their father asked.

"Heu... non."

"She didn't want us to come," Micheline said. "I'm ten, I can take care of myself."

Bernard and the others would have laughed, if it hadn't been so sad. Julie and Charmaine squeezed a chair between them and made the two children sit and eat.

The quiet conversation ebbed when Bérangère put a platter of fresh bread cut into thin slices on the table and Charmaine unscrewed the lid of the pot of strawberry jam Léonie had brought. To the family's surprise, Marie-Ange burst into the kitchen.

Bernard stood up and offered his chair to her. "Please sit, I've finished."

Marie-Ange looked around the assembly and reddened, but sat down in silence. Jacques joined Bernard leaning against the wall. The table conversation resumed, though Marie-Ange didn't take part. Paul and his sister had finished the meatless stew and were about to run off to the playroom. Julie slathered jam onto a slice of bread and covered it with another while Charmaine did the same. The two children held their bread carefully, so they wouldn't lose a crumb, and took off.

There was a question on everyone's lips, but that no one dare asked until Gontrand exploded. "Can you do something about my sister?"

Julie caught a lightning flash of satisfaction in Marie-Ange's eyes. So did Bernard. He used a forceful tone of voice. "Not now, father!"

Bérangère stood up. "Let's adjourn to the sitting room. Charmaine, will you bring the simili-coffee, please?"

Startled, Madeleine, conscious of the tension in the room but not understanding the reason for it, hesitated. "I'll go and supervise the children in the playroom."

Brigitte and Julie gathered up the dishes. Léonie made a move to help.

"Leave them to us. Go and spy on Bernard's wife." Julie turned her friends in the direction of the door.

Shoulder to shoulder with Brigitte, Julie spoke quietly. "Did you notice her eyes when poor Gontrand asked about Lorraine?"

"I'm stunned. It's like if she was happy that the Gestapo got her, Yolande and Jean-Luc."

Charmaine joined them, and the dishes waited a while longer. "I saw that too. Do you think she has anything to do with the Gestapo raid?"

A dead silence fell over the three friends as they stared at one another.

Brigitte spoke first. "Remember, she'd asked me if she should denounce her husband?"

"Mon Dieu, oui! Then Bernard moved out," Charmaine said.

Julie chewed her lip. "We know she is mean enough to take revenge, but I don't believe she'd actually denounce her husband."

"She didn't act after I told her it'd be devastating for their children. She does love them."

Julie scoffed. "If she loved her children that much, she wouldn't prevent them from coming to the Sunday lunch and playing with their cousins."

"I managed to convince her to let them come with me a few times but the last four or five Sundays she refu..." Charmaine stopped eyes wide.

"Since the raid." Julie finished her friend's sentence.

Stupor left them speechless.

All at once they said, "It can't be."

Brigitte dropped the dishcloth into the water. "Let's do the dishes. Do you think that she decided to take revenge by denouncing members of the family? The printshop was an obvious choice since they'd be raided once before?"

Charmaine nodded. "I wouldn't put it past her. Julie's next."

"No, she knows Meinhard is after Julie. She'll turn on you, next."

Julie finished drying a plate. "It would have been interesting if Yolande had been able to come today. Imagine Marie-Ange's face. But Yolande's lieutenant is actually helping her with a couple of children."

Brigitte held a glass up to the light and wiped it again. "You're joking."

"Nope. He's totally aware of the escape line the Auzellos run from the Ritz, and when it comes to children, he's on hand."

Charmaine tilted her head. "Why don't all those soldiers who are against the Nazis revolt?"

Julie hung the towel. "Not enough of them. The SS are fanatics beyond belief."

"What do we do about Marie-Ange?"

"We tell Bernard."

Charmaine turned when the ouside door opened. "Hello, Pierrette. You missed lunch, can I get you something?"

"I worked at the soup kitchen. It's awful, really. Mothers with scrawny babies and children that are just skin and bones. Yesterday I went round hotels and restaurants begging for food. Some restaurants serving the Fritz are actually throwing food away. We're organizing a team to collect it every day."

"I saved you some bread," Brigitte said. "Here, have some stew."

"Thanks. What's with my brother? He's sitting on the attic steps with a big book and looking very studious."

"That's Bérangère old anatomy book. We heard that François is studying to be a doctor," Julie put the pile of plates into the china cabinet. "His time in the maquis has changed him."

"Is that what they call the places where the men gather to escape the STO?" Charmaine asked.

"That's the name," Julie said. "Borrowed it from Corsica. Bandits used to hide in the hills, shrubs, whatever grows on those plateaus, and they call it maquis. Our résistants, escaping the compulsory labor, are organizing like an army to fight and liberate our country and hide in the hills and mountains. They form the maquis."

An angry-faced Marie-Ange marched past them and let herself out, slamming the door behind her.

Lyse-May was picking out a tune on the piano and singing to it. François abandoned his book and joined his cousin with his violin.

"Listen." He played two lines. She played them.

The simple but heart-wrenching melody attracted the family to the music room. They remained motionless by the door. François sang.

"Ami entends-tu le vol noir des corbeaux sur nos plaines,
Ami, entends-tu les cris sourds du pays qu'on enchaîne,
..."

The last note died in the silence. A moved Gontrand asked, "Who wrote it?"

"Joseph Kessel and a friend, Maurice Druon," Charmaine replied. "And Anna Marly wrote the music."

"Kessel, the writer?" Jacques asked.

François smiled. "Oui. It has become the hymn of the Résistance."

"The Marseillaise of the maquis," Julie said.

Moments later, adults, adolescents and children were singing the anthem that told so well their aspirations and determination.

"Friend, do you hear the ravens' dark flight over our plains,

Friend, do you hear the mournful cries of our country in chains...

... Friend, if you fall, a friend comes out of the shadows to take your place..." Jacques murmured.

Gontrand put a hand on his friend's shoulder. "Teach it to your gendarmes."

***

"Another meeting?" Julie asked.

"Not about deporting Jews this time. Did you know Stülpnagel hates having to sign the deportation orders?"

"He's Wehrmacht. Those career officers may have a shred of humanity hidden in their hearts, but in the end it makes no difference. He signs. Anyway, what about that meeting?"

"It's like that other meeting you supervised. Ces messieurs are pretty pleased if not to say excited. Starts at ten."

"Fine, I'll go and inspect the room."

"The boardroom next to Otto Stülpnagel's office. I'll go to the kitchens to order."

Madame LePlouhëc hurried downstairs.

Chef Raoul delegated his sous-chef, Anstett, an Alsace native, to serve food and drinks in order to give Julie more time to listen, and read documents, should she have the opportunity. She soon found out the reason of their good humor. Hitler himself had given the go-ahead to produce, in France, the super weapon which would bring England to her knees.

The officers trusted Julie to collect the documents on the

sideboard and bring the maps and plans to them. She saw clearly the location of Moyecques, in a small municipality of the Nord department, facing England.

The meeting was over by late afternoon. Stülpnagel ordered Oberleutnant Schäfer to put the documents in his office. Manfred Schäfer motioned to Julie to help him. He went first with the large maps and plans. There was a smaller sketch of the new construction location, which Julie slipped under a serviette. Anstett nodded. She carried the documents to Stülpnagel's office. Manfred came back into the room and looked around. The table was cleared, and the young sous-chef had just left with the trolley of debris from the last refreshments.

Satisfied, he bowed to Julie. "*Danke*. It was good."

She smiled and listened. As soon as the elevator had reached the ground floor, she took the stairs to Madame LePlouhëc's office. Anstett was already there. He took out the map from under his chef's jacket. Julie folded it and inserted it into the secret pocket of her large purse.

"Do you want to write it all down or go now to deliver the info to your chief?"

"I think I'll write it while it's fresh in my memory. Anstett can tell you about the meeting. I'm going to change my dress and purse to look summery."

In her private room, she shrugged into a simple summer dress and low-heeled pumps. She transferred the contents of her purse's into a white crochet purse. In telegraphic style, she hastily wrote on the blank back of the map all what she'd learnt. Then, she folded it as small as she could and put it into her purse. Thanks to the heat wave, she wore a wide-brimmed hat, which did much to hide her face. She took the cellar route to the Hôtel Saint-Raphaël. In the foyer, she came face to face with Oberleutnant Schäfer.

"Madame Gonthier, what a pleasure."

She smiled. "My pleasure, too, Herr Schäfer."

"Do you also work here?"

"No, I only came to tell the management we cannot spare any of our kitchen staff." The lie didn't even make her heart beat faster, as it would have done in the early days.

"May I escort you home?"

She couldn't refuse, but she wasn't going to let him know where she lived, and couldn't go to the Manoir without compromising her identity. "Actually, I'm about to take advantage of this beautiful day to go to the Basilique du Sacré-Coeur."

"I would be happy to go there too."

Julie ranted inwardly about her bad luck. "It's a long way from here."

"I'll have a car brought round."

A few moments later, they were on their way to Montmartre. How could she get rid of him now? They climbed the steps to the basilica. Julie told him all she could remember about the famous monument, as they visited like a couple of tourists.

Suddenly, he looked at his watch. "Oh!"

"Something wrong, Herr Schäfer?"

"Your company is so delightful, I forgot the time. I have an appointment."

Julie hid her relief. "Then you should go right away and not be late."

He frowned. "But I must take you home now."

With her most pleasant smile, Julie reassured him. "You're very courteous, but I intend to walk in the park to cool down among the trees before going home."

He looked perturbed. "I am failing in my duty."

"Not at all." She held out her hand. He bent and kissed her gloved fingers and hurried away. She walked to the edge of the square and watched him fly down the steps to the waiting car. Only when the car moved away did she turn to go. A woman went past her and spat in her direction.

With a half laugh, Julie murmured, "Spit all you want, lady. If you only knew!"

The woman turned back. "If I knew what?"

"That appearances are deceptive. Now, excuse me, I have an important meeting."

Leaving the woman open-mouthed, Julie sped off toward rue Azaïs. A last check to ensure she was alone and she made her way to rue Norvins and Bernard's lodgings. She tapped the code on his door.

"Julie! What's so important that you come here yourself?"

"This." She pulled the map from her purse.

He perused the document while she made some ersatz. "Have they started construction?"

"They've done preliminary work and got the orders today to go full ahead. They're bringing in miners from the Ruhr region. I can't remember which companies they hired for the project, but they're all German."

Bernard read her notes again. "They plan a massive underground installation with a bunker above. It's all chalk in that area. Easy to dig tunnels."

"You're sending this to London?"

"Right away. The Brits can make contact with the local Résistance."

"Careful. There were direction finding vans in the area."

"Armand has moved his pianist. I'll go straight there."

"How do you send the map?"

"We'll code it with coordinates to give them an idea of how big the project is. Then someone will take it to London. They have maps there too."

Bernard left first, Julie fifteen minutes later.

In the morning, Bernard adjusted bifocal glasses on his nose and set off to his work at the Credit Lyonnais. There, he greeted employees, and as expected, was called into the manager's office. The two men didn't talk much. The manager signed the transfer of several securities to be deposited in the accounts used by the réseau. They shook hands.

Despite the warm and sunny day, Bernard's worries didn't melt. The map was burning through his briefcase's secret pocket. On the way to Armand's, he changed his mind and turned toward rue Norvins and home. He couldn't shake off the feeling that he had outsmarted the Gestapo one time too many. That's when he noticed the slow moving, unmistakable black Citroën. Only four doors to go, but he wouldn't hurry. With the same measured gait he continued, but braced himself for an assault. It didn't come as he expected.

"Monsieur de Montregard!"

He kept on walking.

The call came again. He ignored it.

"Wait!"

He stopped and looked around, a puzzled look on his face. He faced the traction-avant.

A man in a dark suit jumped out. "Monsieur de Montregard, please come with us."

"Sorry, sir. You're mistaken. I'm Jean-Marie Letellier. Allow me to show you my identity card."

The man took it, looked at it and put it in his pocket. "Bernard de Montregard, don't lie and come with us."

"I don't know what you mean, I'm Jean-Marie Letellier."

"Don't make any fuss. Come with us."

"If you insist."

He took note that he wasn't being manhandled. So, they believed he was a de Montregard. Perhaps nobility still carried a little respect among the SS. His father would laugh. He had long dismissed the title of count even though it still appeared in the Bottin of the Tout Paris. How did they associate him with his real identity? He reviewed incidents and actions, and couldn't find any connection. He'd been well-trained in England in the early days. His ruminations came to an end as the car pulled up in front of Number Eleven, rue des Saussaies, Gestapo headquarters.

Bernard was taken to an empty cell. They had left him his briefcase. He checked that there were no compromising documents, and that the secret pocket was indeed invisible unless you knew it was there. The papers were nothing but bank jargon and figures. He made a show of studying the papers in case they'd spy on him. At noon, a tray came with a bowl of soup, a slice of bread and a cup of ersatz coffee. He was puzzled by this deferential treatment and wondered what came next. In the afternoon, he was led straight to the office of an Obersturmführer.

"Good morning, Monsieur de Montregard. I am Obersturmführer von Meier. I won't keep you long. Just tell me who are your contacts and you will be free to go."

"I'm sorry, sir. I don't know what you mean. My name is Jean-Marie Letellier."

"I have it on good authority that you left your wife to work in the Résistance. Very misguided of you. I'm only asking you to tell us who your contacts are and, of course, to cease all your terrorist activities."

The man who arrested him put Bernard's identity on the desk.

The Obersturmführer examined it. "Accountant at the Crédit Lyonnais?"

"Yes, sir."

"Why were you not in the office?"

"I'm in charge of checking the branches' books, sir. I have to travel."

The man who had arrested him raised his hand to hit Bernard. "You're lying!"

Obersturmführer von Meier stopped him. "None of that here. Monsieur Bernard de Montregard will tell us what we need to know." He addressed Bernard. "Your wife already reported you are a résistant. You do not want her, and your children, to be taken into custody, do you?"

Bernard smiled. "I'm not married. I've never been married." He kept himself rigid, with stooped shoulders and humility. His identity, a dead man, and his job at the bank were foolproof. His interrogator had just revealed an important information.

Marie-Ange wanted him dead.

Whatever description she gave them no longer matched his appearance. He sported a typical bourgeois mustache, slightly longer hair with extensive gray, expertly done by his barber, and bifocal glasses that aged him.

"Berger, did you verify the identity, the place of work?"

"Yes, Herr Obersturmführer. They appeared to be correct. Only our informant certified this Jean-Marie Letellier is Bernard de Montregard."

"And your informant is some gutter snitch hoping for a handout."

At that moment, a voice called, "Bernard!" behind him. He didn't flinch, didn't even move an eyelid and mentally thanked the hard training he received from the SOE in England.

The SS soldier leaned over. "We have ways to make someone talk."

Bernard remained silent. He knew that.

Obersturmführer von Meier twisted a photograph in his hands. "Last chance, Bernard, to tell me who are your contacts and you can go."

"I'm really sorry, Monsieur von Meier, but I really don't know of any Résistance."

von Meier looked again at the photograph on his desk, then threw it at Bernard. "Who is this man?"

Bernard adjusted his bifocals, the bottom half simply being a magnifying lens. Paul had snapped the photograph at the zoo. He had been eight and enthusiastic about photography at that time.

Normally, Bernard took all the photographs and, consequently, there were very few of him. It wasn't very clear, but recognizable for someone who knew him well. "I'm quite sure I have never seen that man, Monsieur von Meier." He put the right amount of awe and respect in saying the name of the Obersturmfürer knowing that SS or not, he was proud of the von in front of his name and his noble origins.

By this time Obersturmfüher von Meier was becoming annoyed. He barked a stream of orders where the words idiots and incompetent were prominent, as well as "get this man out of my sight."

"Go! I don't like wives that tattle on their husbands."

Bernard stood up. "Good evening, Monsieur von Meier."

A guard showed him out. Bernard forced himself to stroll away, even though his insides twisted painfully. Having assured himself he wasn't being followed, he went down to the Métro.

Back in his one room apartment, his strength left his body. He sat for a long while, head in his hands. So Marie-Ange denounced him, thus endangering not only his life, but that of the children and her own. She didn't realize that if the Gestapo had succeeded in identifying him, she too would have been pulled in for interrogation. They would have taken her on the belief that if she knew he was a resistant, then she, too, knew other people. He had vowed to die rather than talk. A timid knock on the door drew him from his somber thoughts. His neighbor, an impoverished artist, poked his head through.

"What happened?"

"I've lost my job." Would the famished painter be the informant? He only knew Jean-Marie Letellier's identity. Could he have found out somehow?

"I was doing portraits on rue Cortot when we heard the car. So we watched."

"The Gestapo invited me to their offices."

"But you're here."

"They thought I was somebody else, so they let me go."

"Unusual, isn't it?"

Bernard narrowed his eyes. "I wouldn't know. I keep my nose out of other people's business."

The artist didn't get the hint. "You were lucky."

"That's for sure. But they'll be back."

The painter stroked his scraggly beard. "The Gestapo never release their prisoners unless they agree to work for them."

Bernard made a throwing up noise. "I'll kill myself before I sink that low."

"What are you going to do now they know where you live?"

A frown creased Bernard's forehead. Was the painter the snitch? He was always short of money. It would be easy for him to confirm the man on the photograph was his neighbor. He'd agree to anything for a few francs. Bernard sighed. "Should I move?"

"I really appreciate your share of the rent."

"You'll find somebody else."

"Do you know anyone? This isn't a luxury palace."

"When the Fritz took over my apartment building, I was glad to find you. With this last bombing, there are more people looking for a place. You won't have any trouble."

"But I'd prefer if you could recommend someone. You've got contacts."

His words again roused Bernard's suspicion. Why should the painter talk about contacts? "I'll look for something else, first."

The painter left and Bernard went to his sink to splash cold water onto his face. He wasn't naïve enough to believe that von Meier had given up, even if he appeared to believe him. Did he think he'd go and confront his wife? He couldn't rule out that possibility. This meant the children were in danger. He picked up the poinsettia that persisted in having red leaves year round and grew to the size of a bush until he trimmed it. He pulled the lace curtain aside and carefully settled the plant on the window sill. He closed the lace curtain and the drapes behind it.

Those in the réseau that were allowed to contact him at home, would see the high alert poinsettia and take measures to put his children to safety as needed. It was imperative to let his contacts know Marie-Ange had betrayed him.

A concentration headache began to form. There was another person involved. He just couldn't figure out who it could be. Perhaps, Marie-Ange had followed him. He dismissed the idea. He was well-trained, and she wasn't. He'd have spotted her. The only time he had the feeling of being followed, was by a young Wehrmacht soldier in the Montmartre area, but that wasn't surprising. With Pigalle nearby it was a favorite place. The young soldier was trying to chat up girls. There were enough people coming and going that it was difficult to be sure whether anyone was following someone or not. A second time, the young soldier was interested in a street artist.

Bernard dunked his dry bread in the cabbage soup he'd just made. His mind worked feverishly. A picture was forming. He had seen the young soldier before. Although, in Paris, there were thousands of young blond and blue-eyed soldiers, this one seemed closer to home. The man's shape and manner of walking reminded him of someone inconsequential, but someone he knew.

Then it hit him. The Manoir. General von Trennen's driver. Bernard finished his soup and washed his plate. He ate his last piece of Camembert with the rest of the stale bread.

According to Pierrette, the young driver didn't have much brain, but he wanted to prove himself. Like the rest of the family, Marie-Ange was aware of his ambitions. When she was last at the Manoir, she could have talked to him.

Bernard closed his fists. Now he had the link from Marie-Ange to his address. Quietly, he tore all the documents in his possession into tiny pieces which he dropped into the communal Turkish toilet on the landing and flushed. He repeated the tearing process but got himself ready to flee before going to flush the pieces.

Although it was warm, he stuffed his coat pockets with underwear, put on an additional shirt, rolled his two pairs of pants tightly and added them to a filet with cabbage and rutabaga. Ten minutes before curfew, he went to the W.C. and flushed the last of the incriminating documents, leaving his door unlocked to avoid the clunk of the key in the lock. Not that it would awake his neighbor who was probably sleeping off the effects of some illicit liquor, like most of the artists living in the building.

While he remained acutely aware of his surroundings, he bicycled in a hurry. Everyone else on the street wanted to be home before curfew. He reached Passage Lepic with minutes to spare. After pulling his bicycle inside the lobby, he climbed the stairs and knocked his code on Julie's door. Seconds later, already in her pajamas, she opened the door and promptly dragged him inside. She relocked the door, repositioned the draft curtain, checked the window's blackout curtain and switched on her flashlight. Bernard followed her to the kitchen. Julie made sure the curtains there were secure and tried the electricity. It came on. She pulled down the ceiling lamp on its chain to just above the table to keep the rest of the room in semi-darkness. She put a pan on the stove.

"I have some black market coffee. Since you're wearing a coat on a summer night, I think you need it."

"Thanks, I do." He deposited the filet on a chair and took off his extra clothes.

"What's the story?"

"Marie-Ange denounced me to the Gestapo."

Stunned for a moment, Julie remained still, spoon in the air. "We thought she might want to do that but didn't believe she would go through with it. Brigitte told her the Gestapo would take her and the children, too, but that was a long time ago. How did she find you?"

"I think she enrolled Karl."

"That little spy? Yes, he'd do a thing like that. Why did the Gestapo wait so long to act?"

"I don't know when she'd have gone to them. And Karl would have to see me... *Merde!* I sneaked into the Manoir a week or so ago to give mother some money. I was in and out in no time."

"But Karl is always watching the west wing. So he followed you and reported to Marie-Ange and she went to the Gestapo."

"With a photo of me dating five or six years ago."

She laughed. "You've changed!"

"I saw Karl in Montmartre a couple of times but didn't recognize him at the time."

She poured the coffee, draining the very last drop. "How did you get out from the interrogation?"

"The Obersturmführer wasn't enthusiastic. He didn't like the idea of wives snitching on their husbands. My lucky day."

She took a dish of cold meat out of the larder and a piece of bread. "You must be hungry. I am."

"I won't ask you where you got it."

An air of innocence spread over her features. "My butcher keeps me supplied. He fears I'd turn him in if he didn't. Although I told him I'd never denounce him, he feels sufficiently guilty. I accept the offerings."

"Any other arrests in the Nebula cell?"

"None. Everybody is being more security conscious. Popaul said he'd wring their necks himself if they didn't observe the rules."

"Good. Armand will take over while I'm gone."

Elbows on the table she held her cheeks. "Fine, we get along. But you'll stay in England. You can't come back. Anyway, I think the allied landing won't be long now. Did you get Armand to send a message?"

"That's what I was on my way to do. Now, I'm counting on you to see to it in the morning. So in the end I'll take the map myself." He exhaled a tired breath. "It's been a long day. The couch is waiting for me."

As soon as the clock marked six, Julie dashed to the boulangerie. The baker's wife slipped an extra bâtard into Julie's bag and whispered, "My son's ready to go."

"Tomorrow. I've someone who'll take him." She didn't think Bernard would mind having the company of a young man eager to join the maquis. At the épicerie, the storekeeper had just come back from the Halles wholesale market and Julie was able to buy two ticket-free cabbages.

In the apartment, Bernard had tidied up. She went and changed into her Majestic finery. "I'm on my way to spread the word. Stay in."

"Anybody wanted to contact me this morning will have seen the poinsettia and taken cover."

"I'm calling on Armand first."

Rue de l'Abreuvoir was deserted. It gave her goosebumps. She climbed the three flights at speed. Armand was waiting on the landing.

"I saw you from the window."

"Olive was denounced by his wife, arrested and released. His identity held up to scrutiny. He's at my place."

"What a miserable woman she is! We need to get him to England. I'll send a message. Where should they pick him up?"

"I'll get Popaul to send a message to Pedro who will get back to you. He'll give you the coordinates."

"What do we do about Marie-Ange?"

"We'll talk about that at lunch tomorrow. You can come."

"No need for me to be seen where I don't belong."

She nodded. "We'll discuss that, too. I'm off to Popaul's."

Café Popaul wasn't yet open. She went through the hotel entrance and knocked on his apartment door. Bertrande opened, but remained silent. All knew, that there were times when words were superfluous. Popaul came into the kitchen.

"Olive was denounced by his wife. He was arrested and released. But he's burnt. No one is to go to his rendezvous. Popaul, contact La Combe-aux-Loups to arrange for a plane."

Popaul reacted with fury, "*La putain!* Selling out her own husband! We'll take care of her."

"Be careful of the children."

"Get them to stay with their grandparents."

She sighed. "I'm going there tomorrow. I'll let you know how we want to proceed."

"Of course. Do you want transport to the Majestic? If you wait five minutes while I open the establishment, Fredo's the first customer for a petit Calvados before he delivers the produce to the hotels."

"Illicit spirit?"

He laughed. "No perfectly legal, from the Fritz's supply."

Chapter Eighteen

Surrounded by the family's warmth, Yolande joked that her boss had driven her and would pick up her at three o'clock. Hughes had brightened up since his sister had come back and he made no objection to joining the other adolescents outside where, again, Madeleine supervised the young children. Jacques and the rest of the family sat close together around the oak table in the kitchen.

Maude arrived late. "Next I'll sign up for the Tour de France. It only took me one hour to come from Meudon."

Laughter drowned her last word. It was only six kilometers. She took it with good humor.

"Where's Bernard?" Bérangère asked.

All eyes went to Julie. "He's traveling for business."

Gontrand fingered his unlit pipe. "You mean he's gone to England?"

Julie sighed. "It's safer for him."

There was a silence. Then Julie related the events. Cries of horror punctuated her last words.

Jacques held his chin in his hand. "What are your plans?"

François raised his head. "Traitors are eliminated, but Marie-Ange didn't cause anyone's death or imprisonment."

Pierrette turned on her brother with vehemence. "She's at the root of the raid on the printshop!"

There was a collective gasp.

Yolande nodded. "It was a denunciation. Thanks to Jacques, it was traced to a close family member."

"And besides, we don't know whether the two couriers who were arrested three days ago were the result of the same betrayal," Pierrette said.

François lowered his head. Julie noticed the hardening in Yolande's look and the silent tears that escaped Bérangère's eyes.

"We're going to have a meeting," Julie said. "We must remember she has two children."

The afternoon ended along with the family gathering.

***

In the Cave, the discussion became heated. Popaul and the kidnapping squad were adamant that traitors didn't deserve to live. As head of the réseau, Armand reserved his decision for the end of the discussion. Dr. Bignon and François held a private colloquy. Julie knew they would oppose having Marie-Ange eliminated, even if an accident was staged. She watched how Léonie looked at Armand, perhaps ready to support his decision, yet when her gaze went back to Popaul, Julie thought Léonie was agreeing with him. She didn't have to look at Pierrette to know what her stance was, but she didn't know what Maude would say. Auntie Maude could either be overly generous or ruthless. She could tackle a group of rowdy German soldiers and send them on their way as meek as lambs. What would Armand decide? Trained by the SOE, and having already taken lives, Julie feared he would weigh on the side of a radical solution.

As for herself, she was still trying to come to terms with the need to have a traitor removed from circulation and protecting a mother. Though, what kind of mother could she be? What example would she be to her children after condemning their father to a certain death, which he escaped as if by miracle? Julie's instinct was to protect life, but deep down a hardening around her heart was growing.

Armand requested silence. "We all agree that she mustn't be allowed to do any further damage. Popaul, it is not practical to kidnap her and lock her up in the abandoned house. We won't stage an accident. Jacques?"

"We must arrest her. She could stay in prison until the end of the war. She'd have time to reflect on what she did."

"No!" Maude's tone was unequivocal. "She'd wiggle her way out by giving away the rest of us. You know the Gestapo doesn't need a lot of evidence to act."

Julie straightened. "We must arrest her and send her to Drancy or Compiègne."

Armand inclined his head in agreement. “That is a good suggestion. Give her a taste of what life is in the camps.”

“Then she’ll be deported to the labor camps in the east.” A certain satisfaction colored Yolande’s voice.

Pierrette’s brightened up. “Especially if she is classed as Jewish.”

Jacques nodded. “It can be done. I have two gendarmes who’ll help, but we cannot go into the building to make the arrest. Popaul, your men can bring her to rue du Port in Boulogne-Billancourt. Many bombed-out buildings there, it’ll be easy for us to take her into custody.”

A consensus was rapidly reached and a plan to seize her was elaborated for the next day. They’d sew a yellow star on a set of clothes and they would have her change into them.

Maude raised her hand. “No need to do any sewing. I have genuine clothes from a woman about her size with a yellow star already on. Luckily, I hadn’t yet got rid of them.”

Maude undertook to tell Charmaine to take the children to their grandparents and have them stay overnight.

Dr. Bignon addressed Popaul. “Can you proceed without the need for chloroform?”

“Absolutely.”

Julie shrugged. “Even if she screams, neighbors are used to hear her shouting at the children.”

“Then I won’t need to be there,” Dr. Bignon said.

François nodded. “Nor I.”

Close to ten the next evening, Popaul and his men arrived in the grocer’s van. Maude, Armand and Léonie were in the back too. Julie and Pierrette came out of the shadows and in silence climbed to the third floor, followed by the squad. The others remained downstairs and kept watch.

Pierrette knocked.

“Who’s there?”

“Me, Pierrette.”

Marie-Ange opened the door. Ace and Bobard pounced and gagged her before she could make a sound. She struggled to get away and knocked over a vase on a pedestal table in the vestibule. It shattered on the tiled floor. While they were tying her hands and feet, Paul and Micheline appeared in the vestibule. The two men froze. Julie gasped.

"What are you doing?" Paul asked.

He was trembling. At thirteen he was tall and skinny but had authority in his voice. Julie opened her arms and Micheline rushed into them.

"Your mother is being taken to prison," Pierrette said.

Marie-Ange made unintelligible sounds behind her gag.

"Why?"

"Your mother denounced your father to the Gestapo. He was arrested. But he's safe now."

Horrified, the children turned to their mother. "You didn't, did you?"

"She did, and she was going to denounce the rest of us."

Paul took a step toward his mother. "Then you can denounce me and Micheline too, because we, too, are working for the Résistance."

Micheline broke away from Julie's arm and ran to her mother. She aimed a kick at her shins. "I hate you! I hate you."

Julie motioned to the door. "Take her away."

They did, and the two women comforted the now crying children.

A wobble in his voice, Paul asked, "What will happen to her?"

Pierrette put her arm around his shoulders. "She is going to prison."

"Why did she do it?" Micheline asked.

Julie brushed the tears from the ten-year-old's face. "Sometimes, sweetie, it is difficult to understand adults when they have different opinions."

They packed the children's clothes.

"You'll stay at the Manoir," Pierrette told them. "You were supposed to sleep there tonight."

"We came back because we'd forgotten our homework."

In the west wing, Bérangère, under Lyse-May watchful eyes, was making hot chocolate with the other half of the chocolate bar. François joined them.

Lyse-May was full of concern for her cousins. "You want to bunk with me, Micheline?"

Micheline turned to her brother. He looked at his grandmother.

"There's room for you, too," Bérangère said. "You three can talk all night if you want to."

When they had gone to the bedroom, Pierrette asked, "Is grand-papa asleep?"

"He has retired, but I doubt he's asleep. He guessed something was going on."

"Léonie will come here to report," Julie said.

They didn't have long to wait. When Léonie entered conversation ceased.

"It all went according to plan. She's wearing her new clothes and is now in police custody. There's a raid in the Marais tomorrow. She will be in the police van that will take the Jews to the camp. I'm sorry for them."

***

On Sunday, Ernest brought in a load of potatoes from the garden to the women in the kitchen of the west wing. When they finished admiring the large potatoes, he casually mentioned that Karl hadn't come home.

"Should we be concerned?" Charmaine asked.

Ernest smiled. "He had a night on the town."

Suspicious, Julie weighed a potato in her hand. "You wouldn't happen to know if he was alone?"

Ernest shrugged. "He was with two soldiers. Actually, they were from the milice."

"I wonder if he'll ever come back." Julie's tone carried all the fatalism of the world.

A smirk on his lips, Ernest ambled out. As she remembered Lyse-May's abduction, Bérangère sighed. "He was good with little children."

Jacques grumbled as he made his entrance. "As if I didn't have enough work already, I now have a dead German soldier on my hands. Apparently he fell into the Seine and drowned after being drunk, according to the coroner's report. And it so happens he is the general's driver. No, I didn't find his drinking companions. Soldiers too, so they are probably lying low and will never tell."

"Just as well." Pierrette sighed loudly.

They looked at her.

"I mean, just as well because he was a mean bastard."

"Didn't he save your life?" Gontrand asked.

"Not really. He wouldn't leave me alone, so I had agreed to meet him. Unfortunately, we changed Métro line at that fateful Barbès-Rochechouard station that day in August two years ago."

"Didn't he pull you away?"

“No, he ran off, and I followed like hundreds of other people with quick reflexes.”

“But you said...”

“He helped me out of the crush of people at the top of the stairs, but I let him take credit because von Trennen was angry with him for some other reason.”

Jacques stroked his chin. “I spoke to Ernest when I arrived. He said he has seen the young man with a couple of other soldiers, or rather militiamen. I’ll do my best to investigate. It’s going to be slow, very slow. We are overworked and we have better things to do than chase drunken soldiers.”

Chapter Nineteen

Paris, Monday, September 13, 1943

Yesterday, we had electricity from eleven to twelve. I had soaked the beans overnight. They took less than an hour to cook. I wish I could help Brigitte. She needs to buy more food on the black market but her allocations are still the same as three years ago but food has tripled in price. I make so little money I can't buy much on the black market either. I wonder if she's pregnant. She and Julie spent a lot of time talking in a corner. Madeleine of course had brought more food than needed, and Brigitte accepted to take some home. And if I'm not mistaken, my daughter-in-law appeared to promise more. We'll see.

The greatest joy of the day came with the BBC messages. We heard "I ate the whole chicken." I couldn't contain my happiness. I said, "it's Bernard! He's in England!" Gontrand didn't believe me. He said it could be anybody. I had to remind him when Bernard was about nine, he had gone into the dining room while Philippe and Sylvain were chasing the runaway dog. The Sunday roast chicken was on the table. With the dog crisis, we were all outside except Bernard who picked at the chicken and, bit by bit, ate most of it. Then my husband remembered. We teased Bernard every Sunday for a long time afterward.

It is official. Italy has surrendered to the Allies. The unfortunate part is that the Chleus have invaded the region of the Alpes and the Côte d'Azur, which were quite happy with the Italians. I suppose the Chleus are also taking over Italy. I believe we have reasons to hope that the end of the war is near. The Allies have landed in Italy. It shouldn't be too difficult to land in France. It wasn't Alexandre's opinion and he patiently tried to explain why.

When he was talking I suddenly realized he was the only man of the family remaining in Paris. Sometimes I think that losing a leg was a blessing. Not that he isn't living dangerously forging all those papers, but he claims he's well organized.

François had to take an exam and being successful was admitted into the Faculty of Medicine. I'm proud of him. I saw how mature he has become, and I noticed how the boys gravitate to him. For Daniel and Hughes, it's pretty normal being in the same age bracket and coming of age too. Paul, Baptiste and Damien have lost their boisterous little boys' ways and are eager to sit and listen. They ask such serious questions. At that age my sons were more concerned with playing marbles, climbing trees and riding horses.

***

The somber and somewhat angry discussion in the boardroom meeting filled Julie with satisfaction. Clearly, her message had got through. The Tausendfüssier project had been bombed by the RAF. The Militärbefehlshaber wanted to know why. It was so well disguised. They were sharing photographs of the project before and after the bombing. Julie only caught a glimpse of the damage, but it was enough to know that the installation would be out of action for a while. At the same time, she saw the irony of the camouflage being haystacks. She wasn't so happy hearing that the Germans intended to bring in slave labor, in particular prisoners from the Russian front. Her ear prickled when she heard that the secret weapon was to be a rocket. She wished she could understand more about the talk of tubes and canons. The first launch was set for March 1944. She had to get that information to London so they would keep bombing the site.

She debated whether to go to Armand's or just leave a message at the café letter box to meet her at the Cave the next day. While she changed into a skirt and blouse, she decided to leave a message at the café. Unless it was urgent, a simple meeting at the Cave always signified the next day at twenty hours.

The rue Lepic was aptly named for its steep slope, bemoaned Julie as she gave up pedaling and wheeled her bicycle. Her hope for a cool glass of water was dashed when she arrived level with the café and saw the blue curtain among the white curtains. The danger signal. Her heart sank. She kept on going, reached the rue de la Mire on her right, lifted her bicycle on her shoulder and grabbed the handrail to get down the stairs. She remounted at the bottom and freewheeled to rue Ravignan, turned right and freewheeled all the way to the small park and stopped at the Fontaine Wallace to drink. Now feeling more secure, she made her way home, all senses on high alert. Moussou was in conversation with a boy. They greeted her.

"Is everything alright, Moussou?"

"Yes, madame Anna. We're just trying to find a job, but we're told our skin is too dark."

"Maybe you're too young. How old are you, really?"

"Eleven, but I can work, for sure. My maman can't with the little brother."

"And your friend?"

"Ahmed's ten. He can work too."

There was so much hope, hope born of desperation in his eyes, that Julie's heart pinched. She thought of Damien just ten, but with a mother who provided the essentials.

"I just wonder if the two of you could take on the job of cleaning our building, the stairs, the lobby and of course the sidewalk?"

Hope and gratitude illuminated the children's eyes. "Yes, we want to do it. You'll be paying us?"

"Absolutely. What will you do with your money?"

"Buy food."

Although Damien knew money was very tight, he still would ask for a toy plane. "Then it's a deal. I'll get you some brooms and pails."

"There's all that in the closet by the basement stairs."

"Good." She pulled a ten-franc note from her pocket. "This is an advance for you to buy breakfast before you start work tomorrow morning." Ten francs wasn't much, but the boys were ingenious and could haggle like the best of adults in backrooms where deals were made.

Eyes shining with renewed hope, they scampered off. Julie trusted them to buy food. More than once she had witnessed the hunger in their eyes. And more than once she had let them have her bread. Right now, she was only too happy to have escaped danger.

There was no electricity, but the cooking gas was working. By the light of a candle, she reviewed her options while cooking the lentils she had soaked that morning. If the café on rue Lepic displayed the danger signal, something must have happened. Anxiety twisted her insides. At least, the café didn't appear to have been raided.

Although she was not expected at Café Popaul, she decided to go there after she finished eating. A knock on the door paralyzed her for a moment until she heard the code. She rushed to the door and helped an exhausted Maude inside.

After giving her water, the rest of her supper and a cup of ersatz coffee that Maude made no objection to drinking, Julie asked, "Who? Where? When?"

"I was to meet Armand, Xavier and Léonie at Hector Berlioz's tomb in the Montmartre cemetery. I saw the Citroën cars, saw Armand and Xavier turn back, but Léonie was already at the entrance. She was early. They got her. Then a car came toward me. I don't know whether they assumed we were together. I didn't wait to find out. I ran into a dead end street, with stairs, and kept running. The car had to give up. I didn't hear footsteps behind me. I walked and walked, round and round for over an hour, until I was sure no one was behind me."

"Were there many people in the area?"

"No more than usual. It's not late and people were still trying to shop or were going home from work."

Julie hid her anguish. "What are the chances of Armand and Xavier having escaped?"

"As good as mine."

"I was going to leave a message at the boîte aux lettres, but they had the blue curtain up. I high-tailed it."

"Someone must have seen the Gestapo activity."

"What do we do now?"

"I'm going to bed. My old bones are not meant to run and walk for hours."

"Take my bed. I'll sleep on the couch."

In the morning, Maude agreed to remain in the apartment massaging her sore muscles while, before going to work, Julie went to find out what happened. Since she had dresses and shoes in her private room at the Majestic, she put on her ordinary clothes to bicycle to the next letter box. The florist was just opening. As there was no one in the store, Julie didn't make any pretense. She went straight to the potted geranium and pulled the marker explaining how to care for the plant. On the back was a simple C tonight. If ever questioned, the florist would say it was a reminder to water the flower in the evening. After twenty-four hours, the florist erased any uncollected messages.

As she joined a flow of bicycles, Julie wondered who had left the message. When she arrived at the Champs-Élysées her anger mounted. The so-called service d'ordre, none other than the milice, were marching fully armed in a large column. As if there were not enough parades with the Fritz. Her musings were interrupted by explosions. Once more, someone had thrown grenades or some explosives into the middle of the parade. Gunfire resonated, screams, shouts, people running, cars roaring, all happened at once but Julie didn't wait. She couldn't run to the nearest building, so she threw herself as flat as she could on the pavement, letting her bicycle fall over her, imitated by cyclists around her. The noise died down, now replaced by the familiar two-tone sirens. Julie lifted her head, judged it was safe enough to stand up. There was no point in trying to cross the Champs-Élysées. She turned round in the rue Balzac and made her way through the streets around the Arc de Triomphe to cross over at the avenue de la Grande Armée and finally reach the back of the Majestic.

The guard came out of his sentry box and barred her way. She despised the Feldgendame and showed it as she calmly dismounted. "I work here, you dumb ass."

He didn't understand French. She repeated, "*Arbeit.*" The concierge came to her rescue, took her bicycle and motioned for her to go in while giving the guard a malevolent look.

The agitation on the Stülpnagel's floor stopped Julie in her tracks when she exited the elevator. The problem, she soon discovered, wasn't the attack on the French milice but an order from Berlin to close all the so-called Buying Offices run by French crooks, after complaints that the German Buying Bureaus were losing customers. The problem facing the Militärbefehlshaber was that many SS officers were involved with the French agencies. Julie decided she wasn't needed and went back downstairs. Madame LePlouhëc agreed that the Buying Bureaus' mess would keep the occupants of the hotel busy for some time and Julie could attend to other business.

At the Cave, Julie met with Armand and Xavier to discuss how to get Maude to the safety of Montauloup.

Julie laughed. "She doesn't understand the meaning of safety, unless it involved her friends. She wants to go to the maquis. They need a nurse, she said."

Armand nodded. "They probably do. Léonie was taken to avenue Foch. We're monitoring it. Popaul and Jacques are ready to act as soon as she's transferred to a prison."

"A man was caught at the same time. He was carrying newspapers and they ended up strewn all over the pavement," Xavier said. "I've never seen him before."

Armand raked his fingers through his hair. "With the right travel papers, can Maude get to the Auvergne by herself?"

"She'd hit you on the head if she heard you question her abilities."

The two men smoked in silence.

"Can you get travel papers from the MBF?" Armand asked.

Julie gnawed her finger. "If she were to travel on official business, it could be arranged. I think so anyway."

Armand chuckled. "If you went with her and brought back cheese for the hotel?"

"No cheese! But I know ces messieurs are partial to the Meursault de Bourgogne, which is now practically impossible to get in Paris since Bernard had stopped working for the Vander-Veken wine firm. If I promised them a case, I'd get all the papers we need."

"You're on."

"Send a message to Dédé."

The muffled explosions of bombs penetrated the thick walls of the cellar. They listened for a while.

"The industries on the north and west side of Paris again!"

Another huge explosion was heard. "That's a bit close!"

When the all-clear sounded, they rushed home before the second wave of bombers would trigger a new alert.

The next morning news was grim. Julie and Madame LePlouhëc pored over the newspaper opened on the desk.

"A Lancaster bomber got hit by flak, burst into flames and

crashed on La Samaritaine department store. Débris were spread around a large area. They recovered the remains of six crew members. The pilot parachuted out, but was killed landing on the roof of the Louvre museum."

Madame LePlouhëc crossed herself. "*Que Dieu ait leurs âmes.*"

"God takes care of their souls. We take care of their mortal bodies."

***

Three days later, in the morning, Brigitte knocked on Julie's door.

"Brigitte! Come in. You're a long way from home."

"Is my bicycle safe with the boys downstairs?"

Julie nodded.

"You couldn't live on a flat street, could you?"

They burst out laughing. Maude hugged Brigitte and made her sit. "Let's make you some of that horrible black stuff."

"Merci. I have a message. Dédé is in town and will take Maude to Montauloup. Then, he'll be coming back with twenty cases of Meursault Premier Cru. He wants the travel documents to be made for him and his clerk, that is, Maude."

"Fantastic! I'm on my way to work and will make sure to get the needed papers."

An alert sounded. They went to the window and opened it. They could hear the drone of the approaching planes. It grew louder and louder. The first explosion made them jump.

"It's the Renault factory again," Maude said. "Do we go to the shelter?"

People scurried in the street. Some appeared to shrug.

"I'm more worried about uncle Eugene and aunt Berthe living in Suresnes close to the rail yards," Julie said.

Maude shook her head. "I gave them the keys to my apartment in Paris, but I don't know whether they moved there. I've been staying in different digs."

They sat and drank the ersatz Julie had prepared.

Brigitte twisted her hands several times. "I have a confession to make."

They looked at her.

"I'm pregnant."

"Gerhardt must be happy," Maude said.

"He is. I am not."

"He will support you all the way. Are you going to stay in rue Mignard?" Julie asked.

"I'd have gone to stay with your friends in the country, but now that the Huns are everywhere, there's no point."

Maude reached for her purse and pulled out a ring of keys and jingled it in front of Brigitte. "Ruelle Bagnolet, Meudon. Only one neighbor, a good one. Forest all around. Plenty of dried food and pickles from the garden produce."

"Thanks, but what about you?"

"I'm going to join the maquis. It's getting too hot for me here."

"Now, smile Brigitte. I know you're delighted to carry Gerhardt's baby."

"Honestly, yes, I am. But I'm also married to a husband who is fighting to send the Germans home."

Maude scoffed. "We'll cross that bridge when we come to it. Julie, don't be late. We need those papers."

Julie left. Downstairs she gave Moussou twenty francs. "You already did a great job cleaning everything. You are appointed the official cleaners. I hope you haggle with the black marketeer."

Moussou threw his shoulders back. "I do and I win."

"My mom said she'd cook for us, but we'd have to share. I have two little sisters."

"Good for you. Go and shop wisely."

There was no crisis when Julie arrived at the Majestic. Madame LePlouhëc called the quartermaster to her office.

"How is your supply of wine?"

"Very low, madame. I am running out of legitimate suppliers." His French was textbook correct.

"I could provide you with as many as twenty cases straight from the country at the regular price. Our supplier and his assistant are about to leave Paris. If you could arrange to make out a requisition order and add all necessary forms and passes, you could have the wine next week."

"Madame, you are my savior. I'll go to my office straight away. Please write the names for me."

Julie was already writing the information on a hotel notepad and handed him the sheet of paper. After he left, she said, "That went smoothly."

***

Early on a Sunday morning, Julie wondered whether she ought to go to church. She hadn't been since Claire had been killed. The pain cut her heart to shreds. The heel of her hands blocked her eyes. She refused to cry, but the longing for her adopted Claudine and her baby Mathieu exacerbated her anguish. So much of their lives was happening without her.

When the knock on the door drew her attention, she almost didn't open.

"Dr. Bignon! Were you in the neighborhood?"

"Two calls, one of them in this building, on the top floor."

"And no elevator. I make a mean ersatz. Would you like some?"

"Actually, I thought to take a trip to the country and wondered whether you'd like to come?"

Her eyes widened. "My babies."

He smiled. She threw her arms around his neck. "Thank you!"

No more was said as they drove off.

The sun shone. The birds sang and Julie spent her happiest day yet.

***

On a Sunday morning, Charmaine and Julie met at Brigitte's in order to help her pack to go to Meudon before Captain Langen arrived. Sylvestre was crying.

"What's wrong, poppet?" Charmaine asked.

"He's been having a fever over the last few days. Today is the first day he cries. Something hurts, but he can't say."

With a soft hand, Julie palpated his legs and arms. "In my building, one child went to the hospital because the doctor suspected poliomyelitis."

A wounded cry died in Brigitte's throat just as there came a knock on the door. Charmaine opened to Gerhardt.

"What..." At a glance he took in Sylvestre cocooned in Julie's arms and the distraught Brigitte. Christiane grabbed her mother's skirt.

"We need to go to the doctor. It could be poliomyelitis. One child in my building is in hospital."

"I'll take him to Hôpital Lariboisière." He held his arms out.

"But it's a German hospital," Julie said.

"As my son, he will get good care. Brigitte, you come with me."

While his mother fetched a coat and a blanket for Sylvestre, her friends stared at each other. Julie reacted first. "We'll take the children to the Manoir."

"Merci. Will it be alright that I don't speak German?"

Gerhardt smiled. "Not a problem, I shall be there."

He picked up Sylvestre who had stopped crying and looked content in his arms.

Bemused, Julie and Charmaine dressed the children warmly and were soon on their way to the Manoir.

They had to explain the new development. The news colored the usually boisterous family gathering. Even the young children were subdued and concerned.

Gontrand hit the Gerbe newspaper, spread over the end of the table, with his fist. "Is it true that a bomb fell on the Auteuil race course the other day while a race was on?"

Jacques heaved a deep sigh. "Alas, yes. A real massacre! Don't read this rag. Read Libertas. Not sold in stores, but it's still being produced."

"The Gerbe! Bunch of fascists! See what they say, *A new crime from Churchill!* and here, *People denounce the English assassins.*"

"But people are accepting the casualties because they understand that it can't be avoided, as long as the Allies are making progress, and they are. I hear that from my neighborhood," Julie said.

At the knock on the door, everyone jumped.

Reynard entered carrying a gingerbread cake. "I have just received news that Sylvestre is feeling better. His parents will stay with him overnight."

"Thank you so much, Reynard," Bérangère said. "Please, share the cake with us."

Marie came into the west wing kitchen, pushing the door open with her derrière, her hands filled with a tray laden with a cafetière and more food. "Lunch, madame Bérangère. The gingerbread cake is for the children."

There was a chorus of thanks, and Reynard accepted to share the meal with the family.

Always practical, Pierrette asked, "How will you get to work tomorrow without your car?"

"Maybe I could play truant."

Laughter erupted.

"Well, if you need a driver, I can drive. There's even a nice Hispano-Suiza hidden if you need it."

"Did you get a license?" Jacques asked.

"Yes, I did. And I'm good. With all the bombings and other attacks, I thought I should drive an ambulance."

Gontrand shook his head. "What on earth are young women doing these days instead of taking care of their homes? Or their studies? Driving ambulances!"

"Don't you remember who drove you from the battlefield to the hospital? Don't grumble at me and recognize that it was a woman, an English woman who had volunteered to drive an ambulance."

"Alright, alright."

Later Reynard thanked Pierrette. "I'll get a car sent over. You don't want to be associated with working for the Germans. Many French people are getting more and more upset with those who do."

"True. I just didn't see it that way."

***

Moussou was waiting for Julie, as she was on her way to work. "A message for you. Meet François at Parc Monceau."

"Do you know at what time?"

He looked contrite. "I think I forgot."

She smiled. "Never mind, I'll find him." She gave him a five francs coin.

The October sun warmed the drab street. Since there were no meetings scheduled for the morning, Julie decided to walk the couple of kilometers to the Parc Monceau. François knew she more or less went to work mid-morning by Métro. She concluded he'd be at the park. He was sitting on a bench, his violin case at his feet. Here and there, golden leaves floated down on the breeze.

"Aunt Julie! I'm glad the message got to you. I have..." He looked around. They were alone except for a mother with a small child happily rolling in the crinkling dead leaves. He lowered his voice. "A microfilm to be passed on."

He reached in his pocket. Their hands came together against their thighs and Julie closed her hand on the tiny canister. Nonchalantly, she repositioned her hat while pushing the microfilm under a roll of hair and resetting the hairpins. They stood up and walked to the gate to go their own ways. A gunshot made them stop in their tracks while, stunned, they watched a woman take the Walther pistol from a German soldier lying on the sidewalk, jump on a bicycle and disappear in mere seconds. The moans from the soldier brought them to action. A few hurried steps took them to the victim. François rapidly put his red cross armband on his left arm.

"Shot in the chest from the back," François said. With surprising strength, he turned the victim over onto his back.

Julie knelt and held the soldier's head. "*Alles wird gut.*" She stroked his forehead. He was so young. She repeated he was going to be alright. He looked at her and tried to smile through the pain.

François wasted no time in opening the soldier's jacket and shirt. The exit wound was wide and jagged. Blood spurted out. He opened his violin case and grabbed a cloth, immediately applying pressure on the wound in an attempt to stem the flow. Booted feet came running toward them. Julie handed François another cloth. In a moment, they were surrounded, three rifles pointed at their heads.

"Get an ambulance," Julie commanded.

Her authoritative tone brooked no argument from the soldiers. One of them ran off immediately.

Soon the familiar pulsing sirens of French ambulances were heard. The medics helped François tighten a bandage around the soldier's chest, and they were away. The remaining soldiers had long since shouldered their arms. Julie and her nephew stood up. François wiped his bloody hands on his handkerchief and Julie looked at her elegant dress, now splattered with blood. A Gestapo car pulled up.

Ignoring the new arrivals, and in German, Julie addressed the corporal in the group. "The medic here has used all his supplies to help the wounded soldier. Can you get him some more, please?"

A big argument rose between the Wehrmacht soldiers and the Gestapo men. Julie listened carefully while apparently being concerned with her spoilt dress. The soldier's belt that François had undone lay on the ground, the holster devoid of its pistol. One of the soldiers noticed her gaze, crouched and promptly rolled the belt and put it under his arm. The corporal finally convinced the SS that the car from which their comrade had been shot had sped away to the north. The Citroën peeled away from the curb to the relief of soldiers and civilians alike.

The corporal looked into the violin case, “You need a doctor’s case.” He then invited François to follow them. Julie squeezed his shoulder before continuing toward avenue Kléber. Her nephew now managed well enough with the language that she wouldn’t need to be there and translate. People in the streets tended to avoid looking at anything abnormal. She wasn’t stopped by anyone seeing blood on her dress and inquiring if she needed help.

Chapter Twenty

After Julie turned the corner on place des Ternes, an unease came over her. She put a hand on the wall to take off one shoe. While shaking the shoe as if she had a pebble in it, she glanced around, but didn't detect anything unusual. Still sensing eyes on her, she adopted a casual air and walked to the Café du Clos where she knew a message could be passed on even though she had never used that letter box. She directed her unhurried steps toward the café.

She looked inside her purse for her compact to use the mirror to see behind her. To her dismay, she realized she'd forgotten it on her dressing table. Then, two men framed her.

"Come with us."

They escorted her to the car, which had just pulled up. No other words were exchanged. She didn't resist and carried herself with a haughty air. The men ordered her to sit in the black traction-avant.

"Messieurs, could I know why you forced me into your car?

"You will find out."

A mixture of fear and anger roiled through her, but she steeled herself to remain impassive. She expected to be taken to the infamous avenue Foch and was surprised when the car turned into rue des Saussaies and stopped in front of Number Eleven.

They took her purse and her watch. One of her guards moved her forward without undue force to a bare-walled room and sat her on the chair in the middle. A chair and a table were against the far wall to her left, a desk in front of her. A man in shirt sleeves stood behind her. A SS officer reading a file came in and took the chair behind the desk. She registered he was only an Untersturmführer.

"Mademoiselle Anna Gonthier?"

"Oui."

"Who were you meeting in the park?"

Hope surged. They didn't associate François with her. "My lover."

"Who is he?"

They don't appear to know much. "An officer. A German officer."

"Who? His name."

"I can't give you his name and get him into trouble."

The slap knocked her off balance. She righted herself and the chair.

"His name! We watched you at the Majestic."

She should have paid more attention to the civilians who looked like office clerks. "I was fired from the hotel because the staff is forbidden to have relationships with the officers."

"You went back. You don't have a lover."

She didn't reply and another slap landed on her head, but she was expecting it and didn't lose balance.

"Who were you meeting? Why did you go into the park?" Impatience colored his voice.

Julie wondered where she had made a mistake of not noticing anyone watching her at the hotel. Give them half-truths that don't implicate anyone.

"I was waiting for him."

"You are lying. You were waiting for the terrorist."

A fist hit the side of her head and made her ears ring. "No, sir. I was waiting for my lover when I heard the shot. I ran to the street and helped the soldier."

"Why?"

Hold out for two days and everyone has time to hide. She resolved to bear it. Her hands went to her ears. "I can't hear. My ears are ringing."

Another slap followed her comment.

The interrogator near shouted. "You knew a terrorist was going to shoot our men!"

"No, sir. I'm sorry. I couldn't have known."

This time, the fist landed on the back of her head, projecting her to her knees. She was rudely picked up and sat on the chair again. As dignified as she could, she adjusted her hat making sure the pins were secured around the canister.

"You are a terrorist. You don't have a lover. You were meeting a résistance leader."

"No, sir. I want nothing to do with those people."

Another blow made her dizzy. She grabbed the seat of the chair to keep upright. The now angry officer pointed with his chin to the door and the SS soldier, who had brought her in, went out. Julie hadn't forgotten the day when they brought battered Sylvain to make her react and give away his identity.

The SS soldier came back pushing a youth with a bruised face in front of him. The guard threw a violin case onto the table.

François!

Julie's heart sank, but her face didn't betray any emotion. François didn't look at her. Pride overcame her for her nephew. So young and yet so full of resolve, already knowing they had to ignore each other as if strangers.

"Mademoiselle, do you know this terrorist?"

"He's the medic who saved the soldier's life."

The officer stood up, opened the violin and shoved it under Julie's nose. "What is this?"

She looked at the case, then at the officer. "It appears to be a first aid kit."

"Why do you think a terrorist travels with a first aid kit?"

Remain polite. "A medic is not a terrorist, sir."

"I will tell you. It is to nurse the terrorists that were shot."

"More likely to nurse victims of the bombings."

She didn't know what hit her as she sprawled onto the floor. Will over matter. Will over matter, she repeated to herself as a mantra. She got to her feet and sat without help from the brute. The officer turned to the SS goon hovering by François' chair.

"One last time. Who do you work for?"

"Nobody. I'm a medical student."

The SS goon grabbed François' right hand and slapped it on the table. He seized his little finger and bent it back. A sickening crack made Julie flinch. François let out a throaty noise.

"Who do you work for?"

He panted. "Nobody. I'm a medical student."

The SS goon seized his ring finger and bent it back. The youth swallowed a scream.

"Mademoiselle, who were you meeting?"

"My German officer lover."

The SS goon broke François' middle finger. Julie couldn't help but blanch. Holding herself erect, she darted a look of despise at the Untersturmführer.

The officer smiled. "We will break all his fingers unless you tell us who you were meeting."

"My German officer lover."

"It will hurt him. Do you not like children, mademoiselle?"

It suddenly hurt. She would have preferred another slap. A flood of emotions rushed through her. She gritted her teeth. "You think you are the master race, but you're just barbarians. You're torturing a child because of your inadequacies—"

The blow unbalanced her. The chair swayed. In the space of a second, the door was thrown open and slammed back against the wall. General von Trennen strode up to the officer.

"How dare you arrest my daughter? Return her effects immediately unless you want to go to the eastern front."

The SS man who had brought Julie in beat a hasty retreat.

von Trennen threw his arm out, pointing his finger. "What? Breaking a child's fingers? I will have you arrested, leutnant. Have him taken to the hospital. Now!"

Despite her hearing sounding like noises wrapped in cotton wool, Julie noticed how calling him leutnant had a demeaning effect on the officer. He definitely did not want to offend a Generalfeldmarschall. The Untersturmführer took the phone and barked an order for an ambulance. The other SS man came back with Julie's purse and watch. On the point of fainting, François was put on a stretcher and carried to the waiting ambulance.

Without another word, von Trennen piloted Julie to his car. A chauffeur opened the doors, and Reynard helped her inside.

Minutes later, the car stopped in rue Chantemesse. Reynard took Julie's arm to lead her into his office. Although her jaw was hurting, she forced herself to speak.

"Thank you. I just don't know how to thank you. What will happen to François?"

"Always thinking of others first, Julie. He has been taken to the Lariboisi0re German hospital with an order to repair his fingers—"

The telephone rang. Julie listened to the furious argument.

Without hearing all the words, she understood that whoever was at the other end of the line was powerless to avoid the boy being taken to Fresnes after he would be discharged from the hospital. The argument died down and civilities were exchanged.

"Frannois told Dr. Katzenberg to call me. He is about to set his fingers, but he has orders to send the boy to prison right after he is done. We agreed that he would keep him as long as possible now that he knows he was the one who saved the soldier's life."

At Julie's questioning look, he nodded. "The young soldier is recovering. François' prompt action did save his life. Everyone now knows it at the hospital. He will be well-treated. The surgeon-major promised to let me know of any further development."

She breathed a sigh of relief. Günter had come in with coffee and an ice bladder.

"We had a delivery of ice blocs this morning, mein Herr.

Bruises were appearing on Julie's face. She inhaled the aroma of the coffee. Before putting the rubber bladder on top of her head, she carefully took off her hat. Her hair was about to unroll and fall loose. She took out the microfilm canister.

Reynard held out his hand. "That was on its way to Armand. I must find another courier."

"I'll take it."

"No, you will not go out until you are healed."

She frowned and stared at him for a moment. "Do not involve my mother-in-law."

He chuckled. "Your mother-in-law's secret life."

She was stunned. "You mean she has..." Julie was speechless.

"You do not think a woman as patriotic as Bérangère would just accept her son's admonition to stay home."

"I'm afraid I always saw her as the rock, always home for everyone." Julie sighed. After a moment, she looked up at Reynard. Once more she had a strange feeling when looking into his blue eyes. "Why did you say I was your daughter?"

"Because you are my biological daughter."

"No! No! It's not true." She stayed rooted to the chair.

Günter discreetly came in with a towel soaked in ice water. Grateful, Julie held it against her sore jaw.

"It is the truth."

While Julie absorbed the revelation, Reynard looked toward an invisible horizon.

"Your father was a rising star in the diplomatic corps at the French embassy in Berlin, as you know. I was a military attachι. Your mother did not speak any German. William was ambitious, Monique supported him, but was lonely and unhappy. We became close friends." He paused, his gaze lost in the past. "I loved her."

Her heart beating uncontrollably, Julie closed her eyes. "Does my fa... my papa know?"

"He does. We were and still are best friends. This war has separated us. Monique wanted her own child, the child that William could not give her. You were a gift."

She breathed deeply. "Why did she stay with papa if she was in love with you?"

"Do you believe it is possible for a woman to love two men? I do."

She thought of Brigitte in love with Gerhardt and still loving Hubert, despite their arguments.

"You never married because for you there was only one woman."

"Indeed. And William went on to make a brilliant career."

"Did you meet again when he was promoted ambassador to Germany?"

"We always remained in touch."

The ice bladder shifted on Julie's head. She took it off. "Papa loves me like his own. I know that. He encouraged me to study in Germany."

"It is natural. Even if you had been adopted from an orphanage, he would have loved you just the same."

"In a way, he did adopt me." She was silent for a while. "Why was I not told?"

"I don't know and I was not going to interfere. I was happy enough to follow your progress. I saw you at a distance many times when you were studying in Heidelberg."

Her eyes widened. "My German literature professor was a von Trennen, Herr Andrès von Trennen!"

"My father."

"My grandfather..." She paused for an instant. "Is that why I got on so well with him when other students didn't?"

"He is a stern but fair man. You succeeded on your own merit."

Her bruised face showed a sudden revelation. "Once he told me to close my eyes and listen with my ears wide open. And that is when I understood Kurt Meinhard's Nazi beliefs and all Hitler's followers. I broke up then. Were you behind it?"

"You made your own decision based on your own discoveries, but I did feed my father with enough information. I was top of my class in the intelligence game."

She shook her head and immediately regretted it. "You risked your life and career to get me out of the Gestapo's clutches. They won't forgive you."

"Oh, they are already after me and my friends for a bit of anti-Nazi plotting in the past." He sighed. "This war is the result of a delusional, psychotic man. I was not about to let them send you to a death camp."

She looked appalled. "That's true. That's what they are. Not labor camps, but death camps."

"Some of us career officers are once more planning to remove Hitler, but it's not him alone. His SS henchmen also need to be removed. We will act at the appropriate time and I hope sooner than later."

Reynard remained thoughtful for a while. "François should remain for a long while in the hospital. I think I should take him his violin to help rehabilitate his fingers."

"The surgeon-major won't be able to keep him forever. They'll take him to Fresnes."

"I have information on Sturmbannfóhrer Baumbach, who is the Fresnes director, which he would prefer that no one knew about, but I do not have enough influence to get François released. The SS have stripped the Abwehr of much of its authority."

"We hear that Hitler is losing the war."

"True. However, you need to stop your Résistance activities."

She folded the wet cloth as it was no longer cold. "How can I? I'm French and all French people want you Germans to go back home."

He stroked his chin. "Not all as you know. For the moment, it is still war."

"Agreed, some Frenchmen are profiteering from the Occupation. As you say, it's still war because the puppets in Vichy never signed a peace treaty. An armistice is only a temporary respite from the hostilities. So, all of us who don't agree with the situation will do our best to send you home."

He tried hard not to smile. "I would love you less if you were not so spirited. You are half German, though."

"My allegiance is to the country that I have always known as my own and where I was born."

"We are in agreement. You should remain quiet until the bruises fade."

"I'll try."

"Do you hate me?"

Julie closed her eyes. "No, I didn't hate you when you moved into the Manoir. You showed respect. Looking back, I'm glad you weren't some braggart SS man."

"Beware of Meinhard. He is not done yet. He spends much time in Berlin currying favors, but he is like a dog with a bone."

"He's watching you. The liaison was just an excuse, wasn't it?"

"Of course, but he knows I know his secret."

She sighed. "I want to kill him."

"So do I for what he did to you. Do not let him know about the baby."

"I'm sure it is not his." She had no hesitation. She had repeated to herself time and time again that Mathieu was Sylvain's. No matter what, the innocent baby was not responsible for his conception.

He chuckled. "Ah, yes, Sylvain managed to see you when he was here the first time."

"You're well informed."

"Just a little side business to military intelligence."

"He too wants to kill Meinhard."

"One of us will get him."

Julie stood unsteadily. Reynard offered his hand. She took it.

"If the situation were reversed, I would do what you are doing for my country." He led her to the west wing.

Julie let herself be pampered by her in-laws. Her bruises weren't deep and by Sunday, they had faded. She privately told each member of the reduced family about Reynard being her father to avoid Madeleine learning about it. They admitted she'd tell Philippe, and that wasn't a good idea.

While Jacques spewed his scorn on the collaborators, who were recruited by the SS to form the Selbstschutz, a group of self-defense, Brigitte arrived with Sylvestre, looking healthy and happy. Both Gerhardt and Reynard came in.

"We must all be grateful to Captain Langen for his intervention when my little boy fell ill. It wasn't poliomyelitis as we feared, but anemia due to a lack of vitamins."

Bérangère held out her arms for Sylvestre. "We're all happy that he's feeling so much better. Now you need to go to the country where you can get him better food."

"Maude has offered me to stay in Meudon." Brigitte had no doubt that Bérangère knew about her pregnancy, and she had just given her the opportunity to go without anyone knowing about her condition.

Julie noticed moisture in Reynard's eyes as he watched the children eating the rutabaga and cabbage stew topped up with beans.

He held up his hand. "Marie is about to bring something."

Hardly had he spoken that she walked in with a platter of roast meat and vegetables. At the murmur of protest, he silenced the family.

"The children need proper food. Please."

"It's French food anyway!" There was always a streak of defiance in Pierrette's tone when she believed it was an injustice.

After lunch, Gerhardt drove Brigitte and her children to Meudon. Brigitte quickly settled their possessions while the children explored the house and garden. Gerhardt kissed her with the promise to return with the baby carriage. He had just driven away when a woman flounced into the garden.

"What are you doing here? This is Madame Pleynet's house."

"Yes, Maude. She gave me the keys."

The woman's suspicions were not assuaged. "You know the family?"

"I'm part of the family. Maman-Bérangère practically raised me."

"What's your name?"

"Brigitte Marchand."

The woman dropped her belligerent tone. "I'm Gisθle Fournier. What about that kraut who drove you?"

"He's living in my papa-Gontrand's house. He's Wehrmacht, not SS. And I'm pregnant."

Gisèle pulled a face. "You don't show much."

"What do you expect with so little food in Paris?"

Gisèle glanced at the children who stood waiting on the doorstep, except for Christiane busy watching something in the grass. "They are rather thin."

"Alas, that's the reality in the city."

"How old are they?"

"Damien has just turned ten and Estelle is eight. Sylvestre is five and Christiane three."

"There's a boy's school and a girl's school within walking distance."

"Good. Damien and Estelle can go."

"I don't want to go to school. I'll stay home and help," Damien said.

Gisèle shrugged. "You need your schooling, but the boy's school is a rowdy place. Some fascist elements in there since half the male teachers have gone to escape the STO and women teachers have replaced them. I was a teacher. Although the education authorities are asking for retired teachers to come back, I am not."

"Then we'll see about school after the Christmas holidays—"

They turned to look at the Citroën traction-avant that stopped in front of the garden gate.

"Where is Maude Pleynet?"

Brigitte steeled herself. "I don't know who she is. I live here."

"You are lying!"

She took an outraged air. "I am not! I live here."

"You are lying. Come with us. We want to ask you questions."

Damien pulled himself as tall as he could next to his mother. "Hauptmann Langen will have your ass if you don't leave my mom alone."

Stunned, the SS man stared at the defiant boy and raised his hand. Damien ducked. The man's hand, carried by his violent motion, hit the doorjamb, audibly cracking a few bones. A howl of pain burst from his mouth. His companion repressed a smirk and seized the injured man's arm and dragged him back to the car.

"Well done, young man!"

Brigitte didn't agree. "He, or the rest of them, could come back and take us all to prison. What do we do now?"

"Sorry, maman."

"You go inside and I'll get you some eggs. My hens are still laying, sometimes."

"How can I thank you?"

"We have to help each other. Maude is a good friend. As soon as my three sons got demobilized, they went to England. I've had no news. I don't even know whether they got there or not." Gisèle sighed. "I see you're too polite to ask. My husband was killed right at the beginning of the war." She left to fetch the eggs.

Chapter Twenty-One

Jacques dropped into a chair. "You must find the house empty! I do. I miss everybody talking at the same time!"

"It's just us three men," Gontrand said.

Alexandre rolled a cigarette but put it away when Charmaine frowned at him. "Lyse-May has nobody to play with."

Julie lifted her eyes from the hem of the dress she was repairing. "She has books she found in the attic and Brigitte gave her some of her children's books. She reads them two or three times over and acts them out too."

Madeleine looked around. "Where is she? She wasn't in the playroom."

"Ernest made a windmill on a stick with her help. Last I saw her she was running around the courtyard, her whirligig held high," Bérangère said.

"Brrr... it's rather cool!" Pierrette entered and collapsed onto a chair. "The soup kitchen ran out of food before everyone waiting could be fed. And the portions were so small."

A silence settled. Julie wondered if, like her, they were considering themselves lucky to have work and a little money. Except Madeleine, of course, though she saw a few signs that would indicate her sister-in-law was becoming more aware of the war situation. And her compassionate nature was being bothered.

Jacques broke the silence, unmistakable pride in his voice. "At least we have some news to cheer us up. The members of a maquis unit held a parade at Oyonax, in the Auvergne, on the Eleventh of November. The whole town turned out, and the French tricolor flew everywhere."

Gontrand shrugged, anger in his voice. "And in Grenoble, people went to the monument of the Diables Bleus, but the Feldgendarmes surrounded them and hundreds of them were arrested."

Bérangère shook her head. "The résistants are worthy of the Diables Bleus. They retaliated by blowing up the munitions depot. That's quite a coup."

"What's the Diables Bleus?"

No one had heard Lyse-May come in.

Gontrand lifted her on his knee. "They are the Chasseurs Alpins."

"Do they hunt?"

Chuckles were heard. "No, poppet. They are a military unit for the mountains. They don't hunt, but they chase bad people. Well, used to, we no longer have an army."

"So, why are they the blue devils?"

Gontrand pulled a face. Julie came to the rescue. "They have a blue uniform and béret, and when someone is fearless, we often say he's a diable in a nice way, like daredevils."

This explanation satisfied the little girl and she went to play mother with Félicité.

Madeleine smiled at seeing her adopted daughter getting along with her cousin. "Philippe received a package the other day."

Jacques stiffened. "What was in it?"

"A miniature coffin. It's stupid. It's not a toy or a useful gadget."

"And no sender's name."

"No. Philippe said it was a joke."

"A joke in bad taste." Julie bit her lip. She had heard of other collaborators receiving the miniature coffin, a death threat.

Grunts of approval underscored her statement. Pierrette and the older children came down from the playroom and everybody fitted around the table.

"Isn't your mother coming today, Daniel?" Charmaine asked.

"She's looking after Madame Ducharme's *guest*."

All but Madeleine understood the emphasis on the word guest.

"Pierrette, did you go and see your brother?" Madeleine leaned over, eager to hear what her daughter had to say.

"Oui, maman. He's doing well."

Julie admired her niece cool lying. Pierrette had told her mother that he'd had a bicycle accident and had to stay in hospital for a while.

"Why can't I go and see him?"

Pierrette cleared her throat. "Because there are many cases of poliomyelitis and you could bring the germs back home to our little sister. It's young children who are affected. Not old ones like us."

"I brought some chocolate. Can you take it to him next time you go?"

"I will, maman."

Sometime later, they heard the Citroën Rosalie pull into the courtyard. Madeleine bundled up Félicité in a small fur coat and fur-lined boots. An elegant fur bonnet completed the outfit. One of Bérangère's designs. Unwilling to go, Félicité pouted.

Unsmiling, Lyse-May held her precious doll and watched the car roll away. "Angélique doesn't want Félicité to go away."

Charmaine gave her a hug.

Pierrette unwrapped the chocolate. "Here everyone, come and share."

***

Paris, Saturday, December 4, 1943

Soon it'll be Christmas and New Year's Day. What will the next year bring us? I hate to say that there are signs of famine, even in our upper-class district. Bombs are falling close-by, but people are more concerned about food than the destruction.

The poor workers in those repeatedly bombed factories are the first casualties. They have to work to feed their families, even when they would prefer not to work for the Germans. But they don't have any options. When you have a couple of children, or more, you have to swallow your pride and do what you can to feed them and keep a roof over their heads. And they are the first to lose their homes. In reality, we're all working for the Boche.

I believe that the crews of the bombers are showing a great sense of duty by keeping up the bombings even if it leads, not only to material destruction, but loss of civilian life. It can't make them happy to know their bombs also kill innocent people. That's what Gontrand was on about. The crews suppress their feelings in the name of duty. In a way, it's a permanent reminder that we are not alone, that the British and the Americans are fighting for us.

We have received our invitation to the Christmas reception at the German embassy· I wish they would lose our names· We know already that Meinhard will be there· Julie asked Gontrand how she could kill that lout, and my idiot of a husband gave her the derringer that had belonged to his mother· It only kills at close range· He gave her a lesson· It's absolutely crazy· How can she kill him and not be immediately arrested? What if he is only wounded? I'm so worried· She said that at a big reception, she'd have the right opportunity and get away with it too· Why is it that grandmothers can see what their children don't? Like the impracticability of this proposed assassination· My insides are so tight that I'm sure I don't need a corset· That's another thing· All my daughters-in-law, and my darling B and C, abandoned their corsets at the start of the war· "It's like being in a cage" was their argument and they couldn't bicycle with them· I don't have any problems·

***

"What are we going to do?" Madame LePlouhëc threw up her arms.

"Nothing. If they don't want the waiters in the meeting room, we'll just stay out."

"Don't you think it's a meeting of great importance if they don't even want food to be served? We need to know what's going on."

"Have the waiters bring the food on the carts to the door and stand back. I'll join them. Before long, one of the officers will be hungry enough and request something. I'll volunteer to serve."

The staff brought the carts up and lit candles under the silver dishes to keep the food warm. They placed the carts so that anyone coming out of the room would have to stop and detour. Julie's gamble paid off. Half an hour later, Oberleutnant Schäfer had Julie supervise the serving of the dishes. The officers moved to the dining table. While they ate, they chatted and those conversations, Julie considered, were more revealing than the official meeting.

Late in the evening, Julie, thoroughly exhausted, sat in Madame LePlouhëc's office.

"What do we have to communicate to London?"

"That the bombings on the rocket site at Moyecques are not

effective. They are proud of the strength of the concrete bunker and they have five thousands men working to repair and finish the installation. But, there is enough damage to delay the construction and the launch of their V2 rockets or that super weapon they're still talking about. Though, they still believe they will launch that super rocket in March next year."

"Chef Raoul and I made some invisible ink with onion juice and a bit of water. Use it."

"Good" Julie finished writing on the back of a grocery list and handed the paper to her boss.

"What else?"

"Other news for the Gavroche réseau. Let me write it down while the figures are fresh in my head. There's a bit of ink left." On a torn piece of paper she wrote in pencil: buy artichokes, if possible, and potatoes. On the other side, she wrote her message in invisible ink.

When she arrived home, Moussou was waiting for her. "Madame Julie, you're to go to the meeting. He didn't say the time or where because you know it. He gave me a *thune*." He showed the coin to her.

"Very good. I'll get changed and bicycle to the rendezvous. You're a good messenger boy."

He smiled, happy with his five francs coin.

In the dimly lit Cave, Armand was in an animated discussion with Xavier. Without noise, Julie slipped in.

"I could be enemy and you wouldn't notice."

"But I knew when I heard steps on the stairs that it was our beautiful Julie," Armand said.

"Touché."

"Now tell us about the results of switching the trains."

Xavier corrected. "Only the paperwork, not the trains."

"We need a candle to heat the ink on my report."

Armand produced a candle and matches. He held the paper close to the flame. Xavier took brief notes as the numbers appeared.

Julie confirmed her report. "The switch resulted in hours of discussion about who was responsible. *Ces messieurs* believe that they made a mistake in numbering the trains. So Convoi 62 left Drancy, but Convoi 63 never did. Now they are up in arms because they should see Convoi 64 going to Auschwitz, but the last Convoi to depart was Convoi 65. They're missing two trains that ought to have carried one thousand Jews each, but they didn't realize that. They believe a clerk messed up the numbers. Xavier and his men are safe."

"And some poor souls got a reprieve," Pierrette said.

Armand blew a smoke ring. "Any news of Léonie?"

"None. I went to see my gendarme at Drancy but he was unable to approach close enough to a prisoner. The new Feldgendarmes guarding the camp are really obtuse."

"We continue to monitor. Xavier, do you have access to the dispatch papers?"

"Not with people's names, only train requirements."

"Julie, can you get lists of names? It's all done at the MBF, right?"

"They stay in Stülpnagel's office. His own men clean it. And I haven't been able to seduce the officer who carries them to the camp commander."

Her dark humor drew sighs. An hour later, they left in pairs, Xavier and Pierrette first.

***

Julie spent the night at the Manoir so that Bérangère could alter her dress to hide the derringer.

"Do you really want to carry out that assassination? It means taking a life, despicable as it may be."

"We're at war."

"But you are not a soldier on the battlefield."

"I am a soldier of the shadows."

"You are not part of a mission. For you, it's only revenge."

Julie bent her head and kept silent.

"Don't you have some intelligence that you could casually let one of those officers at the MBF discover?"

"Maybe you're right, belle-maman. I'll have to think about it."

"Do you still want to go to the reception?"

"Absolutely! And if I meet Meinhard, I'll spit on him."

"My defiant Julie!" Bérangère laughed just as Reynard knocked. "Mesdames, the carriage is waiting."

Her mother-in-law gave a small push to Julie while she locked the derringer in a secret drawer of the china cabinet.

At the embassy, Julie met an alarmed Charmaine. “He’s here!”

“I know.”

“Don’t tell me you are going to...”

“No. I am not. I have been told there’s a better way. I’ll work on that.”

“But he’ll collar you asking for the baby.”

“Even under torture, I couldn’t reveal where he is because I don’t know the place. Do you realize it’s a year since Mathieu was abducted, recovered and taken to safety? I only saw him and Claudine once since then. I was driven and couldn’t find the way again if I tried. I really don’t know where it is.”

A waiter bowed to Julie and held out his tray on which a paper was folded in two. “Message from General von Trennen.”

“*Danke*.”

Charmaine sighed. “Please, stay close to us or your father. What’s the message about?”

A glance at the paper in her hand made her heart beat faster. *Get him into the garden*.

Julie smiled. “Can you imagine the bombshell if we were to announce we are related?”

They laughed, but it failed to alleviate Julie’s nervousness.

“It’s time for my performance. See you later.”

Meinhard stepped in front of Julie. “I am glad to see you, *liebling*. You have been avoiding me.”

“Not at all. Our paths simply didn’t cross.” In the corner of her eye, Julie saw Reynard move sideways while maintaining her in his sights. Warmth invaded her. She was protected.

“Where are you hiding our baby boy?”

She acted alarmed. “What do you mean? You kidnaped the baby I adopted and now you tell me I’m hiding him?”

“You disappoint me, *liebling*. You had my son removed. I could not find him or you.” He grabbed her arm in a tight grip. “I will not let you go. We are going to fetch him, and we are going home to Germany.”

“Not ever! Let go of my arm. You’re disturbing the audience.”

Without a word, he dragged her into the unlit adjoining room so fast Julie’s reflexes were delayed. “Now, where is our baby?”

“There are many blond and blue-eyed babies fathered by German soldiers and abandoned in the orphanages. I adopted one to remind me of my daughter Claire.”

"I know it is my son. I made you pregnant."

The darkness was both an ally and a danger. "I can't have any more children. That's why I adopted two." The lie flowed easily.

Without letting go of her, he wrenched open the French doors. "You lie!"

Julie kicked him, all the while regretting she had left the derringer behind. He shook her. She saw a silhouette move to one of the other French doors, and hoped it was Reynard coming to her rescue.

Meinhard kept pulling her down the steps to the garden. She saw her chance. If the shadowy figure was to help her, she had to make the first move. Julie purposely missed the last step and let herself fall. She heard a dull thud and Meinhard fell to the ground next to her. Men blending with the night moved around her. But she was free from her tormentor's grasp. She struggled to her feet, picked up the hem of her long dress and ran up the steps.

Back in the foyer, Julie found a ladies' room. Her heartbeat calmed down. She re-pined her hair and straightened her dress before slipping back into the grand room where she could hear Wolfang playing the piano.

She blinked in the bright lights and jumped when a Luftwaffe officer stepped in front of her. "Herr Schäfer."

He bowed. "Would you care to sit?"

"Yes, thank you." Her voice a mere whisper to match his.

He led her to the back and they sat together. Now, she was safe from her nemesis, if he had got away.

The rest of the evening passed in a blur. Oberleutnant Schäfer didn't leave her side.

"I insist you call me Manfred."

"Very well, Manfred." She wasn't going to displease him as he had unwittingly helped her. Now she could say she had been with Manfred Schäfer the whole evening, had she been seen going out of the room with Meinhard. She didn't know why that was important, unless the black shadowy figures killed him. It was that primeval instinct she always obeyed. Besides, Manfred was, if not directly her boss, someone who could get her fired. Her work at the Majestic was too important to risk it.

When he led her into the ballroom, she graciously accepted. Other officers whom she knew at the Militärbefehlshaber also asked her for a dance. While she kept up the role of Manfred's protégée, her ears were attuned to extraneous noises that would indicate Meinhard was looking for her.

Long after midnight, Reynard led her onto the dance floor for the last waltz. "The waltz I had not been able to dance with you at your wedding."

She smiled with warmth. When it was over, he took her and her in-laws back to the Manoir.

***

Friday, December 24, 1943

Livid, Gontrand flung the newspaper to the floor. "It says that we are allowed an extra ration of potatoes and turnips! As if that was food for Christmas."

"Stop grumbling, it doesn't help."

"Why shouldn't I? Children have had no milk since August. Milk is not available. The Boches send all the production to Germany."

"Nothing we can do about that. How many were killed in this last bombing?"

"Do you want to cheer me up?"

"Oh, I hear the door. Must be Julie."

Julie came in with Jacques and soon afterwards the Lebeaus, followed by Rose and Daniel. Madeleine and Félicité were not far behind.

Charmaine and Julie busied themselves in the kitchen.

"I saved last week's meat ration. The butcher gave it to me ground up. It's not much, but we could make a sauce with it."

"Perfect, I stole some turkey from the Majestic."

"You didn't!"

"In truth, Chef Raoul gave it to me. Even the Fritz are not getting all the food they're so fond of eating."

"Shall we cut the turkey pieces small and add them to the sauce? It'll liven up the Jerusalem artichokes and the turnips."

"I wonder what Reynard will bring."

"You don't call him father?"

"I can't. I'm still processing the revelation. But we have developed a bond. Yes, a strong bond."

Marie and Ernest preceded Reynard with platters of chicken, roast potatoes and brussels sprouts. They went back to fetch the traditional bûche de Noël, much to Lyse-May's delight. She explained the log structure to Félicité, telling her three-year-old cousin that since they were the youngest ones, they could eat all the mushrooms and the elves. That was what one did at the réveillon de Noël.

"Gerhardt went to Meudon to see Brigitte, and take her the carriage, among other things." Reynard said.

It was no longer a secret, except to Madeleine, why Brigitte had gone to live in Maude's house. Madeleine turned to Pierrette.

"Were you able to take the parcel to François?"

"Oui, maman. And Herr von Trennen added a few things."

Everyone kept up the pretense for Madeleine's sake.

"Ah, merci monsieur."

Once the dinner was over, they adjourned to the ballroom decorated with the Christmas tree with its neatly wrapped presents. While the delighted children played with their presents, the adults gathered around Reynard.

"I have heard that Kurt Meinhard, who had too much to drink at the embassy reception, was found dead in his bedroom... from an overdose of heroin. Nobody knew he was addicted."

Julie swallowed hard. It had Popaul and his men's signature written all over it. Jacques and Alexandre commiserated politely. Julie wanted to sing out loud. Instead, she looked into her biological father's eyes. An understanding passed between them. She sighed. Earlier on, Karl's death had left her indifferent, but tonight, she rejoiced in the death of a man. Was her heart becoming encased in a sheath of ice?

A piano melody rose under Lyse-May's fingers. More music and singing followed.

Midnight rang its twelve strokes. Reynard stood, his violin under his arm. "This is the last Christmas we will spend together. The Allies are winning. I believe they will be landing in France long before next Christmas. I, too, am rejoicing with you, even though I am saddened by the death and destruction that will inevitably ensue. The Abwehr may soon cease to exist."

Then he played Chopin's Étude n.3 opus 10, known as *Tristesse*.

Chapter Twenty-Two

The New Year Eve's réveillon took place in the cellar. Wave after wave of bombers unloaded their deadly cargo on all the industrial areas around Paris. Bombs strayed. The ground shook. In the weeks that followed, the rescue services were overwhelmed by the number of casualties and the destruction of houses.

With dark circles around their eyes, Pierrette and Xavier along with Hughes, Daniel and Marianne entered the kitchen. The younger children watched in awe as the adolescents collapsed on chairs and sank their heads into their arms on the table.

Bérangère shooed Baptiste, Paul and Micheline out to the playroom. "Find something to do. I'll call you when lunch is ready." She had swallowed her pride and accepted a basket of food from Reynard. Günter was no longer able to obtain the best cuts of meat and the quantity of other foods was reduced, but compared to the family, it was plenty. She made a stew to stretch the meat, adding potato purée mixed with rutabaga. It didn't take long to disappear from the young people's plates.

"A couple of bombs fell on Place de la République," Xavier said. "That's where I was posted until the trains were ready to roll again."

"I drove an ambulance," Pierrette said.

"She had it good," Hughes said. "We cleared cement blocks and debris off the streets so she could drive through."

"Did you pick up dead people?" Lyse-May asked.

They looked away.

"No, sweetie," Pierrette said. "That's the work of the medics and regular rescue people. We're only volunteers."

The answer satisfied her curiosity. She took Félicité's hand to go and play in her room.

Daniel looked at his scarred hands. "It was hard."

They all put their hands on the table to compare them.

Yolande pointed to her brother's hand. "Is that printer ink around your nails?"

Sheepish, Hughes bent his head. "We have nothing to clean our hands with."

"Get sand from the sandbox. It works," Gontrand said.

"How do you get into the shop's basement," Yolande asked.

"Monsieur Pascal knew about a hidden door. Daniel and I fixed up the small hand press. Our contacts pick up the documents we leave outside under pieces of the equipment. It hasn't been cleared away."

"I thought you registered at the university."

"We did. We got our student cards."

"But you aren't attending class."

"We attend the chemistry class. The prof understands."

Yolande shook her head and joined her hands in prayer. "I know I can't say anything, except do be careful."

"What about you, Marianne?" Julie asked.

"I helped with the injured. My dress got rather dirty."

"Don't worry, chérie, I'll wash it. Maman-Bérangère and I made some soap."

Gontrand tilted his head. "Where did you get the lard?"

"There's no lard or fat or oil anywhere. We improvised with ground horse chestnuts. Ernest helped grind them fine. They're a little bit oily, and they contain saponin. Just what you need to make soap. Well, close enough to soap."

Eager to take part in the discussion of domestic matters, Madeleine announced, "I grew horsewort in the window box. I mix the flowers with water and it makes soapy water. I use it for Félicité's clothes because it is so soft."

Bérangère nodded. "Yes, it makes a nice soft soap."

Madeleine looked at the women. "I'll give you a plant each. It grows non-stop."

A chorus of feminine yeses answered her.

***

Armand knocked the code and let himself into Julie's apartment. "You're taking too much risk!"

"Good morning to you. Would you like to share my breakfast?"

He threw up his hands. "Seriously, Julie, you cannot gather intelligence and courier it as well as taking messages from Popaul and myself, not to mention transporting a case of grenades. It is too dangerous. You're playing with fire. You're a group leader. Your men have to do the work, not you."

"They do. But unless the group can be increased to six, I have to pitch in."

She poured the ersatz and cut slices of stale bread. "We don't have anybody. Until you can recruit someone, I have to do it. Besides, Herr Schäfer is very keen in escorting me and stopping for coffee at Le Procope or at the brasserie Au chien qui fume, or anywhere I need to go."

He raked both hands through his hair. "Don't take him to the brasserie Zimmer. Résistants meet there."

"Is that the place with double cellars and a third one below?"

"How do you know that?"

"Unfortunately, some members are not as discreet as you are."

He jumped. "Who?"

"I told him that I'd strangle him myself if he speaks again about things he shouldn't. He belongs to Yves Lamont's cell."

"A communist. I thought they were so disciplined."

"He's young. You can tell Yves. He'll probably know who he is and discipline him."

"Why do you go out with Schäfer?"

She tilted her head and frown. "I don't go out with him. I'm showing him the sights. He's quite happy to buy me flowers while I put messages into the watering can. And when he pleads with a garçon to bring real coffee, I slip messages under the tablecloth. You should admire the art of conversation our garçons have developed to lengthen the time they keep him looking the other way. But you didn't come here to talk about my escort."

"No. There's no trace of Léonie in any of the prisons, and she isn't in the Compiègne camp."

"Drancy?"

"Not there either."

"Nacht und Nebel."

At his questioning look, Julie sighed. "Résistants are made to disappear as if they had never existed."

"Are they deported first?"

"Some must be."

"We'll keep trying to find her. We've learnt that Lorraine went to a camp called Auschwitz."

"A death camp. When the prisoners can't work any longer they are killed."

He grimaced. “I hope she has the strength to survive. The Boches are losing the war.”

Julie sighed. “But it isn’t anywhere near finished.”

“The SOE is now collaborating with the OSS to prevent a communist takeover. The coco are their bête noire. However, they’re also planning the role of the Résistance in a landing in France.”

“So the American Office of Strategic Services has finally realized that cooperation brings better results. That’s good. I should go to work now. Ces messieurs might have a meeting late morning unless they take time to have coffee and croissants. Informal talk is very revealing. By the way, the RAF is still bombing the Moyecques site. It’s a sore point with the MBF. Unfortunately, the damage is quickly repaired.”

“As long as it interrupts the work and delays the launch of those awful missiles, it’s worth it.”

Chapter Twenty-Three

A hand on Jacques' shoulder, Bérangère forced him to sit. "Calm down, you're going to burst a blood vessel."

"How can I? That Joseph Darnand, a man who fought bravely in 1940, pledging allegiance to Hitler!"

"He's a traitor!" Gontrand's yell made everyone jump.

"He has been appointed head of all the police forces. I'm off to join the maquis."

Xavier drummed his fingers on the table. "That may be one way to fight the Boches, but you're much more useful here, especially in Paris."

"Why? Because my men forget to lock the doors of the panier à salade when we pick up the *cheminots* who are suspected of belonging to the Résistance?"

"A dozen railroad workers quietly walking off the police van was impressive. They're back at work now."

The subtle irony about their work wasn't lost on the audience.

Pierrette laughed. "They do very a good job, uncle Jacques. They need you."

"The gendarmes and policemen who are with you, Jacques, need their leader. Without you, they'd be like a car without a steering wheel," Julie said.

Jacques scratched his head. "I so much resent receiving orders from a Nazi. Because, make no mistake, the milice is a Nazi force."

Gontrand pulled his mouth down in a grimace. "You can receive orders, but that doesn't mean you have to obey them slavishly."

Stupor was written on every face.

"I never thought I would hear civil, or rather military, disobedience being encouraged from my the-law-is-the-law husband." She lifted the soupière off the stove. "Enough talk. Sit and eat."

But the talk didn't cease. Jacques wasn't done. "As if we didn't have enough trouble with the damned Gestapistes!"

"What are they?" Madeleine asked.

Jacques spat venom. "The French Gestapo!"

Madeleine looked bewildered. "I thought the Gestapo was German."

A groan was heard. With a slight gesture of the hand, Julie reclaimed silence. "Yes, Madeleine, The Gestapo is a Nazi police force. Now there are French individuals from the underworld who have joined the Nazi organization. And a word of caution, those Gestapists are worse than the SS."

"That's not right. But I understand. I won't talk about them."

A conversation about food started. Julie noticed it made Madeleine uncomfortable.

After lunch, Rose and Julie wiped the dishes.

"You shouldn't take messages to the letter box, Rose. Your French is excellent but you still have an accent and it could be fatal if you were stopped. The militia are getting a reputation for harassing people without provocation."

"It's the only way. We need to exchange information about madame Bernadette's special guests. I take my knitting and put a pattern book on the table. The waiter always takes a long time to bring my food. Women are interested in the knitting so when our courier comes, it's just another curious woman. She slips the papers into the pattern book and I slide them into my knitting bag."

"You're brave."

"I want to get rid of the Nazis and their deadly regime."

Julie squeezed her arm. "Wc do too."

Hughes balanced himself on the edge of a chair. "Is there any news of my mother?"

All heads turned to Julie.

"We know she was on a train that went to a labor camp called Auschwitz." Her heart twisted. She wasn't going to say it was a death camp where the chance for survival was very slim.

Yolande squeezed her brother's hand. "My friend Oberleutnant Lohse is trying to find out if she is actually there. His friend Ziegler is in charge of workers. When they find her, he might be able to get her assigned to an office job."

As they dressed to go home, Charmaine asked Julie, "Are you

going to move back to rue Victor-Hugo? It's closer to the Majestic."

"Among other things, my apartment is being used by guests. I'm fine in Passage Lepic, especially now that I can come and go without having to worry about a particular individual, whose name must never be mentioned."

***

Pierrette counted the last of her money and walked into the florist store. It wasn't quite enough for the two dozen carnations she wanted. The florist scrutinized Pierrette's ravaged face and red eyes. She added five white carnations to make up twenty-three. "Friends?" Too choked up to speak, Pierrette nodded. She took the bouquet and walked toward place de la République to a closed newspaper kiosk where a large red poster depicted the execution of twenty-three young people. She knelt and deposited the bouquet below the poster.

A car's brakes screeched by the curb. She didn't look up. Xavier lifted her and despite her protest pushed her into the Citroën Rosalie he was driving. He ran to the driver side and put his foot on the accelerator.

He turned into the Manoir's courtyard and cut the engine.

"Did you steal Philippe's car?"

"Why did you disobey orders? You put everyone at risk by going to put flowers under the posters."

"Didn't you see all the flowers everywhere?"

"Didn't you see the collabo ready to call the milice?"

"We had friends among those martyrs."

Xavier drew her into his arms. "I know and I hurt too, but you have to think about our réseau and our people. If you were caught, you know what would happen. Another red poster with our names on it."

"I'd never talk!"

"Chérie, the Gestapo's methods are beyond what a body can endure. Ask Yolande. She spent six days in their hands. Ask Julie. She had to witness her husband beaten to a pulp, not to mention François' fingers. Could you have had her courage denying knowing him when they were breaking his violinist fingers?"

"If she could, so could I."

"My love, you haven't seen and experienced what your aunt

has, which gives her an inner strength none of us has yet acquired. At the same time, she ensures that none of her actions can endanger the réseau. You are brave, but you also need to use your brain."

Pierrette lowered her chin to her chest. Xavier kissed away her tears.

"I'll be careful. I promise. By the way, how did you manage to steal Philippe's car?"

"Easy."

"How did you get the key to start it?"

"No need for keys when you know which wires to connect."

"You'll show me?"

"Oui. Go in now, I've got to do something with this car."

"He'll just get another one if you keep it."

"Then the Résistance will acquire two cars. Go now."

***

Paris, Friday, February 25, 1944

What is that milice going to do next? Sadistic individuals, all of them, not only arresting but shooting their compatriots!

I don't know what Pierrette was up to. Xavier drove her and she went quietly to her room. I can't remember if I ever saw Pierrette subdued. All to do with those red posters.

I'm afraid that Paris is heading toward a famine. We can't even travel to the country to get food. First, the farmers are being raided by the milice and the Fritz. Then most of them are feeding the maquis. They don't have anything left for city people, whom they tend to dislike anyway. But even if a farmer could sell a little food, traveling is too dangerous. When the trains are not being bombed by the RAF, they are being derailed by saboteurs. Xavier mentioned that German troops are traveling in regular trains too. That doesn't stop the Résistance from blowing up the trains. I am appalled by this disregard for human life.

The Americans drop bombs from a high altitude and lack precision. Why can't they be like the RAF and fly lower? The RAF is much more precise and cause fewer casualties. The Résistance is all abuzz with the daring RAF coup to break the walls of the Amiens prison to free important résistants. Of course, there were casualties. Oh, have I just written this? Am I accepting that for one small gain we must ignore the greater losses?

The Ricains are not endearing themselves to the population with their bombing, although everybody is quick to laud them for entering the war and coming to help. The lives of French people are like a teeter-totter. One minute we clap, the next we cry. One minute we cheer the bombs falling onto Germany, the next we deplore the bombs falling on French towns. One minute we get angry at the Germans, the next we are sorry for their bombed out families.

I should go and rehearse for Reynard's reception next month instead of ranting on. One piece of cheerful news, Captain Langen gave us news of Brigitte. She is doing well.

And Julie is practicing the flute again.

***

In a silk and lace dress, with two braids falling down her back, Lyse-May looked as pretty as a picture. For the first time, she was allowed to attend Reynard von Trennen's reception and would be playing a couple of pieces.

Although Oberleutnant Lohse was in the audience, Yolande was in the kitchen helping Marie, along with Pierrette, to keep out of sight of the few SS officers also in attendance. Marianne supervised the children with Hughes. Gontrand sat with Xavier in the shadows at the back of the music room. Officers of all three arms kept arriving.

Behind the closed glass doors of the music room, quiet conversations unfolded.

"All the top brass is here," murmured Julie.

Wolfang nodded in agreement. "*Ja*, I have never seen so many at one reception."

"Perhaps they sense this is the last reception I will be hosting," Reynard said.

All eyes turned to him.

"The Abwehr has just been disbanded. It is now under the control of the Ausland-SD. Admiral Canaris has been re-assigned to some inconsequential department."

"What will you do?" Bérangère asked.

Reynard sighed. "There is still paperwork to be taken care of.

That should last until the Allied landing, which is not far off now. The Résistance is already being given directives. We will soon be out of here."

Charmaine was puzzled. "How, or rather, what do you know about the French Résistance?"

Reynard chuckled, but it was Wolfang who replied. "The Abwehr's main occupation was spying on résistants, spying on the German armed forces, spying on the SS and spying on foreign powers."

Julie repressed a laugh. "Quite an assignment! Morale is low, even at the MBF."

"Many of the troops and commanders are nervous," Reynard said. "So many officers, especially those who come on leave, are anxious about what Berlin is saying, and what they see in the field. It doesn't match."

"They came en masse tonight to hear intelligence from you."

"I am keeping to the official line. I do not want to be arrested."

Charmaine tugged on Julie's sleeve. "It appears the guests are taking their seats. Captain Langen is ready to announce the musical interlude."

The evening unfolded successfully and no one received more applause than Lyse-May's thoughtful interpretation of Bürgmueller's *Pastorale*.

Chapter Twenty-Four

"Morning, Armand. Is breakfast becoming a regular feature?"

He laughed. "Your stale bread tastes better than mine. Here, take this."

He handed her a cloth bag. Julie looked inside. "Day-old bread and... one egg! Shall we cook it for breakfast?"

He chuckled with glee. "They do in England, with bacon too, but that's not available here."

"We should always eat when we can. We never know whether it's going to be our last meal." The sobering thought was a daily reality. They had survived longer than most in the underground. She poured the last of the oil in a pan, adding the bread sliced thin and the thoroughly beaten egg mixed with leftover potato puree.

"Is it awkward that your real father is a German?"

"The whole family liked him since the day he moved in. He has protected and helped us. Sometimes we forgot his nationality, especially at Christmas or when we celebrated, like Lyse-May's rescue. I've been drawn to him. It's my mother I can't figure out. Was it love or was she just using him? My papa remained friends with him. I just don't understand." She paused. "But you don't come here, despite your own rules about meeting, to talk about philosophical topics."

Armand couldn't help but laugh. "Right. Maude had a transmitter for her réseau. Six weeks ago, when the Gestapo was closing in, her pianist moved the transmitter once more and had just enough time to hide it before she was caught."

"Oh, mon Dieu!"

"She didn't talk and since they didn't find the radio in her apartment, they let her go, obviously keeping a close watch on her."

"What do you want me to do?"

"Two things. Recuperate the transmitter and help her to safety."

"What's her cover story?"

"She's a maid at the Château de Bellevue. One wing is still standing. The *Soeurs de la Charité* have taken it over since the war started and are running an orphanage, *Le petit monde*."

Julie pursed her lips and drummed her fingers on the table. "Could she have taken the transmitter to the château?"

"I don't think she'd endanger the children by hiding it there."

"I remember Maude talking about the Couvent des Capucins, once. It's been demolished a long time ago, but there are ruins. She has taken us to see the Bastion des Capucins. It provides a fantastic panorama of the Seine and Paris. She wanted to take us to a grotto, but we were too tired to go."

"If it's that beautiful, the Fritz must be occupying it."

"It's part of the Château's property. I think they respect the nuns and their work. Though I'm sure they'd have inspected the grotto. Such an obvious place! There's an internment camp nearby and there are the underground limestone quarries. They're used as shelter during the bombings, but I doubt the Fritz shelter there, or even want to inspect them."

"They're rather scared of the Paris quarries and Catacombes, but maybe the Gestapo aren't."

"Oh, I don't know. They're scared of diseases and residents are prompt to spread rumors about what's under our feet. To sum up, you want me to find the radio, put it on my bicycle and ride back here after I ensure the safety of... what's her name?"

"Antoinette."

"I'll go tell Madame LePlouhëc and Popaul."

"I'll tell him. He'd take the opportunity to give you some messages. You're to concentrate on this mission."

She gave him a sweet smile. "I will, sir."

Later in the afternoon, Julie made her way to the Manoir. Lyse-May helped her put a change of clothes in the panniers and waved goodbye.

In Meudon, Julie struggled to open the gate until Damien spotted her. He held the gate open and helped push her bicycle inside.

"Tante Julie!"

The children ran to her, and Brigitte, attracted by the noise, came out. The two friends kissed and hugged.

"It's so good to see you. I feel so isolated here." Brigitte buttoned up Christiane's light coat. "Damien, chéri, can you take your siblings into the garden until dinner time, please?"

He complied willingly.

"They're digging the garden for the spring planting. So, what brought you here?"

Brigitte took out potatoes and carrots from her cold pantry. Julie pulled a whole saucisson from the pannier. "Courtesy of my favorite chef at the Majestic."

"Wonderful."

They started cooking.

"I have to find Antoinette, who I believe is a maid at *Le petit monde* orphanage. Next she has to tell me where she hid the transmitter so I can take it to Paris."

"My neighbor Gisèle and I take a rabbit to the château from time to time. I'll give you one and you can go. I've never met anybody there other than the nuns."

"Arrested six weeks ago, released a few days ago, she probably needs a lot of care. She didn't talk as far as we know."

"You'll go tomorrow. Some of the hens have started laying again, not every day, but there'll probably be two or three eggs."

In the morning, Gisèle brought the rabbit over. She had taken on the task of teaching school to the children. They happily followed her to what they called the school room. Brigitte and Julie went to the château.

The sister recognized Brigitte and opened the door wide. "Thank you so much. Our little ones are in such need of good food."

The pre-schoolers crowded around the new arrivals. Brigitte played with them.

"You've arranged this old ruin pretty well, ma soeur," Julie said.

"We were fortunate and had a lot of help." The nun looked pointedly at Julie. "You have a reason for coming other than bringing food?"

"Yes, I have something to ask you. I'm looking for Antoinette."

Suspicion flashed in the nun's eyes. "Why?"

"I know she was tortured by the Gestapo for transmitting important information to the Allies. Now, we need to take her to safety and I must find the radio." Julie hadn't planned to tell the truth to the nun. She didn't try to analyze why she did.

"I'm glad you're not beating around the bush. If you had, I'd have sent you away. Come and see Antoinette. Her physical wounds have been taken care of, but she's in a catatonic state."

"Mon Dieu!"

"Pray for her. This is her room."

Although Julie expected it, the sight of the young woman sitting in bed made her sway. She dropped to her knees by the bedside. Both Antoinette's legs were encased in plaster, as was her right arm. Her half-shaven head showed two long rows of stitches and her purple, puffed up face bore several more stitches. Her eyes stared, unseeing, beyond this world.

"We did what we could. We don't know whether the Gestapo released her because she was useless to them, or because they're hoping to catch someone else."

"Merci, ma soeur, for saving her life."

Gently, Julie held Antoinette's swollen and lacerated left hand in hers. She feather-stroked the back of it. A tiny pressure of the young woman's fingers on hers sent Julie's heart soaring with hope.

"I will get you to safety. Be strong, Antoinette."

Again the tiny squeeze on her finger. For a brief moment, the young woman's eyes focused on Julie, pleading.

"I'll take care of it." Julie didn't know whether that brief recognition was to urge her to take care of the transmitter, or begging to be taken to safety.

She whispered she'd be back, then went outside and played with the children for a while.

Back at the house, Gisèle took the children, including Christiane, outside for a game of cat and mouse.

"Alright, now, what about Antoinette?"

"I have to arrange to have her taken to Bérangère. The nuns are so good, but can't spend time with her other than for the physical care. And the Gestapo knows she's there. Right now she cannot speak and tell where the transmitter is hidden, but maybe they hope the Soeurs de la Charité will heal her and then they can start all over again. They want that radio and they want her to transmit for them. They've done it with another radio-operator."

"What happened?"

"She asked for a drop of arms and an SOE agent. The Lysander came. The Gestapo was at the rendezvous."

"Oh, no!" Brigitte absorbed her friend's words for a long moment. "The radio could be hidden anywhere in the forest. There's a spring and people go there to get water when the pipes get damaged by bombs. I'm lucky I have a deep well..."

They looked at each other.

"What if there was a dry well?"

"Let's go look while Gisèle is teaching the children in the house. Even Christiane is eager to learn with her."

They each took a jug and walked to the spring, leisurely in the belief the house and its occupants might be watched. A riot of buds had sprung everywhere in the warm spring air. Julie walked off the path to examine the emerging flowers. She held a branch here or there while her eyes darted around the forest floor, looking for a sign of ancient habitation. They arrived at the spring, Julie filled her jug and spun round to see that the SS soldier of the day before was striding up the flagstone path from the town. The injured soldier was nowhere to be seen.

"What are you doing here?"

He didn't just speak but barked in bad French. She pulled herself tall and disdainful. Behind her, she could hear Brigitte's short breaths.

"As you can see, we're fetching water." She turned, took Brigitte's jug and began filling it. At six months pregnant, Brigitte wasn't showing much, but she pushed her belly forward.

The soldier looked nonplussed. Julie carried both jugs and, closely followed by her friend, started nonchalantly on their path. He didn't follow. Moments later, they heard his booted steps retreating on the other path.

"You have nerves of steel! I was already wetting myself."

Julie laughed. "No, you weren't. Gisèle said you sent him off when he came to the house. Now, let's stop for a moment. I want to see those flowering bushes by that space between the trees."

She put the jugs down and fought her way through the brambles and thick brush, while Brigitte scanned the surroundings. Julie's foot hit a large stone and she nearly tripped. She stood still. Although it was regrown, a lighter space in the denser forest was still visible to the searching eye. If there had been a house here, some fifty years ago, there must have been a well. With caution, she stepped to the side of the stone and found a small heap of the same sort of limestone blocks devoid of moss. That indicated they had been moved in the recent past. She identified the heap as the remnants of a chimney. Heart beating fast, she crouched and lifted a smaller stone, then another and another. In the hollow, where the hearth had been, was a dark shape that didn't look like stone. Her hand fitted in the space and touched hard, angular edges which she recognized as a suitcase.

Full of joy, she carefully put the stones back. She didn't retrace her steps but continued in a leisurely arc to rejoin the path farther along to keep up the pretense of botanizing in case they were watched, even though she didn't have that unmistakable brooding she had at other times. With a jug in each hand, Brigitte hurried to catch up.

"I'll have a premature birth if you keep disappearing from my sight!"

"I had to come out in a different place so as not to leave too much of a track. Not that I think your SS idiot would be able to follow through the shrubs and bushes, but Olive pounded into my head that whatever you do, you leave no trace."

"Your eyes are shining."

"I found it! Maude had said her pianist radioed from the forest and changed location every other day. It made sense that Antoinette would have a hiding place in the forest, but not too far from her place of work and Maude's."

"So we're coming back tonight?"

"I am. On my own. I'll tie the suitcase on the bicycle and I'll be out at dawn, or whenever the curfew is lifted."

"I never thought I'd say this, but I hope they bomb the Renault factories again, so no one will wonder why you have a suitcase on your bicycle rack."

The alert sounded after midnight. The bombs were not directed at the Renault factories, but a few strayed far enough from their targets to enable Julie to leave under the guise of a refugee fleeing the destroyed buildings. She didn't think wise to cross Paris with her precious cargo and opted to go to the Manoir.

While she was still in Boulogne-Billancourt, she had to stop behind a crowded bus. A young harassed woman with two young children and a baby in her arms was being harangued by a couple of militia men who tried to get her off the bus' open platform. One of the miliciens grabbed her arm, making her lose her balance. The baby began to cry.

Julie couldn't help herself and addressed a man on the curb. "Can't you do something?"

The six-year-old child screamed to let his mother go. The militiaman slapped him. The man on the curb shouted, women joined him and in a few seconds the waiting crowd, as well as the crowd inside the bus, threw insults at the militiamen. The situation grew threatening. They hesitated. On the other side of the street, Julie noticed the arrival of two gendarmes and expected them to intervene. The now angry crowd surrounded the miliciens. They looked around and seeing an opening, ran, punches raining down on them. The gendarmes strolled away.

The ticket collector stepped onto the platform and pulled the bell cord to signal the driver to drive on. The crowd on the sidewalk discussed the incident with animated gestures. Julie pedaled away. She'd never been so glad to roll into the Manoir's courtyard. Suitcase in hand, she knocked and entered the kitchen.

"Belle-maman, this suitcase needs to be hidden."

Gontrand leaned against the doorjamb. "Take it to the cellar and the tunnel entrance."

Julie took the suitcase down and placed it inside the tunnel. She'd have to walk to Popaul through the quarries with the heavy radio, but the prize was worth the effort. Maybe she could get one of the men to come and help.

When she emerged from the cellar, Bérangère had put a plate of heated soup on the table. Lyse-May waited patiently before throwing herself into Julie's arms. Julie finished her soup and kissed her niece. "I have to go now, but I'll be back later."

The little girl went back to her book and Bérangère accompanied Julie to the courtyard.

"I'll be back with a friend for the suitcase and we'll leave via the quarries. I have to arrange transport for a young woman in need of nursing care. I'd like to bring her to you."

"Of course. I'll arrange the spare room. The children don't play there anymore, the playroom upstairs is more to their liking."

At Popaul's, Julie glanced at the patrons. The usual soldiers had been replaced by older men with ill-fitting uniforms. They weren't interested in the rooms upstairs or anything else in the establishment and spent most of their time eating and drinking.

"I'm not needed here. Is Armand home?"

"You can find him at the cemetery du Père Lachaise. Frederic Chopin's tomb. There's a meeting." He glanced at the clock, "At five. Use the rue du Repos entrance. Easier."

"We're going to need Ari later tonight for a trip through the quarries."

"I'll see to it."

Although hunger twisted her stomach, Julie didn't stop at home for a piece of stale bread, as she wanted to make it to the cemetery on time. She couldn't fathom what type of meeting it could possibly be. Fantasy took over. They were assembling an orchestra and would play Chopin's music. She chased the idea and watched the Métro stations so she wouldn't miss the Bagnolet station, as she wasn't familiar with the area.

She found rue du Repos and the tomb of the renowned composer. Pierrette and Xavier sat on the steps next to the tomb. On the other side, Armand and another man leaned against the railings. When he turned toward her, she nearly cried out, Dédé, but bit her tongue. They looked surprised to see her.

"I've just been told. I came back this morning from Meudon."

They came closer while keeping themselves half turned to monitor the area. Leaves were sprouting on the trees and shrubbery. Buds were bursting everywhere. Armand motioned her to continue.

"The transmitter is at the Manoir. Antoinette needs to be taken there by ambulance."

"I'll borrow an ambulance," Pierrette said.

Worry hadn't left Julie since seeing Antoinette. "Is it possible to get Dr. Bignon involved?"

Armand nodded. "Is it bad?"

"She didn't talk. You'll see." She paused. "The Gestapo is watching the woods behind Maude's and I'm quite sure the château where the Soeurs de la Charité have their orphanage. They took her in and I think the good sisters stitched her up. The stitches appeared to be just sewing cotton thread and a lot more irregular than if there were done by a doctor."

"So an ambulance would be too obvious," Dédé said.

Xavier tapped his cigarette ash with his index. "I think a hearse would be more convincing."

"Very good idea," Armand said.

They looked at Dédé whose ingenuity had helped them many times in the past.

"My van is black. I could get black cloth tomorrow morning and drape the windows on the back doors and hang a curtain behind the front seats. We need a coffin."

Pierrette grimaced. "Gruesome!"

Julie shook her head. "It'll have to be a stretcher. She couldn't survive the handling to put her into a coffin. If we cover the stretcher with black cloth, it should be convincing enough."

"I'll contact Dr. Bignon."

"I think Dr. Bignon and Pierrette with her Équipe nationale armband and her Red Cross armband should travel in the back. I'll ride in front to guide Dédé. I should be able to find a black outfit in my mother-in-law's attic."

"About the radio," Armand said.

"I propose to take Ari through the quarries to help me take it to Popaul's cellar. It's heavy."

"It's an hour and a half's walk," Pierrette said.

"Don't I know!"

"People coming up. You move away, we'll cover," Xavier said.

Nobody bothered lovers. He took Pierrette in his arms while Armand, holding Julie by the waist, and Dédé walked in the alley in the opposite direction. They came out on boulevard Gambetta where Dédé had parked his van.

After dropping Armand at his place, Julie left a message with Popaul for Ari to go to the Manoir for eight o'clock. Dédé then drove to the Manoir.

"I was so lucky! Those FTP left a bomb at the entrance of the supply depot, but I was still at the other end of the street."

"I don't know why they keep throwing grenades at the Germans. It doesn't make any difference and then hostages are shot."

"Scare the Fritz?"

"Hardly. They are still living it up and having fun in Pigalle."

Two days later, an imitation hearse left the Manoir with Julie in a long, old-fashioned black dress, complete with hat and veil, while Dédé looked solemn in a black suit and top hat from the previous century. Pierrette, sporting a white nurse's apron, and Dr.

Bignon sat on cushions in the back next to the stretcher and a length of black cloth.

It didn't take long to arrive at the Le petit monde. Julie opened the gates to the château. Dédé backed up to the front door, while she pulled the bell.

"Bonjour, ma soeur. We've come to take your patient to safety."

"*Dieu soit loué*." With that blessing, she held the door wide open.

Dr. Bignon and Pierrette followed Julie and the nun. Antoinette had no reaction until Julie took her hand and stroked it as she had done the previous time. With tender care, Dr. Bignon assessed her injuries. Julie's heart sank at seeing his grim face. He slid the injured woman onto the black cloth over the stretcher that Pierrette and Julie held, carefully wrapping his patient with the cloth. He then took Julie's place. She carried his black bag and put her veil down. She gently pulled the flap of cloth over Antoinette's face when they reached the door.

The nun held it open. "I'll close the gates behind you. Don't stop. Sister cook saw the SS men when she came back from the market."

Julie had the distinct impression that eyes were following their every movement.

Dédé drove slowly as a hearse would, while Julie kept her eyes glued to the side mirror. She began to relax when they reached boulevard Flandrin. If the situation hadn't been so dire, she'd have laughed as German cars gave them the right of way. Pedestrians looked the other way or made the sign of the cross.

Once in the courtyard, Ernest, who was conversing with Günter, closed the gates. In no time, Antoinette was in a bed with pillows supporting her legs and arm. Bérangère gave her water from a syringe. Lyse-May watched with a mixture of fascination and distress.

Gontrand took his granddaughter's hand. "Let's go for a walk."

"It looks that she has internal damage, maybe lacerations on the spleen and liver considering the swelling and bruising. I need to operate, but I don't have enough supplies for this delicate operation." Dr. Bignon held his head with both hands.

"I'll ask my father to get you what you need," Pierrette said.

Bérangère shook her head. "He'll blabber about it. He always talks too much."

"I'll ask my... Reynard." Julie looked at her watch. "He's still in his office. I'll tell Günter to phone."

She didn't know what the adjutant said, but two hours later, Reynard arrived with several large boxes and a Wehrmacht doctor. There was a moment of silence.

"Surgeon-Major Katzenberg has brought a field hospital. He set François' fingers."

"The best light is in the kitchen," Bérangère said. She took the white apron from Pierrette, sent her to fetch a sheet for the table and washed her hands. Julie helped Dédé reconvert his van and he left to deliver wine to the supply depot.

In the kitchen, Dr. Katzenberg took the lead. Pierrette held a bucket for the discarded swabs. Julie went back into the kitchen and watched from the door, ready to translate if need be.

Dr. Katzenberg called her over. "Monitor breathing. Mirror."

Julie took a small ornate mirror off the china cabinet. The doctors applied chloroform to her nose and mouth, then gave her an injection of morphine.

"*Ja*, I stitch spleen. Liver still big enough to grow."

Dr. Katzenberg was throwing torn pieces of liver into the bucket. He and Dr. Bignon worked with precision, without words. Bérangère handed the needed instruments and stanched blood.

Pierrette paled, but her hands held the bucket steady.

"Raped. No stitch. So we clean infection and stitch."

Last, the surgeon checked Antoinette's jaw. "Broken. No chew. Give much liquid food."

"Will it set properly?" Bérangère asked.

Dr. Katzenberg nodded. "*Ja*, already set. Just time now."

The two doctors transported Antoinette back to her bed while Julie helped clean the kitchen.

"Take the bucket to the garden and ask Ernest to dig a trench for the contents," Bérangère said.

Pale and sweating, Pierrette complied.

Marie came in. "General von Trennen asked everybody to the dining room."

"Where's Lyse-May?" Julie asked. "Beau-papa's back." She and Bérangère tip-toed to the spare room only to find the little girl kneeling at the foot of the bed, hands joined in prayer. Gently, Julie motioned her to come. “Antoinette will sleep for a while. Come and eat.”

Chapter Twenty-Five

Monday, April 17, 1944

Another Easter, and no end of the war in sight. Last month the Boches decimated a maquis on the plateau of Des Glières in the Alps. My heart goes to those young people's mothers. Bombings everywhere. We are lucky to have our own shelter. When the sirens shriek at midnight, many people have to run to an official shelter. I heard the women in the queue yesterday. They have a case or a bag by the door with their most precious possessions, photos, jewelry or souvenirs of loved ones. Some said they pack all the food they have every evening. Others go to bed fully dressed, while the general opinion is that night bombings are done by the RAF so they feel safe. I don't know. The newspapers reported some shelters being hit.

Antoinette is finally recovering, emerging from that catatonic state. She doesn't talk yet. Lyse-May spends hours with her, reading her stories and when the brave young woman falls asleep, the dear child spends another bout of time on her knees praying for her.

Gontrand hasn't yet come to terms with the dreadful parade on the Champs-Élysées of the Légion des Volontaires Français against Bolchevism. The parade that was headed by our son Rodolphe, no less. What a shame it is for us! Where did I go wrong bringing him up? He was such… No, I can't say a wonderful boy. Only his way was the right way. He hit and kicked until his brothers gave in or thrashed him.

I read in the newssheet Libertas that the SS have arrested and deported over a hundred children hidden in a place call Izieu. I've never heard of it, I'll go and look in the

Atlas. There, I found it. An out of the way place on a hill, at the foot of the Alps, not far from Lyon and Chambéry. Children! Those SS are not men. They're machines. Machines don't have hearts.

Time to feed Antoinette.

***

Friday, April 21, 1944

Shortly before midnight, Julie awoke to the strident sound of the sirens. Soon after bombers were overhead. It was unusual, they normally were heard over in the suburbs. The German flack rang out in repeated short bursts. She opened the north-facing kitchen window only to see the sky illuminated by the blinding light of a circle of flares. The deafening noise hurt her ears and she closed the window. Still, bombers kept coming. Bombs fell and exploded. Fires now projected their deadly reddish light.

Julie picked up her bag and, after ensuring there was no warden in the street, ran to Popaul's café. He must have guessed she'd take refuge in his solid cellar because Bertrande was holding the door ajar. Julie was barely inside when there were hurried steps. Armand bolted in. The building shook. The thundering of exploding bombs prevented them from speaking. In the cellar, shock waves destabilized the wine racks that Popaul was hastily securing to the walls. Armand lent a hand.

"It must be the marshalling yards at La Chapelle," Armand said.

Julie hit her forehead with her finger. "La Chapelle! That was the message, *La Chapelle au clair de lune*."

"It probably was for the railroad workers résistants to clear out."

"We heard it but we didn't understand it. If we had, we could have urged inhabitants nearby to take refuge somewhere else."

"You know people don't heed warnings, even if Marjane herself had been singing the song."

She lowered her head. He was right. An hour later, all of a sudden, the intense din stopped. They waited for the all-clear. It had barely begun to sound than it was cut. A second wave of bombers approached and dropped their payload of death. Shock waves made the ground shudder. Dust and plaster fell on them.

"That one fell on Montmartre," Popaul said.

They lowered themselves into the quarry below. The roar became muffled but went on and on. At least, the rock didn't move. They didn't dare sit down. Popaul held his wife in his arms. Armand drew Julie into his. She laid her head on his shoulder. He rested his chin on her head and breathed in the light scent of her hair.

"You smell good," he whispered.

She smiled. "We make soap with flowers."

The next explosion made the rock tremble. They held each other for another hour. Finally, the all-clear sounded. They climbed back upstairs and looked into the street. No damage close by, but they could now hear the two-tone sirens of the ambulances and the firefighters. The sky was ablaze over a huge area. Buildings collapsed as the conflagration reached them.

"This is bad," Julie said.

"I'll go and volunteer."

"Me too."

"Stay here. There's too much danger."

"Armand!"

"Sorry, chérie, I don't want anything happening to you."

"I promise to be careful, if you make the same promise."

He kissed her and they set out. They saw with relief that the basilica of the Sacré-Coeur, reflecting orange glows, was still standing at the top of its hill, but as they approached craters pockmarked the streets and ruined buildings became evident among the sputtering of flames under the firefighters' hoses.

Julie was assigned to the triage and comfort of the survivors, Armand to help carry the injured. The smoke burned the eyes. They tied wet handkerchiefs over their noses and mouths. At the end of the long day, as dusk enveloped the tragedy in a veil of misery, Julie saw Pierrette driving the last ambulance. Exhausted and grubby, they trudged to Popaul's in silence.

***

Before Jacques could enter, Lyse-May stood in his path. "You can't yell uncle Jacques because Antoinette needs quiet."

"Very well, mademoiselle Lyse-May. I'll be as quiet as the proverbial mouse." He picked her up and kissed her on the cheeks.

When Madeleine arrived, Lyse-May took charge of her little cousin.

"I brought liver and eggs for Julie's sick friend. Is she doing better?"

"She is thanks to the food you brought. We're grateful, Madeleine," Bérangère said.

"I can give you more ration tickets, if you need to."

"You're very kind. We still have some, but there's no food in the stores except for rutabagas, turnips and sprouting potatoes. Even the dry lentils and peas have run out."

"I know. My usual suppliers find it difficult to get produce and milk. Eggs are one hundred and ten francs a dozen, but the storekeeper only gives half a dozen for that price."

"A worker only earns eight hundred and seventy francs in a month. His family cannot buy eggs." Pierrette's voice carried traces of her anger.

"It'll get better." Charmaine's conciliatory tone, in keeping with her quiet nature, usually soothed tempers.

"I've got news," Jacques announced. "François has been transferred to Fresnes prison."

"Why?" Madeleine stood up.

"Calm down, please. When he had his accident..." Julie threw a pointed look at Jacques. "The Gestapo wanted to deport him."

"But why? He didn't do anything wrong."

Pierrette snapped. "That's what they do. Thousands of innocent people were deported just because the Nazis didn't like the look of them."

Madeleine opened then closed her mouth.

"He is safe in prison. He has his own cell," Jacques said.

To distract Madeleine's attention, Bérangère asked, "Are Hughes and Daniel upstairs?"

"They'll be in later," Rose said.

Julie raised her eyebrows. Gontrand came in with Lyse-May and Félicité.

"These two sparrows are hungry. Feed them and we'll go to the pond to see if some ducks have come back."

If any ducks had returned, they were probably already in someone's pot, but nobody was going to say this aloud.

Gontrand and his granddaughters had just gone when the backstairs door opened cautiously. Daniel poked his head into the kitchen.

"Come in. Don't just stand in the doorway." Bérangère said.

"I have friends with me."

He turned round. Julie and Charmaine went to the backstairs. Xavier, Hughes and Daniel were helping two airmen out of the cellar. One of them had burns on his face. Bérangère sprang into action and put the first-aid case on the table. Chairs were pulled out for them. Charmaine rummaged in the pantry and added a jar of preserved beans to the stew.

They gave their names but asked to be called by their nicknames.

Sergeant Hortie's eyes were half-closed by the swelling of his face. "Thank you. Mrs. Caron has cleaned the burns, but she and her husband had to send me along. A woman friend of theirs guided me to Paris, and another woman to a café. And here I am."

"You can stay here until you heal, boy," Gontrand said.

"I'm Sergeant Moss. I came down in Saint-Mandé next to an anti-aircraft battery. I could hear the Germans talking. They shot a few times. I crawled away. I got to a place called Champian and decided to avoid the village, but I had been seen by two men. I told them who I was and they told me to hide in a haystack, and they'd come back within two hours. I didn't like the look in their eyes. So as soon as they had gone, I walked away as fast as I could across the field and through the woods. On my way toward Longjumeau, I met a man who said I must hide. He took me to his house and fed me. Then a young woman came to fetch me and we arrived in Paris at a café."

Julie tilted her head. "Are you Canadian?"

"I am. I flew with the RCAF."

"The Royal Canadian Air Force." There was pride in Paul's voice.

"You are safe here. We will get you on your way back to England as fast as we can, Sergeant Moss," Xavier said.

Julie shook her head. "I have heard that now our escapees are being concentrated in a camp near Fréteval because the British can't ensure their transport to England. What about joining a maquis?"

"A Résistance unit? I'm game. You take me to it."

"We will."

"And when I'm healed, I'll join you," Sergeant Hortie said.

"In the meantime, they can sleep in my brother's room," Pierrette said.

***

As Pierrette had predicted, her father had a new Citroën Rosalie, though when she examined the car, it didn't look entirely new.

"If you have nothing better to do at the moment, come and see Gontrand. He's asked for you."

Philippe glanced at his desk and the heap of untouched files. He closed the door and followed his daughter.

Dressed in his Sunday suit with tie, Gontrand acknowledged Philippe's awkward greetings. Pierrette slipped out.

"I asked you to come to inform you your son is in the Fresnes prison."

Alarm came over Philippe's face. "What happened?"

"He saved a German soldier's life."

"You don't make sense."

"According to the authorities, a terrorist shot the Fritz. It happens a lot these days. François, who was with Julie at the time, rushed to the soldier's aid. Now that he's a medical student, he carries a first-aid kit."

"When did he go into medicine?"

"Recently."

"If he saved the soldier, why is he in prison?"

"Your Nazi friends didn't believe he didn't know the terrorist. So they broke his fingers before throwing him in jail."

Philippe blanched. "His fingers? But... but..."

"Fortunately, we have connections. He spent time in the hospital getting his hand fixed. But your friendly Gestapo still sent him to prison."

Philippe cupped his face in his hands.

"No words? The future Germanic Europe isn't working anymore? Can you get your son out of prison or is this where your influence stops?"

Philippe heaved a groan of despair. "Things have gone wrong. I believed following Marshal Pétain was the right thing to do. You thought so too. I know you have changed and no longer support him, but it's not right. He is still our head of state."

"You're too stupid to understand, or are you so greedy that you didn't care about anything except lining your pockets?"

"I was working hard, employing people."

"Throwing Jewish business owners out to take over their enterprises and stores. Is that what you call employing people?"

"I paid them. If I hadn't done it, the German would have confiscated their businesses."

"Cretin! The time of reckoning is coming. The Allies are winning and the French are helping. Do you know how many chose to join the maquis? They formed the FFI. You don't know what it means? Forces Françaises de l'Intérieur. An army of nearly two hundred thousand men. They don't like collaborators like you."

After a moment of silence, Philippe said, "I received another miniature coffin in the mail."

"I see." Gontrand paused. "You have two choices. One, you go and confess your sins to a FFI commander and join them. Or, two, you keep on until we win, and you follow your masters when they run back to Germany. You can go now. In fact, you can go and applaud Pétain. He's visiting the bombing of the marshalling yards of La Chapelle. You heard about that, non?"

"I'm sorry, father."

After his son had gone, a single tear fought its way over the old man's wrinkles to lose itself in his white mustache.

***

Armand kept changing the meeting day and time. Although there wasn't much Gestapo activity in the sixteenth arrondissement, except for prisoners being brought to Number Eighty-Four of the avenue Foch, he didn't want to take a chance.

The kidnapping squad and even Popaul were present.

"First the bad news. Yves Lamont and a couple of his men have been captured by Gestapistes, tortured and shot. Yves' body was recovered by pious hands for burial. While alive, his eyes had been gouged out."

A hush of horror came from every chest.

"There were other gross mutilations on other résistants by the milice."

All bent their heads for a minute of silence.

"Although we don't work with the Francs Tireurs Partisans, I cannot stress enough the need for tight security. Popaul?"

"We successfully retrieved two of ours from a police van on the road to Compiègne."

He was cheered.

"A man, not so young, has asked many times to join my réseau. I told him I don't have a réseau. He insists I'm part of a réseau. The squad has taken turns following him. He goes home until he comes back to see me, or go out to shop."

"Your feelings?"

"I'd call him a résistant of the last minute. I'd like to know if he was involved in black market or something more nefarious. Many people, seeing the Allies are winning, want to change camps."

"He isn't short of money, like most of us are," Jambon said.

Bobard sighed. "No sign of a job."

"Take him to the country, next to a lake or river, and ask him," Xavier said. "If you don't like his answer, throw him in."

Julie raised a hand. "That's getting down to the Gestapo level."

"Not at all. He'll get back on shore and will know what can happen if he's trying to cross us." Pierrette's vehement words drew smiles.

"Actually, not such a bad idea," Armand said. "But before you do that, find out from the concierge and other neighbors how he spends his time. They might be willing to tell."

The squad agreed to take charge of that operation.

"Next what can be done about the children being deported from Drancy? That Alois Brunner is the most sadistic man in the Nazi organization."

Julie gritted her teeth. "He wants to cut down the next generation of Jews. The adults die and no children to keep procreating. That's his solution to the Jewish problem."

"Could the Red Cross not intervene?" Pierrette asked.

"It has been shut down by the authorities." Julie's hands emphasized her words.

Popaul made a fist. "It makes my blood boil! I could hit each one of them."

"When I was there, I saw a couple of ambulances in the compound," Pierrette said. "They take the sick to the prison hospital Rothschild."

A long discussion ensued.

"Could we persuade the next ambulance to take some children

along?" Julie asked.

Armand pursed his lips. "Supposing the nurses agree, what do we do with the children?"

"We can find families for them," Pierrette said.

Julie reddened with anger. "Remember, it's the Union Générale des Israélites de France who provides the authorities with lists of Jews for relocation. Jews selling out Jews to save their own skin!"

"Pierrette, since you know your way around Drancy, can you try to talk to an ambulance nurse and find out whether anything is possible?"

"I'll go tomorrow."

A few other matters were discussed before the meeting broke up.

Chapter Twenty-Six

Thursday, June 1, 1944

Dr. Katzenberg and Dr. Bignon came today to remove the plasters from Antoinette's legs and arm. She has been healing nicely. Julie and Pierrette have been getting her up every day to walk a few awkward steps. So she has been able to share some meals with us. Antoinette becomes tired after ten minutes, but I admire her determination. Julie is staying tonight.

The streets are not really safe. There's a strange current in the air and people are getting both anxious and excited. Yet, we're all exhausted. I don't know whether it's because four years of Occupation is causing so much food shortage and death, or because we keep running from store to store to get the bare minimum for the children.

The Germans must be feeling it too, because they only move in groups and they don't sing anymore. Not so many young blond gods. In fact, the majority we see on the streets are much older. They must be reservists, but they still go to Montmartre and the cabararet despite all the attacks by the FTP.

My husband is hollering at the children to keep quiet. It must be BBC time.

As usual, the voice announced personal messages. Among them, *Les sanglots longs des violons de l'automne*. The familiar voice repeated the message, but it was drowned by the cheers and hurrahs from Julie, Hughes and Pierrette.

"This is it! The message that the landing is imminent. This is the first part, we have to get ready." Julie's excitement was contagious.

"Chut! There's more. *Le premier accroc coûte 200 francs*." Pierrette jumped up. "That's for the railroad Résistance Green Plan to get ready!"

"What does the first rip costs 200 francs mean?" Bérangère asked.

"It's the green baize of a billiard table. That's for the sabotage of the railroad system," replied Pierrette.

"It's taken from the title of a book," Julie said.

Bérangère nodded. She considered it better not to try to understand the relevance.

***

Early in the morning Julie called in at Popaul's in case he had news she ought to know, but before they could talk, Armand entered the kitchen.

"Glad to find you, Julie." He extracted a wad of papers from his salesman's briefcase. "Plans of action to be distributed. Take them to the bookstore in rue de la Pompe."

"I will, this minute. First tell me where I can contact you should something go wrong?"

Armand scratched his head. "Nothing will go wrong, but I'll be in the Église de la Madeleine at ten. I'm meeting several leaders separately and expect to be there about an hour."

"We must always be prepared for the worst," Popaul said.

"My sentiment," Julie said. "So if you see me in the church wearing this mantilla over my hat, take cover, it means danger." She showed him the black lace scarf, then put it back in her purse next to the documents.

"Smart as usual. Popaul, here are yours."

Armand left as fast as he came in. Julie followed, excitement coursing through her veins. It was finally happening.

Many unsmiling faces and dull eyes in the Métro alerted Julie. She couldn't explain to herself why it bothered her. Another glance at her traveling companions didn't make the feeling evaporate. She changed line at the Trocadéro station for rue de la Pompe. Once at the top of the stairs she turned her head as if to orient herself. Only a few of the passengers that were in her car had come out. At a normal pace, she started toward the rue de la Pompe. There she stopped on the sidewalk, watching for German traffic. Others did it too. What she saw farther down the street was a too familiar sight.

She crossed the street without delay. Several black traction-avant and an ambulance in the vicinity of the bookstore signified disaster. She kept walking, saw a queue at a grocer's store and joined it. People came behind her. It didn't take long for her to learn that a group of soldiers had been fired on and the Feldgendarmes had shot whoever was in the vicinity, including the owners of the bookstore, the fishmonger and an unfortunate woman with her baby, innocent people, bystanders, who had nothing to do with the assassination carried out by the FTP.

Julie had no intention of staying long in the queue. Her large purse slung across the shoulder, she checked her ration tickets. A woman turned to her.

"Aren't you Madame Marchand's sister?"

Though startled, Julie recovered quickly. "Yes, I am Brigitte's sister." This was her friend's usual shopping area.

"We haven't seen her in a long time. Is she alright?"

"She had to go to the country, we have family there, because Sylvestre, the younger boy, was sick and we thought it was poliomyelitis."

"Oh, dear! Was it?"

"Non, fortunately, it was only a lack of vitamins."

"Not surprising with the food our children have to eat these days. And now it's even less."

"Who's that man back there? He isn't from around here," someone said.

Julie tensed, but like every woman turned her head to stare at the only man in the queue. She only needed one glance to identify the better fed man, the sharp features with a spiteful crease of the mouth. She was first to resume her position. "*Milicien*," she whispered.

Her words didn't have the quiet effect she expected. The women's eyes sent daggers toward the man. A phrase was being repeated, "What is he doing here?" louder and louder. Julie joined in. The militia man knew better than to confront a crowd of angry women. Perhaps he had been told about the women of the rue de Buci. Though it was two years previously, it was still being talked about. He strode past and away.

Time was passing and Julie needed an excuse to leave. She looked at her watch.

"Got somewhere to go, my dear?"

"As a matter of fact, today I have a few hours work in a hotel. If I wait for my turn, I'll be late, and there might not be anything left in the store anyway."

A chorus of sighs responded to her sorry tone of voice.

"You can go ahead," one woman said.

"Thank you, that's very kind, but if there's anything left, you better have it for your children. I'm alone. I'll manage."

Warm words of thanks followed her as she turned back toward the Trocadéro. Unless Oberleutnant Schäfer was in an important meeting, he'd be delighted to escort her to one of the most beautiful churches in Paris. At the bottom of avenue Kléber she spotted a vélo-taxi and climbed in.

Madame LePlouhëc greeted her, but Julie cut the civilities short.

"Is Schäfer around?"

"In his office. Something wrong?"

"I nearly got caught. If he's with me, I'll be safe."

"Ah, couriering instructions. Go, when *ces messieurs* ask for you, I'll tell them you were requisitioned."

Julie chuckled all the way to the Oberleutnant's office.

Although the weather wasn't auspicious for strolling, Julie felt safer to walk than take the Métro. They entered the forecourt of the church by one of the spaces in the low wrought-iron railings. Manfred Schäfer stopped at the foot of the steps to admire the classical Greek façade adorned with its eight fluted Corinthian columns. Once inside, Julie began to breathe easier and she took her time to arrange her mantilla over her dainty hat.

"Why the veil over the hat?"

"Some might consider it too frivolous for church."

Manfred gallantly put coins in the alms box. At that moment, the organ unleashed a Bach cantata.

"This is so beautiful. Such a huge organ," Manfred said.

With measured steps, Julie guided her escort around the church, murmuring all she knew of its history, which, she suddenly realized, wasn't much, but Manfred appeared totally entranced by the music and the beauty of the light pouring through the lunettes in the roof, light which illuminated the intricate sculpture over the altar and gave warmth to the many-hued marble.

While his head was looking upward, Julie's eyes searched the few people sitting in the pews. They were the regulars who came to listen to Édouard Mignan's organ practice. On the edge, by the side of the magnificently sculpted pulpit, sat Armand and a man. She adjusted her mantilla. He saw her. His head tilted and gave a nod.

Finally, back at the Majestic, Julie was asked to supervise the staff for a small meeting. She had difficulty controlling her impatience, though it was rewarding to ascertain that the Germans had no idea where the landing would take place.

"They cannot land without a port, so it has to be Calais or Dunkerque."

"Or Boulogne."

"We have reinforced all the batteries in those areas, and the majority of our frontline troops are waiting there."

Carl-Heinrich Stülpnagel shuffled the papers in front of him. "What is the progress on the Moyecques site?"

"It has been abandoned. The English dropped an earthquake bomb on it at the beginning of July. Hundreds of workers were entombed. Many of our engineers too. But the work continues on the German site. It will soon launch the first missile. Then there will be no talk of landing."

Guffaws greeted the speaker's words. The meeting broke up and Julie hurried to the office where she wrote down the comments she'd overheard in the meeting.

"They are delusional."

"Then it's to our advantage, non?" Full of glee, Madame LePlouhëc left to get the message sent to London.

Julie wondered how she could get the documents that were burning a hole in her bag either back to Armand or to an alternative letter box. She didn't look forward to traveling in the Métro with them.

Madame LePlouhëc came back. "Still here?"

"I'm carrying dynamite in my purse. I don't know whether any of ours have been caught in the vengeful retaliation of the rue de la Pompe."

"Go to your in-laws. If someone comes here for you, what do they say?"

"This week, it's, *I have a recipe for topinambours*."

"Good. I'll be here until after supper. Here, have some money. Go out front and take a vélo-taxi. It's raining. And take my umbrella, I have another one."

When Julie came out and crossed the road, the guards didn't move from the shelter of their black, white and red sentry boxes, on either side of the hotel's lion statues. The chance of a vélo-taxi was slim. She strode on. A little way farther, she heard the splash of wheels.

"I can get you home faster, ma'am."

"Yes, please."

The wiry driver of a certain age jumped off the bicycle and unhooked a tarpaulin off the trailer. She sat and he pulled it over her legs. She gave the address and while hanging onto the umbrella, she reached in her purse for the bill Madame LePlouhëc had given her. Her thoughts whirled around her head. She had become aware that the young men who used to run vélo-taxis had given way to much older men. Had they all joined the maquis? She hoped that was the case and not that they had been caught and sent to work in Germany.

In the west wing, she was pleased to see Antoinette's progress. Gontrand had taken it upon himself to retrain the young woman to walk.

They were about to sit down to a carefully apportioned supper when there was a knock on the door. Lyse-May jumped off her chair to open it.

"Armand!" Julie stood. "Belle-maman, beau-papa, meet Armand. He's a good friend of Bernard's." She then introduced Antoinette, Lyse-May and her cousins.

Before he sat, he pulled out a black market Camembert from his briefcase.

"Did you substi... subtilized it from the Fritz?" Lyse-May asked.

He chortled. "Absolutely. I'm a magician."

"You're not Arsène Lupin?"

They laughed.

"Sometimes I am, other times I use magic."

"Good, you'll have to show me."

They shared the meal and the Camembert.

Lyse-May, Paul and Micheline went to revise their lessons with Antoinette.

Bérangère took her knitting and Gontrand sucked on the stem

of his empty pipe. Julie could no longer contain her impatience.

"Did anybody get caught?"

"All accounted for except Milou. One of our contacts. The concierge next to the bookstore thinks he was one of victims. We're all meeting tomorrow night at Hôtel de Saint-Simon. Our friendly waiter will collect the plans from you in the menu and distribute them to my lieutenants as they arrive. It's going to make a dent in our funds, but with the activities of the Feldgendarmes and the milice, it's the safest way."

Hughes and Pierrette made a noisy entrance.

"Oops! Sorry."

"What did you learn?" Armand asked.

"Milou took a bullet in the arm but played dead. The ambulance took him to the Bichat hospital. I'll take him out tomorrow to a safe house until he heals. The two couriers that were arriving were far enough away and hid with other people in an apartment block," Pierrette said.

"We've been lucky."

Julie made a face of distaste. "Not only do we have to be on our guard from the Gestapo, we also have to look out for the FTP's irresponsible actions."

"That man that wanted to join the réseau? He checked out. He laughed at being dunked into the pond and said he understood. He had a thriving black market business. Not a particularly bad individual, more of an opportunist. His concierge said he never spouted Vichy propaganda."

"I'll tell Popaul to send him to our contact in the FTP. We don't want him to overhear sensitive intelligence accidentally."

Armand departed, but Julie stayed for the night.

***

When Julie arrived at the Hôtel de Saint-Simon, she worried about the preponderance of men in the restaurant.

"It's fine." Armand stood and held a chair for her. "We've been assured the Fritz don't come here. It's too much out of their way. They've been avoiding narrow streets and especially cul-de-sacs."

"The milice may not have such qualms."

"The FTP put a target on their backs."

"I never thought I'd say good, but... Anyway, it's not long now before our Allies land."

Armand sighed. "The Boches won't give up without a hard fight."

She chased a small piece of meat around her plate. "We'll help. This is rabbit, I'm sure. But it's good."

"Eat, then we'll go and listen to the radio."

***

Monday, June 5, 1944

Julie dropped into a chair at the Manoir. Armand had already arrived with Pierrette and Hughes. "It's incredible that those Fritz are still talking about victory, the losses in Africa and in Russia just being setbacks. They don't have enough men to occupy our country, so they're sending veterans of the First War and sixteen-year-old youth."

"It sounds to me like desperation," Bérangère said.

Armand was quiet. Julie frowned as she looked at him. He sighed.

"One of ours happened to walk into a Gestapo raid. They turned him in no time and he spilled all he knows. Word has got out. No one is to use the letter boxes and everyone is moving out. I have new digs."

"Where?" Julie asked.

"Rue de la Faisanderie. You know the apartment. Pierrette gave me the keys."

They all nodded. Bernard was in England. As for Marie-Ange, they preferred not to think about her.

"What about you, Julie? Where can you stay?"

"She can stay here, of course," Gontrand said.

"It's too dangerous for you, beau-papa. I'll stay in Maude's old apartment."

"Aunt Berthe and uncle Eugene have moved there since the rail yards in Suresnes were bombed."

"It's about time I get back to my apartment on rue Victor-Hugo."

"Hughes and I always make sure we leave from the Sorbonne as if we'd been studying all day."

Hughes grinned. "Sometimes we do."

"About the children in Drancy? When an ambulance goes there, they load a few children," Pierrette said.

Gontrand stood and uncovered the radio. "News time, silence, everyone!" Static garbled the announcer's voice until he adjusted the frame antenna of copper wire.

"And now for the personal messages. Les carottes sont cuites. Armand seized Julie's hand and squeezed it hard. Her eyes were shining. The carrots are cooked indicated the location. "Normandie," she whispered. Next, "bercent mon coeur d'une langueur monotone."

"This is it! Tomorrow, it's tomorrow! The Allies are landing!"

They all stood in the kitchen and embraced one another. The children ran in, followed by Marie and Ernest. "Is it true?"

"It is."

"Madame Julie, would you go and tell monsieur Reynard?"

She untangled herself and hurried into the Manoir. von Trennen was in his office. He too had listened to the radio and knew something was happening.

"It's real, Reynard. The Résistance got their messages. It's for tomorrow."

"I deduced as much. In Normandy, isn't it?"

"Indeed. Thank you for the map of the defensive batteries along the beaches. It did get to the Allies."

"The High-Command couldn't believe they were bringing an artificial port." He chuckled. "Too full of themselves. Now it is just a matter of time."

"What about you?"

"I shall be alright, for the immediate future, at least."

Julie went back into the kitchen and Armand took his leave. Julie helped Bérangère prepare lentils for the next day.

"That man Armand is in love with you."

"What?" Dumbfounded, Julie stood still.

Bérangère chuckled. "I thought you'd be the last one to notice."

"I'm sorry for him. I only have one love and I know that Sylvain went back to England after Jean Moulin, the leader of the Résistance, was betrayed and died last July. The Gestapo have a price on Sylvain's head."

"This awful business is coming to an end now. You'll soon be reunited."

In the morning streets witnessed a feverish activity as Julie made her way to avenue Kléber. People rushed to the stores, shoving and pushing before running back home with whatever food they were able to obtain. At the Majestic, too, officers ran about, shouting, slamming doors and barking orders.

Julie navigated between the harassed clerks and irate officers.

"Thirty-four loaded trucks for the Normandie front burnt to the ground by those terrorists!"

"Where?"

"Rue Picpus."

She retreated to Madame LePlouhëc's office. Chef Raoul joined them with boxes of canned food, which they piled against the wall. Much later, when the ruckus diminished, she went to Stülpnagel's floor. Behind his closed door, voices were raised but not enough for her to make out the words.

Around noon, she descended to the main dining room where officers adopted a more philosophical view to the news that the Allies had tricked them.

"Let the generals organize the troops. We only need to keep administering France and making sure that our troops can reinforce those in Normandie."

"We have to get road signs made. It takes a while."

"Surely you can get some boards and paint them with *Zur Normandie Front*. Not too difficult."

"Let's not worry, our troops will throw them back into the sea."

"My dear Schäfer, why are you not out there bombing the hell out of the English?"

"Not enough planes."

They laughed, believing it was a joke. Julie knew it wasn't. Manfred had told her it was a real concern for the Luftwaffe, but their pilots were the best.

When she left in the evening, the streets were deserted. On all the houses, the shutters were closed. It was a reminder of the Exode of 1940. She sighed and climbed the stairs to her apartment, carrying her bag of cans from Chef Raoul's stash. She hoped that one day, Léonie would be back to surprise her as she put the key in the lock.

There were so many instructions to communicate, Julie spent most days bicycling to all parts of Paris. Once it was known that the Allies had landed, but that it would take several weeks before they'd arrive in the city, Parisians came out again. The hand-painted *Zur Normandie Front* cheered them no end, especially when some daredevil youths repositioned them to point north.

At a meeting in the Cave, Julie noticed there was a number of men and young women she hadn't met before. No introductions were made.

Armand opened the meeting. "The *Comité Parisien de Libération* is calling for the formation of *Milices Patriotiques.* Urgently."

"But the communists have been trying to organize the patriotic milice since last summer."

"Not to be mistaken for the Vichy milice. This is the Parisian Committee for Liberation."

Armand flicked his hand. "The SOE now thinks that the Milices Patritotic are a good idea and they will depend on the *Conseil National de la Résistance.* They will be put under the command of the *Forces Françaises Libres* and organized along military lines. Obedience and discipline are of utmost importance. We're going to have a tricolor armband with M P in the white. Daniel?"

He picked up the bag at his feet and stood. "My mother has already made some." He showed one to the assembly and handed it to Armand.

"There's one for each of you," Armand said.

"Will we participate in the action with the FFI?"

"Like in an army, there are different levels. The *groupes francs* will be at the forefront."

"Like the guerilla units in the maquis?"

Armand nodded, though Julie wondered if anyone could see him through the haze of cigarette smoke. He must have read her thoughts. "Right. The objectives are to impair the movement of German troops, the recuperation of arms and vehicles. We'll enhance our communications and create a health service as well as a supply chain."

"What are you going to be?"

"I've been appointed second-lieutenant in the FFI and will command a platoon. I'll be able to select some of you. When I'm not available, Fox, my second in command, will be in charge."

Julie rose and acknowledge the introduction with a nod.

"You have all heard de Gaulle's speech that we must fight the occupiers by all the means at our disposal. He has also formed the provisional government of France while still in Algiers. If you are not sure why I'm telling you all this, here is the reason. The Americans do not want Général de Gaulle to govern France. They, themselves, want to occupy us and set up an American military government in France."

Armand had to stop speaking until the boos directed to the Americans died down. "They have actually already printed money to replace our French francs, without the familiar République Française." Another volley of boos exploded. "We, Frenchmen and Frenchwomen, must liberate ourselves." Cheers rose with enough strength to chase the smoke to the ceiling. "In the country, the maquis are fighting battles and weakening the enemy. Fortunately, the SOE is ignoring the politics and supplying the Résistance with arms and expert advisors. We will win!" A burst of applause erupted. "We'll review our organization. Each chef de groupe will command four men. Group leaders do not take part in any action." The discussion went on for a while until Armand called an end to the meeting.

A voice rose singing. "*Ami, entends-tu le vol noir des corbeaux sur nos plaines,*" which was taken up by all the voices, "Friend, do you hear the raven's dark flight over our plains,

Friend, do you hear the mournful cries of our country put in chains...

...Friend, if you fall, a friend will come out from the shadows to take your place..."

The song over, Julie and Pierrette collected the spent cigarette butts in a bag.

"Pretty awful tobacco," Pierrette said.

"But some old men will be happy to roll new cigarettes out of that lot."

"Ugh!"

***

"Madame Julie!" The concierge hailed Julie as she was taking her bicycle out. "A boy brought an envelope early this morning. It's so nice to have you back. I'm locking the gate and the front door. The Fritz are stealing bicycles."

"I noticed a few soldiers actually bicycling."

"Back to Germany. Can you believe it? That's what they're doing. Trying to get home before the Ricains arrive here."

"I won't leave my bicycle outside anywhere. I've been so busy I didn't even stop to chat."

Madame Durand smiled. "I've seen you rush out. So is it really true, the Ricains have landed?"

"Oui, madame. The Americans, the English, the French and others of our Allies are now fighting the Germans on French soil."

The lugubrious wail of the siren cut short their talk. Soon after, the rumble of the flak had them shaking their heads.

"It's in the north of the city," Madame Durand said. "Shall we go to the cellar?"

"The Mahut family isn't going?"

"It's only Monsieur and Madame Mahut. Their sons have joined the maquis."

"Any special guests?"

"Two in Madame Bodénan's apartment, one in the apartment opposite. Dieu I was so glad to see back of those SS men. Though, I must admit they never bothered anyone here. They left the apartment clean and tidy. Monsieur Albert Sagot is still in prison. We don't use his apartment, but I did let a Jewish family use the Bizinzskis' apartment. Have you found out any news about Madame Bodénan?"

"Alas, no. Léonie seems to have just disappeared."

Madame Durand shook her head. "Such a nice woman. But I'm keeping you. Off you go."

Julie climbed on her bicycle, a smile on her lips. A couple of hundred meters away, she saw Charmaine leaning on her bicycle.

"La pipelette can talk forever!"

"Blame Victor-Hugo's legacy. He made the concierge Pipelet in *Les Misérables* talk and gossip exceedingly."

"Anyway, I was going to see her to find out how many guests are there, and if they have some photos with them."

"Go ahead, she'll be happy to introduce you. Here, have my compact and take a picture of each of them. It saves a lot of trouble."

Charmaine whistled. "What a beauty! Don't you need it to photograph secret documents?"

"There hasn't been much need or opportunity of late. Leave it with Madame Durand when you bring the papers. I'll get it later. You're not still singing with Wolfang, are you?"

"Oh, yes! Would you believe Otto Abetz is having a reception in a couple of days? They exist in a different world, I think."

They kissed and went on their separate ways. As Julie arrived at the Champs-Élysées, she had to stop. Stunned, like several other cyclists, she heard, then had to watch the men of the First Sicherundsregiment as they marched up the Champs-Élysées playing *Preussens Gloria.* After they passed, she heard someone say, "They are totally oblivious to anything!" Murmurs of agreement were heard. Julie pedaled on, darting looks around, aware of all noises, especially vehicle engines.

Her last call was to Yolande to tell her about the Bizinzski apartment. Lucienne, the new concierge, greeted Julie.

"Mademoiselle Bourgmestre has just come back."

"No need to be so formal, Lucienne."

"I haven't been a concierge for very long. Some of the tenants want to be called by their titles. I thought we did away with counts and barons after the Révolution."

Julie laughed. "Vanity, that's all it is, vanity." She climbed the stairs slower than usual, her legs heavy after pedaling for most of the day.

"You can use the Bizinzskis' apartment. Here are the keys."

"Great. We need more safe houses. The Gestapo and the milice have unleashed their fury on us."

"Retaliation for the Allied landing."

"Go home, they've advanced the curfew again."

"Are you coming to tomorrow Sunday lunch?

"Of course. I wouldn't miss it."

Chapter Twenty-Seven

A somber atmosphere reigned over the west wing. Not only had they just heard that, in Tulle, the Das Reich Division had hanged ninety-nine men and adolescents and deported another three hundred, but they had committed another atrocity in Oradour-sur-Glane.

Jacques shook himself. "They shot all the men and burned all the women and children alive in the church for no reason at all. There were no maquis there."

"The maquisards had attacked the garrison in Tulle and won. The town was liberated. The Germans had surrendered. No one knew the Das Reich division was on its way north toward Normandie, killing and burning its way," Julie said.

"What makes me so angry and want to scream is that this hardened criminal Laffont went from Paris to Tulle with a hundred of his sadistic convicts and carried out those gruesome hangings, gratuitous killings, alongside the Boches," Jacques said.

"So the massacre was premeditated!" There was so much anger in Julie's voice it made her shudder.

Lyse-May leaned against her. "What's a massacre?" The adults remained silent. "I know. The bad men killed a lot of good men."

At that moment, Madeleine arrived. One or two tears were promptly wiped out and the children were encouraged to go and play.

Later, Julie took Madeleine aside. "You should move to the Manoir with Félicité. The streets are not safe. Philippe has been threatened."

"What do you mean?"

"He has received miniature coffins in the mail. They are death threats."

Madeleine looked alarmed. "He said it was a joke."

"Not at all. Many people want to punish collaborateurs."

"But he only did what Marshal Pétain ordered."

Julie shook her head. "He did, but please consider moving for Félicité's sake."

Madeleine made no reply. She gave Julie a worried look. She picked up Félicité and left.

Pierrette sidled up to Julie. "What will it take to convince my mother the situation is serious?"

"I've run out of arguments."

Pierrette sighed. "I'm going with you."

Julie winked. "Xavier didn't come today."

"He had to work. Oh, here's Mireille." Pierrette went to her sister. "You heard that the Allies have landed and that the Germans are being pushed back to Germany?"

"No, they are not! Don't you know how powerful the German army is?"

"Not anymore. I just want to warn you of what will happen to you and women like you who cavorted with the Germans. Your Baron Dieter von Hauffen won't be there to protect you."

Mireille looked down at her shorter sister. "You and your little sabotages, you'll soon be in prison. The Germans have been very tolerant with your sort, but it's over now. Time for a crackdown." She turned her back and continued on to Count de la Ferrière's mansion that the baron had requisitioned.

Pierrette shrugged and caught up with Julie. "A fat Fritz came to the café where I work sometimes and asked if I knew who could sell him a civilian suit."

"I saw a clerk from the MBF exchanging money with one of the waiters and going off with a bundle of dark cloth, definitely a suit."

"They want to desert, but they'd be instantly recognized. They are too well fed to pass for Parisians."

With a laugh, they climbed on their bicycles and went their various ways.

***

Friday, July 14, 1944

We agreed that we wouldn't go to the Arc de Triomphe for the national day, not just because the military command forbade it, but because it'd be an unnecessary risk. The antsy Boches are trigger happy. We stood in the street and watched people go and put flags at the windows. We mostly weren't using the word Boche anymore, but I noticed its use has crept back in. Women in the queue who were careful to use Fritz, Fridolins, Chleus, Frisés and Doryphores are now calling them Boches, and that's definitely pejorative and showing our hatred for them. I was saying we wouldn't join the parade for Bastille Day, but the communists have organized a parade and just about everyone wanted to join in and get the flags out. I couldn't hold our young people back. Of course, Julie promised to look after Lyse-May. I know she'd give her life for my granddaughter. Thankfully, all that banner waving didn't end in disaster. The police didn't intervene. They just watched while people sang the Marseillaise. It seems that the population has been galvanized into action to do its part to fight the Boches.

The allied troops are still in Normandie, still too far away to make any difference here. In the meantime, Xavier reports that trains filled with Jews are still going eastward. Damned SS sending little children to those camps. We heard about the atrocious conditions. It's so inhumane.

I should go and read what the Boches have prohibited this time. Next it will be forbidden to breathe.

"In the event of action:

· it is prohibited for the population to circulate in the streets and public places between sunset and sunrise

· public entertainment venues will be closed

· it is forbidden to serve alcohol

· giving information to the enemy will be considered treason and dealt with as such

· any civilian taking part in combat will be considered a partisan and dealt with accordingly."

Not much different from what it has been up to now.

***

On Sunday, a few minutes before lunch, Marie entered pushing a dessert cart loaded with canned foods, bags of peas, beans and flour, as well as bottles of oil. Reynard followed. Julie introduced Armand.

"Gerhardt has gone to Meudon with Günter and hopefully they can bring madame Brigitte back. I think she will be safer among you. Günter, my driver and my groom have cleaned and repainted her apartment, but I want her to be persuaded to stay at the Manoir. The Francs Tireurs et Partisans are calling for an insurrection. It is too early for that. There is no back up yet. I hope they understand."

"Please, stay and have lunch with us."

"Thank you, madame Bérangère. I have dismissed my staff, but Günter does not want to go. My days are hanging by a thread. You've heard that there has been an attempt on Hitler's life a couple of days ago, on the twentieth. Admiral Canaris has been arrested. I shall be next."

"No! We're going to hide you!" Julie said.

He shook his head. "No, not hiding. I hope the Americans or the French arrive soon enough so I can surrender to them."

"They're too far away. You can surrender to FFI Second-Lieutenant Armand when the time's right."

All eyes turned toward Armand. "I'll accept your surrender in due course."

Bewildered, Madeleine helped her daughter off the chair. Antoinette and Marianne volunteered to supervise the youngsters outside.

Unsure of herself, Madeleine sat next to Julie. "I think you're right. I should come and live here, but I'd be in the way. There's not enough room in the west wing."

Reynard overheard. "You will take a room in the Manoir, like you used to before..."

"Won't it be awkward, Mr. von Trennen?"

He smiled. "Not at all, I had only wanted to rent a room in the Manoir when I came here. I still hope you will retake possession of your home, madame Bérangère, even before I leave."

He was duly thanked.

Gontrand put down his fork. "We might do that. You're part of the family. I see no problem sharing."

When the adults had finished eating, Lyse-May strolled in and leaned against the table in front of Jacques.

"Uncle Jacques, what's *Honneur de la Police?*"

"Where did you hear that?"

She looked at him for a second or two. "I don't know."

No one believed her, but they kept it to themselves.

"I think you already know about the Résistance."

"Of course."

"Well, *Honneur de la Police* is the name of a Résistance group. Now what will you do with this information?"

"I'll keep it to myself. I'm seven and three-quarters. It's the age of reason."

"I trust you."

Spontaneously, the little girl threw her arms around his neck, then scampered off.

Gontrand scooted his chair close to Jacques'. "How did you survive the purge of the high-ranking officers?"

"I have an impeccable record... on paper anyway."

Reynard was the first one to laugh. "Alexandre doesn't only do photography."

Pierrette started washing the dishes. Julie and Charmaine dried them.

"Yolande didn't come today."

Pierrette took her eyes off the china in the sink. "She worries me. She heard that there was an order from that awful man Alois Brunner to round up all the Jewish children in the orphanages to be taken to Drancy for deportation. Then when I went to the Ritz, I was told she'd left."

"Mon Dieu! She's going to try to save as many as she can," Julie said.

Charmaine stopped drying with a plate in mid-air. "Don't tell Hughes. He'd join his sister right away. I fear for her."

"I'll try to find out what's going on," Julie said.

Pierrette dried her hands. "Me too."

***

The director of the Louveciennes children's home didn't believe Yolande.

"Surely, this home was created by the UGIF. So they wouldn't hand it over to the SS."

"Please believe me. The sources of my group are adamant. The commandant of the Drancy camp has ordered that all the children, from the homes belonging to the Union Générale des Israélites de France, are to be taken to Drancy for deportation. We have time to save most of the children here."

"It's inconceivable. They wouldn't take two-year-olds."

An alert sounded. Yolande pitched in to help take the children to the cellar.

When the all-clear sounded, it was past supper time. Yolande helped feed the little ones whom she had comforted during the bombing.

"It's too late for you to go back to Paris. Would you like to stay?"

"Thank you. I'll stay."

In the gray dawn, Yolande jumped up from the narrow bed she'd been given. She ran to the open window and heard the distinct rumble of buses. With haste, she dressed and finished tying her hair while she ran to the director's room. "They're here!"

The director crossed herself as the buses screeched to a stop. Soldiers surrounded the large old house.

***

"Where's Hughes?" Pierrette's scream brought Bérangère and Julie running.

"Why?"

"He didn't come home."

A gasp was followed by silence.

Pierrette slumped. "I went out early to try to get some bread. I met a friend. She was crying. She said on Sunday several youth groups were going to collect arms and ammunition, but it was a trap. They were taken to the Bois de Boulogne yesterday and executed. Hughes had said he was going to help a friend unload an ammunitions truck."

"Did she say where in the Bois de Boulogne?"

"At the Cascade."

"I'll go and see Jacques to find out what happened."

Julie was climbing on her bicycle when a police van pulled into the courtyard. A gendarme helped Hughes out and supported him. Julie rushed to them and took Hughes' other arm. With their help, he hopped into the west wing kitchen and sat on a chair. Pierrette and her grandmother had been watching. They rushed to his side. His clothes were filthy and torn.

"*Merci, monsieur le gendarme*," Bérangère said. "Anything we need to know?"

He drew his sleeve across his eyes. "Your nephew was lucky.

Thirty-five of his comrades were massacred yesterday. They were lured by a Gestapo agent, shot and killed with grenades. I must go now."

After he left, the women waited for Hughes to finish an ersatz with a little of the sugar that Bérangère had hoarded. They undressed him and washed him. Marie came in with clean clothes. Bérangère and Maude examined his swollen knee and ankle. He winced.

"Not broken, I think," Maude said.

The two nurses bandaged the knee and ankle. They succeeded in sliding the leg into his shorts. Antoinette attracted by the commotion had looked in and taken the children outside, despite their protests.

Hughes sighed. "I'm sorry. Thursday evening I was to help a friend. We climbed into trucks. I wasn't comfortable and looked outside. I began to recognize the quartier. The truck started along rue des Saussaies and I realized, it was a trap. I told my friends and slipped under the canvas by the tailgate. I let myself fall and roll into the gutter. My leg hurt, but I bit my arm and remained immobile, like dead. By the noise, I knew the boys in the truck were taken into the SD offices. Another truck almost ran over me. The boys were thrown back into the trucks. I could hear them. They drove away. I didn't move until there was no more noise. I crawled into a building and hid in the courtyard in the bicycle shelter all night. The concierge found me this morning. He said not to move, he was getting help from a résistant. He came back with the gendarme."

Gontrand put his hand on his nephew's shoulder. "You acted like a man. I'm proud of you."

***

Madame Durand waited for Julie. "There's a letter, but not a post office letter. A boy brought it early this morning."

Julie took it, examined it, and frowned.

"What is it?"

Dear Madame Durand, still as curious as ever. "This is my cousin Yolande's handwriting."

"Well, open it. You need a knife?"

Julie gave up and followed the concierge into the lodge. Her eyes widened. She read aloud.

Dearest Julie, I hope this note will reach you. I'm in Drancy. I was helping at the Louveciennes orphanage. All the children and staff have been brought here. They came for us at four in the morning. I stayed with the children and I'm taking care of seven of them. The youngest is barely two. A young woman, Denise Holstein, is taking care of nine. Send a parcel and paper if you can. Yolande.

"Poor mademoiselle Yolande. Can you get her out?"

"I'll try. I must go and consult our team." She folded and inserted the letter into her dress pocket and mounted her bicycle. Pierrette was still at the Manoir when she pulled into the courtyard.

Pierrette, her grandparents and Julie sat close together at one end of the big oak table.

"I knew she wanted to try to save those children, that's what she's been doing with Blanche Auzello at the Ritz. She'd heard that that monster in charge of Drancy planned to kill every single Jewish orphan in and around Paris. I'll take a parcel." She turned to Julie. "Can you write to her? We might be able to get her out, she isn't Jewish."

"I hope so. Though, she might have the idea that if she goes to Auschwitz, she could find her mother." Julie became worried.

Bérangère handed her a sheet of paper and a pen. "I think you may be right. We made some ink. It's not too bad. Keep the blotter on the paper."

Pierrette fetched her backpack. "Do we have a bottle of wine to bribe my gendarme? And a can of Olida ham? The ham is for his children, the wine is for the Feldgendarme, who has a gimpy leg and would prefer to be home with his wife."

Gontrand had already gone to fetch a bottle of Beaujolais. "But it's Sunday."

"Don't worry, grand-papa, they don't go to church." With that last quip, she departed.

Brigitte settled in one of the bedrooms in the Manoir, and baby Étienne won everybody's heart. Not surprisingly, Gerhardt spent much of his time at the Manoir.

The Citroën Rosalie pulled into the courtyard. Charmaine and Julie were betting on ten suitcases. There were only five. Madeleine took the same bedroom she had used in times past.

At dinner time, Pierrette came back. "Parcel delivered. I'll go back Friday, when the gendarme goes back to work at the same time as his Feldgendarme friend."

Gontrand rubbed his chin. "I do have another bottle of Beaujolais. Not many bottles of wine left, though."

"We'll manage. Don't worry."

Friday evening reunited the family. Consternation reigned as they read again how the milice and SS soldiers had liquidated the Vercors maquis.

Fatigue accentuated Bérangère's wrinkles. "More than six hundred good people killed. Is that advancing the liberation?"

Her bitterness was echoed by Charmaine. "They killed the wounded and the medics. They killed the villagers who live on the plateau du Vercors. It's barbaric!"

Pierrette put Yolande's letter on the table and pushed it toward Julie. "Please read it."

Julie opened the envelope. "*Dear Hughes...* Maybe you want to read it to us, Hughes?"

He hesitated. "You read it, tante Julie."

Thank you for the children's clothes. My team was only half-dressed when we were pushed into the buses. The director of this dreadful Drancy camp was there in person and wanted it to be over before curfew so the townfolk wouldn't know about the raid. When we arrived at Drancy, the internees were appalled to see so many children. Many more had come from other homes. Over two hundred, I think. Maybe two hundred and fifty. It was heartbreaking to see how those little children were so disciplined. They didn't make any noise and did what they were told. They knew that they were in danger and instinctively did what they could to remain alive, to adapt. Some five-year- olds took care of three-year-olds. The internees helped us settle our charges in unused stairways. The conditions in the camp are abominable, the filth, lice and bedbugs incredible. We are scheduled to leave Monday 31st of July. It's train convoi numéro 77. The staff helpers from Louveciennes were released as they are not Jewish. I intend to accompany the children along with Mademoiselle Holstein to Auschwitz and I will try to find our mother. This is probably the last letter I can write. Be strong, Hughes. I'm strong and determined, I remember about the train slowing down at the Lérouville hill and will tell some résistants I met who will be on the train too. The war is almost over. I will come back with maman.

A long silence hung over the family. Hughes broke it. "I want to join the FFI and fight that scum of the earth."

"When the allied armies reach Paris, you can join the French," Gontrand said.

"I'm nineteen. Old enough to go now."

"It'd be impossible to travel to the front. If you're going to die, make sure it's worth it. And going to the Normandie front isn't."

Hughes pulled a face.

His grandfather couldn't hide his pride. "There is no doubt that there will be fighting in the city before long. You're already a member of the Milices Patriotiques. Armand will assign you a fighting role."

"Yes, we will have to fight because the Americans said they have no intention of liberating Paris. It's not on their way to Germany, and that's where they are going." Bitterness colored Pierrette's voice.

Stunned at the revelation, Bérangère said, "What do you mean they aren't coming to Paris?"

"We heard it directly from London. The High Command, that's mostly the Americans, don't consider Paris a strategic position, so they will let us starve and die fighting alone. I don't know what's wrong with the Americans."

Incomprehension spread over Bérangère's face. "But they did land thousands of men in Normandie."

"Yes, and we are grateful, but they don't understand that Paris is France. All eyes are turned on Paris."

"Pierrette understands the politics behind all this better than we do. However, in the meantime, it is of vital importance that we transmit intelligence reports, particularly of troop movement and numbers, to the allied armies," Julie said.

Not only Hughes but the other adults looked defeated. "What's the point of sending them intelligence if they are not coming?"

Julie raised both hands. "We don't know exactly what's happening, but you don't think General de Gaulle will sit back and wait until the Americans have taken Germany and come back for Paris, do you?"

"Oh, so he will take his own army of the Forces Françaises Libres that he put together in London, and come to liberate Paris," Charmaine said.

Gontrand snorted. "The Parisians will go to the barricades before that."

Hughes limped to the coat rack and came back in wearing a black béret, on his head, tilted over his right ear, a cross of Lorraine in evidence. "That's the FFI béret. Madame Rose has made lots of them."

"I hope you're not wearing it in the street," Bérangère said.

"Of course, not."

***

When the news that the Operation Walkyrie plot had failed and Hitler was still alive, Reynard joined the family. He carried a small case.

"The Gestapo is arresting everyone involved in the Schwarze Kapelle. They will come here, so I must be gone."

Armand accepted the surrender of General von Trennen, Captain Langen and Adjutant Klein.

"For your safety, I will take you to an empty apartment on your word of honor that you will not escape."

Reynard smiled. "You have my word."

Julie snapped her fingers. "My apartment is safe. Madame Durand will see to their needs."

Armand nodded. "We'll go as soon as it's dark."

"I'll drive the general's Mercedes. And I'll bring back a suitcase to stay here."

***

In the morning, all available hands moved effects and furniture from the west wing into the Manoir. As Reynard had requested, they took up to the attic the boxes he and his staff had to leave behind. By the end of the day, the reinstallation was complete. Hughes remained in the spare room while Antoinette and Lyse-May, who had been sharing a room, asked to remain in the west wing.

In the tense atmosphere of the capital and the incessant bombings around the city, life continued with fear and excitement for Parisians and ruthless determination for the couriers of the Résistance.

Armand and Jacques arrived together.

Jacques mopped his brow. "A heat wave! That's all we needed!"

After those years of living in the crowded kitchen of the west wing, it was natural for them to gather in the big kitchen of the Manoir. Marie was happy to resume cooking for the family, but now she had many helpers. The young children had finished eating. Madeleine ate with them and took them outside with the adolescents, except Marianne who, at sixteen, had begun to courier the false papers her father produced.

They heard the squeal of brakes before the pounding started on the front door. Ernest rushed followed by Jacques. They opened and five Gestapo men burst inside. They spread into the downstairs and upstairs rooms throwing doors open, and climbed up to the attic. One kicked the kitchen door. "Where are they?"

Bérangère stood up and, in a most haughty stance, glowered at them. "This is Count de Montregard's residence. If you're talking about the Germans that had requisitioned my home, they have fled."

The Unterleutnant was taken aback. Brigitte's youngest children had decided this was a time for crying loudly and they did soon joined in by the baby.

The SS officer recovered and opened his mouth. Bérangère didn't give him time to speak.

"You can leave now and don't slam the door behind you. It upsets the children."

"Madame, we have to know where the General von Trennen is."

"All we know is that they stole my husband clothes. They were no longer on the premises when we awoke."

Another SS man had come to stand behind the Unterleutnant. "*Niemand.*"

"Nobody?"

'*Niemand.*"

They turned round and left. The cars roared away. Ernest closed the front door.

Julie laughed. "Well done, belle-maman."

Then they inspected the rooms and straightened the mess the SS had made when looking into the wardrobes and under the beds.

Conversation resumed.

***

The tip of his cane angrily striking the ground, Gontrand ranted against the Germans. "That Choltitz ordered gendarmes in the north-east districts to be disarmed! And to add insult to injury ordered a parade with all the military vehicles they have."

Bérangère shrugged. "He's trying to intimidate the Parisians."

"That was fine. We had people counting them and finding out where they are stored. We sent the information to the Allied HQ," Xavier said.

Armand rubbed his chin. "The allied armies are still stuck in Normandy and Brittany."

Jacques straightened in his chair. "In a few days' time the police will go on strike, so will the Métro. Get everything you need tomorrow and then keep the children inside."

"The *cheminots* have gone on strike a couple of days ago. We were the first to strike."

"The Americans have parachuted into Provence to prepare a bridgehead for a second landing," Armand said. Cheers greeted his words. He continued, "An insurrection in Paris is inevitable. Please, don't do anything until I give the order."

"We already have no cooking gas, and the electricity is on and off, more off than on. Not to mention the air raid alerts day and night." This dismal pronouncement didn't curb Bérangère's enthusiasm.

"It's only the beginning, my dear."

Red and panting, Julie came in. Her mother-in-law gave her a glass of water and Charmaine put a plate in front of her.

"What took you so long?" Armand was teasing her and she knew it.

"The heat wave!"

They chuckled.

"No, really, I hurried. The bureaucrats are packing the documents they don't want us to find and piling them into any vehicles they can commandeer. Orders have gone out to destroy anything they can't take, whether it's a painting or a vase de Sèvres. Some officers have been reassigned to Normandie. They never thought they'd have to see combat. The pro-Nazis were vehemently telling the anti-Nazis they were defeatists and to get their boots on for the front. I saw soldiers stealing bicycles from under people's feet. One man didn't let go of his and passersby crowded the Boche. He cleared off in a hurry."

"Charmaine, you should leave the children here." Bérangère had a worried frown across her brow.

"We'll close the store and stay in. My photographic equipment is already stored away."

Baptiste and Marianne immediately clamored that they were going home with their parents.

"Not surprising," Julie whispered to Pierrette. "There's so much uncertainty they need to be in familiar surroundings with their parents."

Chapter Twenty-Eight

Paris, Tuesday 15, August 1944

A meeting had been called at the Manoir as Armand suspected the Cave might be watched. The Gestapo were not giving up. Deportation trains still rolled out of the city, heading east. The last person they expected to arrive was Maude, weary and limping, in a worn nurse's uniform. With her, two men helped a limping young man with his arm in a sling. Jacques thanked the two gendarmes in civilian clothes. They were given bread and a slice of canned Olida ham with a glass of red wine.

Bérangère was still hugging her friend. Finally, she sat her down and provided her with bread and ham.

"Meet Guillaume, a friend of François, who became our cook. He threw himself on me and took the shrapnel from the blast of a hand grenade."

"Guillaume, you're my hero for saving my best friend!"

His pipe in his hand, Gontrand looked worried. "Gendarmes out of uniform?"

"A company was in uniform and they were immediately arrested. So, yes, we're all in civilian clothes."

Bérangère was impatient to hear Maude's news. "Tell us more."

"The maquis of La Combe-aux-Loups successfully repelled an attack. Then Pedro led the men into a very successful counter-attack. No Boche left in the area so they went to harass the back of the army corps fighting the Americans in Provence and since they have fully-staffed hospital units, I wasn't needed. I'll be more useful when the fight starts in Paris. Guillaume was hoping to come to Paris and see François. So we made our way back. The Fritz were quite happy to give us a ride, and they weren't going to the front to be sure."

They laughed.

"And at the Porte de Paris, we were taken under the wing by these gentlemen. The tragic news now. Jean-Jacques was executed. You know he'd become a milicien. He refused to join the maquis."

Gontrand shook his head. "My poor brother, and Huguette, losing Mathieu in the war and now..."

"I saw them before I left. Arnaud couldn't understand why his son hadn't seen the light like he did. Young Reine is such a comfort for them."

"And we can't even write to my brother."

Maude took a deep breath. "What's this business about the American generals wanting to bypass Paris?"

"They believe they'd have to fight house to house and that it will turn into another Stalingrad, but with American troops. They believe Choltitz will blow up the city. And next, that they will have to bring in tons and tons of supplies for the starving Parisians."

"Bunch of weaklings. We'll do the fighting ourselves!" It was typical of Maude's vehemence, but no one laughed. Heads nodded in agreement.

***

The next couple of days passed in a blur. Pierrette and Hughes came in shaken.

"Those damned Boches opened fire on the crowd on boulevard Saint-Michel!" Pierrette struck the table with her fist.

"We'd just left the Sorbonne and we were lucky."

Hughes was still limping but eager to join the fight.

Julie slid onto a chair. "But here's the biggest news. Consul Nordling of Sweden, negotiated the release of three thousand political prisoners."

Charmaine clapped her hands. "Will that include François? We haven't been able to take him parcels over the last few days."

Jacques shook his head. "You can't simply open all the doors and tell them to go. The wardens will have to go through the registers to make sure they only release the politicals. Remember, the Germans are still in control."

"Not for long, though. And those résistants are needed." Pierrette's body language was the epitome of determination.

Jacques took his leave. "You won't see me now until it's all over."

"Why?"

"Because tomorrow, the seventeenth, we're going to take the préfecture de police and you bet the Boches will fight us. But I will have the honor to arrest Amédée Bussière, our Vichy préfet de police."

A chorus of best wishes accompanied him.

Julie looked worried. "Be careful, Alexandre. The Saint-Germain quartier is hot. The FTP are out in force."

She was right. Fierce fighting broke out in several quartiers and in particular in the Quartier Latin.

In the morning they heard that von Choltitz had declared a cease-fire. Gontrand took the flag out and was fixing it into its holder when Pierrette rushed to him.

"Take it down. The Boches shoot into houses that have French flags out!"

Reluctantly, Gontrand folded away the flag and went back in followed by Pierrette.

"People have started pulling up pavé and building barricades to prevent the Boches from circulating."

"How close are our troops?"

At that moment, Julie arrived. "The French are passing Clamart. The Americans are in Fontainebleau. Armand is directing the fight on the boulevard Saint-Michel. There's a barricade there. Maude's in the rear with a medic."

"Lyse-May! Where are you going with that bag?" Bérangère called out.

"It's food for Hughes on the barricade."

Julie smiled at the child's thoughtfulness. "*Oh, non*! You are not going. First of all, boulevard Saint-Michel is too far to walk. Bullets are flying all around. Next, you don't know whether Hughes is still there. He could have been assigned somewhere else."

The young girl bent her head. "You take the bag. You don't want me to be in the fighting. 'snot fair!"

"I know, but you have to be much older to go to the barricades."

"But it will be over by the time I'm old enough."

"Yes, and that's a good thing. Fighting with guns is pretty awful, sweetie."

Pierrette reappeared with her backpack. "I've got two nurses' outfits. Let's go."

As Lyse-May, still pouting, watched them disappear down the

street, Antoinette took her hand. "Guillaume promised he'd tell us another story from the maquis."

***

Hot and dusty, Pierrette slid onto a chair. "Now that the Vichy government is gone and the police are on strike, the FFI and the FTP are increasing their attacks on the Germans. You should see all the posters calling for the insurrection to start!"

Gontrand adjusted the dial of the radio by a millimeter. "The FFI seized the radio station and the printing press. Isn't that good news?" He didn't wait for a reply. "They have a tank from the 1940 campaign that some mechanics repaired. It's proved very useful. There's fighting everywhere."

With a smell of cordite hanging on her, Julie hurried in and deposited a bag on the table. "That's all I could get, two leeks from someone's garden and one rutabaga from the grocer. There's no fighting in our quartier, but FFI are out patrolling. The few Germans that are still here are staying inside."

"*Chut!*"

They leaned toward the radio. "The SS have shot twenty-five passersby at the Gare de Lyon, for no reason."

"*Les salauds!*"

Bérangère swearing was such a rare occurrence that it stunned her relatives into silence.

Julie finally broke the silence. "You should know what Madeleine Riffaut did."

Pierrette pricked up her ears. "She belongs to a communist cell."

"That doesn't make any difference. We're all fighting together now. She was short of manpower so I joined in with two men of her group. We seized a munition train and took eighty Germans prisoner."

Gontrand frowned. "Just the four of you?"

"Sometimes it's not just armed confrontation that wins a battle. We carried her stock of ammunition and hid in the trees by the tunnel de Sorbier, in the Buttes Chaumont. The train was halted while the Germans inspected the rails leading into the tunnel. Madeleine Riffaut ordered us to open fire and we threw threw all our grenades, dynamite, just everything. The Germans ran into the tunnel. So Madeleine ordered to throw all the smoke bombs in it at once. The Germans came out with hands up and surrendered. They thought they were being attacked by a whole army."

Gontrand sniffed the air. "That's why you smell of gunpowder!"

Pierrette's hands waved circles in the air. "I wish I'd been there!"

"That took some nerve!" Bérangère shook her head.

Julie shrugged and looked away. Her mother-in-law looked at her shrewdly conscious of the change in the young woman.

"You did well."

"We had to do it. That train was going to the Gare de l'Est and would have supplied the Prince Eugene barracks on the Place de la République. Many troops there, and with all that arms and ammunition, it was heading for a blood bath, both for the résistants and the Allies who are arriving as I speak."

***

General Leclerc's avant-garde fought the Germans at Fresnes, and the prison's doors were thrown open to the political prisoners that were still held there. François stumbled out into the sunshine. He saw a young woman with an FFI armband.

"Do you have a car to take me home so I can rejoin my unit?"

"Come and see my leader."

"You belong to Armand's réseau?" There was admiration in the chef de groupe's voice. "I'll get you someone."

Ten minutes later, François was on his way next to the young woman driving with couple of résistants newly freed in the back. "Nice cars, these traction-avant. I like the paint work."

She laughed. "We do our best. We painted 'Police' on ours because there were some rowdy youths who didn't want to listen to reason. Now they do."

Fançois smiled, looking at her. She wasn't even twenty. "You're doing great while I was rotting in a cell."

"Was it bad?"

"It's a squalid place and the food was unrecognizable. Turn left, that's my grandparents street."

She let him off in front of the house but declined to come in. "I'm needed elsewhere."

He climbed the steps two by two, punched the bell push and opened the door. He was engulfed in a forest of arms and led to the petit salon where a young man threw aside the book he was reading and stood up.

François' mouth fell open. "Wilhelm? It can't be."

They embraced. "I'm Guillaume now."

"How come you're here? I thought you were dead."

"Your captain didn't kill me."

"But I heard a shot."

"That was a wounded German who took his own life rather than surrender. The maquis took care of me. I became their cook. One day, your aunt Maude arrived. Beside, being the cook, I became her assistant medic. She is as good as any doctor. She fixed me up when I was wounded in the last attack on La Combe-aux-Loups and I'm healing well. I plan to study to become a doctor if the new government will give me French citizenship. The captain made a file on me and hopefully will be back to vouch for me."

"I'll vouch for you too. Then we'll study together. I"m enrolled in medicine, though I spent most of the year, first in hospital, then prison."

"Your sister gave me your room—"

"Good, will share."

***

Julie brought two cans of Olida ham. "Rısistants broke into the factory. I didn't order it. I was given these. The food situation is dire, but Gınıral Leclerc's 2ème DB is at the Porte d'Orléans. They will enter Paris in the morning."

Friday, August 25, 1944

Bérangère had to give in. Brigitte's children were determined to go and welcome Leclerc's French soldiers. Antoinette offered to stay and look after baby Itienne.

"No, your legs are working well, you're strong again. You come with us."

"We'll look after you," Damien said.

Marie stopped them. "Take these sandwiches. They're small but you'll be hungry."

Lyse-May thanked her and carried the cloth bag. They went toward the Hôtel de Ville. Brigitte kept looking around. "Where is Julie?"

Charmaine motioned with her head over her shoulder. "I believe she's gone to the Majestic."

"Surely, she doesn't work there anymore?"

"The MBF will have to surrender, she'll help the management.

There must be tons of sensitive documents to seize before the Germans destroy them, even though lots have already been taken away by those who fled early."

Guillaume and Franηois halted in the middle of the street. "There's shooting ahead. We should take shelter."

They shepherded their family group into a building, along with other people, until it was quiet again. Then church bells pealed out all over Paris.

"Mon Dieu, isn't it wonderful to hear the bells again? Silent for the last four years. Listen to that booming sound. That's the huge bourdon of Notre-Dame de Paris. They'll hear it all the way into the suburbs." Bérangère couldn't control her emotions, neither could Gontrand.

"Why you cry, pépère?"

"Tears of happiness, sweetie. We are free again."

Exhausted, they turned back through the middle of the crowd toward the Manoir.

Pierrette caught up with them. "Tomorrow is a grand day. Général de Gaulle is going to walk to the Arc de Triomphe then go to mass at Notre-Dame. By the way, Cardinal Suhard was told not to be at the mass, filthy collabo!"

Since, inwardly, Bérangère agreed with Pierrette she didn't ask her to respect the clergy as she would have done in earlier times. Maude openly laughed.

In the morning, Bérangère and Brigitte ironed everyone's best clothes. Lyse-May held out her tulle and lace dress with excitement. It had been made from an eighteenth century petticoat her grandmother had discovered at the Marché aux Puces. There had been enough material to dress Estelle and Christiane, too. Brigitte had made blue, white and red ribbons and a wide one to go with the girls' dresses.

"I love it!"

Christiane chimed in. "Me too."

"Hughes, Daniel and Xavier are with their FFI unit. They want to enlist." There was a trace of envy in Pierrette's voice.

"Not surprising." Bérangère shook her head slowly.

The approaching sound of a gasoline engine had them rush to the door. A black Citroën traction-avant liberally painted with white FFI and crosses of Lorraine had stopped in front of the

Manoir. A man with a FFI armband and a béret jumped out and helped the passengers. Two other FFI men stood guard with their submachine guns.

"Julie!"

She waved and turned back to the car. A two-year-old boy was passed to her and Colette exited along with Claudine. Lyse-May shrieked with joy. The résistants put two suitcases on the sidewalk and seeing that the women had run down the steps, saluted, kissed Julie and roared away.

"You made it!" Brigitte hugged her friend.

Ernest took the suitcases up to the bedrooms and came back downstairs. "Madame Bérangère, I have checked the Hispano-Suiza and got some gas from the troops. We painted FFI on the front and back, just in case, as mademoiselle Pierrette suggested. I propose to take you and the children from the Arc de Triomphe to Notre-Dame. It's too far to walk for the little ones in this heat."

"You'll be alright walking, François?' Julie asked.

"I want to be there! Anyway I was better off than most of my comrades there thanks to the parcels you sent, even after I shared with others."

Lyse-May, carrying her precious doll, Angélique, held Gontrand's hand. With Alexandre, they had gone ahead. Brigitte, with Itienne in her arms and Julie carrying Mathieu, rode with Ernest to the Place de l'Étoile at three o'clock. They waited for their in-laws to arrive with the other children and the young people.

"Children, take a good look at that very tall man. His name is Général Charles de Gaulle. He is the one who has filled us with hope for the last four years. Never forget him. He's the symbol of the Résistance." The pride in Julie's voice was contagious.

When the ceremony was over Julie, Brigitte and the younger children piled into the Hispano-Suiza, while Gontrand and Alexandre got a ride with an FFI car. They reunited with the others on the approaches to Notre-Dame. Lyse-May took Gontrand's hand to cross the square and come closer to the cathedral.

Général de Gaulle had barely reached the cathedral gate when a rifle shot rang out from a nearby rooftop. Gontrand pushed Lyse-May to the ground and collapsed on top of her. Another shot was heard. People around them slid on their bellies. A couple of FFI men rushed into the building, emerged on the roof and chased the sniper. They took aim and fired. The sniper swayed, lost balance and fell off the roof to the sidewalk below.

Julie got to her feet holding a crying Mathieu. "Here, take him!" She thrust the toddler into Bérangère's arms. Then she ran to where Lyse-May and Gontrand lay. Lyse-May raised her head and struggled to extricate herself from under her grandfather's weight.

"You're heavy, pépère."

He didn't move. Julie crouched down and shook his shoulder. He didn't budge. Dread settled over her as she pulled the girl from under him. Lyse-May managed to get to her knees, but the skirt of her white dress was still caught under Gontrand's big frame. Julie helped her pull her dress free. The girl screamed when she looked down and saw the blood-stained fabric. "Pépère!"

Julie wrapped her in her arms and checked for a pulse on her father-in-law's neck, even though she knew it was futile to do so. François and Guillaume were already by her side. Very professionally François turned Gontrand over.

Tears welled up in François' eyes. "A bullet went straight trough his heart."

Lyse-May freed herself from her aunt and threw her arms around her grandfather's head, her sobs rending the air. The family group didn't need to hear the words to know that his booming voice would never be heard again.

Dressed in white coats, medical students-turned medics arrived on the scene. Gently, they pried Lyse-May's arms off the dead man. They lifted Gontrand onto the stretcher. Bérangère closed his eyes and pulled the white sheet over his face.

"We'll take him to Hôtel-Dieu hospital."

Bérangère followed. Brigitte and Julie looked at the stunned children. The little ones, not understanding but scared by the silence, clung to the adults.

"We'll go with grand-maman," François said.

Lyse-May broke away from Julie and, running, caught up with Bérangère. Angélique, its porcelain head shattered, was left forlorn on the pavement.

Ernest tapped Julie on the shoulder. "Everybody in the car." He led the way.

Later in the evening the sirens wailed their warning. Alert?

The incredulous family mourning in the grand salon with Bérangère, didn't move. They heard the drone of bombers overhead. Damien and Baptiste, who had been allowed to stay up, jumped to the open window. The first quarter of the moon shone bright in a clear sky. "Germans! They don't sound like the Americans. They're German planes. We can see the silhouettes—" Almost immediately they heard the explosions of falling bombs. Everyone sprang to action, rushed to the bedrooms and swept the children into protective arms. They hurried down the cellar.

"*Salopards* until the end!" Bérangère's lip curled in disgust.

"Yes, real bastards."

***

Next morning, the family gathered around the radio, only to hear there were two-hundred fatalities and some nine-hundred wounded. Over a thousand buildings had been damaged. It had been so unexpected. Since the Germans had surrendered in Paris, the defenses were slow to react. Only two Luftwaffe planes were downed. The announcer began listing the streets where bombs had fallen and was at Boulevard Saint-Germain, when Maude rushed in. "Somebody fetch the Lebeaus, the photographic shop is besieged by self-appointed justices."

"Ernest!" Julie hollered. She grabbed her armband. Brigitte handed her a captured German Walther pistol and gave an armband to Ernest. Minutes later the Hispano-Suiza, honking loudly, forced its way through the crowd on Boulevard Saint-Germain. Julie seized control of the situation. Pierrette, with a Luger in hand, and Xavier in a French uniform and holding a rifle, barred the door of the store and the door to the apartments. The crowd hurled insults.

"Let's have that *putain* who slept with the Boche!" was the refrain of the angry neighbors.

Julie jumped in front of them. With her voice raised but not shouting, she addressed the crowd. "Alexandre Lebeau provided false identity papers and ration cards to the Résistance. His singer wife was blackmailed by the Gestapo and obliged to perform for the Germans to save her husband and children. Yet, she couriered vital documents all over Paris for the Résistance. Now go home, you've got the wrong people."

There was a wavering through the assembled mob.

Pierrette clinched it when she shouted, "My aunt never slept with that Boche. He was a homosexual."

Several people turned red at this embarrassing sexual revelation and left. In the meantime, Ernest had slipped in by the door of the apartments. Gus who had stayed with Alexandre and Charmaine to protect them and the children, stepped out. He had a string of invectives for the remaining neighbors, while Ernest pushed the children into the car, promptly followed by Charmaine. Alexandre calmly walked around the Hispano-Suiza and climbed into the front passenger seat.

Pierrette put her pistol into her satchel, took out two placards with FFI in large black letters and stuck them on the door and window of the store. "And if any of you touch this store, we shall know who did it and we will come back for you."

Julie lowered her firearm and took a seat next to Charmaine. Ernest drove back to the Manoir. This time at a more leisurely speed.

Marie had prepared a lunch. Although the garden was producing, she thriftily used and preserved the food. She served the meal in the dining room. Just as they were sitting down, the doorbell sounded. Julie got to her feet but before she could leave the table, the door opened. Sylvain, in captain's uniform, strode in followed by Bernard, whose uniform displayed the insignia of a medical officer. She threw herself into her husband's arms. For a while a glorious chaos reigned. Then sadness tempered the joy. Her eyes damp, Bérangère ordered everyone to sit. "There will be time to cry later. Right now we must share this happy moment."

Room was made at the table for the new arrivals, who handed army K-rations to Maric bcforc sitting down.

"We just have a two-hour leave. We met Hughes as he signed his enlistment papers with the army."

During lunch, Sylvain kept looking at Mathieu in the highchair. When the meal was over, Julie plucked her son from the chair, wiped his face and placed him in her husband's arms in the petit salon. "Meet your son Mathieu, named after your uncle and aunt's son. He's two years and four months."

Sylvain held the little boy, who was babbling in a language of his own. "Blond and blue eyes, like Claire's." He looked at her.

She knew there was a question in his mind. A doubt remained in hers, but she buried it away. "My biological father is blond and has blue eyes."

Shock registered on his face. Julie recounted the events. At that moment, Claudine trotted in.

"Meet Claudine, my adopted daughter. She's three and a half."

She ran to Sylvain. "You're my papa?"

"Yes I am, and I love you."

"I love you too, and Mathieu." She poked her little brother and said something in that strange language they shared between them.

Mathieu laughed and kneeled on Sylvain's lap. "I love you." His little hands touched his father's face.

Both children moved to another armchair where a toy carrousel lay. Sylvain took Julie in his arms. They kissed and hugged, happy and brokenhearted at the same time, for what they had lost and gained. Then it was time to go.

Goodbyes had to be said. Bernard gave an extra hug to Brigitte, and Ernest drove the two captains back to their unit.

Antoinette, Colette and Marianne called the children and the toddlers to go and play outside. In the kitchen, Julie and Charmaine looked at Brigitte holding the letter that Bernard had given her.

"It's a letter from Hubert. His plane was shot down but he made it to England and is injured in hospital."

"And you don't want to open the letter?"

"For the longest time, he was out of my life. The letter brings him back and I don't know whether I like it or not." She sighed and took the kitchen knife from Charmaine and slit open the envelope. She began reading, tilted her head and looked at her friends, then at the letter and read aloud.

Dear Brigitte,

By now you must have been told that I am in hospital recuperating. I was planning to come and tell you in person that I wish to end our marriage. I have met a wonderful woman who means everything to me. I know this is hard on you and I regret that the children will be disappointed, that is, if they even remember me. I hope you can forgive me. As soon as I am discharged, I will fly again to help finish the war. When it's over, perhaps we can meet and reassure the children that I love them. Will you please tell them?

Brigitte tossed the letter to the floor. "That's that. The end."

"What do you feel?" Concern colored Charmaine's voice.

"Frankly, nothing. When he was away with the air force, I

remember being happy until he came back. Then we argued, but made up before he left again. I was happy again alone with the children. Then came the war."

Julie chewed her lip. "What will you tell the children?'

"I realize now that I never talked about their father. I suppose Damien remembers him. Estelle maybe a little, she was five when the war started. Sylvestre was too young to have any memories and Christiane was just a newborn. I think I will tell only Damien and Estelle, but only if they ask about him."

"At least until the war is over there's no need to make any changes."

Julie nodded. "They have already lost Gerhardt, the only father figure they know."

A dreamy smile settled over Brigitte's lips. "He and Reynard were whisked away to the American High Command. They're cooperating by providing much useful information to the Allies."

"How did you learn that?"

"Julie and I received a short verbal message passed on by an influential rısistant."

***

Bérangère and the family were about to sit down for lunch when Pierrette arrived, dejected, her eyes red and puffy followed by François equally down. They each put a hand on their mother's shoulders. Pierrette spoke.

"Philippe was gunned down as he was leaving the house in Neuilly."

Madeleine jumped up screaming. "No!"

Bérangère took her in her arms. As the screams persisted, she moved with her to the petit salon and closed the door behind her.

François made to follow. Pierrette stopped him with a hand on his arm. "She must process the news on her own. Grand-maman is the best person to help her." She turned to the rest of them. "Mireille was dragged from the mansion next door."

"We heard the commotion," Charmaine said. "What was it?"

"My sister has been taken to the public place where the vigilantes are shaving the heads of women who slept with the enemy."

Marie crossed herself.

Charmaine was angry. "Revenge. The self-righteous will shame or kill those who didn't join the Résistance or didn't boast about it."

They knew she talked from experience.

Pierrette took a deep breath. "Of all the collaborateurs, Philippe was one of the better ones, if that is not a contradiction in terms."

Bérangère and Madeleine returned to the table. Félicité held out her arms to her mother.

"Gontrand's funeral will be Monday. We'll hold Philippe's on Tuesday."

Julie admired her mother-in-law's fortitude. She drew Lyse-May closer to her. The little girl had lost her joie de vivre.

In time, life resumed. A government was installed and the police regained control of the streets. They put an end to the savage reprisals of the vigilante justice.

Jacques came to see Bérangère and was relieved to find Julie with her in the music room. "I am the bearer of more sad news. We found Rodolphe in his Waffen-SS uniform. He took his own life."

Bérangère lowered her head. "Is it ever going to stop?"

War destroys roads, buildings, factories. It also destroys families.

Epilogue

Tuesday, May 8, 1945. The war is over but the wait has just begun for the return of the deported.

Every day, Julie and Daniel, or François and Guillaume went to the Hôtel Lutetia, which had become the center for the repatriated, hoping that this time they would find Lorraine, Yolande and Léonie.

They became angry that some deportees arrived, still wearing their striped prison camp clothing, and were given a Métro ticket and left to fend for themselves. Pierrette and Julie organized a group of women to help the returnees.

And one day, thin and drawn in an army uniform, Yolande stepped off the bus. Yolande announced that she had been with her mother to the end but that she had died of typhus, only days before the camp was liberated.

Oberleutnant Lohse had found Yolande. She refused to be freed unless her mother was too. Chagrined but understanding, he obtained them a job in one of the camp offices. After the liberation of the camp, she accepted to stay in Germany as a translator for the Americans Forces in Germany until it was all over. When it was, Ernst Lohse was waiting for her.

The wait continued for Léonie. She arrived, also in uniform, one afternoon after escorting internees too sick to travel by themselves. She was going back immediately for there were others in need of help.

One day, she escorted Marie-Ange to the hospital. Paul and Micheline came to see their mother. When Marie-Ange asked for forgiveness, they granted it to her and she died in peace.

Bernard, Sylvain, Armand, Xavier and Hughes wrote letters until the day they were demobilized. Reynard and Gerhardt also wrote letters until they were allowed to come back to Paris.

Julie became a reporter for a major magazine, while Colette looked after the children.

Lyse-May became a fiction writer.

François and Guillaume/Whilhelm, who was granted French citizenship for saving Maude's life in the maquis, became surgeons.

Daniel journeyed to Germany. He found no living relatives. Appalled by the destruction in both countries, he came back to Paris to study architecture.

Wolfang Ziegler became accompanist to Charmaine, who achieved her dream of becoming an opera soloist.

Alexandre was decorated. He sold the photographic studio and opened one in a different location in Paris.

Jean-Luc repaired the printshop, which grew into a successful printing establishment.

Pierrette finished her studies at the Sorbonne and immersed herself in political life.

Madeleine took up residence at the Manoir and, with Félicité, was a great comfort to Bérangère.

Maude Pleynet went back to live in Meudon and came frequently, by bicycle, to visit Bérangère.

Rose continued living under her false identity with Bernadette Ducharme. The two having become fast friends created a thriving knitting and sewing business.

Pedro was granted French citizenship for his heroic action on the battlefield.

Charlot, always first to take risks, was decorated. He went on to work for a humanitarian organization.

Monsieur Biquette and Dédé were briefly questionned. Their actions to help the Résistance were well documented.

Jacques visited Bérangère every Sunday and continued his police work until he retired.

Michel Curie, the gendarme-passeur, was promoted.

Popaul's café became the rendezvous of many former résistants.

Dr. Bignon continued with his regular practice.

Antoinette regained strength and became a nurse.

Madame Durand remained as concierge in Julie's apartment building.

Author's Notes

The Paris I knew has changed drastically, new buildings, particularly where the bombs fell, new streets, new names to honor heroes of the war. Wherever possible I located my characters in places that still exit with their original names. If some readers care to look at a map to see where actions take place, they will find them.

France bore the greatest toll of the Allied bombing, with cities, like Caen completely flattened. The Allies broadcast a justification of the bombing on the BBC: "*A horrible necessity. At no time in history has an ally inflicted such bloody and painful wounds on an allied and friendly country. Yet, during the Occupation, 3,000 airmen downed over France were rescued, hidden and exfiltrated by the French people they had just bombed.*"

In this series, many personal memories came to life in a fictional form. The unfolding events are backed by years of meticulous research that grew as the archives were being opened and new material came to light.

I chose to include some true incidents and put my characters into them. I named, but only by their nicknames, Sgt. Hortie, and Sgt. Moss to tell their true stories from their recorded account. I named real-life nineteen-year-old Denise Holstein for her devotion to the children with whom she was deported to Auswichtz (and survived). I based Yolande's long letter on Denise Holstein's own account. I named Bernard-Émanuel Lefschetz, who founded a network of volunteers to care for children of deported parents. I also named Madeleine Riffaut, the nineteen-year-old resistant whose admirable action probably saved thousands of lives. The only fictional part is my character Julie taking part to that daring action so she can narrate it.

As for me, the war and its aftermath stole my childhood. I lived through the German occupation of France, in Paris and neighboring Suresnes, very much alone with the grandparents who raised me. Since I had no one to play with, and being gifted with a vivid imagination, I invented a large family, which is brought to life in these pages.

The initial trigger for the first story was a photo depicting children who were separated from their families during the Éxode. This is why Julie's work with the Red Cross is to reunite children with their parents. Since the early days, when no one would talk about the Dark Years, I had collected books and documents about the war in France, in particular, the Occupation of Paris. There was, for me, a deep need to know what had happened and why.

To this day, I have a profound admiration for the men and women who refused to accept defeat and Nazi rule and formed the Résistance. In recent times, some historians and writers have tried to analyze the Résistance and often diminish its role and importance, totally ignoring the heartfelt motivation of the ordinary, untrained people behind it, and the thousands who lost their lives to the cause.

I repeat General Eisenhower's quote from the beginning of this series. It sums it all: "***The French Résistance was the equivalent of ten divisions.***"

Write to Geneviève Montcombroux at solitudepublishing@gmail.com
genevieve-montcombroux.com
Follow her on FB

All the Silences:
Book one, The Tears
Book two, The Rage
Book three, The Hope

Covers by stunningbookscovers.com

Some other books in English by Geneviève Montcombroux

* Non-fiction: The Inuit Dog of the Polar North — A detailed work about the Inuit dog, its history and provenance, its role in the Inuit life in the Arctic and its place in modern society. The North and South Poles were conquered by explorers using Inuit dogs. Surveyors and geologists mapped Antarctica with the help of Inuit dog teams.

* Romance:
Northern Lights and Sled Dogs — Kelly dreams of long distance dog races. Tyler let his problems overcome him, until Kelly comes into his life in a remote cabin in the Yukon Territory. Dogs, puppies, racing, winning, a powerful mix leading to a happy ending.

Northern Skies — Mattiesoon (Mattie), a First Nations biologist in the Canadian North. Josh, a helicopter pilot and owner of a remote fishing lodge. They belong to opposite poles. Dramatic events bring them close until they find their happy ending.

Pizza for Two — Piers has known the depth of despair. Nicole carries the burden of a troubled past. Their road ahead is strewn with untruths and deceit until they find their happy ending.

The Magic of Music — Marina, a concert pianist, sees her life shattered. Trent's life revolves around his daughter Sophie who is blind and suffers from selective mutism. Trent carries an enormous guilt. Drama evolves in Otter Lake, a small prairie town. Music soothes the souls and leads to a happy ending.

* Children books

A Dog Named Tezzero — Two smart dogs. Two eager boys. A doggy adventure that brings people together.